Marius & Delia

Marius & Delia

Or, A Pleasant & Profitable

History of the Times

by D. M.

ATTRIBUTED TO

DEBORAH MILTON

Definitive Text with Critical Commentary

Edited by Margo Quigley

SpringStreet Books

SpringStreet Books
www.springstreetbooks.com

Copyright ©2021 SpringStreet Books
All rights reserved. Published 2021.

ISBN: 978-1-7357957-0-6

Printed on acid-free paper.

Contents

INTRODUCTION

SOMETIME IN the mid-1690s—some twenty-five years before *Moll Flanders,* more than forty years before *Pamela*—Deborah Milton, daughter of the poet John Milton, wrote *Marius & Delia,* the first English novel. Its astonishing literary quality and iconoclastic originality have yet to be fully assessed, as the critical essays included in this new authoritative edition will attest.

The story of the novel's recovery is, like the work itself, one of suspense and surprise. A single surviving copy was discovered in a private library and subjected to a hurried hugger-mugger transcription. That discovery remained almost unknown for nearly two decades. An unexpected assertion of copyright to the transcribed and privately printed work limited its circulation to photocopies of photocopies, passed back and forth among a few specialists and their graduate students. Only now, with the successful resolution of that legal challenge, is it possible to introduce this remarkable novel to a broader audience.

The title page of *Marius & Delia* designated the author as D. M. The only known surviving copy amplified this byline in a crabbed but legible contemporary hand, inserted above and sloping clockwise around the initials:

[D.] ebora [M.] ilton yᵉ Regicides doughter

Even without this contemporary attribution, we might well have inferred the identity of D. M. from what is known about John Milton's youngest child.

Deborah Milton was born on May 2, 1652. Her mother, Mary Powell Milton, died just three days later. Her father was by now totally blind. In 1656 he remarried but his second wife, Katherine Woodcock, died in early 1658. Five years later, in February of 1663, he married Elizabeth Minshull, who proved to be an unsympathetic stepmother to the three daughters of his first wife, Anne, Mary and Deborah. By 1670 household tensions had reached a breaking point.[1] John Milton moved out of the house into temporary lodgings with Edward Millington, a bookseller. His wife Elizabeth was thereby given a free hand to deal with her refractory stepchildren.[2] The elder two sisters, Anne and Mary, were apprenticed to embroidery workers. Deborah's mode of escape, or expulsion, is less certain, but she also left home and settled in Ireland as a lady's companion.

After her father's death in November of 1674 an oral will surfaced, purportedly declared to her uncle Christopher Milton, an attorney, well before John Milton's final illness, but only written down and produced after his death. This will disinherited the deceased's "unkind children," leaving the estate entirely at the disposal of their stepmother. The will was contested by the daughters. The deposition of Christopher Milton established that Elizabeth Minshull Milton had promised him a share of the estate if the will passed probate. She would collect the first thousand pounds, then the balance of the estate would be paid to *his* children—an arrangement which he explained as an additional oral bequest that John Milton had confided to his wife. The only other deponents were an illiterate servant, still in the employ of Elizabeth, and that servant's sister. Their evidence consisted of remarks purportedly made by John Milton, confirming that his wife would get all when he was gone and that his children were disobedient and neglectful of their father. The ludicrous testimony of these obviously suborned servants has been taken seriously by too many John Milton scholars. It is irresistibly comical, all the same, to picture Milton, smacking his lips over a tasty dinner, telling his wife to keep the good food coming so she can get all his money when he's dead: "God have mercy Betty I see thou wilt performe according to thy promise in providing mee such Dishes as I think fitt whilst I live, and when I dye thou knowest that I have left thee all."[3]

This hazily documented oral will could not survive legal scrutiny, as Christopher Milton must have realized in advance.[4] But Elizabeth Milton landed on her feet: as widow and administrator, she was entitled to two-thirds of the estate; her three stepdaughters each received £100.[5] The two elder sisters signed releases on February 22, 1675, acknowledging receipt of payment. The release signed by Deborah is dated March 27 and written in a different hand, suggesting it was prepared and executed elsewhere, most likely in Dublin.[6] Deborah's release stipulates that she received, in addition, "severall Goods late of ye said John Milton Deceased." It may be that she bargained a little harder than her sisters. Or, there may have been a family understanding that these items had been designated as Deborah's by her father. One of these articles, according to Masson, was "a silver seal which Milton had used, bearing the family arms."[7] This intriguing bequest may signal a recognition of Deborah's potential as a writer whose work would carry on the family name.

The receipt for Deborah's small share of her father's estate was signed by both Deborah and her new husband, a Dubliner named Abraham Clarke, whom she had married on June 1, 1674, according to parish records.[8] He was said to be a silk mercer by John Aubrey, her father's earliest biographer; in the parish register his occupation is given as weaver.[9] We know nothing more about him or about their life together, except that they would have ten children, seven sons and three daughters, most of whom did not live to adulthood.[10] Deborah left Dublin for London not long after the birth of her daughter Elizabeth in November of 1688.[11] Boatloads of Protestants fled Dublin for England and other safe havens from late November through February of 1689, due to widespread fears of a Catholic uprising.[12] We know that the newborn, Elizabeth, was left behind in Ireland, and we never hear again of Abraham Clarke, her husband. The scanty facts available suggest that Deborah returned to London on her own, leaving her surviving children and her husband in Ireland. He may have died around 1702 or 1703, since the children dispersed at this time.[13] Elizabeth, now fifteen, came to England. A son, Caleb, was in India in 1703, where he remained until his death in 1719.[14]

Alternatively, Abraham Clarke could have died in 1688, prompting a homesick Deborah to return to London, leaving her children (the eldest could be no more than fourteen) with her husband's family, who would be better able to maintain them. It is possible that husband, wife and older children migrated together in 1689, leaving the infant behind because she was sickly. That hypothesis would leave unanswered the question of why the family, if intact and thriving, would postpone Elizabeth's immigration until her sixteenth year. An Abraham Clarke was admitted to the London Company of Weavers on May 9, 1709.[15] That's the right name and the right occupation, although it would take an unusual set of circumstances to explain a twenty-year delay in his admission. But even if this Abraham Clarke was Deborah's husband, the couple may have been estranged, since we have additional information to indicate that Deborah was on her own during these years.

At some date between 1704 and 1708 Deborah Milton Clarke addressed a petition for financial aid to Robert Harley, then Secretary of State, later 1st Earl of Oxford. This petition is summarized as follows in a record of manuscript material in the possession of William Cavendish-Bentinck, the 6th Duke of Portland:

> Deborah Clark, "only daughter of John Melton, author of *The Paradice Lost.*"— Petitioner "is in a very low and destitute condition, but is far more desirous to maintain herself by her care and industry than to be burdensome to any honourable person who generosity might induce to relieve her for the respect had to her late dear father." Is capable of gaining her living had she a small stock to put her in a way to do so, and humbly prays his Honour to compassionate her distressed condition as shall seem meet.[16]

It is fair to assume that this précis excerpts and paraphrases the petition itself. It must have been a difficult document to compose, yet the excerpt exhibits literary skill in coupling words of ordinary speech to a crisp Latinate syntax. Deborah had the discernment to address her petition to a statesman who was also a major patron of the arts. At this early date, many public figures would be unlikely to compassionate the child of John Milton, whose post-Restoration reputation was as the infamous defender of regicide (witness the annotation to D. M.'s title page).[17]

No mention is made of husband or children: Deborah was living alone, dependent on her own earning power, and sought only to obtain the "small stock"— probably money to be spent on books and writing materials—that would enable her to make her own way again. In 1721, the engraver George Vertue sought her out to ask about portraits of her father.[18] He most likely learned her whereabouts from Oxford or from his son, Lord Harley, who was Vertue's patron. He found her "in a mean little street near Moorfields, where she kept a school for children for her support." Possibly Oxford had helped her start her school.[19] This mean little street must have meant home to Deborah. It is the neighborhood where she had lived with her father and sisters from 1661 until she left home in 1670. Age and failing eyesight eventually forced her to give up her school. She took up residence in Spitalfields with her daughter Elizabeth, who had married Thomas Foster, a weaver, in 1719.[20]

We next hear of Deborah, again in much reduced circumstances, near the end of her life. In April of 1727, a letter in *Mist's Weekly Journal* feelingly described her situation as a frail, destitute old woman, dependent upon her daughter and her son-in-law, a journeyman-weaver, for her support. An accompanying appeal to public charity on behalf of the surviving daughter of the immortal John Milton produced sufficient bounty to improve the family's comfort and provide a decent funeral. She died four months after that public notice, on August 24, 1727, at the age of 75.

The energetic wording of this public appeal is worth reviewing, if only because Deborah must have read it and considered its implications for how she should conduct herself. In it, two actions are demanded of the reader by the pseudonymous author, "Philalethes," for two distinct motives. First, go visit the great poet's daughter out of curiosity, as I did: she looks so astonishingly like her father. Second, don't go visit the great poet's daughter "out of mere curiosity, without a design of assistance." The word *curiosity* occurs three times: Deborah Milton Clarke is presented as both an object of compassion and a novelty well worth viewing:

> I could not hear that a daughter of Milton was still living without a curiosity of seeing her, and making some enquiries about her father. I was not, indeed, without some doubts before I went, that she might have usurped the title of such descent; but the traces of her father's features appear so strong through her venerable age, that they immediately silence all doubts. The resemblance strikes you with that force, that I dare engage, any one who looks on the print of Milton in metzotinto, and then would go to see his daughter, should be able to pick her out from amidst an hundred other women of equal rank, and equally strangers....
>
> ... I am persuaded the same good-natured curiosity which prompted me to go and see this old matron, will excite crouds to follow the example; and that the finest geniuses and fairest faces in this great metropolis, will not be ashamed to meet one another in the kind office of lending her a little comfort. The same circle of coaches which glitter at one evening's ring in Hyde-Park, making a tour to the quarter of her residence, and leaving but the scanty pittance of relief, might set her above all future anxieties.[21]

Come one, come all: Take a good look but don't forget your pocket money. You'll find her at Mr. Foster's, next door to the Blue Ball, Pelham Street, Spitalfields. Suggested donation: "the expence of a single masquerade or opera ticket"; or, as a lesser amount, "the price of a pantomime and rope-dancing."

The language might be embarrassing, even humiliating, but it let Deborah know precisely what was expected of her. In order to win financial support for her family, she needed to enact the role of daughter of the author of *Paradise Lost*. Her performance was constrained by the fact that many of her visitors would have had definite expectations and must have cued her responses with leading questions. The family narrative had already been scripted by her father's biographers, only they did not agree on her role. Four biographical accounts of her father had been published by this time, all making some mention of Deborah.

The earliest biographical information consists of notes recorded by John Aubrey, talented antiquarian, crank polymath, and avid collector of anecdotes. A perpetual bankrupt, Aubrey made ends meet by doing the odd literary job and by cultivating a set of friends and patrons who would invite him to stay, at least for dinner, sometimes for a year or two. He knew many members of the elder Milton's circle and was well situated to gather information. His manuscript notes for a life of John Milton, dating from 1681, state that "Deborah was his Amanuensis, he taught her Latin, & to read Greeke to him."[22] Further in his notes Aubrey returns to her again with the statement that Deborah was "very like her father" and "could read to him Latin: Ital. & French & Greeke," an elaboration that indicates he had encountered an additional source for his facts among John Milton's circle.[23] Without the later comments of Edward Phillips (see below) to bias us, the straightforward interpretation here is that Deborah knew Latin well enough to read it and to take dictation in that language. For the other languages mentioned, she presumably had a decent reading comprehension but lacked fluency. Aubrey, a genial Royalist with no strong religious leanings, was unlikely to have been on any intimate footing with Milton, but his notes do contain a few first-hand observations and recollections.

In the annals (*Fasti*) printed with his *Athenae Oxonienses* (1692), a chronicle of Oxford-educated bishops and authors, Anthony Wood incorporated an account of the Cambridge-educated John Milton, primarily for the sake of denouncing his republican and regicidal politics.[24] Although he characteristically fails to name the friend who was his source, Wood drew his information directly from Aubrey, who, he says, was well acquainted with Milton "and had from him, and from his Relations after his death, most of this account of his life and writings." Wood omits many details acquired by Aubrey but follows him in declaring that Deborah was "trained up by the Father in Lat. and Greek, and made by him his *Amanuensis*."[25]

The Milton family narrative changes abruptly when we come to the biography written by Edward Phillips, the son of John Milton's sister. It appeared anonymously in 1694 as the preface to an underground edition of Milton's letters of state.[26] In his biographical sketch of his uncle, Phillips denies that Deborah understood any language other than her own and implies she was incapable of wielding a pen. He presents Deborah and her elder sister Mary as compelled (his yet more strenuous verb is *condemned*) to perform a servile and passive task as readers of incomprehensible texts in a half-dozen languages. As Phillips underscores at the outset, this intolerably tedious task was redundant and unnecessary. Milton already had intelligent males in attendance, both men and boys, who were eager ("greedily catch'd at the opportunity") to serve him as readers:

Those [children] he had by the First [wife] he made serviceable to him in that very particular in which he most wanted their Service, and supplied his want of

Eye-sight by their Eyes and Tongue; for though he had daily about him one or
other to Read to him, some persons of Man's Estate, who of their own accord
greedily catch'd at the opportunity of being his Readers, that they might as
well reap the benefit of what they Read to him, as oblige him by the benefit
of their reading; others of younger years sent by their Parents to the same end;
yet excusing only the Eldest Daughter, by reason of her bodily Infirmity and
difficult utterance of Speech, (which to say truth I doubt was the Principal
cause of excusing her), the other two were Condemn'd to the performance of
Reading, and exactly pronouncing of all the Languages of whatever Book he
should at one time or other think fit to peruse; *Viz.* the *Hebrew* (and I think
the *Syriac*), the *Greek,* the *Latin,* the *Italian, Spanish* and *French.* All which
sorts of Books to be confined to Read, without understanding one word, must
needs be a Tryal of Patience, almost beyond endurance; yet it was endured by
both for a long time; yet the irksomeness of this imployment could not always
be concealed, but broke out more and more into expressions of uneasiness;
so that at length they were all (even the Eldest also) sent out to learn some
Curious and Ingenious sorts of Manufacture, that are proper for Women to
learn, particularly Imbroideries in Gold or Silver.[27]

Phillips is not yet done with the topic. He insists that John Milton's daughters
knew nothing, nothing!

It had been happy indeed if the Daughters of such a Person had been made in
some measure Inheritrixes of their Father's Learning; but since Fate otherwise
decreed, the greatest Honour that can be ascribed to this now living (and so
would have been to the others, had they lived) is to be Daughter to a man of
his extraordinary Character.[28]

Thus, if we are to believe Phillips, Fate decreed that Deborah—the "this now living"
who is conspicuously not named—was the inheritrix of £100, plus a useless facility for pronouncing six or seven languages without the slightest comprehension.[29]
Phillips skirts the question of who took dictation for the blind Milton, implying that
there was no amanuensis regularly available and that *Paradise Lost* was, accordingly,
"written by whatever hand came next."[30]

Now, this is a remarkably detailed account of three unimportant, uneducated girls
in their relationship to their father, one that jars with the overall tone of Phillips'
memoir of his uncle, whom he styles "the Ornament and Glory of his Countrey."[31]
Phillips' wooden exordium (which wears its learning like a prisoner's chains) purposes an edifying biography of a great man. Yet, counter to this encomiastic intent,
the family apologist makes an abrupt shift to pity his female cousins as untaught,
ill-treated and overworked by a demanding father, until finally released from an
unnatural servitude to learn something proper for women to learn. Phillips' vivid,
avoidable portrayal of an unhappy family circle had a lastingly negative influence
on posterity's judgment of Milton's character. Samuel Johnson, for one, read it as

demonstrating that John Milton was reprehensibly misogynistic even by the dismal standards of his day:

> His family consisted of women; and there appears in his books something like a Turkish contempt of females, as subordinate and inferiour beings. That his own daughters might not break the ranks, he suffered them to be depressed by a mean and penurious education. He thought woman made only for obedience, and man only for rebellion.[32]

Later biographers of John Milton have given primacy to Phillips' account among the early lives because he had firsthand knowledge of some of the events he reported: along with his younger brother John, he lived in the Milton household from 1640 (age ten) until 1646.[33] Intimacy does not foster objectivity, however, and Phillips gives us several hints that these were for him acutely unhappy years. Uncle John was a stern, relentlessly driving schoolmaster, one who was stingy with the food to boot.[34] Aubrey, an adept interviewer, captured one telling detail under the heading "from Mr E. Philips." In it we find Phillips fusing his own experiences with those of Milton's first wife, Mary Powell, who "found it very solitary: no company came to her, often-times heard his Nephews beaten, and cry." Phillips' ambivalence towards his uncle seeps into the formal biography again when he gratuitously speculates that the infirmities of Milton's eldest daughter and the death of his young son may have been due to neglect or negligence.[35]

Phillips clearly projects his own resentments, his bitter memories of emotional neglect and loneliness, on other members of the Milton household. What he writes of his female cousins has a striking parallel to his account—anonymous, it will be recalled—of how John Milton educated his two nephews. Instead of the traditional regimen of Cicero, Virgil, Ovid, Hesiod and Homer, Milton made his young nephews serviceable by putting them through the performance of reading (possibly with little comprehension) obsolescent texts on geocentric astronomy, geography, physiology, agriculture and other technical subjects: "Thus by teaching he in some measure increased his own knowledge, having the reading of all these Authors as it were by Proxy."[36] John Milton's eyesight was already failing, even as he was collecting notes (no doubt dictated to his nephews as they stumbled through their lessons) for an ambitious Latin thesaurus that remained fragmentary at his death.[37] As with the daughters, so with the nephews. They were unable to benefit from exposure to John Milton's genius.

> Had they received his [Milton's] documents with the same Acuteness of Wit and Apprehension, the same Industry, Alacrity, and Thirst after Knowledge, as the Instructer was indued with, what Prodigies of Wit and Learning might they have proved![38]

We must also question how much direct knowledge Edward Phillips could have of his much younger cousins' daily lives. His residence in the household ended before Mary and Deborah were born. In the early fifties he was living in Shrewsbury, although he visited London from time to time.[39] After 1660 he plainly distanced himself from his notorious uncle. He and his brother John were obliged to scrape out a living as tutors, translators and hack writers. In the years immediately following the Restoration, the Milton connection could only hurt them. John Evelyn notes in his diary for October 24, 1663, that Edward Phillips came that day to be his son's tutor: "this gentleman was nephew to Milton, who wrote against Salmasius' Defensio: but was not at all infected with his principles, though brought up by him." Without this repudiation of his uncle, Phillips could not have made it past the job interview. In early 1665 Phillips improved his place by becoming tutor in the household of the Earl of Pembroke, a position he retained until about 1670, which would have kept him in Wiltshire for most of that period.[40] We can be certain that he did not visit Milton during his final illness and did not attend his funeral, since he dates his uncle's death as "the year 1673, toward the latter end of the Summer" when in fact Milton died in early November of 1674.[41] It is easy to slip up over numbers (Phillips makes many such blunders), but people will generally remember the weather or season for important events in their lives.

The volume of state papers bearing Phillips' memoir of his uncle was sufficiently obscure that subsequent Milton biographers, writing on deadline, could make free use of it, paraphrasing or flat-out plagiarizing extensive portions. John Toland claimed to have done original research for the biographical preface he contributed to the 1698 edition of John Milton's prose works. In fact, he follows Edward Phillips closely throughout, even in mistakenly dating Milton's birth to 1606 rather than 1608. With a noteworthy lack of candor, he never cites Phillips as his source, nor does he acknowledge the existence or priority of his published life of his uncle— instead alluding vaguely to having perused "the Papers of one of his Nephews."[42] His account of the daughters' education follows Phillips with slight if significant alterations. Toland, a fervent admirer of Milton's republicanism, neutered Phillips' commentary ("a Tryal of Patience almost beyond endurance") and softened his "condemn'd" to a "forc'd," coupled with the implication that Milton promptly released the girls from further performance once he "understood their Murmurs" as signifying a lack of enthusiasm for their task.

> He had no Children by this last Wife, nor any living by his second; but of his three Daughters by the first, he made two very serviceable to himself, and, in so doing, to the rest of the World. For tho many sent their Sons to read for him, and several grown Persons were ambitious of obliging him that way for their own Improvement; yet he taught these young Women to read and pronounce with great exactness the *English, Italian, Spanish, French, Hebrew, Greec,* and *Latin* Languages. So that whatever Book he had occasion to use, one of 'em was forc'd to read it to him, tho neither of 'em understood a word of those Writings, except *English* their Mother Tongue. This Drudgery could

not but render them in time very uneasy; and accordingly, when he understood their Murmurs, he dispens'd with their Duty in this case, and sent them out to learn other things more becoming their Sex and Condition.[43]

From Toland the story descended to Elijah Fenton, who supplied a biographical foreword to the 1725 edition of *Paradise Lost*. Fenton's only original contribution is an error. He assumes, logically enough, that the task had been imposed on the two elder sisters (since Toland did not distinguish them). Fenton further glosses over any trace of paternal tyranny. His version unintentionally highlights how much effort would have been needed, by father and daughters, to acquire competency in a tedious task that, according to Fenton, was soon discontinued.

> Three daughters by his first wife were then living; the two elder of whom are said to have been very serviceable to him in his Studies. For having been instructed to pronounce not only the Modern, but also the Latin, Greek, and Hebrew languages; they read in their respective Originals whatever Authors He wanted to consult; though they understood none but their mother-tongue. This employment, however, was too unpleasant to be continued for any long process of time; and therefore He dismiss'd them to receive an Education more agreeable to their Sex, and temper.[44]

Alone among the eighteenth-century biographers, Samuel Johnson must get the credit for confronting the absurdity head on. Quoting in full Edward Phillips' account of the daughters' training in exact pronunciation, he sagely remarked, "A language not understood can never be so read as to give pleasure, and very seldom so as to convey meaning."[45] We know that Milton was sensitive to maladroit reading. Thomas Ellwood, who volunteered to read Latin for Milton in the hopes of polishing his own educational attainments, said that Milton would instantly recognize when his comprehension failed him, and would construe the passage for him.[46] If Deborah and Mary were in fact programmed to function as seventeenth-century analogs of text-to-speech software, their usefulness to a blind scholar would be marginal at best, since they would be unable to verify a reference or locate a passage by its context.

We know also that Milton chose to employ a tutor for his daughters rather than send them to a typical dame's school, where they would have learned little more than to sew and to read. He clearly expected them to attain a degree of literacy and general learning that would render them useful to him. William Riley Parker proposes that Milton set high humanistic standards for the education of his daughters, which failed because, he says, they were either too stupid or too rebellious to learn:

> They had the benefits of private tuition, but they seem to have profited little. Perhaps they were incapable of learning much; perhaps they were rebellious.... What they were taught, we do not know. Remembering Milton's own theories of education, his emphasis in actual practice upon rapid learning of many languages, and his natural eagerness to have his daughters serviceable to him

in his blindness, we may reasonably infer that any tutor whom he employed to teach the girls was instructed to prepare them quickly in Latin, Greek, Hebrew, and some modern foreign languages—just as John and Edward Phillips had been prepared. If such was the fact, we know that it resulted in failure—and some would add, 'of course'.[47]

Parker isn't paying attention to the implications of his own words. Milton wanted his daughters to learn languages not, say, metaphysics or math. Acquiring a reading competency in one or more languages requires no special intellectual gifts. Anyone can do it—even girls! It is equally absurd to suppose that Milton, who whipped his nephews freely, would spare the rod with a rebellious daughter who refused to memorize her *hic-haec-hocs*. Biographers, such as Parker, who accept Phillips' representation of the daughters' ignorance are forced to discount Aubrey's biographical notes (often because they *are* notes, rather than a developed and potentially biased narrative) or to strain Aubrey's words, "could read to him Latin: Ital. & French & Greeke," by redefining *read* to mean *pronounce*. In fact, Aubrey had a keen relish for the vivid or telling anecdote. If his informants had said Deborah and Mary were trained to pronounce languages they could not understand, he would not have failed to record such a strange and revealing detail.

Parker feels obliged to accept and rationalize Phillips' story because Deborah Milton Clarke confirmed it in 1727, when curious Londoners—those "finest geniuses and fairest faces"—came to inspect her remarkable resemblance to her father and to pay her the price of a pantomime and rope-dancing. To Phillips' unlikely narrative Deborah added an incredible performance. Not only did she know how to pronounce Latin, Greek, Hebrew, French and Italian without a jot of comprehension, but she could still repeat passages of Greek and Latin poetry that she had last read to her father nearly sixty years ago! Perhaps it is preferable to say that Deborah *apparently* confirmed Phillips' story. Although, as we shall see, she was much visited following the public appeal in *Mist's Weekly Journal,* and nicely compensated, there are no contemporary first-hand accounts to tell us how Deborah entertained her visitors. In February of 1738, when he was in the final stages of preparing a new edition of Milton's works, Thomas Birch solicited an account of Deborah Clarke from his friend Thomas Ward, who duly passed on his decade-old recollections. Birch patched Ward's information into the final pages of his preface (the first section—heavily plagiarized from Phillips—was already at the printer's):

> Mr. Ward saw Mrs. *Clarke, Milton*'s Daughter, at the House of one of her Relations, not long before her Death, "when she informed me," says that Gentleman, "that she and her Sisters [*sic*] us'd to read to their Father in eight Languages; which by practice they were capable of doing with great readiness and accuracy, tho' they understood what they read in no other Language but *English;* and their Father us'd often to say in their hearing, *one Tongue was enough for a Woman*. None of them were ever sent to School, but all taught at home by

a Mistress kept for that purpose. *Isaiah, Homer,* and *Ovid's Metamorphoses* were Books, which they were often call'd to read to their Father; and at my desire she repeated a considerable number of Verses from the beginning of both those Poets with great Readiness. I knew who she was, upon the first sight of her, by the similitude of her Countenance with her Father's Picture. And upon my telling her so, she informed me that Mr. *Addison* told her the same thing, upon her going to wait on him. For he, upon hearing she was living, sent for her, and desired, if she had any Papers of her Father's, she would bring them with her, as an Evidence of her being Mr. *Milton's* Daughter. But immediately upon her being introduc'd to him, he said, *Madam, you need no other Voucher; your Face is a sufficient Testimonial whose Daughter you are.* And he then made her a handsome Present of a purse of Guineas, with a promise of procuring for her an annual Provision for her Life; but he dying soon after, she lost the Benefit of his generous Design. She appear'd to be a Woman of good Sense and a genteel Behaviour, and to bear the Inconveniencies of a low Fortune with decency and prudence."[48]

Ward made one obvious error in summing up his conversation with Deborah Clarke, and he is an untrustworthy source generally.[49] Here he may well have refreshed his memory by dipping into Toland or Fenton. But there are comments gathered by yet another Milton biographer, Jonathan Richardson, which serve to support Ward's account. Deborah's many visitors, all asking more or less the same questions, got the same answers. Is it true that you and your sister could read to your blind father in a half-dozen languages? Yes, we could. Is it true also that you couldn't understand a word of what you read? Now, what should Deborah answer? Are her visitors going to reach into their purses with pity and compassion if she demonstrates her intellectual superiority? Perhaps she feinted with a half-truth: she and her sister were often obliged to read works they didn't understand. Then, when asked if she could remember what books she had read to her father, Deborah amazed and astounded her visitors by reciting passages from Homer, Ovid and Euripides.[50]

It may have happened by chance, acting on an intuition that it would be wiser not to disabuse her pity-prone visitors of their cherished assumptions. Or, scrutinizing the language that Philalethes employed to urge the fashionable elite to leave Hyde Park and line up their glittering coaches in humble Pelham Street, Deborah may have determined that she needed to provide a show. After all, her visitors had been asked to retrench the price of an opera or masquerade, or of a pantomime and rope-dancing. They ought to get something for their money. In the spirit of carnival, she gave them an elderly bluestocking masquerading as an idiot savant.

Acting again as a touchstone for Miltonic mythos, Johnson forcefully expressed his skepticism regarding Deborah's ability to recall incomprehensible texts read to her father over a half-century ago:

This is the daughter of whom publick mention has been made. She could repeat the first lines of Homer, the Metamorphoses, and some of Euripides, by having often read them. Yet here incredulity is ready to make a stand. Many repetitions are necessary to fix in the memory lines not understood; and why should Milton wish or want to hear them so often! These lines were at the beginning of the poems. Of a book written in a language not understood, the beginning raises no more attention than the end; and as those that understand it know commonly the beginning best, its rehearsal will seldom be necessary. It is not likely that Milton required any passage to be so much repeated as that his daughter could learn it; nor likely that he desired the initial lines to be read at all; nor that the daughter, weary of the drudgery of pronouncing unideal sounds, would voluntarily commit them to memory.[51]

Incredulity has made its stand, but without stating its position. Presumably Johnson suspected Deborah had been coached—a possibility Parker also hints at.[52] There is no obvious motivation for Deborah and her unknown prompter to undertake such a tedious task, when she might readily and more naturally entertain her visitors with anecdotes, real or manufactured, of her father.[53] Few people manage to be word-perfect—in this instance phoneme-perfect—when reciting from memory. If Deborah was repeating something truly incomprehensible to her, her slips would have been painfully conspicuous as gibberish; on the contrary, her visitors seem to have found her ready recitations of Greek and Latin adequately accurate.

In any case her visitors were gratifyingly entertained. The glittering coaches of the finest geniuses and fairest faces did stop at her door, and the shillings and occasional guineas piled up—though hardly to match the hyperbole of Voltaire, who must have been among the curious: "I was in London when it became known that a daughter of blind Milton was still alive, old and in poverty, and in a quarter of an hour she was rich."[54] No doubt Deborah had frequent occasion to reminisce about Addison and his purse of guineas. Her visitors must, one and all, have made predictable remarks on her Miltonic features. If any among them were at risk of neglecting Philalethes' stipulation that they were to pay a standard price of admission, they had Addison's splendid precedent set before them as reminder.

Philalethes had been confident that his tear-wringing appeal would "excite crouds" to visit and reward "this old matron." In fact, we have decided hints that Deborah Milton Clarke was in the public eye during her last months. "That Daughter," wrote Richardson in his 1734 life of her father, "who a few years since was So much Visited and Reliev'd for her Father's Sake, and for the Share She had in Producing the *Paradise Lost,* Reading and Writing for him."[55] Richardson expresses his regret that "an Accident" prevented him from meeting Deborah Clarke, for which he compensates by painstakingly accumulating second-hand reports. Contradicting Edward Phillips' claim that *Paradise Lost* was dictated to random early morning callers, Deborah let it be known that she was her father's chief amanuensis. As Richardson learned from her visitors, the blind Milton would lie sleepless or awake early with new lines shaping themselves in his thoughts: "Then, at what Hour soever, he rung for his Daughter to Secure what Came."[56] Of course, Deborah's claim might have been fabricated to increase her cachet. (Her stepmother had apparently put out a rival claim with *her* visitors.)[57] However, Richardson acquired two unique descriptions of John Milton in dictation mode, which sound genuine and which most likely came from visitors to Deborah's Spitalfields salon:[58]

> Other Stories I have heard concerning the Posture he was Usually in when he Dictated, that he Sat leaning Backward Obliquely in an Easy Chair, with his Leg flung over the Elbow of it. that he frequently Compos'd lying in Bed in a Morning.... I have been also told he would Dictate many, perhaps 40 Lines as it were in a Breath, and then reduce them to half the Number.[59]

From the perspective of a Deborah Miltonist, establishing the identities of her father's amanuenses is hardly crucial. Nonetheless, it is worth pointing out that Edward Phillips' contention that *Paradise Lost* was "written by whatever hand came next" is not plausible. First drafts are intensely personal creations: Milton would not have submitted to being "milked" by casual callers.[60] Ellwood was a daily visitor during some of the period in which *Paradise Lost* was composed, yet he knew nothing of the work until Milton loaned him the completed manuscript in 1665.

Richardson appeals to Deborah's testimony to refute opinions that John Milton was "a Severe and Cruel Father," a topic that occupies him for seven pages, more space than he devotes to defending Milton from the charge of Arianism. Deborah clearly made a strongly favorable impression on her visitors that was communicated almost by contagion to Richardson. Now it is the father, not the daughter, who must be defended against a charge of undutifulness:

> It has been said, This Daughter not only withdrew her Assistance in Reading, &c. but went away to *Ireland,* where She Married, all, not only without her Father's Consent, but even his Knowledge. but I never heard 'twas upon Occasion of any Unkindness of His, Unless as having Married.[61]

These two cluttered and eccentric sentences are hair-pullingly ambiguous. It has been said—by whom? By Deborah's visitors, who had it directly from her lips? Or by some unnamed others who passed it third-hand, with their own interpretations, to Richardson, who dutifully hands it on to us? Richardson's "Reading, &c." reminds us—as if we needed reminding!—that the etcetera is a point in dispute among Milton's many biographers.

Despite his stylistic idiosyncrasies, Richardson was a diligent, shrewd and independent biographer. If "an Accident" had not prevented their meeting, we would certainly be able to know a great deal more about Deborah Milton—and about her more famous father. Richardson read Toland and Wood (not Phillips) but never copies them. He was sufficiently perceptive to dispute the claim (derived from Phillips) that Milton experienced writer's block for half of every year:

I cannot Comprehend ... that a Man with Such a Work in his Head can Suspend it for Six Months together, or but One; though it may go on more Slowly, but it must go On.[62]

In the course of his lengthy plea to find Milton innocent of the charge of paternal cruelty, Richardson hits upon the probable kernel of fact underlying Phillips' much-repeated story. Milton's multilingual daughter Deborah had merely been asked to read dull and difficult books which could not interest her:

What is there in All This Much more than what is done very Commonly, That of requiring a Child to read what He or She as little Understands, or takes Pleasure in as these Girls did his Latin, Greek, Hebrew, &c?[63]

For all his interest in Deborah Milton Clarke, Richardson never mentions her daughter, Elizabeth Clarke Foster, in his 1734 biography and apparently never sought an interview with her. Richardson was effectively the last of the early biographers to acquire fresh information. But the biographies kept coming, commissioned by publishers wishing to distinguish new editions. Successive biographers maintained a façade of diligence and originality by attributing old information to new sources. In 1738, when much of his preface was already at the printer's, Thomas Birch made a last-minute visit to Elizabeth Foster in search of supplemental information for his highly derivative biography:

I visited Mrs. *Foster,* her Daughter, from whose Mouth I had the following particulars, which she had often heard from her Mother; who meeting with very ill treatment from *Milton's* last Wife, left her Father, and went to live with a Lady, whom she call'd *Merian.* This Lady going over to *Ireland,* and resolving to take *Milton's* Daughter with her, if he would give his Consent, wrote a Letter to him of her Design, and assur'd him, that *as Chance had thrown his Daughter under her care, she would treat her no otherwise than as his Daughter and her own Companion.* She liv'd with that Lady, till her Marriage, and came over again to *England* during the Troubles in *Ireland,* under King *James* II.[64]

In 1742 the Fosters relocated to Lower Holloway, then the rural outskirts of London, where they were most likely forgotten, moving back to outer London early in 1749. In 1750, when Birch paid her several visits, Elizabeth Foster resumed her mother's life story, giving her interviewer further details, which he neglected to record except in summary form:

She gave me a particular Account of the Severities of her Grandfather's last Wife towards his three Daughters by his first, the two eldest of whom she bound prentices to Workers in Gold-Lace, without his Knowledge, and forc'd the younger to leave his Family. Mrs. Foster confess'd to me, that he was no fond Father, but assur'd me that his Wife's ill Treatment of his Children gave him great Uneasiness; tho' in his State of Health & Blindness he could not prevent it.[65]

Elizabeth Foster is our sole source for the information that Deborah, after leaving home, became a companion to a lady called Merian. Barbara Lewalski assumes that Deborah's patroness was an unidentified Irish aristocrat, a Lady Merian; Parker takes Merian to be a surname, possibly a mistake for Merrion, Meryon, or Meriam; Shawcross simply states that Deborah went to Ireland around 1672 as companion to a Mrs. Merian.[66] None of them could have tried very hard to identify her. She is surely Mary Stapleton Fitzwilliam, wife of Thomas Fitzwilliam, 4th Viscount of Merrion. Contemporaries would have commonly referred to her as Lady Merrion. The Fitzwilliams were Catholic royalists who took up arms to defend the thrones of Charles I and James II. Such a family might seem unlikely to host the child of John Milton, unless one gives a sinister interpretation to the words, "treat her no otherwise than as his Daughter." However, the Fitzwilliams had hedged their bets by making politically prudent matches with daughters and sisters of prominent Parliamentarians. Oliver Fitzwilliam, the 2nd Viscount (later Earl of Tyrconnell), married Eleanor Holles, daughter of the 1st Earl of Clare and sister to Denzil Holles. The marriage of his nephew Thomas, who became 4th Viscount in 1673 at the death of his father, may have been arranged or facilitated by the Holles family. His wife Mary was the daughter of Sir Phillip Stapleton (died 1647), a leader of the Presbyterian political party who had been closely associated with Denzil Holles. As a consequence of these useful family ties, the Fitzwilliams were among the very few Irish Catholic families who managed to regain or retain their estates within the Pale despite the punitive confiscations that took place under Cromwell and again after the Williamite Revolution.[67] (They possessed 2923 plantation acres, equaling 4735 English acres, in County Dublin.) Had James II managed to recover his crown, the Fitzwilliams might have had an opportunity to return the favor.

I have not been able to find a date for the marriage of Thomas Fitzwilliam and Mary Stapleton, but some point in the early 1670s seems likely. A portrait in the Fitzwilliam Museum in Cambridge bears the inscription "Mary Stapylton Wiffe of Thomas Ld Visc^t Fitzwilliam 1679." It was a second marriage for her, the widow of a man identified as Bigges of Gray's Inn. Foster's description of the letter written by Lady Merrion to John Milton suggests by its wording that she knew him, at least through shared connections, which is likely enough given her background. The phrase "as Chance had thrown his Daughter under her care" emphasizes that this relationship was not formally arranged or planned. When life with her stepmother became insupportable, Deborah may have shuffled among family and friends before she found a home with this lady.

Parker, who always attempts to follow Phillips, supposes that Deborah *was* apprenticed to embroidery workers but broke her indentures.[68] If that were the case, there is no reason for Foster to have suppressed this portion of her mother's biography; even supposing that she and her mother viewed such an apprenticeship as demeaning, it would serve as an another instance of the stepmother's malice. In contradicting Phillips' insistence that the three sisters were sent out together as apprentices in embroidery work, Foster gives a markedly different spin to the same set of facts.

From E. Foster: "the two eldest of whom she bound prentices to Workers in Gold-Lace, without his Knowledge"
From E. Phillips: "at length they were all (even the Eldest also) sent out to learn some Curious and Ingenious sorts of Manufacture, that are proper for Women to learn, particularly Imbroideries in Gold or Silver"

Phillips' "even the Eldest also" is a clue that he is engaged in gilding and embroidering the family history. Five years later, when her signature was required to acknowledge receipt of her share of her father's estate, Anne Milton put on paper a shaky scrawl that is either entirely meaningless or a failed attempt to form the letter M. We do not know whether her disabilities were mental or physical or both, but she was manifestly incapable of curious and ingenious needlework. This seems a clear instance of what contemporaries termed apprenticeship for labor, as opposed to apprenticeship for education. The sisters were not sent out to learn a ladylike craft but rather put to work as menials.

Elizabeth Foster certainly ought to be a more reliable source for her mother's life than Edward Phillips. But Birch also reports her as saying that Deborah was prevented by her father from learning to write.

That he kept his Daughters at a great distance; and would not allow them to learn to write, which he thought unnecessary for a Woman.[69]

This is pushing Phillips' theme to the point of absurdity. Even if Milton had held such a belief, he would have consulted his necessities and made use of his daughters as scribes, as Aubrey informed us he did with Deborah. In any case, this assertion is easy to disprove because the three releases from 1675, acknowledging their stepmother's payments, signed by the sisters and by Deborah's new husband, have survived.[70] Anne's pathetic scribble has already been described. Mary wrote her name clearly enough, but her handwriting has a labored appearance suggesting inexperience and a too tightly held pen. She formed her first name with relative ease compared to her last name, "millton." Although it's possible this was her preferred spelling, the thick strokes of the second *l* and the *t* betray a slip of the pen that she didn't know how to fix. Her writing also slants strongly upward. Deborah's signature has a different character altogether. It is a legible, no-nonsense hand, written in a loose, rapid style without ornamentation. She too makes a mistake with her last name, writing C-l-a-r-k, then beginning another upstroke before catching herself and putting in the final *e*. Her father's biographers condescendingly attribute the error to a lack of familiarity with her married name. But there is a more obvious and meaningful explanation for anyone who is interested in understanding Deborah's life and experiences.

She and her sisters had fallen out of touch. We know that because they used Deborah's maiden name when listing her as a party to the dispute over the oral will in December of 1674. If her sisters did not know she had married, then Deborah may not have learned of her father's death until some later date. Perhaps someone got word to her in February of 1675, when the widow settled accounts with Anne and Mary. She has not had much time to recover from the shock when the release was prepared for her signature one month later. Her father is dead, her stepmother is cheating her, and there's nothing she can do about it. She makes a mistake because she's upset; the signature, especially in the first three letters, has an agitated appearance.

The implausible assertion that Milton kept his daughters from learning to write may have originated in a misunderstanding on Birch's part. Foster was perhaps speaking of the education of Christopher Milton's daughters, not John's. One of them, Catherine Milton, lived with the Fosters in Lower Holloway from about 1742 until her death in 1746. On some surviving documents, excavated by industrious John Milton scholars, she and her sister signed with a mark.[71] Thomas Newton likewise states that Elizabeth told him that her mother was not allowed to learn to write. However, given that Newton's statement is word-for-word identical with Birch's, this apparent confirmation is only another instance of the mutual cribbing that is rife among Milton's eighteenth-century biographers:

> That he kept his daughters at a great distance, and would not allow them to learn to write, which he thought unnecessary for a woman.[72]

For the preface to his 1750 edition of *Paradise Lost,* Newton, like Birch before him, attempted to give a fresh look to stale facts with a visit to the Fosters, who had recently moved back to London from Lower Holloway. Describing Elizabeth Foster patronizingly as a "good plain sensible woman," he cites her as his source for a disconnected series of Miltonic trivia, ranging from John Milton's eating habits to his financial losses at the Restoration to the birthplace of his father. His handling of the familiar tale of the daughters' ignorance achieves a certain originality by fusing elements of Phillips' original narrative (including some of his phrasing) with details gathered by Birch from Foster:

> His daughters were not sent to school, but were instructed by a mistress kept at home for that purpose: and he himself, excusing the eldest on account of an impediment in her speech, taught the two others to read and pronounce Greek and Latin and several other languages, without understanding any but English, for he used to say that one tongue was enough for a woman: but this employment was very irksome to them, and this together with the sharpness and severity of their mother in law made them very uneasy at home; and therefore they were all sent abroad to learn things more proper for them, and particularly imbroidery in gold and silver. As Milton at his death left his affairs very much in the power of his widow, tho' she acknowledged that he died worth one thousand five hundred pounds, yet she allowed but one hundred pounds to each of his three daughters."[73]

The last bald statement is surprising. Even if Elizabeth Minshull Milton was the termagant Richardson termed her ("a woman of a most violent spirit" says Newton), she was unlikely to make such a frank admission of fraud. Newton is mishandling the ambiguous phrasing Birch picked up from Foster, inheritrix of her mother's bitterness towards the stepmother: "*Milton*'s Widow, tho' she own'd, that he died worth 1500 *l.* yet allow'd his three Daughters but 100 *l.* each."[74] The phrase "she own'd" could be construed either as "the stepmother admitted" or as "my informant Mrs. Foster claimed," with the latter surely representing Birch's sense. We have here a particularly inept example of the biographers' practice of rifling each other's facts and phrases.

Having rediscovered Milton's last surviving descendant, Newton makes one final use of her to set out the hackneyed observation, beloved by John Milton's biographers, that it's tough to make a living as a poet:

> In all probability Milton's whole family will be extinct with her, and he can live only in his writings. And such is the caprice of fortune, this grandaughter of a man, who will be an everlasting glory to the nation, has now for some years with her husband kept a little chandler's or grocer's shop for their subsistence, lately at the lower Holloway in the road between Highgate and London, and at present in Cock Lane not far from Shoreditch Church. Another thing let me mention, that is equally to the honor of the present age. Tho' Milton received not above ten pounds at two different payments for the copy of Paradise Lost, yet Mr. Hoyle author of the treatise on the Game of Whist, after having disposed of all the first impression, sold the copy to the bookseller, as I have been informed, for two hundred guineas.[75]

These sentences yoke together disparate notions that comprise a single, highly prized theme of Milton's biographers, one they are at considerable pains to uphold in their selection of the evidence: let's call it the *sui generis* topos. It can be detected as an influence upon readings of Milton from his times down to our own, and it contributes to the persistent underestimation of the intelligence of his daughter and granddaughter. It goes like this: Milton was unique, inimitable, in multiple literal, biographical and figurative applications. He left no monetary inheritance to his offspring because he himself was poor and unappreciated; he had no offspring capable of inheriting his genius because his children (all daughters) were pathetically stupid; his line (artistic and familial) is extinct, though he himself will live forever in his writings.

Newton is notably precise about the occupation and current address of Elizabeth Foster and her husband. There is an implicit appeal for patronage, if not outright charity. Her grandfather was cheated by his publisher and so she must keep a miserable chandler's shop to eke out a bare subsistence. There is an echo here of Philalethes, who also drew an ironic link between the poverty of Milton's descendants and the affluence of his publisher.[76] The least you can do, reader, Newton implies, is send your housemaid to Cock Lane to buy you your candles and soap.

Ultimately, Newton's paragraph brought the Fosters more than just a little extra custom to their shop. As a postscript to his attack on Milton as a plagiarist of obscure neo-Latin poets (the inversion of the *sui generis* topos), William Lauder fastened onto Newton's words as displaying callous disregard of the sufferings of Milton's granddaughter:

> That this relation is true, cannot be questioned:—but, surely, the honour of letters, the dignity of sacred poetry, the spirit of the *English* nation, and the glory of human nature, require—that it should be true no longer. In an age, in which statues are erected to the honour of this great writer, in which his effigy has been diffused on medals, and his work propagated by translations, and illustrated by commentaries; in an age, which, amidst all its vices, and all its follies, has not become infamous for want of charity: it may be, surely, allowed to hope, that the living remains of MILTON will be no longer suffered to languish in distress.... And, surely, to those, who refuse their names to no other scheme of expence, it will not be unwelcome, that a SUBSCRIPTION is proposed, for relieving, in the languor of age, the pains of disease, and the contempt of poverty, the grand-daughter of the author of PARADISE LOST.[77]

Lauder's over-the-top adoption of Elizabeth Foster's cause is dripping with irony and malice, yet it was not without positive consequences for the Fosters. The subscription, plus a benefit performance of *Comus,* held April 5, 1750, yielded £130.[78] Lauder was soon shown to have forged his best evidence for labelling Milton a plagiary. Strong-armed by Samuel Johnson into penning a formal confession, he subsequently offered a curious good-from-evil defense:

> And, lastly, may I beg leave to remark, that *Milton*'s only surviving Posterity, Mrs. *Elizabeth Foster,* reaped more real Advantage from a Proposal of mine, addressed to the Public in her Favour, in a Postscript subjoined to my Dissertation, than from the Writers of the highest Encomiums and formal Panegyrics on the great Author, or his Works, put all together.[79]

She did reap real advantage but she may not have needed it so direly as Milton's biographers, pursuing their theme of deprivation, wished to believe. Elizabeth Clarke Foster was not in fact impoverished. She and her husband had inherited at least £350, perhaps more, from their cousin-once-removed, Catherine Milton, who died in 1746.[80] There may have been debts to claim some part of it, but the remainder (£200 were settled on Elizabeth) would still be a substantial nest-egg for a childless couple—not that the extra £130 from the benefit would have been unwelcome. Thomas Birch's journal entry for January 6, 1750, provides an insight into Elizabeth Foster's awareness of the commercial value of being granddaughter of the great poet:

> I Visited Mrs. Foster, Grand-daughter to Milton, who keeps a chandler's shop
> in Cock-Lane near Shoreditch-Church. ... I presented her 5 Guineas from Mr.
> Yorke. She shew'd me her Grand-Mother's Bible ... in a Blank Leafe of which
> Milton had enter'd in his own Hands the Births of his Children.[81]

Birch had previously visited Foster at least twice, but on neither occasion had she
allowed him a look at this relic, which Ward (who probably had the street smarts to
tip her an admission fee) had seen in 1738.[82] In the same journal entry Birch notes:

> Dr. Newton had been with her, & given her a Guinea some time ago; Mr
> Lauder lately, & Dr. Foster within these few Days.[83]

It's unclear from this cryptic entry whether the latter two callers paid visits only or
guineas too. There were occasional granddaughter gifts still coming to Elizabeth
Foster. Birch visited her again in November of 1750, bringing with him a present
(amount unspecified) from a friend. In December another subscription in her
behalf was announced in *Gentleman's Magazine*, but the proceeds are unknown.
She died on May 9, 1754. Birch, who seems to have taken a liking to her, or else
a longing for that family Bible, presided at her funeral. The silver seal that had
belonged first to John and then to Deborah Milton was kept by Thomas Foster
and acquired after his death by Thomas Hollis. The Bible passed down by Mary
Powell Milton to her daughter and granddaughter went missing in the late eighteenth century.

The attentive reader will have noted that my biographical account of Deborah Milton
Clarke is derived from the secondary sources devoted to cataloging every attestation of her father's earthly existence. There are undoubtedly additional primary
sources—constituting The Life Records of Deborah Milton—to be discovered and
analyzed by scholars seeking traces of her life in Dublin and London. The original petition to Robert Hartley, presumably surviving among the Portland Papers
now at the British Library, ought to be transcribed and published in facsimile. A
paleographic examination of the petition and of Deborah's signature might lead
to the discovery of other samples of her writing. A careful scrutiny of archival
correspondence and diaries from the period might turn up allusions to Deborah
Milton Clarke or to D. M., the author of *Marius & Delia*. It would be sad to think
that, among Deborah's many visitors in the last months of her life, no one showed
an interest in her for herself or elicited her personal history.

    In sketching Deborah's life from the sources devoted to her father's, I have also
presented the most conservative interpretation of the evidence. There are alternative,
possibly more persuasive explanations for Edward Phillips' insistence on Deborah's
intractable stupidity. His hostility might stem from a fundamental disapproval of
Deborah for not limiting herself to occupations and endeavors "that are proper for
Women." He may have felt the honor of the family required him to expunge the
transgressive image of an educated Deborah Milton with pen in hand, replacing it

with that of an semi-literate girl mouthing words from books which she could not comprehend. Certainly there was an estrangement between the two cousins that is unmistakable in the clumsy wording of his concluding fillip: "the greatest Honour that can be ascribed to this now living (and so would have been to the others, had they lived) is to be Daughter to a man of his extraordinary Character."

Having exercised such exemplary restraint in presenting the scanty biographical information currently available, I will now venture to speculate on Deborah Milton's formative experiences, with their impact on her views and her motivations as a writer. I am well aware that I am teetering on a two-legged stool: extrapolating from a bare set of names, dates and events, and, yet more treacherously, from my own reading of her novel. I should state at the outset that I do not suppose *Marius & Delia* to be autobiographical, except in occasional details, and even these have been transformed and repurposed by artistic imperatives. Although chapter 6 presents a parodic version of Deborah's life with father—a parody in which both father and daughter are caricatured and distorted—very little else in the novel can be assumed to be taken from life.

Generalizing from Edward Phillips' experience, we can presume that John Milton was not affectionate with or interested in children except as subjects for pedagogical experiments. His daughters would have gotten very little of his time until or unless they were capable of demonstrating intellectual abilities above the average. Deborah must have been left under the charge of nurses and housemaids of varying levels of competency and kindness until her fifth year. A sudden change for the better came at age 4½ when her father married the young Katherine Woodcock, who defied convention and folklore by proving to be "very indulgent to her children in law."[84] This happy interval came to an end fourteen months later when her kind-hearted stepmother died. Now approaching her sixth birthday, old enough to be able to read and to write a simple join-hand, Deborah may well have exerted herself, as child and scholar, to get her father's attention and affection.[85]

The always-interesting Aubrey, having recorded in his notes that Deborah was "very like her father" and could read several languages, added: "The other sister is Mary, more like hr [*sic*] mother."[86] (Anne died a few years before Aubrey did his interviews.) More than mere physical resemblance is implied here. If Aubrey found these observations worth recording, they must have been communicated to him with some degree of emphasis, as a facet of family lore, implying a good daughter/ bad daughter dichotomy. Given the incompatibilities of that unhappy first marriage, there is a hint of opposition or antipathy between Mary and her father, and perhaps also between Deborah and her elder, less favored sister. Mary, whose handwriting shows her to be no scholar, may well have been burdened with extra household responsibilities, sandwiched as she was between a handicapped older sister and a privileged younger one. In the dispute over the oral will, the gossipy testimony of the maids smeared Mary as the most culpable of Milton's "unkind children." She is reported as reacting to her father's remarriage in 1663 with bitter adolescent sarcasm, "that was noe News to heare of his wedding but if shee could heare of his death that was something."[87]

With the restoration of the Stuart monarchy in 1660, Deborah's father lost his pension, lost most of his savings, and nearly lost his life. Knowing himself to be at risk of suffering a traitor's death, Milton absconded for four months, leaving his daughters—to fend for themselves? Under the care of their maternal grandmother or their uncle? No one knows. He resurfaced after the promulgation of the Act of Oblivion, when, to the surprise of many, he was not one of the exceptions reserved for trial and execution. Late in 1660 Milton was imprisoned on an old warrant for some unknown time, perhaps a month or two, and again his daughters presumably had to cope on their own. At some point in the upheaval of this year, Deborah, now age eight, must have come to understand that their father, who had been a great man, honored and admired by so many distinguished visitors, was in fact despised by a large and now very vocal majority of those who knew his name. In August his books were burned by the common hangman at the Old Bailey. Richardson reported that he was afraid to go out of doors for fear of assault.[88] In print, and possibly in the street, he was name-called a poison-spitting blind adder, a blind beetle, a base mercenary scribe, an impudent and blasphemous libeler and, more broadly, a filthy beast with a vicious mind. Deborah must have heard some of the abuse being applied to him. Mary, who turned twelve in November, was old enough to understand what their father's infamy meant for their future.

The family moved twice in the six months after the Act of Oblivion. Perhaps Deborah's father was still adjusting to his straitened circumstances. After settling in the house in Jewin Street, it must have occurred to him that a wife is cheaper than a servant. In February of 1663 he married for a third time; his bride, Elizabeth Minshull, was thirty years his junior. A good-natured widow with some savings would have been a more rational choice, but Milton had a visceral distaste for taking an experienced partner to his bed. He may have believed a virginal young woman would be more pliable. If so, he was destined for disillusionment (again). We don't know how well or ill the stepmother initially got along with her new husband's daughters (ages 16, 14 and 11½). Mary was certainly of an age to resent the sudden introduction of a stepmother. If there is any truth to the servants' gossip about Mary, she may have launched the hostilities, to which Elizabeth Minshull Milton responded with loaded cannon and with all the tactical advantages of the in-charge adult.

Deborah was spared the worst horrors of 1665, the plague year. Her father, or perhaps her stepmother, responded to danger in a more timely fashion than he had in 1660. The family got out of town in time, probably in late June or early July. Thomas Ellwood, Milton's young Quaker friend, obligingly secured a rental for the family in Chalfont St. Giles, Buckinghamshire. They would stay in this pleasant rural retreat for seven or eight months, until the plague abated in late winter. This sojourn may have been Deborah's first experience of rural life, of woods and fields, of air untainted by the sulfurous coal smoke of London. She would also have had, potentially, an exposure to Fifth Monarchists as well as Quakers, as both sects had a presence in this village.

The Great Fire of 1666 did not reach beyond the city wall at Cripplegate, sparing the Milton family's neighborhood altogether, although it destroyed the house in Bread Street that John Milton had inherited from his father. On August 15 of 1666, two weeks before the fire, Milton dictated an overdue but hardly urgent letter, including in it a complaint about his amanuensis *du jour,* a boy with no knowledge of Latin, to whom he had to spell out his words. Deborah must have been absent or ill, presumably for more than a few days, or her father wouldn't have undertaken such a tedious chore. Perhaps he had come to rely upon her so entirely that he had no backup assistance. In 1662 Thomas Ellwood had been accepted as an afternoon visitor and reader, but let to understand that his presence was superfluous:

> I [was] admitted to come to him; not as a Servant to him (which at that time he needed not), nor to be in the House with him: but only to have the Liberty of Coming to his House at certain Hours when I would, and to read to him what Books he should appoint me.[89]

Illness might seem more likely than absence, given the family's straitened means and her father's need for her to supply (in Phillips' highly depersonalizing phrase) his want of eyesight with her eyes and tongue. However, she probably had some opportunities to exchange visits with her cousins, Christopher Milton's daughters, in Ipswich. Thus, it is unclear whether Deborah was home during the terrible four days of the Fire. It is perhaps significant that *Marius & Delia* registers its impact through the second-hand accounts of fleeing survivors.

We don't know how rapidly the relationship between the stepmother and the three sisters soured, or if all three were equally in her bad graces. Deborah did, after all, make out better than her sisters in the settlement of their claims to their father's estate. When Aubrey collected his notes in 1681, some of his positive report on Deborah as her father's favorite seems to have come from the widow, whom Aubrey had sought out and interviewed. Certainly, though, the feuding had made for general household misery by 1670, seven years into the marriage. The coincidence of Milton's lodging with the bookseller Millington at roughly the same time that his two elder daughters were apprenticed out by their stepmother is too great to be ignored, although John Milton's biographers have in fact ignored it.[90] It certainly appears as if he deserted his daughters, although a blind man suffering from severe gout can perhaps be pardoned for showing the self-absorption of the invalid. That seems to have been Deborah's mature viewpoint, as presented by her daughter to Birch eighty years after the family breakup: "he was no fond Father, but [she] assur'd me that his Wife's ill Treatment of his Children gave him great Uneasiness, tho' in his State of Health & Blindness he could not prevent it."[91] In the course of the same conversation, Foster told Birch that the stepmother compelled

Deborah to leave ("forc'd the younger to leave his Family"), but one hardly knows how literally to take the verb. Elizabeth Minshull Milton might have only made it unpleasant for Deborah to stick around, especially after her father had taken off to seek his own peace and quiet in bachelor's lodgings with his friend Millington.

We don't know the date of Deborah's departure for Ireland with Lady Merrion. When George Vertue visited her in 1721 to ask her opinion of the various portraits of her father, she explained her lack of familiarity with the Faithorne portrait, done in 1670, by the fact that "she was several years in Ireland, both before & after his Death."[92] While we might interpret this remark as indicating she went to Ireland with Lady Merrion very soon after leaving home, it is equally possible that she remained in London for some unknown time without visiting, perhaps fearing that her father would demand her return to full-time duty as amanuensis and assistant caretaker. She was now eighteen. She may have wanted her freedom, or as much freedom as a moneyless, mostly friendless young woman could enjoy in seventeenth-century England.

Mostly friendless: I believe Lady Merrion would have treated Deborah as a friend and companion rather than a servant. Elizabeth Foster's passed-along comments about this lady suggest that Deborah had fond recollections of the relationship. On her side, Lady Merrion, the former Mrs. Mary Bigges, must have valued the company of a woman from her own background as she adapted to life in an aristocratic Irish Catholic household and to Ireland itself. One hundred and forty years of English effort to eradicate Irish law, custom and culture had produced uneven results, even within the Pale. Outside Dublin, which was a compact, bustling imitation of London, the country people kept to their traditions, to their language and to their religion. There were nucleated villages—Deborah likely saw them—that still practiced the rundale field system (comparable to the communal open-field agriculture of medieval England) along with booleying, a communal system of seasonal grazing.[93] The Fitzwilliams were thoroughly anglicized, with a tradition of sending their sons to Gray's Inn, but their tenants and many of their servants must have been Gaelic Irish. If Deborah accompanied her lady on the family's rounds of visits to other noble households, she would have witnessed, upstairs and downstairs, castle and village, the divergent life of seventeenth-century Ireland.

Compared to their English counterparts, Irish Catholics enjoyed a certain degree of toleration, or at least of only intermittent repression. A family as wealthy and powerful as the Fitzwilliams of Merrion would have had a resident priest and private chapel, in which they would not have stinted a ritual magnificence appropriate to the family's status as well as its piety. In her *Making Ireland English,* Ohlmeyer instances this family for a lavish keep-up-with-the-Butlers-and-Boyles lifestyle.[94] Although Deborah's status in the household may have been that of an upper servant, she would have witnessed, and partly enjoyed, life in the grand aristocratic style, enthusiastically aped from French, Italian and English models. Dublin's artisans and merchants brought London and European fashion to their wealthy customers as imitations and imports. It is reasonable to suppose that Lady Merrion had an account with a Dublin silk mercer named Abraham Clarke, and that her companion managed the details of her purchases.

We don't know whether Deborah married for love or for a home of her own. I will venture to guess that it was a prosperous, well-to-do home, going on little more than her husband's confident, flourishing signature and his upscale trade in silks and other luxury textiles. We know that they had ten children and that their last child, Elizabeth, was born in November of 1688. Some weeks or months later, Deborah took ship for England, apparently leaving her newborn, her husband and her older children behind in Ireland. Of the many possible explanations for her solo departure, from sudden widowhood to a simple cut-and-run, her daughter's words "during the Troubles in *Ireland,* under King *James* II," suggest a motive as well as a date.

The OED defines *the troubles,* with or without a capital *T,* as public disturbance, disorder or confusion; and, more specifically, as referring to any of the various Irish rebellions and civil wars from 1641 down to 1919. In the more general sense, *the troubles* began soon after James took the throne and began distributing honors and offices to his fellow Roman Catholics. His Irish viceroy, Richard Talbot, newly created Earl of Tyrconnell, pursued an aggressively pro-Catholic policy, remodeling army, judiciary and town corporations to obtain a Catholic majority—which would yield a Catholic-controlled parliament at the next elections. No one, Protestant or Catholic, had any doubt that Tyrconnell aimed at overturning the 1660 Act of Settlement, which had confirmed Protestant possession of lands seized from Catholic royalists under Cromwell. The settlement was in fact repealed in the 1689 parliament by an act that additionally authorized the seizure of land belonging to rebels to James' rule (with rebellion defined so broadly as to include anyone who had corresponded with family or friends in England).

In such a climate of who's-in/who's-out uncertainty, few people would have felt it was the right moment to splurge on luxury goods. Moreover, there was an ongoing exodus of affluent, at-risk Protestants carrying their wives, children and movables back to the homeland. Some may well have neglected to settle their accounts with the greengrocer, the chandler and the silk mercer before they left. Once *the troubles* intensified to civil war there was an almost complete cessation of trade. Since most of his textiles would have been imported, Clarke would have had few goods to sell, few customers to buy them, and many bad debts on his books. There was even a shortage of good money for settling such debts. English monarchs from Henry VIII onwards had routinely forced an inferior underweight coinage on Ireland. Desperate for cash to equip and maintain his army, James II took this tactic to a new extreme by striking vast quantities of brass coins, from sixpences to crowns, which were radically devalued after the defeat of James' army in the battle of the Boyne.[95] A business failure, precipitated by the troubles of Jacobite Ireland, would explain the permanent breakup of the Clarke household. No longer able to maintain a large family—an eleventh child would be disastrous—Deborah and Abraham parted ways and had their children parceled out to relatives able to take them in.

Let's suppose that Deborah Milton Clarke, dispossessed and effectively widowed, came back to London with the intention of making a living as a writer and translator. She happened to have one good contact who could help her get a start on Grub Street. Her cousin John Phillips made a living with his pen and was a talented writer of burlesque. In his 1705 memoirs the publisher John Dunton gave a pungent assessment of John's abilities and disabilities as a hack writer:

> Mr *Philips,* a Gentleman of good Learning, and well born. He'll write you a *Design,* off in a very little Time, if the Gout (or Claret) don't stop him.[96]

It's possible John helped Deborah find writing and translating work, or subcontracted some of his own to her, and there is one interesting coincidence to support this conjecture. Gout or claret or disease put a stop to John Phillips' prolific career not long after Dunton published his tweet-sized character sketch. Phillips' last bylined piece (of a lifetime total near fifty) appeared in 1706; his death thus falls within the period in which Deborah petitioned Harley for financial support. Alternatively, Deborah may have managed well enough on her own until failing eyesight forced her to quit writing and translating. She had needed glasses since she was eighteen and she must have greatly feared undergoing her father's fate.[97] A thorough scrutiny of pseudonymous and anonymous publications from 1689 to 1708, including translations, might hope to identify samples of her bread-and-butter writing. I suspect she would have signed herself D. M. only on her best work. Those initials, like the silver seal which she salvaged from her father's estate, mark her as the literary inheritrix of the great prose stylist who had signed J. M. to his own prose works.

Those twenty-odd years in Dublin leave no obvious trace in Deborah's novel; yet her immersion in Anglo-Irish culture must have heightened a sense of dislocation and alienation upon her return to London. After the Great Fire, residential rebuilding began within a few months but proceeded fitfully. The grand public and institutional buildings under the plan of Wren took shape during her years in Ireland. The ramshackle London of her childhood, the unplanned, essentially organic growth of a millennium, swept away by an apocalyptic conflagration, had been replaced by a new city of brick and stone and of a relentlessly symmetrical and uniform design. It must have been disorienting, quite literally bewildering, to wander about a rebuilt London that had been shorn of the landmarks of her youth. There were other changes too: less material but no less significant. The slow, fitful transformation of England from an agrarian economy of independent small producers to a world power with a permanent underclass of impoverished wage-earners took place over the course of two centuries, roughly and crudely datable as the period from 1640 to 1840. Yet the years from 1666 to 1696 registered cataclysmic changes that would be strikingly manifest to someone returning from a long absence. The rebuilding of London had generated great fortunes for successful speculators, thus widening the divide between rich and poor. There were also immense profits, ruthlessly achieved by bribery and jobbery, involved in equipping the army and navy during the Nine Years' War (1688–97). New, complex financial systems had to be developed to handle the strain of William III's endless war, which, together with the increasing concentration of wealth, combined to propel England into the capitalist and consumerist era. The founding of the Bank of England in 1694 signalled the end of the old ways of direct exchange and of small-scale buying and selling. Culturally, too, it was not the England of 1670. An abrupt *volte-face* to an obsession with order and propriety—mirror-image of the *joie-de-vivre* license of Restoration London—came in with William and Mary. The 1690s saw the foundation of the Society for the Reformation of Manners and the passage of laws increasing the penalties for crimes against property. Even the character of English prose was affected. The inventive exuberance of Burton's, Browne's and the elder Milton's prose was blue-penciled into the desiccated, no-big-words-please clarity of Addison and Steele's essays, attuned to the market for more accessible work. This aesthetic shift to a plain style has been credited to the influence of the Royal Society, but it also constitutes a capitalist venture to provide a more vendible product. Propriety, profit, property: the watchwords of the new era. Deborah's outsider status shaped and sharpened her awareness of this shift in values.

We do not know when *Marius & Delia* was written. There are certain clues in the text to help us hazard a date for it. Reference in chapter 13 to a reward of forty pounds for informing on coin-clippers would date the text after April of 1695 when the law was passed. The business of coin-clipping and counterfeiting depicted in that chapter, along with the mock dedication's references to "a newfangled bank note" and "the new silver late come from the Mint" position the fiction within the years of the "Great Recoinage Crisis," 1694 to 1696, when the undervaluation of silver relative to gold incited an epidemic of coin-clipping. The resulting loss of confidence in a debased coinage was remedied by the drastic step of a complete recoinage, in which the old hammered silver coins that were so easily abused were called in to be replaced with milled coins—and by the coincidental introduction of bank notes, the crucial innovation that made capitalism both possible and inevitable. However, I do not wish to imply a topical trigger, à la Dickens, for Deborah's emblematic exploration of the themes of duplicity and fraudulence. Counterfeiting and coin-clipping, though savagely punished, were widely practiced as amateur money-making operations in late seventeenth-century England. Moreover, the second half of the text, in shifting to a contemporaneous timeframe, abandons the meticulous chronicling of political events that characterized the first five chapters. The conspiracy in which Sir John Herewige and Major Boyle are engaged bears a generalized resemblance to the many abortive attempts to spark a revolt against William III. No allusion is made to the infamous 1696 assassination attempt, suggesting perhaps that the text was largely complete before February of 1696. It may be that Deborah took advantage of the lapse of the Licensing Act in May of 1695 to get her defiantly unconventional work published. However, the act had been allowed to lapse because it had failed to control a thriving underground press. Controversial authors who opted to publish anonymously or pseudonymously could always find a printer, provided their work was not frankly treasonable. Until further biographical or bibliographic research provides fresh evidence, we can only hazard a circa 1695–96 date for the novel. At a minimum, we can say that some date *after* early 1695 seems certain.

Although published without an imprint, much could potentially be learned by applying the methods of textual scholarship to a close examination of paper, printer's ornaments and initial capitals, along with other printing techniques, but the location of the original, if it has not been destroyed, is unknown.

In the late 1960s, a University of London doctoral candidate named Angus Burdock, who was researching a doctoral thesis on John Gauden, obtained access to a number of private libraries that contained copies of various editions of the *Eikon Basilike* (purportedly written by Charles I but believed to be the work of Gauden). In one of these libraries—we do not know which—he discovered a slender volume, plainly bound, with no identifying marks on the cover or spine.[98] Chancing to look inside, Burdock saw the title page with its now-famous annotation, "Debora Milton yᵉ Regicides doughter." He at once put John Gauden aside and began to read.

In 1975, Burdock published his transcription of *Marius & Delia*.[99] In his foreword to the text he provided a partial and frankly misleading account of his discovery (see Appendix 2).[100] This 1975 publication ought to have launched a paradigm shift in our understanding of the history of the novel. But the anomaly (in Kuhnian terms) of a previously unrecognized woman writing the first English novel could not be assimilated by what was still a male-dominated scholarly elite. The publisher Burdock chose was obscure and Burdock himself did little to publicize his discovery. He distributed a few dozen copies among his colleagues and acquaintances, who appear to have viewed the work, dismissively and self-defensively, as a joke or a stunt or an imposture.[101] Deborah Milton had not yet found her audience.

To his credit, Burdock did not absolutely abandon his attempt to rescue Deborah Milton from an undeserved oblivion. In 1984, at a University of Leeds reception following a presentation by the late Angela Pruitt on the recovery project for neglected eighteenth-century women writers, Burdock approached Pruitt and presented her with a copy of the novel. Pruitt was not slow to realize the significance of the text for feminist studies and for literary history. As word—and photocopies—of *Marius & Delia* spread, Pruitt was contacted by a major university press soliciting a scholarly edition. She and her prospective editor were assembling an editorial board, on which Burdock had been offered an honorary position, when a cease-and-desist letter was issued by an attorney retained by Burdock. The letter was little more than legal boilerplate, asserting intellectual property rights on behalf of Burdock while offering no rationale to defend such a claim. By any plausible interpretation of copyright law, Deborah Milton's work, though lost to readers for nearly three hundred years, was as much in the public domain as her father's writings. But the legal threat, however toothless, discouraged the publisher. Pruitt then attempted to interest other publishers, but none were willing to undertake the project in the face of a potential lawsuit, however unwinnable or even frivolous in its basis.

The lack of a suitable and readily available text had a stifling effect on Deborah Milton scholarship. Burdock's litigious stance left many scholars reluctant to provide copies to colleagues or even to admit to possessing a photocopy of his edition. All the same, a few committed Deborah Miltonists continued to include *Marius & Delia* in their graduate seminars. In the early 1990s, a more restrictive definition of the fair use provision of US copyright law required that permissions be obtained for all copyrighted materials included in photocopied coursepacks. I can recall attempting to convince my college administration (as well as the campus copy center) that only Burdock's preface was in fact copyrightable, and that the text itself was as open to free dissemination as *Bleak House* or *Hamlet*. In vain: the fact that Burdock or his publisher had asserted a copyright claim meant that formal permission must be sought and obtained. The obscure publisher was now untraceable.[102] Burdock, when contacted for permissions, responded by setting an excessively high fee, payable as a wire transfer to his personal UK banking account. The demand proved too great a hurdle for most, and as a result our students were again denied the opportunity to encounter *Marius & Delia*.

Until he began to receive permission requests, Burdock was apparently unaware of the extent of interest in Deborah Milton's novel among North American scholars. Extraordinary as it may seem, having presented Angela Pruitt with a copy of the 1975 edition, he again abandoned any attempt to publicize his great find. Having discovered, however belatedly, that there was a Deborah Milton "market," in 2004 he took the step of arranging for a scan of his 1975 edition to be published as a print-on-demand title. This was certainly an advance, of sorts: the text was now more readily available for classroom use, although students were obliged to order it from the publisher's website, which lacked a distribution system. But Burdock's latest edition could not meet the requirements of contemporary scholars. It perpetuated the transcriptional errors of the original while introducing additional errors due to faulty optical character recognition. In the absence of a creditably edited text, there would continue to be resistance in the broader academic community to acknowledging the authenticity of *Marius & Delia*, as well as obstacles to publishing scholarship. Without a well-prepared edition for study and citation, Deborah Milton scholars would have little chance of establishing her place in a revised canon. However, it was clear that Burdock, now earning royalties from his print-on-demand reprint, would contest any attempt to publish an authoritative edition—for that matter, any new edition at all.

After extensive discussions with colleagues, I took the initiative of contacting Carol Hart at SpringStreet Books, a small niche publisher specializing in scholarly editions of neglected authors. *Marius & Delia* was certainly within the press's scope and arguably fit its list. After some deliberation and a consultation with their at-torney, the publisher agreed to undertake it, providing Burdock's legal challenge could be resolved without protracted litigation. Accordingly, the publisher notified Burdock of their intent to publish a new edition, observing that the work was in the public domain. Burdock's response was another cease-and-desist letter. After a further exchange of correspondence, Burdock filed suit in US federal court, in which I was named as codefendant and required to undergo the surreal experience of a four-hour deposition (during which I was asked whether I had ever been con-victed of a crime and if I had a history of drug abuse or mental illness). Burdock's own deposition took much less time, as he rapidly sank into contradictory claims, then refused to answer further questions. (Appendix 2 provides a transcript of his testimony.) An out-of-court settlement was subsequently reached, and publication of *Marius & Delia* was allowed to proceed without further challenge.

As the terms of the settlement are not confidential, some readers might be in-terested in knowing them. Briefly, the publisher granted Burdock a half-share of the editor's royalties—a proviso I was under the necessity of accepting if I did not wish to see my efforts go for nothing—in exchange for which he dropped all present and future copyright claims.[103] Moreover, as a rationale for his royalty share, Burdock granted permission to reprint "his foreword to the first edition, or other pertinent document produced by him or otherwise providing his views or opinions, unless subject to copyright by a third party not granting permission to reprint, as selected by the editor as suitable for inclusion in the edition currently in production and all future editions derived from it." As editor, I saw no merit in providing space for Burdock's verbose, self-involved and frequently irrelevant foreword: its only point of interest lies in his account of finding the unique copy, as summarized above. He has produced no other scholarship worth reprinting, and I doubted his ability to produce original work on a level with the five critical essays commissioned from leading scholars for this edition. I was apparently obliged to include something "providing his views or opinions." Accordingly, having carefully reviewed the terms of the settlement agreement cited above, I selected Burdock's deposition for inclusion as an appendix.

Although hardly a *Jarndyce v Jarndyce,* these legal maneuverings were sufficiently protracted to upend the original publication schedule. They were, additionally, a considerable drain upon my own time and resources so that I was unable to supply the endnotes and glossary as originally planned. Instead, I made this task the group endeavor of my Fall 2019 Honors English seminar. We collectively decided, through chapter-by-chapter class discussion, what required annotation or glossing. In the interests of fairness, and at the risk of some degree of redundancy, I randomly assigned responsibility for specific endnotes and glossary entries to my eleven students, but they were free to exchange assigned annotations with their classmates. The submitted annotations (signed with the contributor's initials) were subjected to peer review by means of Google Docs, with each student being responsible for reviewing thirty annotations submitted by his/her classmates. While not without the usual flaws of student efforts (some read as bald paraphrases of class notes, others as Wikipedia copy-and-pastes), I believe the results are of value. These students were, at a minimum, highly qualified to decide what required annotation in a text that would be aimed, at least in part, at students like themselves. All in all, the efforts of these future Deborah Milton scholars are commendable, and I recommend this approach to other scholars who are tasked with preparing editions suitable for the classroom. In alphabetical order, my co-editors and annotators are:

Ashley Carter	Chase Hunter
Brandon Cowper	Madison Krueger
Trevor Dale	Cameron Padilla
Hailey Fisher	Hannah Sue Park
Tyler Harris	Paige Smith
Ethan Hill	

In preparing this edition I have benefited from the enthusiastic support of colleagues: some with an abiding, long-term interest in *Marius & Delia,* others who had no knowledge of the novel's existence until invited to share their views and expertise. The five essays included in this edition were all commissioned for this publication. The first generation of Deborah Miltonists, those who were introduced to her by the late Angela Pruitt, are in or approaching retirement. (This edition is the final project of my own career, as I am now emeritus.) In consequence, I decided to reach out more broadly to younger scholars who were, by and large, unfamiliar with *Marius & Delia.* The response to my queries, the outpouring of enthusiastic interest, brought more proposals for critical essays than the planned volume could accommodate. At Kayla Norton's initiative, a proposal has been developed for an open-access, peer-reviewed journal devoted to Deborah Milton scholarship. The inaugural issue, for which several contributions are already in hand, is planned for February of 2022. It has been exciting and gratifying—and a very great privilege—to be the editor responsible for introducing *Marius & Delia* to its twenty-first century audience. As the great majority of readers will be experiencing *Marius & Delia* for the first time, I will refrain from any further comments that may function as spoilers.

Notes

1 The dating here derives from Christopher Milton's deposition concerning the oral will, in which he stated that he knew little of his nieces' situations, "they living apart from their father four or five yeares past," which would put the date of their departure as 1669 or 1670. Given that John Milton was said to be living elsewhere "about 1670," the later date for the family breakup seems more likely.

2 John Milton's departure from the house to temporary lodgings with Millington is reported by Jonathan Richardson in his 1734 life of Milton (Helen Darbishire, ed., *Early Lives of Milton* [London: Constable & Co., 1932], 203, 275). Richardson's informant, who knew Milton, said that he would encounter him in the street, being led up and down by Millington, which certainly suggests his wife and daughters resided elsewhere. Most likely he had taken flight from a distracting domestic crisis, without considering the consequences of leaving his wife in authority over her stepchildren.

3 J. Milton French, ed., *The Life Records of John Milton* (New Brunswick, NJ: Rutgers University Press, 1956–58), 5:220. At her death in 1727 at the advanced age of 89, Elizabeth Minshull Milton's effects included a good deal of culinary equipment (see David Masson, *The Life of John Milton* [London: Macmillan and Co., 1880], 6:748–49 for an analysis). She must have been nettled when her husband, that advocate of a spare diet, ate whatever was put before him without much appreciation. During her long widowhood, most of it spent in Nantwich, Cheshire, she seems to have enjoyed entertaining, although she was not lavish with portions, inspiring a village adage: "Mrs. Milton's feast, enough and no more" (Masson, *Life*, 6:746).

4 To be valid, an oral will must be formally declared in the presence of three witnesses during the individual's final illness. None of these requirements were met in the will produced by Christopher Milton. It is not clear from surviving documents whether the oral will was overturned by the court or the parties reached an out-of-court settlement (William Riley Parker, *Milton: A Biography* [Oxford: Clarendon Press 1968, 1996], 2:1157–58).

5 Edward Phillips, Milton's nephew, gave the value of the estate as £1500 in cash, not counting household goods. ("The Life of Mr. John Milton," in Darbishire, *Early Lives,* 78). Masson and Parker both assume the widow to be honest and so compute the value of the estate as £900 based on the £300 dispensed to the daughters as their one-third share. But the fact that the daughters received a round sum indicates, obviously enough, that no serious accounting effort was taken.

6 Gordon Campbell, *A Milton Chronology* (New York: St. Martin's Press, 1997), 218.

7 Masson, *Life*, 6:742.

8 Campbell, *Chronology,* 216. The record is in the register of the Church of Ireland united parish of St. Peter and St. Kevin; since St. Peter's church was under construction the wedding presumably took place in St. Kevin's, Camden Row. The parish register for the years 1669–1761 was published in 1911 (London: William Pollard & Co.) and is available online in the Internet Archive database. The couple did not, apparently, stay in this parish: there are no baptismal entries for their children.

9 These were overlapping occupations. Silk mercers sometimes operated as master weavers by employing journeymen to produce silks of a specific fashionable and vendible pattern. Aubrey's manuscript notes state, "His da: Deborah *Maried in Dublin to one Mr Clarke [a mercer] ^sells silke etc^ very like her father* could read to him Latin: Ital. & French & Greek." The asterisks indicate an addition put on the next page, marked for insertion with a tallying mark, and the carets mark another addition written above that line. John Aubrey, "Minutes of the Life of Mr. John Milton," in Darbishire, *Early Lives*, 6.

10 Only three children are mentioned as surviving to adulthood: Elizabeth (d. 1754), Urban (d. 1742–50), and Caleb (d. 1719 in India). Our source for the number of Deborah's children is the not very reliable John Ward (*Life Records*, 5:334–35), who says that she married "Mr. Abraham Clarke, a Weaver in Spittle-Fields."

11 This daughter, Elizabeth Clarke Foster, told Thomas Birch that her mother "came over again to *England* during the Troubles in *Ireland*, under King *James* II," (*Life Records*, 5:288). The date of Elizabeth's birth comes from the notes of Thomas Birch, recorded on the day of her funeral in 1754 (*Life Records*, 5:287, 352).

12 J. G. Simms, *Jacobite Ireland, 1685–91* (London: Routledge & Kegan Paul, 1969), 49, 54.

13 I owe this observation to Parker, *Milton*, 1:652.

14 *Life Records*, 5:301.

15 Parker, *Milton*, 2:1163. Though he records this coincidence of name and livelihood, Parker postulates that Deborah's husband most likely died between 1688 and 1702.

16 *The Manuscripts of His Grace the Duke of Portland Preserved at Welbeck Abbey* (London: H. M. Stationery Office, 1907), 8:383. Melton for Milton (likewise Paradice for Paradise) is not uncommon at this time.

17 Milton's recognition as the great English epic poet is attributable to Addison's commentaries on *Paradise Lost*, which appeared in *The Spectator* between January 5, 1712 and May 3, 1714.

18 *Life Records*, 5:314–16; Masson, *Life*, 6:755.

19 A penciled note next to her name in a copy of Wood's *Fasti Oxonienses* that had belonged to Robert Harley, Earl of Oxford, reads: "Her I knew and often releivd" (*Life Records*, 5:110–11).

20 *Life Records*, 5:352.

21 *Mist's Weekly Journal*, April 29, 1727. My text here is quoted from a reprint in *The European Magazine and London Review* 1787; 11 (Feb):65–66 (where it is listed in the Table of Contents by the title, "The Question, whether Milton superintended the Education of Youth from Necessity, or for the mere Pleasure he found in the Employment, answered by a singular Fact," the singular fact being the poverty of his daughter, a retired schoolteacher). Excerpts from the original may be found in *Life Records*, 5:319–21.

22 Darbishire, *Early Lives,* 2–3. Aubrey wrote "and Hebrew" in the list of languages Deborah read to her father but later crossed those two words, either because he felt doubtful or his other source contradicted this claim. Aubrey's manuscript notes include a sheet in Edward Phillips' hand that describes the studies Milton assigned his students and catalogues Milton's works. Next to *Paradise Lost,* Phillips has written "Edw. Philips his Amanuensis" with a corrective "cheif" inserted between "his" and "Amanuensis." When Phillips came to write his own version, however (see p. xii), he claimed there was no regular or chief amanuensis but instead *Paradise Lost* was "written by whatever hand came next."

23 Darbishire, *Early Lives,* 6. Aubrey's "Minutes of the Life of Mr. John Milton" was shared his friend Anthony Wood but otherwise went unknown and unpublished until 1813.

24 Wood includes Milton on the grounds that he was incorporated as an Oxford M.A. in 1635, according to a long-standing procedure for recognizing degrees and granting university privileges to graduates of other universities.

25 Anthony Wood, *Fasti Oxonienses or Annals of the University of Oxford* (1691) in Darbishire, *Early Lives,* 41. Wood's brief life of Milton also drew heavily on an undated, unsigned memoir of John Milton that was preserved among Wood's papers in the Bodleian. As with Aubrey's notes, this life was unavailable to Milton's early biographers and was not published until 1902. Attributed by Helen Darbishire to Milton's younger nephew John Phillips, the authorship has since been assigned to Cyriack Skinner, a former pupil of Milton who remained a close friend. Skinner tells the story of Milton's disastrous first marriage but says little of Milton's daughters, except that he had them, or of his amanuenses, except that he had them.

26 *Letters of State, Written by Mr. John Milton* (London, 1694). The publisher is unknown. Two of Milton's subsequent biographers, John Toland and Thomas Birch, who plundered and plagiarized it, were aware of Edward Phillips' authorship of the life. Birch had access to a presentation copy inscribed by Phillips.

27 Darbishire, *Early Lives,* 77–78.

28 Darbishire, *Early Lives,* 78.

29 Anne died in childbirth between 1675 and 1678. Mary, unmarried, died at some unknown date prior to 1694.

30 Darbishire, *Early Lives,* 73.

31 Darbishire, *Early Lives,* 53.

32 Samuel Johnson, "Milton," in *Prefaces Biographical and Critical, to the Works of the English Poets* (London: J. Nichols, 1779), 2:144.

33 It is not at all clear why two small boys, ages nine and ten, were sent to live with their bachelor uncle. They may have been recently orphaned (the date of their mother's death is unknown), and their uncle may have agreed to take them in order to test his educational theories. John Phillips apparently continued to reside with his uncle until about 1652 (John T. Shawcross, *The Arms of the Family* [Lexington: University of Kentucky Press, 2004], 96).

34 "Hard Study, and spare Diet" (Darbishire, *Early Lives,* 62).

35 Darbishire, *Early Lives,* 67, 71.

36 Darbishire, *Early Lives,* 60. Milton's *Of Education* gives an after-the-fact rationale for this strange curriculum. The first year of study, Milton argued, should deal with applied science, to discover the young student's aptitudes. Study of the great classical authors is reserved for the seventh and eighth years of his academic program. Edward Phillips did not stay the full course and must have had to mug up Virgil and Homer on his own.

37 The memoir attributed to Cyriack Skinner mentions an unfinished Greek thesaurus as well (Darbishire, *Early Lives,* 29).

38 Darbishire, *Early Lives,* 61.

39 Phillips was resident in Shrewsbury from at least 1651 to 1655 (Shawcross, *Arms,* 75–76).

40 Shawcross, *Arms,* 79. It is not certain how long Phillips kept this position. Parker remarks that he may have continued as a tutor in the Pembroke household until July 1674 (*Milton,* 2:1119).

41 Darbishire, *Early Lives,* 76. As Parker notes, in regard to Phillips' errors and general vagueness in discussing Milton's final years, "It is probably significant that, talking to Aubrey, Milton's third wife could not remember Phillips' christian name" (*Milton,* 2:1119).

42 "The Life of John Milton," in Darbishire, *Early Lives,* 85.

43 Darbishire, *Early Lives,* 177.

44 "The Life of John Milton," in John Milton, *Paradise Lost,* 12th ed. (London: Jacob Tonson, 1725), xviii–xix.

45 Johnson, "Milton," 2:122–23. Jonathan Richardson expressed some vague misgivings on this point in his 1734 life of Milton, as he called upon his readers to pity and wonder at the conditions under which *Paradise Lost* was composed by its blind, ill and discouraged author: "not in Circumstances to maintain an Amanuensis, but Himself Oblig'd to teach a Couple of Girls (or as Some say One) to Read Several Languages, and to Pronounce them, so as not to be Grievous to an Ear as Delicate as His, or even to be Intelligible" ("The Life of Milton, and a Discourse on *Paradise Lost*" in Darbishire, *Early Lives,* 289).

46 "For, having a curious Ear, he understood by my Tone, when I understood what I read, and when I did not: and accordingly would stop me, Examine me, and open the most difficult Passages to me" (Thomas Ellwood, *The History of Thomas Ellwood,* excerpted in *Life Records,* 4:369).

47 Parker, *Milton,* 1:585.

48 Thomas Birch, "An Historical and Critical Account of the Life and Writings of Mr. John Milton," in *A Complete Collection of the Historical, Political, and Miscellaneous Works of John Milton* (London: A. Millar, 1738), 1:lxi–lxii. I have modernized the use of quotation marks. It is difficult to feel much confidence in Birch, who begins his biography by criticizing Toland for failing to name his sources, and, in a footnote, by citing and describing Phillips' memoir. Having done so, he proceeds to plagiarize where Toland had merely paraphrased, substituting a few synonyms to disguise his thievery, and decorating the foot of the page with serial citations to Phillips. Occasionally he puts a lengthy passage in quotation marks. There are also lengthy citations, with quotation marks, from Richardson and Toland. It is, in short, a patchwork of acknowledged and unacknowledged pilfering.

49 J. Milton French makes uniformly unflattering comments on his accuracy: "Ward makes numerous errors in his account" (*Life Records,* 5:5); "Ward's notes are so full of errors of various kinds" (*Life Records,* 5:100).

50 It is not clear who, besides Ward, encouraged Deborah to recite, but another account of her abilities occurs in the preface to Thomas Newton's edition of *Paradise Lost* (London: J. and R. Tonson & S. Draper, 1750), 1:lxxxi: "As she had been often called upon to read Homer and Ovid's Metamorphosis to her father, she could have repeated a considerable number of verses from the beginning of both these poets, as Mr. Ward, Professor of Rhetoric in Gresham College, relates upon his own knowledge: and another Gentleman has informed me, that he has heard her repeat several verses likewise out of Euripides." We don't have any further specifics but certain verses of Euripides would be apt to her situation:

But if you are thought superior to those who have

Some reputation for learning, you will become hated. (*Medea,* ll. 294–95)

51 Johnson, "Milton," 2:145–47.

52 "If these were not rehearsed tricks to impress admiring visitors" (Parker, *Milton,* 2:1098).

53 I mention the need for a prompter because Deborah Clarke had inherited her father's eyesight as well as his features. Even if her sight was still adequate for reading, she would have required an accomplice (Philalethes?) to provide her with the texts to be memorized.

54 Cited by Masson, 6:752, from an unidentified letter. I have not been able to track the original in Voltaire's literally voluminous correspondence (fifty-one volumes in the edition of Theodore Besterman). Voltaire may have known of Princess Caroline's generous contribution of £50 to the Deborah Milton Clarke Fund (*Life Records,* 5:319).

55 Darbishire, *Early Lives,* 279.

56 Darbishire, *Early Lives,* 291.

57 Newton gathered a second- or third-hand report to this effect: "I have learned, that she confirmed several things which had been related before; and particularly that her husband used to compose his poetry chiefly in winter, and on his waking in a morning would make her write down sometimes twenty or thirty verses" ("Life," 1:lxxix). Newton may be attributing familiar information to a different (and conveniently dead) source to produce an impression of fresh research. A sample of Elizabeth Milton's handwriting survives in the signature to her 1680 release of rights to *Paradise Lost* to the publisher, Samuel Symonds. As reproduced in Masson

(5:779), it indicates she could only be a last-resort amanuensis for her husband. The letters are large, crudely formed, and modeled on printed characters. She may have been self-taught and unable to write much more than her own name.

58 Of John Milton's immediate circle, only Elizabeth Minshull Milton and Deborah Milton Clarke (both dying in August of 1727) were sufficiently long-lived to have offered intimate details concerning Milton's habits that had been missed by previous biographers. Richardson several times mentions Milton's widow, always in an unflattering light ("a Termagant"), suggesting that his information on the Milton household derived ultimately from Deborah.

59 Darbishire, *Early Lives,* 291. The eccentric use of lower and upper case letters is his.

60 "And hee waking early (as is the use of temperate men) had commonly a good Stock of Verses ready against his Amanuensis came; which if it happend to bee later than ordinary, hee would complain, Saying *hee wanted to bee milkd.*" Darbishire, *Early Lives,* 33. Quoted from the anonymous life attributed to John Phillips by Darbishire, which is now thought to be by Cyriack Skinner.

61 Darbishire, *Early Lives,* 229.

62 Darbishire, *Early Lives,* 291. Phillips' unlikely story that Milton was only able to compose between the autumnal and vernal equinoxes may have been his uncle's polite dodge for dispensing with Phillips' assistance once Deborah was old enough to be relied upon—and when Phillips' royalist sympathies had become distastefully evident.

63 Darbishire, *Early Lives,* 228.

64 Birch, "Historical and Critical Account," 1:lxii.

65 Birch in a letter to Philip Yorke, dated November 17, 1750 (*Life Records,* 5:350).

66 Barbara Lewalski, *The Life of John Milton* (Maldon, MA: Blackwell Publishing, 2001), 459. Parker, *Milton,* 2:1124. Shawcross, *Arms,* 26. Parker (*Milton,* 1:622) also suggests 1672 as the year Deborah went to Ireland but gives no basis for his guess.

67 Oliver Fitzwilliam was evidently a man of many sides. He and his younger brother William fought for the king at Naseby, but he subsequently ingratiated himself with Oliver Cromwell and participated in the short-lived Rota club in 1659 (Francis Elrington Ball, *A History of the County Dublin* [Dublin: Alex. Thom & Co., 1903], 2:17–18). His English in-laws first came to his assistance in the 1650s, helping to recover some of his property, which was then held in his wife's name and leased to another powerful patron and kinsman, Arthur Annsley (Jane Ohlmeyer, *Making Ireland English: The Irish Aristocracy in the Seventeenth Century* [New Haven, CT: Yale University Press], 286). Charles II rewarded his loyalty in 1661 by creating him Earl of Tyrconnell. He had a fresh crisis when the Restoration Court of Claims found against him. His allies mobilized to lobby the king on his behalf, with the result that the subsequent Act of Explanation (1665) granted a full restoration of his prewar estates. Thomas Fitzwilliam, the 4th Viscount, commanded a horse troop in the Jacobite army but nonetheless received a pardon from William III and retained all of the family lands (Ohlmeyer, *Making Ireland,* 322, 357). Over two thousand of his fellow Jacobites were not so lucky, their estates seized and themselves outlawed (Simms, *Jacobite Ireland*, 213).

68 Parker, *Milton,* 1:606–7.

69 Birch, "Historical and Critical Account," 1:lxii.

70 The signatures are reproduced in Samuel Leigh Sotheby, *Ramblings in the Elucidation of the Autograph of Milton* (London: Thomas Richards, 1861), 176–79.

71 Parker, *Milton,* 1:658.

72 Newton, "Life," 1:lxxxii.

73 Newton, "Life," 1:lxxx.

74 Birch, "Historical and Critical Account," 1:lxii.

75 Newton, "Life," 1:lxxxiii–lxxxiv.

76 In issuing a general appeal for charity on behalf of Deborah Clarke, Philalethes singled out Milton's publisher (Jacob Tonson): "I shall hope that industrious and thriving bookseller who has got so many thousand pounds by the copy of Paradise Lost, will not be behind-hand in his contribution: 'twill be but a bad excuse for him to say, that it was her father, not she, who wrote that admirable poem."

77 William Lauder, *An Essay on Milton's Use and Imitation of the Moderns in His Paradise Lost,* (London: J. Payne and J. Bouquet, 1750), 165.

78 *Life Records,* 5:350.

79 Quoted in John T. Shawcross, ed., *John Milton: The Critical Heritage,* (London: Routledge & Kegan Paul, 1972), 2:196.

80 *Life Records,* 5:340–42. By her will, made in July of 1744, Catherine Milton left £50 to Thomas Foster and £200 separately to Elizabeth Foster. Thomas Foster, however, is one of the two executors, who were left two bonds totaling £212, which means another £106 for the Fosters. The executors also split everything left after the individual bequests had been paid. A codicil made in April of 1745 canceled five bequests totaling £80. Interestingly, the bequests left standing (to people other than the Fosters) also total £80 plus one bed (the other, better bed going to Elizabeth Foster). Philalethes' 1727 public appeal for charity might also have overstated the supposed poverty of the Fosters at that time, "who strain so hard, and pinch themselves to give maintenance to an aged parent." The address provided to prospective visitors, "Mr. Foster's, next door to the blue ball, Pelham-street, Spitalfields," indicates that Deborah's son-in-law was a householder, not a mere lodger.

81 *Life Records,* 5:346.

82 Ward had transcribed the dates of birth from this Bible, passing the information on to Birch, but characteristically made an error in one of them.

83 *Life Records,* 5:347.

84 *Life Records,* 4:216.

85 John Milton himself had learned to read and write between ages five and seven. He had every reason to push his daughters and their tutor or governess to be equally quick in mastering skills so essential to his comfort and continued productivity.

86 Darbishire, *Early Lives,* 6.

87 *Life Records,* 5:222.

88 "He was in Perpetual Terror of being Assassinated" (Darbishire, *Early Lives,* 276).

89 *Life Records,* 4:367–68.

90 Parker supposes, improbably enough, that "both Milton and his books" went to live with Millington while his "thoughtful wife" was getting their new house on Jewin Street "in perfect order for him," even though this dating for the move to Jewin Street is speculative (*Life,* 607–08). Lewalski assumes that lodging with Millington somehow simplified the task of selling off part of his library, although it is hard to see how that would work (*Life,* 490).

91 *Life Records,* 5:350

92 *Life Records,* 5:314.

93 J. H. Andrews, "Land and people, c. 1685," in *A New History of Ireland. III. Early Modern Ireland, 1534–1691,* ed. T. W. Moody, F. X. Martin, F. J. Byrne (Oxford: Oxford University Press, 1993), 464–67.

94 Ohlmeyer, *Making Ireland,* 98.

95 Michael Dolley, "The Irish coinage, 1534–1691," in *A New History of Ireland,* ed. T. W. Moody, et al., 418. Simms says the brass half-crown was devalued to little more than a penny under William (*Jacobite Ireland,* 91).

96 *The Life and Errors of John Dunton* (1705), 241, quoted in Shawcross, *Arms,* 240.

97 The information about Deborah's need for glasses was recorded by Birch in an interview with Elizabeth Foster (*Life Records,* 5:344). The problem, as usual, progressed over the years; the 1727 public appeal by "Philalethes" says "the failure of eyes and strength" had forced her to give up her school.

98 One of my graduate students, Augusta Simpson, recently completed a dissertation, "Tracing the Provenance of D. M.'s *Marius & Delia,*" in which she examined a microfiche of Burdock's 1971 dissertation in order to identify libraries visited in his research which may have contained the unique copy of *Marius & Delia.* Her findings will appear in a future issue of *Deborah Milton Studies* (see Appendix 3).

99 Angus Burdock (ed.), *Marius & Delia* by Deborah Milton (Leeds, UK: Scandalon Press, 1975), 240 pp. with a 27-page foreword signed by Burdock as editor. The press run was apparently limited to a hundred copies, few or none of which survive. This text was available as a print-on-demand scan of the original from approximately 2004 until 2017, when Burdock withdrew it.

100 Burdock has subsequently contradicted or retracted key statements concerning the discovery of the text and the circumstances of his transcription. See Appendix 2 for details regarding Burdock's original account as well as his under-oath revisions.

101 Such reactions are not entirely extinguished today. For a more contemporary instance, see the lively discussion recorded at the 2009 East Mississippi State College Conference on Early Modern Women Writers, www.eastmsc.edu/english/2009emwproc.pdf. Regrettably, a permalink is not available and the file may have been removed.

102 In the course of her doctoral research (see note 98 above), Simpson attempted to contact Buford and Sandra Tanker, the owners of Scandalon Press. The couple sold their business in 1989 and moved from Yorkshire to Sarasota, Florida, where they had family ties. Buford Tanker died in September of 2003; his wife, who had served as editor for the press, is now in an assisted living residence in Sarasota, where Simpson attempted to interview her. When asked if she recalled the publication of Deborah Milton's novel and whether the editorial papers of the press had been preserved, Ms. Tanker responded, respectively, "We get macaroni-and-cheese on Tuesdays" and "When are they bringing lunch?"

103 Additionally, the settlement agreement stipulated that the print-on-demand title be withdrawn, along with any remaining copies of the 1975 edition. It prohibited circulation of photocopies or PDF versions of the text, excepting: 1) those of the current edition made available to contributors in the course of preparation, at the editor's and publisher's discretion; and 2) any future electronic editions, derived from the current edition, on which royalties would accrue.

Historical Timeline

1640 (Nov) Long Parliament begins.

1642 (Oct 23) Battle of Edgehill: first major battle of civil war.

1642 (Nov 13) Battle of Turnham Green.

1647 (Jun) Charles I taken captive.

1647 (Nov) Charles I escape to Isle of Wight.

1648 (Dec) Pride's Purge: forced removal of conservative MPs, establishing the Rump Parliament.

1649 (Jan) Trial and execution of Charles I.

1649 (Mar) Monarchy and House of Lords abolished.

1649 (May) Parliament declares England a commonwealth.

1651 (Sep) Army of Charles II defeated at Worcester.

1651 (Oct) Charles II escape to Europe.

1653 (Dec) Oliver Cromwell made Lord Protector.

1654 (Mar) Triers appointed to review clergymen for doctrinal conformity.

1654 (Aug) Ejectors appointed to expel inadequate preachers and schoolmasters.

1655 (Aug) Decimation tax introduced: a 10% tax upon known Royalists.

1658 (Sep) Death of Oliver Cromwell; his son Richard succeeds him as Lord Protector.

1659 (May) Richard Cromwell resigns, ending Protectorate; Rump Parliament restored by army.

1659 (Aug) Booth's Uprising, also called Lammas Day Uprising.

1659 (Oct) Rump Parliament expelled by army ("the Nine Colonels"); rule by army council.

1659 (Oct) General Monck declares support for Rump.

1659 (Nov) Troops under command of Lambert depart London, with intent to halt Monck's advance.

1659 (Dec) Rump Parliament restored.

1660 (Jan–Feb) March of Monck's army from Scotland to London; (Feb 3) Monck enters London.

1660 (Feb 11) Monck sides with City of London in conflict with Rump Parliament: Londoners celebrate with bells and bonfires.

1660 (Feb 21) Monck restores Long Parliament, readmitting MPs excluded in 1648.

1660 (Mar) Restored Parliament dissolves itself for new elections.

1660 (Apr 10) General Lambert escapes from Tower and attempts uprising; (Apr 23) recaptured.

1660 (Apr 25) Convention Parliament meets.

1660 (May 1) Publication of Declaration of Breda, proclamation of Charles II offering general amnesty (excepting the regicides) and occasioning general celebration.

1660 (May 29) Charles II makes triumphal entry to London.

1660 (Oct) Executions of regicides.

1661 (Jan 6) Venner Rebellion of Fifth Monarchists; (Jan 19–21) executions of Venner and fellow conspirators.

1665 Great Plague of London.

1665 (Aug 1) King and Court arrive in Salisbury.

1664 (Aug 3) Sir Henry Danvers rescued by mob in Cheapside on his way to the Tower.

1665 (Sep 25) King and Court leave Salisbury for Oxford session of Parliament.

1666 (Sep 2–5) Great Fire of London.

1667 (Jun) Dutch navy sails up Thames and Medway to burn English ships at Chatham and capture flagship.

1669 (Jan) James, Duke of York, secretly converts to Roman Catholicism.

1673 (Sep) James, Duke of York, marries Mary of Modena, a Roman Catholic; his conversion to Catholicism becomes public.

1675 Green Ribbon Club formed circa 1674–75; grew in numbers and importance over the following years. Wearing of green ribbons first noted in 1676.

1678 (Aug) Popish Plot allegations made by Titus Oates to Charles II and Earl of Danby.

1678 (Sep 27–29) Oates testifies before King's Council.

1678 (Sep 28) Oates swears to the truth of his evidence before Justice Godfrey.

1678 (Oct 17) Body of Justice Godfrey discovered; his murder attributed to Roman Catholic plotters.

1678 (Oct) London papists disarmed; regiment of train-bands posted throughout the city; defensive chains up in the streets.

1678 (Oct 23) Oates makes his allegations of a Popish Plot to Parliament, which thereafter become public knowledge.

1678 (Nov 12) Bedloe testifies before House of Commons.

1678 (Dec 19) Letters of the Earl of Danby read in Parliament.

1679 (Jan) Cavalier Parliament dissolved.

1679 (Mar) New Parliament.

1679 (Apr) Oates publishes *A True Narrative of the Horrid Plot.*

1679 (May) First Exclusion Bill, intended to bar Duke of York from succeeding to the throne; Charles II prorogues Parliament, occasioning civil unrest.

1679–80 Increased press censorship during period between Parliaments.

1679 (Jun 22) Scottish rebellion, put down by Monmouth in Battle of Bothwell Bridge.

1679 (Jul 18) Trial of Sir George Wakeman, accused by Oates of attempting to poison the king; found not guilty.

1679 (Aug) Serious illness of Charles II.

1679 (Aug–Sep) Parliamentary elections; Popish Plot agitation.

1679 (Nov 17) First large-scale pope-burning spectacle.

1680 (Apr) Shaftesbury launches Irish Plot, begins gathering witnesses.

1680 (Apr–May) Nightly meetings of the Shaftesbury circle; publication of pamphlets claiming James, Duke of Monmouth, to be legitimate heir to Charles II.

1680 (Aug–Sep) Tutoring of Irish witnesses, primarily by Oates.

1680 (Oct) Parliament meet; Whig publishing propaganda resume under protection of House of Commons.

1680 (Nov 11) House of Commons passes Exclusion Bill but it fails in the House of Lords.

1680 (Nov 17) Second pope-burning pageant.

1681 (Jan) Parliament prorogued, then dissolved.

1681 (Mar 21–28) Oxford Parliament; last Parliament of Charles II's reign.

1681 (Jul) Shaftesbury arrested, charged with treason.

1681 (Nov 17) Last of the large-scale pope-burnings.

1681 (Nov 24) Shaftesbury acquitted by London jury; celebratory bonfires in the streets.

1682 (Jun) Loyalists win London sheriff elections; major loss of power for Whigs.

1682 (Sep) Tory sherriffs take office; Shaftesbury in hiding.

1682 (Nov) Shaftesbury escapes to Holland.

1683 (Jan) Shaftesbury dies in exile.

1683 (Feb–Mar) Development of Rye House Plot to assassinate Charles II and Duke of York.

1683 (Jun 12) Discovery of Rye House Plot; becomes public knowledge a week later.

1683 (Jun–Jul) Arrests of Sidney, Essex, Russell, Wildman, Hampden, Howard and Grey.

1683 (Jul 13) Trial of Lord Russell; suicide of Essex in the Tower.

1683 (Nov 26) Monmouth pardoned; Sidney sentenced to be hanged, drawn and quartered.

1685 (Feb) Death of Charles II; James II declared king.

1685 (May) Trial and punishment of Oates.

1685 (Jun–Jul) Monmouth Rebellion: (Jul 6) James, Duke of Monmouth, defeated at Sedgemoor; (Jul 15) executed.

1685 (Aug) Bloody Assizes presided by Lord Chief Justice Jeffreys: 300 executed, 800 rebels sold into servitude in West Indies.

1686 Period of strict press censorship begins.

1688 (Jun) Birth of son to James II; opposition leaders invite William of Orange to invade England.

1688 (Nov 5) William of Orange lands at Torbay with small army.

1688 (Dec 11–16) Flight of James from London; (Dec 11) riots and bonfires of looted goods of Roman Catholics; (Dec 12–13) mob attacks on Catholics continue.

1688 (Dec 13) The "Irish Fright": public hysteria at rumors of an Irish attack.

1688 (Dec 16) Return of James; (Dec 23) James flees to France.

1689 (Jan) Convention Parliament declares the throne vacant.

1689 (Feb) Acceptance of crown by William and Mary as joint sovereigns.

1689 (Mar) James II in Ireland, supported by French troops and generals.

1689 (Apr) Coronation of William and Mary.

1689 (May) William and Mary declare war on France, beginning the Nine Years' War, also known as the War of the Grand Alliance.

1690 (Jul) Army of James II defeated in Battle of the Boyne.

1692 Land tax in effect, 1692–1713, main source of revenue to fund war effort.

1692 (Aug 3) Battle of Steenkirk.

1692 Bad harvest causes much hardship; increasing problems with clipped coins and inadequate money supply.

1693 (Dec) Whig Junto now the majority in William's ministry.

1694 (Apr) Bank of England founded.

1694 (Dec) Death of Queen Mary.

1695 (Apr 22) Passage of law providing £40 bounty for betraying coin-clippers.

1695 (May) Licensing Act expires, ending statutory regulation of the Press in England.

1695 (Dec) Passage of Recoinage Bill to address monetary crisis resulting from coin-clipping.

1696 (Feb) Jacobite plot to assassinate William III discovered.

Marius & Delia

Or, A Pleasant & Profitable

History of the Times

by D. M. *ebora Milton yᵉ Regicides doughter*

LONDON

To be Sold at the Sign of the Red Fiſh
in Bride Lane near Fleet Ditch

To Lord ———¹

MY LORD, I was making a memorandum of my debts, when the printer sent for me. Where is the preface, he wanted to know. It cannot go forth without a preface or a letter. —It has a species of preface in its opening, I said. It has, moreover, a vindication and an epilogue; for it is an entirely new thing, never before attempted. Never mind that, said the printer. It must have some pages of stuff in the fore, being a letter to the reader or a dedication to some rich patron. A dedication is more mannerly and impressive-like. —I have no acquaintance with rich patrons, they know neither my face nor my name. Never mind that, said the printer again. (That a man who has the best language of the best authors put daily before his eyes should possess no more words than a parrot!) Never mind that, said he. Scarce one writer in a hundred knows the lord he makes his acknowledgments to. 'Tis only fooling the reader into a belief that the book and its author are something considerable and well worth his shilling.

I took up my pen readily enough but sat musing over the page. My wits were wrung so dry by the sweaty labor of writing my book, that I had none left to eke out a preface. I looked over my list of debts: so much for lodging, washing, beer, bread, coals, candles, paper, for my last good shirt, now well worn; then recalled with a blush the debts left out of my account, owed to the few friends I have, or once had. I excused myself with the reflection that all authors are debtors, if not downright thieves. This thought in turn started a most unblushing and impudent notion of how to accomplish my troublesome dedication to Lord I-Know-Not-Who. Full of my idea, I went at once to my most prosperous acquaintance, whose door has been shut against me these past six months. —I ask only the use of your library, I said, only a half-hour among your books and no more. I stood at the door whilst my entreaty was messaged by the footman to the housekeeper and by the housekeeper to her master, my heretofore friend. At last I was grudgingly admitted. (I would have tried to interest him in a dedication, a very fine dedication, fresh and good cheap, if I but had opportunity.) The insolent servant who admitted me lolled against the wainscot, so to keep an eye on sundry gilded toys of his master's. He gave no heed to the books that I took from the shelves and perused. That was fortunate for me, for I had my pen knife with me to aid in making a collection of choice phrases, certain that the master of the house would never notice the loss. Even supposing that in an idle moment he might open one of his books (most were with pages uncut), he would never look upon the fawning beggarly preface. I took my purloined scraps back to my garret to lay them out upon my table. *Ex improviso,* altogether beyond my expectations, it was good![2] I had the makings of a dedication that would compel any lord to open his purse in pure amazement and gratitude. But alas!, before I could pin the scraps to their places and copy them out, what should befall but that my landlady, bellowing to be paid, let fly the door. My snippets of servile compliment flew off the table and out the open window. There was nothing to do but make the best work I could from the remnants which I swept up from the floor.

My august and munificent Lord ——, the Gaius Maecenas of this mercenary age, who peruses this little book with pleasure and instruction, it is not too late to become D. M.'s patron![3] I have instructed the printer to leave a generous blank so that we may put in your name for the second printing. —God's oons! Damn this scribbler for a ninny! —Oh, my lord, we may know your honorable birth and breeding by your curses: you fear no Society informers.[4] —How the devil may that be, when neither the author nor the printer have put their names to the thrice-blasted thing! —'Tis true my lord, that, by reason of some little trifles that might be misunderstood, the printer and I thought fit to conceal ourselves. However, you have only to let it be known to your bookseller that you seek the author of MARIUS & DELIA. I shall hasten to throw myself at your feet and to accept a suitable acknowledgment. I am not so bold as to ask for guineas; nor would the chandler, the baker, the small-coal man, nor that foggy slut of a landlady, know what to do with a newfangled bank note. So let it be, my lord, of the new silver late come from the Mint. Your name will be instantly entered into the next impression, to your everlasting benefit and my own. In which expectation, I declare myself your much-indebted servant and obsequious well-willer, &c., D. M.

Contents

Exordium Scandali

In plain English, a false start, a stumble at the threshold.[1]

IN THE KINGDOM of Nonestia there lived a gentleman called Marius, of distinguished birth yet declining means; for he was a man of too great character to prosper under the turpitude of his times. The last of his line, he lived very private with only one small daughter and a one-eyed maid for his family. His house, a stately hall of antique beauty, stood close by the great road that led to Illondro, the far-famed capital of the realm. This Marius was a learned man, whose health was impaired as much by his studies as by his misfortunes. He withdrew himself from worldly concerns, forsaking the society of friends and compeers, that he might devote himself to solitudinary contemplation and considerance. His waking hours were spent in studying history, law, divinity, and philosophy, as he sought enlightenment for questions that troubled him to the jeopardy of his health, both of body and spirit. Yet the more he read, the more perplexed and doubtful was his understanding. He grew neglectful of his already diminished estate. His daughter wore rags, and the maid made away with his goods.

One morning Aurora discovered Marius yet at his book, his head lowered upon his arms, not in sleep but deep reflection. He raised himself slowly (he was afflicted with the gout), murmuring of dukes and death and bloody insurrections. (He might do so safely for there was none to hear. The maid snored in a trundle bed by the ashes of the kitchen fire. His daughter lay quietly awake at the maid's side, the side farther from the fire, huggling her puppet.) He paused at the window. The hedge was ragged with fruit, sparrows chirped in its branches, but he neither saw nor heard. The rattling of a countryman's cart mingled strangely with his thoughts. Forebodings of murderous broils and tumults filled his imaginings. As he sat down again, he slapped his hand upon the table and exclaimed: Monmouth pardoned, Sidney sentenced to a traitor's death. Would it were reversed! Hampden clapped up still, peached by base informers. I fear they've done his business. Pray God I am not traced in this![2]

Pox on't! Good paper wasted! My poor artifice exploded the moment my chief character parts his lips to express his thoughts! I must tell the story some other way, and tell it plainly, without the gilt adornments of fable and romance.[3] 'Tis a true story, I promise you, for I had it direct from the old man's daughter, a very ingenuous creature, scarce able to frame a plausible lie, or to comprehend much of what she witnessed. I myself have passed on that road, it is the North Road, and looked up to see the old man at his window.[4]

But I will not tell it after her in selfsame words, which were by turns tiresome and scandalous. She was overmuch concerned with her own sensations in telling her tale, though she was but an inconsiderable actor in the events she related. As for scandal, however delightful to some, I must not allow it for her own and for her father's sake. I must falsify names and features and other such particulars. For many of the persons in her story are yet alive; and, though deserving of the gallows, I would not have their deaths upon my conscience. I shall call the old man Marius Bye; his daughter will be Delia; their maid may keep her right name of Jane. ✠

CHAPTER 1

Marius Bye: his birth and his mother's antipathy to him. His apprenticeship to a London corn-chandler named Boult. His head turned by harkening to violent sectarian preachers and reading seditious pamphlets. After his rebellious scribblings are exposed, he is dismissed to make his own way in the world.

MARIUS **B**YE is a man of vinegar wit and frustrate ambition: a Roundhead of our latter days, a belated but convinced republican.[1] He was born in the first year of the Great Rebellion. In the weeks following the battle at Edgehill, his mother, great with child, was much unsettled by the bands of soldiers tramping up and down the road.[2] Her husband assured her that the broken stragglers were rebels in flight; the well-appointed troopers were the King's own men. The rebellion, he said, was all but vanquished; so that she began to take heart and grow easy. Then it was that the sudden appearance of Hampden's regiment, on the march to Turnham Green, singing psalms with a savage fervor, caused her to shriek and fall down in a swoon.[3] Her womb dropped, her pains coming so quick and strong there was no time to send for the midwife. She turned away when her maid showed her the boy, small and weazen-faced but crying lustily. A fever that turned to a consumption kept her confined to her bed for many weeks. When her babe was brought to her, she felt no joy. She could not look upon him without a resentment of pain and sickness, or a shuddering recollection of hundreds of Roundheads in green cassocks, baying with full-throated fury for the blood of kings and Moabites. In vain did her husband tell her that Essex could not prevent his army of weavers and cobblers from deserting, and that the child was a healthy, likely boy: she only shook her head.[4] From her window she saw routs of masterless men, rampant, unchecked, seizing whatever they could win for themselves by fast legs or stout cudgels. She wept on her knees when the Roundheads conveyed the King, their captive, from Newmarket to Hampton Court, passing upon the road before the house. The news of his escape came on the eve of her son's fifth birthday, when she noticed him with a rare smile and a kiss. 'Twas fortunate Marius was away at school on the day that Parliament struck off the King's head.[5]

From a tardy beginning Marius came to be a tolerable good scholar; whipping made him obstinate in his ignorance, until a chance word of praise spurred him to apply himself. He at last mastered the Carmen de Moribus and had advanced to Tully's Epistles when Cromwell's Ejectors

9

made a visitation to his school.[6] They were not satisfied with the school-master's answers. When they proceeded to inspect his books and papers, they discovered a Book of Common Prayer shelved with the colloquies of Erasmus and Corderius.[7] The school was broke up, the pupils sent home until a suitable master could be found for them. In the event, Marius' schooling was come to an end; whatever plans his father had formed for his education were frustrate by his wife's indiscretions. Her devotion to the Royalist cause became notorious in the parish after she incited her eldest son to fly off to the exiled court.[8] Mr. Bye grieved for this unnecessary hazarding of his heir, and grieved as well that he would now be subject to the decimation tax on suspected royalists. He would have kept his youngest son at home if his wife were not as unfriendly to him as before. Instead he carried him to London, to apprentice him to his mother's cousin, a prosperous corn-chandler named Boult, who had a house and shop on Elbow Lane, and a warehouse close by Queenhithe.[9]

His master was at first well satisfied with Marius. The close, solemn air that so displeased his mother was advantageous to business. His firm gray eye, turned upon ragged loiterers, discouraged pilfering; his headpiece, slow but retentive, could match his master's customers to the numbers in his ledger-book, though the keeping of the accounts was as yet beyond his abilities. Sundays he dutifully accompanied his master to church, where he gave the sermon little attention; for Boult was no precisian and never catechized his family. One such Sunday, when the minister's hard and confounding words of reprobation and predestination had heads drooping and eyes winking, a young man stood up upon a bench and cried out: Heed not the falsehoods of hireling priests! The truth of Christ Jesus is not bound up in the dark sayings of an old book. It is the light within you that is Christ, and the light of Christ shall set you free. Rise up, rise up, I say to you, and come into the light! A pretty Quakeress who stood beside him bared her breasts and lifted her arms to heaven, saying, A sign, a sign![10]

As soon as the responsible citizens were sufficiently roused from their stupor to take in what was happening, they clambered out their pews and rushed down the aisle to seize the wicked blasphemers. The apprentices were on their feet already, jubilant at the momentary triumph of misrule. The young man and woman scampered to the doors, supported by a blue-coated rabble of apprentices and servants. Marius was hurled forward by the throng, and, in the confusion, being shoved, put out his elbow into a farandine waistcoat that proved to belong to his master. That is at least what he told the indignant corn-chandler, who knew not whether to believe him. (He

had been until then a sober, diligent youth, noways prankish.) The boy was
of an age when the sudden view of a woman's breasts might make his limbs
unsteady, and cause his eyes to sparkle so, and his lips to tremble. In truth,
I question if Marius took notice of the woman; he was unsettled rather by
the words he heard, thrilled by their harsh, eruptive sense.

That selfsame day he sought out a Quaker meeting, where he met with
disappointment; as the Friends did nothing but groan or hum to themselves,
or utter a few disjointed phrases. The meeting house was known, however,
and an unruly crowd soon gathered to hurl stones through the windows, a
disturbance which little affected the tremblers, quivering in ecstatic communion. Marius left in some confusion. He had no appetite for martyrdom.
It may be, too, that he did not know to which party he would choose to
adhere; for he, at his young age, must have been stirred more by the mob
without than the mystics within.

Marius was just turned of sixteen. In Somerset House a waxen Cromwell
had at last taken the crown, set upon a graven head, the scepter fixed in
a strengthless hand. His son and heir proved likewise to be a personage
of soft and malleable stuff.[11] Army and Parliament tossed and tousled for
supremacy; no one could say which government was worse. The masters of
London, the lords and gentry of England, felt the frailty of their authority
and were afraid. Soldiers, for want of pay, were dangerous; their officers were
no better, and with less cause. Cottagers broke down hedges and dined on
the lord's venison. Apprentices rabbled wealthy citizens. Merchants feared
to open their shops; their wives and daughters kept withindoors. Sectaries
preached on street corners, in cellars, taverns, and warehouses. Some erected
makeshift pulpits in the church aisle and roared out blasphemies over the
incumbent's sermon. Quakers cried up their unlettered promptings as superior to Scripture and Commandment. Back-lane printers poured forth a
torrent of factious and impertinent pamphlets demanding the abolition of
tithes, titles, and primogeniture, proclaiming the New Jerusalem, pleading
the Good Old Cause.[12]

Marius partook eagerly of it all. His idle hours were spent in Coleman
Street and at Allhallows the Great, or wherever the preachment suited his
humor for extremes.[13] Yet it was the politicians who gained his ear more
than the sectaries. His pennies were bestowed on seditious pamphlets and
pint-pots of mum shared with a knot of like-minded youth, who combined
in a league they called the Prentices Club; for they were ready enough to
riot, though mostly given to grumbling and prating. They united in declaring their opposition to the tyranny of kings, lords, prelates, masters, and

fathers; but all positive principles were still to be canvassed and disputed amongst them. A soap-boiler's boy turned Ranting Quaker said that Christ Jesus was the light and the life within, and he who was guided by that light could never sin. A freshly hatched Fifth Monarchist said that was but prattling bibble-babble: Jesus was a tall handsome man with curling auburn hair, who would shortly return to rule over England as a second Eden. The earth will then bring forth fruit without men's labor and all will share equally, except the saints will be dressed in golden raiment and sit upon thrones.[14]

—Who then will bake the bread and weave the clothes?

—King Jesus himself will clothe his saints, and manna will drop from heaven as in Moses' time.

—The manna that fell upon the City would be too filthy to eat.

—The City will be purged in a holy fire. It will be a New Jerusalem, a city of golden pavements and tall towers gleaming with jewels.

The notion of such a transfiguration held them still, until they began again to wrangle and dispute.

Much about this time, Marius began to keep a commonplace book wherein he recorded a few such dialogues, as well as sentences he culled from sermons and pamphlets. This work, grown to many volumes from years of disputation and study, his daughter saw him often consult. At the top of the first page he wrote down the words of the insolent Quaker who interrupted the sermon. After it came a loose collect of scriptural ill names and fustian rant, then a half page filled with circles, squares and ciphers, which must have been his callow projection of a commonwealth.

That some such commonwealth was nigh at hand Marius did not doubt. His spirits, which heretofore were sluggish and cold, had been kindled to a hectic fever by the violent talk of tub-preachers and renegadoes. The broils and commotions, the calamitous tumults of this year, were to him the birth pangs of a republic that would endure until the end of time.[15] He despised swordsmen as a danger to liberty; but, nonetheless, cheered the fall of the Protectorate and the restoration of the Rump Parliament by the army. The removal of the Rump by the Nine Colonels he in turn applauded. Next he was crying out for a free and full parliament and hurling brickbats at soldiers. He showed already his genius for inventing taunts and jeers, which were eagerly taken up by the rabble about him. He must have heard some voices crying for the return of King Charles; but, in a mob, some call for one thing, some another. As he would say in after-years, Free is a great and lofty word. He did not then suppose it could signify its contrary, or that men would choose to relinquish their liberty only to gape at kings and princes in luxurious trappings.

It is not to be supposed that Boult, the corn-chandler, failed to observe the moonish behavior of his apprentice; but apart from laying a stick across his shoulders once or twice a day, his master let him be. (He himself held no fixed opinion: though he might prefer a settled government, it was undeniable that the late king had been no friend to corn-chandlers, whereas the distractions resulting from the rebellion had brought him great profit.) Boult mistook Marius' distemper for the greenness of his years. When it was time for the boy to take up his indentures, Bolt intended to propose a marriage to his daughter, which he knew would be welcome to the boy's parents.[16] (I take that he was a widower with a daughter only; for that is all his family that Delia knew of.) Thus things stood, until an inquisitive maid fished his commonplace book from its hiding-place. She happened to open it on the page scribbled over with small-figures and circles, whereupon she gave a fearful screech and fell into a fit: for what could it be, if not a spell to summon the devil? When the chandler came to examine the book, it fell from his hand in his fright. It was the words that alarmed him, bitter railings against kings, masters and fathers, along with senseless abusions— "thou vile venomy Rabshakeh, I have new-edged the sword of righteousness to plant it in thy papistical bowels"—a madman's assassinating ravings, it seemed to him.[17]

Marius' father, summoned to deal with the boy, was as scandalized as his master. Boult argued him a lunatic and proposed his committal to Bedlam. Marius then awoke to his danger and, in private to his father, discoursed of his principles and opinions with such efficacy that the father was at once convinced of the truth: his son was not a pitiful madman but something far worse. It seemed that his mother had taken his measure aright, and that the boy was predestinate to discord and rebellion. Incensed and aggrieved as he was, the father did not cast off his son, for fear that he might bring the family name to the pillory or the gallows. In exchange for a solemn promise to conceal his name and kindred in all his future doings, his father granted him a quarterly allowance, sufficient for a bare living and no more. These arrangements having been settled, Marius packed his gear and left, with neither father nor master knowing, nor greatly caring, whither he took himself. ✶

CHAPTER 2

Concerning the Bye Family: Their second son, Ferdinando, ventures life and limb in the Lammas Day uprising. Their lost son Roger returns, much altered. Marius begins his career as a pamphleteer. How he survived the twin scourges of Plague and Poverty. Roger killed in a brawl at Oxford. Mr. Bye goes to seek Marius in London but falls ill upon his return.

To SATISFY my readers, as well as my own curiosity, I have taken some pain to uncover more of Marius his history than he chose to impart to his daughter. His family was respectable though undistinguished: his father's father walked behind a plough and his mother's father stood behind a counter; but the estate was good, and among their neighbors, who were of like extraction, they passed for gentry. For some years, Marius' parents heard nothing from Roger, their first-born, who had obeyed his mother's prompting to offer his services to the King in exile. Fearing his loss, they fastened their hopes upon their second son, Ferdinando, who was, in his natural parts and temperament, much superior to his two brothers. At Oxford Ferdinando indulged himself more in books and less in debauchery than befits a gentleman, but his lively disposition won him many friends. Whilst his brother Marius was in Coleman Street hearkening to Levellers and Fifth Monarchy men, Fernando was home for the long vacation.[1] He had declined an invitation offered by a chum of a great landed family, not wanting to put his father to the expense such a visit would require. When a baronet's son, who left his college to acquire a smattering of law, invited him to his new lodgings in Gray's Inn, he thought he might safely accept.[2] Ferdinando would have cheerfully walked to town; his parents feared that doing so would disgrace him before his friend, and insisted he be mounted. Alas, their good saddle horses had all been taken from them; the clumsy, heavy-paced beast they put him on was only fit for the cart, and for the mockery of his friend, should it be seen.

The Inns of Court buzzed with rumor of an uprising set for Lammas Day. Some said it was to bring in the King; others, only to demand a full and free parliament.[3] During an evening of guzzling with good fellows, a ride to Tunbridge Wells was proposed for the morrow ('twas the last of July), in the hope of joining with the forces said to be assembling there. No gentleman of spirit and mettle could decline such a proposal; certainly none of the young sparks present dared to do so. Near Sevenoaks they encountered an army patrol; several of their party instantly turned and fled, so that it was scarce possible for the rest to pretend to innocence. Whether their numbers and arms were sufficient to make a stand I could not learn: certainly their courage was not. In the rout Ferdinando's dobbin was startled into a gallop, but he was still far in the rear and soon to be caught. To save himself he turned his horse out of the road into a rough coppice-wood. He thus escaped pursuit, only to have his beaten horse founder on a steep slope. Ferdinando, encumbered by his lended sword, went down beneath him. He was found by a woodcutter, who laid him across his horse and bore him home. The goodman set his broken leg; the woodcutter's wife, skilled in herbs, applied poultices to the wound.

When Ferdinando, alone of all the party, failed to return to Gray's Inn, it was thought he had been captured, especially as the poverty of his steed had been generally remarked. His friend the baronet's son employed much of the next day in attempting to trace him among the prisoners being held at the Mews, Petre House, Scotland Yard, and other such places. Having dispatched a brief letter to Ferdinando's father, he considered the bonds of friendship to have been faithfully observed, and gave no further regard to Ferdinando's fate. The anxious parents knew not what to do, except await some word from their son. But he, in his dread of prison and a traitor's death, had begged the woodcutter and his wife for secrecy. His fears, though groundless, did him no hurt; for the bedstraw was clean, the goodwife's plasters innocuous, and his case incurable. The priest who came to minister the last rites took down a letter for his parents, wherein he regretted the sorrow he would cause them and asked forgiveness for his rashness. The honest couple followed the bier to the churchyard and shed some tears for the unhappy young gentleman. He had however left them a serviceable horse and a purse full of silver that was to them a fortune. They could not but reflect, with pious thanksgiving, on how well things fell out for them.

The grief of his parents was great, for he had been his father's favorite and was now his mother's also. His friend's letter said nothing of the party's headlong flight, and his own gave few particulars of his fatal injury. Her fancy, still pursuing its peculiar theme, saw her son beset and cruelly cut down by republican rascals in arms. Her husband consoled and quieted her as best he could; for despite his grief at the loss of his child, he did not fail to discern the risk of a sequestration.[4] With the utmost difficulty he persuaded his wife to curb her loud lamenting and to join him in concealing the circumstances of their son's death. They haggled over each particular, his mother persevering that they not sully Ferdinando's heroic action with base, craven lies. In the end, they fixed upon a tale of a gallop and a stumble that was very near the truth.

Wrapped in sorrow and gloom, they little attended to the turmoil taking place in London and Westminster. How to pay the army tax was the only question of polity or governance to concern them. Upon All-Hallows they awoke to find the road occupied by file upon file of sullen redcoats.[5] These soldiers sang no psalms of vengeance or of victory; for the current quarrel was not God's but that of their officers, falling out amongst themselves. Stragglers and deserters infested the countryside, robbing and pilfering along the way. Another civil war seemed certain: even Mrs. Bye gave up all hope of the King's return. She withdrew to a small upper room in the rear of the house; there she slept and fed and prayed, leaving management of the household to her husband, and refusing all attempts at consolation. She would not be coaxed forth from her retreat. It was in vain to tell her that the Nine Colonels had been compelled to unlock the doors of Parliament House: It meant only that the men who beheaded her king ten years ago were once again in authority. She cared not, she said, whether 'twas the tub-preachers or the swordsmen who ruled. When Lord General Monck took the North Road into London, followed a few hours later by his entire army, Mrs. Bye refused even to look from a window. Eight days later, her husband, their servants and all the neighborhood went atop Highgate Hill to view the smoke of hundreds of bonfires, and, upon returning home, lit one of their own. Mrs. Bye came but half-way down the stairs before mistrust stayed her steps and occasioned a retreat.[6]

She was at last lured to the hall by unparalleled good news: a letter from their long-lost Roger. In it he expressed his hope of a sudden reunion and boasted of the favor of a great man of the Court. His mother's joy was uncontained. She extolled her own sagacity in sending him away, declaring that the family's prosperity was now secure. (Imagination advanced Roger to a knighthood, at the least, poor Ferdinando being now forgot.) She conjectured the identity of her son's patron, guessing at Lord Hatton or the Marquis of Ormonde. Here she was wide of the mark, not understanding which of her son's virtues had commended him to a protector. When, four years before, Roger arrived at the Court without money or friends, deficient in grace, dress, conversation, and birth, he cut no figure at all. What little notice he received was upon suspicion of spying for Cromwell. He might have perished from want had he not ventured his last few coins in gaming. He had in prior days shown superior skill at put, mumchance, fox-mine-host, and other such games, so that it required only his present necessity to develop his genius. Roger shared Dame Fortune's favors with those he would have as his friends; in consequence he was taken up by Sir Phineas Dyce, a gentleman who little cared how he won, provided that he did.[7]

Their prodigal soon made his return. His mother nearly expired of pure joy to see her son; his father scarce knew him. His form was corpulent, his behavior coarse and sowish. Roger bore the news of his brother Ferdinando's death with great calm. He viewed Marius' disgrace and banishment with evident satisfaction, though he could not approve of the allowance money. His mother, no doubt believing her son to be inward with the great during his long residence in foreign lands, wished to learn the characters of the King and the principal courtiers. But Roger's familiarity with the Court was limited to the tattle of servants and hangers-on, all of it scandalous and some partly true. This he repeated with a depraved gusto, amplified by his own lascivious imaginings. (He had indeed a pretty talent as a storyteller of this sort.) His mother never before heard such filthiness, so openly related; but if her son told it, if His Majesty and the Great Ones of the Court enacted it, then such doings must be ala mode, and the fault was in her own rustic simplicity. Mr. Bye, having gauged his son's character, lamented to his friends how unhappy he was in his sons, the one a Libertine, the other a Leveller.

If young Marius felt any compunction for offending so excellent a father, he never acknowledged it in after-years. He may have been well pleased to escape his master and his neglected duties, and to have money all a sudden in his pocket. (He was yet to learn how quick 'twould be spent.) Besides which considerations, he now had leisure and solitude to pursue what he had come to believe his calling. He found cheap lodging in Blackfriars, unpacked his bundle, and at once set to work. He had his theme direct before him: The Long Parliament had dissolved itself at last.[8] Its successor required advice on settling the government, advice which Marius thought himself capable to provide. He wrote off two or three sheets, which he took at once to the stationers near St. Paul's, where he had often bought pamphlets that pleased him with their violence. I expect he had some words in the title about the Old Cause and the commonwealth, for the booksellers gave it but half an eye before they tossed it back to him with a mock. One, a little kinder than his fellows, told Marius to look about his shop to see what was selling. Such republican trash was no more the fashion: the call now was for satires on Cromwell or panegyrics on the martyred king, or on the young king that's coming in. But Marius (with money in his pocket) was no hireling. The printers in the alleys near the bridge were more accommodating, and among them he found one willing to take his virgin effort for a consideration. It must have been irksome to discover that he must pay the printer, but he no doubt expected to recover the charges by its sale. He soon discovered that the petty chapmen would not take it, nor any common crier able to understand the title. He was forced to give his pamphlets gratis to beggar-girls to make any money they could. (Those who did had the wit to proffer Marius' paper at the Fleet and Thames-side privy-houses, where 'twas briskly taken up.)[9]

Marius had a passable good headpiece, slow to take impression but stubborn to quit. He applied himself now to learning his craft, frequenting the booksellers, thumbing the wares of chapmen, reading prints he found lying about in cookshops or alehouses, all the while scribbling in his commonplace book. The news of Lambert's sudden escape from the Tower rekindled his hopes, and he at once joined battle in the only way he could, by penning a pamphlet account of the hero.[10] This remarkable work was above one-quarter true: if the rest were lies, 'twas by no fault of Marius. He was acquainted with two or three cashiered officers, fellow Levellers and fanatics, who told him their stories of the general, which he faithfully related, rounded with blood-and-thunder threatenings of ruin to Cavaliers and changelings. This time he left the bookseller's shop with a purse made heavier by a few crowns. Shortly thereafter, he had the inexpressible satisfaction to see his work (The Life and Principal Victories of Lord General Lambert by M. B.) hawked about London and eagerly taken up by enthusiasts and neuters alike. This green success must have moderated his disappointment when, a bare fortnight later, the captive hero was made to stand under Tyburn tree before a mob that jeered and flouted him.

The Prentices Club broke to pieces about this time. Those whose expectation of a great alteration had caused them to be surly to their masters now repented on their knees. Most belonged to that pliable sect that wish only to shout and throw brickbats from the security of the multitude. They heartily joined in the May Day celebration; they drank of the beer and wine flowing from the conduits; they cheered the King and the Princes of York and Gloucester as if they were heart-whole and perpetual royalists.[11] The only one, beside Marius, who would not serve the time was a journeyman feltmaker named Gowler. The restoration of the monarchy delivered such a shock to his convictions that he would not credit it as lasting, as more than a final, fleeting test of the elect. Every violent storm had him rushing to the window, to look for King Jesus riding the thunderbolt. It was by means of this Gowler that young Marius became acquainted with a knot of Fifth Monarchy men—disbanded soldiers and discontented artisans, like this poor crack-brained feltmaker, that pined for a New Jerusalem in their squalid courts and alleys. The executions of the regicides in October at first stirred up doubt and despair among them.[12] They loudly prayed and loudly disputed to seek the meaning of these events, deciding in the end that Major-General Harrison was one of the two witnesses heralding the return of King Jesus. The identity of the second witness was a dark question over which they quarreled mightily, some saying it was John Carew, others Thomas Scot, and yet others Hugh Peters. They laid a mad plan to recover the heads from London Bridge and the quarters from the Gates, believing, without doubt, that the corpses of the witnesses, once reassembled and committed to burial, would soon be resurrected, ushering in the Fifth Monarchy.[13]

On the Epiphany, after a day of raging sermons, they took up arms to recover the heads and quarters of the regicides, calling out all the while for King Jesus to descend. It was only some forty or fifty fanatics in all, but they possessed the fury and strength of madmen, scattering the train-bands and murdering twenty men before they were at last brought to bay.[14] Gowler was a rebaptized brother in this conventicle, but as for Marius there is no information. His daughter believes he never went out with any rebels to do murders, saying, he in no sort was a violent man, except in his writing, for he struck her but twice in all her life. She thinks he did no more than draft the heads of the declaration that was published for their rising. Notwithstanding her opinion, I read in Baker's Chronicle that the rebels twice hid themselves in the woods near Highgate, and I question whether Marius might have guided them to their lurking-places.[15] Horse and foot scoured the countryside in pursuit, passing up and down the North Road and the by-lanes thereabouts. Mrs. Bye thought certainly that Forty-One was come again.[16] Her husband feared that his youngest son was numbered among the conspirators. Their lunatic attempt came to an end on the third day, and within a fortnight thirteen more traitor-heads were set out to edify the public, among them Gowler the feltmaker's.

The spectacle of his friend's head upon a pike affrighted Marius sadly, but could not still his busy pen. Prudence, as well as his father's command, prompted him to change his name and his lodgings with some frequency. (His daughter insists that he never did so to escape his debts, only from a suspicion of spies, trepanners, and informers.) On quarter days he went to a goldsmith in Cheapside to receive his allowance.[17] His father (hoping for his reformation) said that he might leave a letter with the goldsmith, but he never did so, only noting down his street and his alias. Mr. Bye was unacquainted with the by-lanes of the liberties and suburbs, else he would have observed that his son's frequent changes made a steady progress downwards to obscurer and shabbier lodgings. For Marius was impelled to scribble on every point of controversy that might support his cause. His fellow republicans, when they liked his writing, would subscribe some small sum toward its publication; but often he bore the cost, and withal found few willing to take his waste paper off his hands; so that he was fain to drop his seditious writings in alleys and alehouses. In common with other factious and unlicensed scribblers, he railed against the cruelty of Norman Law, the perfidy of Parliament, and the immorality of the Romish Court.[18] But he had no successes like to his history of the great General. Marius was possessed of a pretty way with insult and invective. A literate tripe-man might have paused over a strongly worded broadside before wrapping up his guts and garbages; the citizen on his seat of ease may have read a few lines before applicating Marius' work to its proper end.[19] Yet he lacked a very necessary talent of the popular pamphleteer: he had no knack for bawdry. His muse was virulent, passionate, yet singularly chaste. If it were possible to pen a dull libel on the intrigues of the court ladies, Marius was the man to do it.

The coming of the plague made at first little difference to Marius.[20] He had no thought of fleeing to the countryside, for there was another plot afoot that summer. He received his quarterage at Midsummer, acknowledging it with his alias and his residence, although I question if he trusted the goldsmith with his right and full abode. If there were any signs of uneasiness, or preparations for departure in the goldsmith's establishment, he did not note it, and he would not have made a long stay. He had the habit, common to conspirators and other malefactors, of skulking in back lanes and alleys, avoiding the markets and the thoroughfares. Shortly after Lammas Day, a drumming and the clamor of a mob drew Marius into Cheapside. A Fifth Monarchy preacher named Danvers was on his way to the Tower, though but poorly guarded. His supporters, abetted by out-of-place servants and apprentices (whose masters left them behind in fleeing the plague), overcame his escort and carried him to safety.[21] Marius must not have taken part in the fray, or at least he had leisure to look about him. He was put in a toss to see that the shop of the goldsmith upon whom he depended was padlocked and boarded up; nor was there anyone who could tell where to find him, for most of his neighbors had likewise departed the City, leaving only a servant or two behind, who would not answer his knock. This was a great blow, for Marius barely eked out a narrow subsistence from one quarter to the next.

When Marius returned to his room, it may be that he intended only to set down his necessary expenses and figure how he might diet himself, or he may have contemplated writing to his father for aid. Once he took up his pen, however, his ideas pursued a different course. His swelling indignation at the goldsmith took possession of his thoughts, mingling with public and impersonal grievances. King, courtiers, prelates, physicians, and magistrates, all had abandoned the poor of London as a sacrifice to hunger and disease. He considered the discarded serving-men and comfortless abandoned boys that mobbed Danvers' guards in Cheapside. In his mind's eye he saw them pushed into the streets with a scanty pittance of their overdue wages, but not before they had obeyed the commands of their masters and mistresses in loading carts and chariots with chests of plate and hoarded coin. He saw the carriages of the great piled high with trunks filled with rich draperies and other household goods. And none but a favored lady's maid or a lapdog, a footboy or a monkey, was allowed a place. There was matter here for a half-dozen pamphlets, which Marius whipped up, one after another. These little works were eagerly read and passed about among the populace; though in truth there were few left in the City who could afford a groats-worth of his satires. He scarce gained more than a few shillings; and now the plague carts were filled, the reeking graveyards were piled with bodies, and even the poorest attempted, in vain, to flee.

A learned apothecary has set down his observation that choleric and melancholy persons, and those with lean and dry bodies, were especially prone to succumb to the contagion. If so, I marvel that Marius survived, for he was all these things. But since he could not afford the apothecary's advice, nor his pomanders, his vesicatories, his diaphoretics or his plague waters, it may be that his poverty saved him, at least from being poisoned. His daughter said that his only antidote was to rub his body with vinegar, and to hold wormwood before his face when out of doors. In truth, I believe Marius may thank his own cunning for his escape. The plague, as is well known, began in Westminster, then struck with fury in Cripplegate and neighboring parishes, before it spread eastward by starts and leaps. By the time the plague was raging in Shoreditch, it had spent its force in the western and northern parts. Marius, who gave careful study to the weekly bills of mortality, quit his room in the Minories at the end of September, returning to a lodging he had formerly taken in Cripplegate.[22]

I doubt his parents gave much thought to him, even though they witnessed in July the northward commigration of wealthy citizens, their coaches and wagons heavy laden with goods. His father had notice of his obtaining his allowance at Midsummer, and that was all they knew of him. Their son Roger visited them about this time: to show a proper filial regard to his parents, no doubt, though these visits never concluded without a goodly number of

guineas passing from his father's purse to his own. He still pretended to be a
courtier, and it may be his mother believed him; but all his years of seeking
favor had procured him no further privilege than that of claiming a place
at the servants table in the household of his dissolute patron. When the
Court removed to Salisbury he followed after. This proved a most profitable
stop for him, as his cogging and foisting tricks with dice, grown stale and
unvendible in London, were new to the loutish roisterers of Sarum alehouses.
When the Court progressed to Oxford, a verminous swarm of hang-bys and
lick-trenchers, Roger among them, made thither as well, by wagon and foot
(all other conveyance being pressed into the service of the Court). By the
time Roger and his fellows reached the town, every inn and lodging-place
was filled up from cellar to garret. They could find for themselves nothing
better than a rough tippling-house in the outskirts of the town, and even
here there were not beds enough for all. A dispute began that grew hot
and then violent. Roger got the bed for which he quarreled, though he did
not lie in it for long. The surgeon was too late to save him; the priest was
never sent for. Some papers found upon him named his parents, to whom
the surgeon addressed his condolences and his bill.[23]

The King came to Oxford about the Twenty-Fifth of September, in
advance of the sitting of Parliament. The news of Roger's death must have
reached his parents close upon Michaelmas. Mrs. Bye wailed and beat her
breast; Mr. Bye was sorrowful but resigned. He saw the necessity of bringing
Marius home, though it was not easy to bring his wife to his view. Mr. Bye
was no politician; yet he understood very well that levelling notions suit
poorly with full purses and fine expectations. He had therefore a reasonable
hope that his heir would discard his quondam principles for a wholesome
self-regard. He looked for the usual notice from the goldsmith, so that he
might know where to send for his son. When no letter reached him, he
began to feel some alarm for Marius, as well as for the deposit which the
goldsmith was holding. He set out for the City, going first to Cheapside,
where he found, as he feared, that the goldsmith was fled the plague. The
goldsmith had last given him an address for Marius that was in the Minories,
a place he did not at all know. Whenever he hesitated at a turning or paused
to inquire the way, pestiferous women and starved children would come up
to beg alms; he gave more from fear of contagion, to keep them at a distance,
than from charity. He began to perceive how pinched and scraping Marius
must be, to take lodgings in a place of such ill aspect. As he was passing
near an open cellar, a stark-naked man, crazed by sickness and hunger,
leapt up and attempted to pull him from his horse. He struck out with his

whip, which the madman seized and turned against him. His cries for help drew a band of idled seamen who beat the poor lunatic off. Mr. Bye was compelled to pay out a substantial reward to rescuers who were not much less threatening than his attacker. Troubled and much discouraged, doubting his son could long survive in such an evil place, he turned homeward. Upon passing through Aldersgate, he remembered that another of his son's shifting abodes had been in Red Cross Street. Turning towards St. Giles, he came upon Marius in the street as he was returning to his lodging.[24]

They did not embrace, this father and son, for each feared from his look that the other was infected. Marius said he could not then go home, but would come within a week. He gave no reason: it must have been some plot or pamphlet that he rated above compliance with his parent's wishes. Mr. Bye regretted having no money to supply his son's needs: For, he said, I have given away all I had to people who begged it from me in the streets. —God preserve you for your kindness to them, was the unexpected reply.

Upon returning to his home, Mr. Bye could not dismount without assistance. He went straight to his bed, and I do not believe he was ever again able to leave it. It may have been the plague; for, though the physician diagnosed a lethargy and prescribed Goddard's Drops, it was observed that he would not come into the chamber unless the maid first made a great fire and fumed the room with rosin. Howbeit, Mr. Bye never developed the fatal tokens, and no one else in the family was stricken.[25] He himself thought that he took a taint from the madman, whose touch had sent such a shudder through him that he sickened in an instant. Fitfully, in his waking moments, he related to his wife all that had happened, and got from her a promise to be kind to Marius and not to reproach him for what was past. When at last Marius came and was brought to his father's bedside, Mr. Bye roused himself to look upon his son, uttered the name of Ferdinando, and never spoke again. ✠

CHAPTER 3

Marius comes into his inheritance. He lives unquietly with his mother, until she leaves to lodge with her cousins, the corn-chandlers. Marius reduces his family to two female servants and devotes his hours to study. Fleeing the dreadful Fire, his mother and cousins come to stay with him. Introducing Hull: the beginning of his rise to great wealth. Marius applies himself to alchemy; but in ten years' time, he is not one farthing the better for it.

HEN **Marius** went to view the estate, he found it weakened and impaired from the exactions of the army, the Protectorate, and his brother Roger. He never recovered the money his father had deposited with the goldsmith, and this remained a subject for animadversion as much as any policy of the King and his ministers. His daughter says that in all his writings there is scarce one where he has not worked in some mention of the dishonesty and greed of the City, or else a sharp allusion to goldsmiths, usurers, and bankers. Here he was unjust in his specific charges, if not in the general. A linen-draper who has long kept a shop in Cheapside assured me that this goldsmith was of honest fame and would have settled his accounts, had he lived to do so. He, with his family, fled London for Maidstone not long after Marius drew his Midsummer allowance. The plague visited that town, no less than the City, where it numbered the goldsmith, his wife, daughter, and son among its victims. His trusted clerk, no doubt considering that death cancels all debts, helped himself to the goldsmith's store of deposits, striking with such expedition that his master's body was scarce cold before he reached the sea-coast and took ship.

The late Mr. Bye may have been correct in expecting the reducement of his son to a prudent conformity, especially as he was now estranged from his fellow plotters, none of whom knew him as Marius Bye of ——. Though it may be true, as his daughter maintains, that he never took up arms against the King, he had otherways risked putting his neck into the pillory, if not the noose. Thus, seeking his own safety, he might have settled into life as a country gentleman of moderate good estate, had his kind father lived to guide him. But it was not possible for Marius to put his past life behind him when his mother was always ready to give a reminder of it. Whether she forgot her promise to her husband I do not know; certainly she found it difficult to honor. Or, she may have interpreted it narrowly; having forgiven past ills, she was at liberty to find present fault, and did so. When she did not speak, she looked her reproaches. They continued together uneasily for much of a year, until Mrs. Bye left to board with her cousins in the City. Marius Bye was at last master of his own house, though pinched to pay his mother's dower. The servants that had shown their regard for their old mistress by their insolence to Marius were dismissed; the land that his father had farmed was leased to tenants. He hired a man to dig his garden and tend the stable, retaining only one superannuate maid to manage his house, the very one who had assisted clumsily at his birth four and twenty years before, and for whom he would elsewise be expected to make some allotment. Decrepit save for her tongue, ears, and eyes (which were admirably active and sharp), she had a poor cottager's daughter for her drudge, to do the work of the house under her supervision. To this child, called Jane, she passed on much useful instruction, in addition to a lifetime's accumulation of malicious gossip and espial. By reason of their extremes of age and their respective infirmities (the child Jane having but one good eye, the other put out in a precocious quarrel), Marius paid them small wages. He made but an ill bargain; for over the many years, these two women, the old witch and the young one, would cost him much money and fret by their thieving and spying. If, in delivering my history, I have given out some of this family's most intimate doings, related with an uncharitable construction, it is owing to the prying malice of this old housekeeper, who related her eavesdropping discoveries to Jane, who repeated them, in later days, to the innocent Delia.

At this time Marius went seldom to London, only once or twice to Fleet Street to purchase books for his library; and so I believe he did intend to shun his former associates. He immersed himself in his studies, attempting to correct the deficiencies of his education, with what efficacy I do not know. Thus abstracted, he gave no regard to the unwonted noise of the road before his house and did not go out, as his two servants did, to gape at the billowing black clouds spreading over the City, or the flame that arched across the sky that night. His earliest notice of the terrible Fire was a violent knocking at his door. It was his mother and Boult, his old master, along with Boult's daughter and son-in-law, seeking refuge with him. They had saved almost nothing except themselves. Mrs. Bye clutched her best petticoat knotted over a few trifles she had hastily snatched up. Else there were only some bedclothes heaped in a barrow containing the worn-out chandler, who they had thus carried all the way from Cripplegate.[1]

The Fire had found them, like so many others, unprepared. The chandler and his son-in-law, whose name is Hull, trusted overmuch that pulling down the houses about Queenhithe would stop the fire before it reached their warehouse. They thought belatedly to hire lighters to carry their stores to safety. Already the prices demanded were almost equal to the value of their grain, which was mostly beer-corn, or so Hull said; but Father Boult said that there would be a dearth after the fire from which they might profit, if only they saved their stuff from the flames. While they haggled with carriers and disputed with each other, the fire grew. Sparks and burning brands shot out widely, so that there were now many fires starting up at once. They obtained two carts, one that belonged to them and another that they hired, and were preparing to load them with corn, when a shrieking maid ran up to tell them that the fire was spread almost to the house. Hull proposed to take one cart to rescue their household goods, reasoning that a parcel of good plate was worth twenty quarters of corn. Boult was stubbornly fixed upon saving his stores, saying that his daughter, Mrs. Bye, and their maids would fill the cart with trash; but would be sure to carry out the silver if they had only their own hands and backs at their service. It was only with promising to fill the cart with goods from the shop that he was allowed to take their cart and horse home. He had to go only a short way along Thames Street, but the press of people, horses and wagons was so great that the house was up in flames when he got there.[2] His wife had put the servants to carrying out the plate and other fine things, but neglected to set an adequate guard over the saved goods. These, put down at haphazard and left to the tendance of a distracted servant, were at once snatched up by thieves that were as quick and fierce as the flames. Little of value remained, excepting a hamper full of bedclothes that Mrs. Bye had sat upon, feeling too fainty to go back for more than she clutched in her trembling arms. Hull vented his fury on the servants, blaming them for disobeying their mistress in order to save their worthless boxes; calling them rogues and thieves, then dismissing them without a penny of their wages. Which, being otherwise a sad injustice, made Delia hope that they had snatched up a spoon in their flight, to save their young master from committing a calumny.

Hull was left with a horse and cart loaded with two wrangling, weeping women, and with just such tenpenny baggage as his father-in-law had derided. It was futile to attempt a return to the warehouse. The multitude of frenzied householders and the heaps of their worldly goods stopped all the lanes leading to the river. He might have sold the cart and horse, which were worth more than their load. Near Budge Row, a grocer catched hold of the reins with an offer of thirty pounds. But the women screeched in horror at the prospect of forsaking the few things they had saved. They were all of them frightened out of their wits. It might be that the end of the world was come upon them: the people praying and lamenting in the streets said so. In that case, what avails thirty pounds, more than turkey-work cushions and coverlets? This man Hull is a wily dealer, who saw there was a fortune to be made in carts and horses that day; but even he was too bewildered by the uproar, smoke, and confusion to make profit of it. He stopped at an inn and went forth on foot in quest of Father Boult.

He found him lying in the lane before his warehouse, flung over a heap of corn, weeping for vexation and smoke. The carman, in his simplicity, had hired himself for only five times the ordinary rate. While still loading his cart, he was importuned by desperate citizens bidding as much as five pounds for his services. He at once threw out his load, telling Boult that, with his ten shillings and his miserly soul, he could hire the devil to carry his corn. Old Boult's headpiece was weakened by calamity; he was obstinate to save some part of his stock, however small. He seemed to believe it would sprout a new warehouse filled with sacks of grain; for he could not be budged from his post until his son-in-law loaded a barrow with a bushel of wheat and began to push his load up the hill, the old man tottering behind him, keeping barely in advance of the flames, with sparks shooting out dangerously all about them. The women had taken a chamber at the inn and called for a dish of cold mutton: none of them knowing where they should go or what they should do with themselves. At nightfall the fire looked so great, the flames bearing down so near, that they passed the night waking, in readiness to flee again. They had by now determined to make their way northwards to Mrs. Bye's son. Departing as soon as it was light, they paid the reckoning, though not without sharp reflections upon the goodness of the mutton and the price of horsemeat. All the ways out of the City were crammed with heavily laden carts and foot-passengers. Fires were starting up all round. Yesterday it had been the Day of Judgment commencing; now 'twas said to be the work of Papists, flinging fireballs in windows.[3] New fires and fresh terrors sent them first one direction, then another. Finally, their horse, a poor hidebound jade not fit for such exertions, fell on its knees and would go no further. Old Boult was so overcome by the smoke and his distresses, to be as feeble in his legs as the horse. Mrs. Bye, too, would have been unable to walk, if not for a fear that they would leave her behind. Hull sold the barrow for twenty shillings that morning, not expecting it would be needed. Now he paid five and twenty for another, into which they put Boult and the bedclothes. They rested a short while at Islington, and came at last to Marius' door about ten at night.

This family was full of their story upon arrival; nor did they cease to rehearse it during the long months of their stay. They talked endlessly of their losses, not without insinuations, or frank quarrels, over who was most at fault. Mrs. Bye ought to have sat upon something more valuable than the bedclothes. Hull was wrong to dismiss the servants on the spot, as they lost the use of their backs. Both carts should have been sent at once to the house. The two women lamented the sacrifice of those treasures that had been preserved from fire, only to be left behind in the abandoned cart—a pair of turkey-work cushions, a cabinet of kickshaws, a warming pan that had been in the family some ages. They looked on the chandler as if measuring his relative worth, and finding him light in the balance. At least that is what Marius' two servants claimed, who pried and peeped at all occasions. It was Mrs. Bye and Hull's young wife who made the most noise; Boult still suffered in his wind, and could vent his reproaches only in gasps and wheezes. (He had bitter words, especially, concerning the wickedness of porters and watermen, who had sought to profit from the general calamity.) Hull had no part in these disputes. He had borrowed a horse of Marius and set out towards the City the very next day, whilst the Fire was still raging. The maids thought he had a secret hoard and was gone to dig it up. That is what Jane said to Delia and she believed it, for the man was notedly wealthy within a few years' time.

If Mrs. Bye, the chandler, and his daughter quarreled and grumbled a great deal amongst themselves, they achieved a perfect accord in their dislike for Marius. Boult envied his prosperity and comfort; Mrs. Hull felt renewed pique that he had not sought her favor when he might. Mrs. Bye, seizing upon the rumor that sectarian plotters had fired the City, accused her son of being a friend to incendiaries, if not one himself. He had an unhappy time of it until Hull at last returned late in the year, restoring Marius his horse, only a little spavined, and carrying off his family to a temporary lodging in the rear of a new-built warehouse. After their departure Marius relieved his feelings with a pamphlet on the Causes of the Late Lamentable Fire in the City of London. In it, he declared that the Fire was caused neither by the Papists, nor the sectaries, nor by the carelessness of a baker in Pudding Lane. A spark escaping from the baker's oven was only an incidental and indefinite cause (here he displayed his newly acquired learning). The material cause by which the Fire grew to waste the City was the Thames-side warehouses and granaries filled with combustible merchandise; and the efficient cause therefore was the avarice of chandlers, badgers, jobbers, and factors, in heaping up these hoards of goods; without which fuel, the fire would have been confined to a few streets. He drew a lively picture of chandlers bargaining with carriers and porters, abusing them as sharking rogues and thieving villains for tripling their price; they answering: Rascal and rogue us not; for we would be pitiful fools, not to have learned from you, our betters, to withhold our wares from the market until we may command the best price. One chandler, a man too close-fisted to pay carriage for his musty corn, fell to weeping and wringing his hands, for woe that there would be a dearth, and he unable to profit by it. By the avarice of these traders, the entire City had been levelled to ashes, great halls and wretched dogholes alike, so that once-wealthy citizens were glad of a blanket to cover themselves.

Marius then declared that the Fire had a final cause in purging the City of greed and inequality. A new city would arise from the ashes of the old one, as goldsmiths and merchants, humbled by their losses, worked beside masons and bricklayers to build a new London that would endure forever. I cannot conceive how Marius formed such a preposterous notion, unless he had been turning the pages of his commonplace book, and recollecting the mad dreams of his apprentice days. He ought to have understood the falsity of his vision, from Hull having already a warehouse new-built. It may be that he, like his two gossiping servants, believed that Hull had a hoard of coin to spend in reestablishing himself. Howsoever, this Hull grew to be a considerable man on the Exchange, where his low beginnings and dishonest dealing are well known to many. He had formerly been Boult's factor in Hertfordshire and Essex. He would never have been thought of for a son-in-law, being of no family, and a trifle deformed, if not for their disappointment in Marius, whereupon Boult's anxiety for a successor, and his daughter's for a husband, led them to pitch him for a substitute.

Before taking leave of Marius and his family, Hull made up a pack containing the coverlets that Mrs. Bye preserved with her backside. In the fields about Islington, he found families that escaped the Fire with their plate, jewels and finery, but little else. Having just passed a wakeful, wretched night exposed to the elements, they were ready to yield to a bad bargain, exchanging rings and other rich toys for something to protect them from the dew. These he took to the goldsmiths and haberdashers of the Strand, where he was no doubt cheated, but not so badly as he had dealt by his desperate customers in the fields. He tarried in the smoldering City only a few hours before setting out for Ware (baiting the horse, for convenience, at its master's own stable).[4] Stopping at the principal inn, he drew a large, gaping audience to hear his account of the fire that had reduced the city to ruins and ashes, and turned its great merchants into beggars. He described the throngs of homeless people camped in the fields, dependent on charity for sustenance, gnawing on ship biscuits soaked in puddle-water. He doubted London would be rebuilt, or not for a generation; its citizens were already dispersing to other parts. He gave particulars of great men, including some corn merchants, who had lost all. That he himself was in prosperous state was certain, from money seen when he took out his purse, and the fine jewel sparkling on his finger. The next day the large farmers came to him with their samples, eager to accept any reasonable terms. He repeated this performance in other towns along the Lea, until he had engrossed as large a supply of corn as he could quickly dispose of to the brewers and bakers that had escaped the Fire, who were as eager to buy as the farmers to sell. From grain Hull turned to getting a supply of brick, and was among the first to rebuild, though it was only a warehouse. He kept house in a portion of it, while he acquired desirable properties both within and without the Walls, faithful to the brogger's precept of buying cheap in a glut. Within ten years' time, dealing sometime in one commodity and sometime in another (he'ld have traded in old boots and besom if he saw a good profit in't), Hull had the means to build a fine mansion-house; so that old Boult and his daughter might ever after bless the day that they turned Marius Bye without doors.

I was curious to know how Marius employed himself after writing his little tract on the Fire, which he published with some difficulty and little success. At this time there would be few printers of a kind to hazard their necks for his troublesome pamphlets. A great many had been ruined; those whose shops survived the Fire were so discouraged by the busy inquisitions of Roger L'Estrange, that they sold their presses and turned to some new trade to keep themselves.[5] Delia was at first strangely reluctant to answer my questions about her father's doings at this time, pretending she knew nothing of the years before her own childhood, though she was well furnished with stories of her grandparents and uncles. Did nothing happen for a full ten years, I asked, whereupon her maid Jane might frame a story? When I so pressed her (for she is of a truthful and trusting disposition), she admitted at last that Jane had said many things of her father's doings, between the time of his mother's departure and his own marriage; but she was sure they could not be true and therefore ought not to be repeated. She said too much already: for certain, I would not let her be until she explained her mystery. I cajoled her into confidence by saying that, if she told it to me, I might assist her in finding whatever grain of truth lay hidden in Jane's malice; and that the wisest course to dispel a scandal, was to examine it dispassionately. Upon this encouragement, she told me that her father was said by Jane to spend his days in the kitchen, engaged in sorcery, burning brimstone and other foul things, in order to summon up the devil to do his bidding. Although it was certain to her, Delia, that her father would do no such thing, Jane backed her story by showing her a cupboard, containing a collection of jars labeled with symbols and hard words, and of glass vessels with long narrow necks, some curved and some straight, whereof she could not conceive a use, but which Jane said were glasses that witches and devils used to drink from.

I knew what such vessels served for, from a demonstration I witnessed at the College. I asked Delia if she never heard of alchemists, and of the vessels, called alembics, cucurbits, and pelicans, wherein they performed their distillations and sublimations, in quest of the Philosopher's Stone.[6] She colored slightly before saying, she had not thought of it, as she had been still a child when Jane showed her the contents of the cupboard. She was only sure, even then, that her father would not be guilty of such wickedness as sorcery or conjuring devils.

I asked Delia, smilingly, how it was that two servants, who could not have known each other, the one a maid in the corn-chandler's family, the other in his own, each separately accused her father of consorting with devils? She took my jest seriously; for, after pausing in troubled thought, she answered, Such women did not understand a book-learned man such as my father is, and were inclined to think evil of someone who passed his time in reading and studying, unless it were the Bible. —Did your father never read the Bible? I asked, to sport with her some more. Again she looked vexed, as if she would take back her words if she could. —He told me to read the Bible, she said, and sometimes he had me read to him, from the prophets Jeremiah and Isaiah or the book of Daniel.

Her thoughts still laboring to exonerate her father, Delia said she was certain he undertook his experiments in the hope of benefiting others, for he greatly pitied the poor and despised avarice. He himself, she said, cared little for money and never indulged himself in luxuries, not even caring, greatly, what he ate or drank or wore upon his back. That much may be true, and Marius may not have aimed at his own enrichment in his alchemical pursuits. I am inclined to believe, however, that he hated great and wealthy men a vast deal more than he loved the poor. He well knew that whosoever possessed the secret of the Philosopher's Stone, would overmaster and vanquish the goldsmiths, the great men of the kingdom, and the King himself too, which was his constant mark in all his pursuits. Whilst he thus chased his gilded will-o-the-wisp, Marius passed some ten years in near solitude, only going occasionally to the City, to buy himself books or powders; and perhaps to consult with others of his kind, who likewise sweated for a discovery that would level all distinction to equality. For when every hedge-smith or strolling tinker can coin himself gold, where will the great men be?

Like most men, Marius did not discourse of his failures; so that it is not possible to know when he abandoned his alembics. He may have discovered that he was running through his income (for some gold must go into the crucible to encourage the transmutation) and getting for it nothing but smoke and stink and scorched fingers. (He was slow to understand that the only sure way to transmute base substances to gold is by the method of Hull.) He by and by began to go to London more frequently. The maids were too ignorant to note when he first stuck a fresh green ribbon on his shabby hat. The token of a great change in their master came when he returned one day with two new sad-colored suits of a rich and rare quality; fine enough for the Court, the maids said; finer certainly than any stuff they ever before fingered. This sudden transformation set the maids to gabbling; and if they were under any uncertainty about their master's doings, it was only in figuring how many whores he had in his keeping. Here they insulted his constancy: for the sole mistress of his heart, that he loved above all else, was the Good Old Cause.[7] ✣

CHAPTER 4

Marius gains early notice of the Popish Plot from his fellow alchemists. He joins the circle of plotters and scribblers under the protection of Lord Shaftesbury. A final quarrel with his mother. The death of his old servant. His marriage. His impolitic scribbling endangers his neck, and he slinks home in fear; until the publication of Oates' narrative of the Popish Plot goads him to take up his pen again.

IN ALL the years since the head of his friend Gowler, the felt-maker, was fixed upon a pike, Marius had little commerce with other commonwealthsmen, other than a few crack-brained chemists, who likewise aimed to level or undo distinction of rank. When he was at last freed from the society of his mother and cousins, and had dismissed the servants, he was content to be solitary, and to settle himself upon his books and crucibles. He had severed long ago all correspondence with those of his fellow-apprentices who had cheered the restoration of the King, and who were now men of mature years, well established in their trades and crafts. The opinions of these men had undergone a revolution with the times. They now spoke ill of a King who squandered the wealth of the nation on his popish whores. When the Dutch sailed up the Medway and fired the ships, they recalled the great victories of Oliver, who had made England feared and respected throughout Europe.[1] Old Rowley, they said, was only the French King's lapdog. After the Duke of York married a popish princess, and by-and-by became himself a Papist, their murmurs grew.[2] They began to express views that seemed not unlike those declared in the Prentices Club long before. So that they might speak more freely, these grumbling citizens formed themselves into cabals that knew each other by some sign or token. The most clamorous and meddlesome clubbed at the King's Head Tavern in Fleet Street, signifying their turbulent intention with a green ribbon, the bygone token of the Levellers. There they voiced their objections to arbitrary government, pensioners, courtiers, Papists, and high-flying churchmen.[3] Marius was at first not much noted in this promiscuous rout of parliament-men, citizens, and mechanics, until his busy pen raised him to notoriety.[4]

By reason of his intercourse with chemical men, Dr. Tonge being one of their number, Marius had particularly good intelligence of the infamous Popish Plot.[5] For a full fortnight, near the end of August in Seventy-Eight, Marius knew as much of the Plot as the King himself. His case was that of the barber who served King Midas, possessing a secret that he yearned

to tell, only he scorned to whisper it to the reeds.[6] Instead, he took it to
his brothers of the Green Ribbon Cabal, who disappointed his ambitions
by advising him not to publish it, telling him, the time was not ripe, as
the Town was empty and there would be nothing done until Parliament
met. However, the opportunity of strife and discord was too fine to be
neglected, so that Marius was put to scribbling counterfeit letters, as from
Jesuits or Romish courtiers, which alluded obscurely to plans nearing
fulfillment, to a great slaughter, a vast army in secret readiness, or an impending conflagration. These papers were copied in different hands, then
dropped in the streets, to be taken up and discoursed in the coffeehouses
and taverns. This was a new species of writing for Marius, wherein he
showed considerable powers of invention and innovation. To excite the
passions of the populace over the murder of Justice Godfrey, he forged a
memoranda of persons, intended to be understood as special enemies of
Rome, which was headed by Dr. Titus Oates and Sir Edmund Berry Godfrey,
whose name was crossed.[7] Lord Shaftesbury was honored as the third man
on the list, followed by the members of his Green Ribbon faction whom
Marius wished to compliment as worthy of assassination. These dropped
papers, which put men from their wits, had a seeming confirmation when
the train-bands were suddenly called forth, and set to guarding the gates,
interrogating travelers, and disarming known Papists. The chains were
up in the streets for the first time since the final days of the Rump, as if
in readiness for an assault on the City. No one knew anything, except by
rumor, and by the sinister papers that were taken up in the street. Marius
may thereby make a claim that he contributed, however modestly, to the
ferment of those times, and to the fears of wakeful citizens, that they
would be fired in their houses, or else have their throats cut in their beds,
by twenty thousand Papists up in arms.[8]

Delia has seen much of her father's writings upon the Plot among his
papers. One of them, writ in his best hand, may have been his first pamphlet on this subject, which he was persuaded not to publish by his confederates. The title is an index to the whole, and to its author's mind: The
Jesuitical Plot Revealed, With their Particular and Secret Plans, to Compass
the Assassination of the King, by Pistol, Poison, Poniard, and Ambuscade.
From which it appears, that Marius was more inclined to encourage than
expose the plotters; for he may well have considered that a regicide would
plunge the three kingdoms into such disorder that James could never hold
his throne in security. And, though his fellows diverted his original intention,
his forged letters also remarked upon the ease with which an assassination

could be effected, from the King's daily walks and excursions, the freedom of the palace, and his keeping few guards about him.

When Marius was presented to the Lord Shaftesbury, the little great man looked earnestly upon him for a long minute, before taking his hand and studying the palm of it with an air of respect and courtesy.[9] He then plunged into a long-drawn speech, whereof I believe neither he nor Marius could give the sense, about the broad, short strength of the heart line, the directness of the head and life lines, and the significance of the Saturnian line, still holding his hand and looking close upon Marius as he spoke. Those who mocked the Lord Shaftesbury for his folly of fortune-telling never witnessed, or never apprehended, how he employed it to attach his followers, and sometimes to discern his foes before they knew themselves to be such. As he prated of the lines of fate, heart, mind, or the mounts of Venus, Mercury, Mars, his eye was keen to see upon which phrase his man jumped. By that means he gained an understanding of his ruling passion, whether it be a desire for pleasure or for gain or, like Marius, for glory. By toying thus with his fortune-telling, enacted with a beguiling familiarity, he made wiser men than Marius his properties. His mother, his master, and even his father all thought Marius to be disagreeably closed, sullen, and secret; but the Lord Shaftesbury laid open his breast in an instant, and spoke words that made his eyes shine and his lips quiver.

It must have been about this time that Marius ordered his new clothes, and with them he put on a better manner, for he was now the intimate of an earl, dining at his table, and acquainted as well with other men of great estate and name. Of a surety his brother Roger never achieved such distinction in all his years of following the Court. I wonder if his mother had any knowledge of his betterment, and whether she looked upon Marius with less severity, by reason of his fine clothes and fine acquaintance. She had stayed only a little while with her cousins before taking lodgings of her own, settling at last in Hatton Garden. On quarter day, when Marius brought her widow's third, the two would pass a few words civilly, inquiring after each other's health, and remarking that the season was uncommonly wet or dry or hot or cold. On one such visit, Marius neglected to remove the green ribbon in his hat, and her eye fell upon it. All her ill will was revived in a moment; she called him a wicked Leveller and commanded him from her house. She lived to see James crowned King, and ended her days as an open Papist, summoning her son to her deathbed so that he might witness a Roman priest anointing her. 'Twas in the violence of their persuasions that they showed their kinship, this mother and son.

All this while, the two maids had the house much to themselves; for Marius took lodging in the City and would stay away for days upon a stretch. When at home, he was so enwrapped in his projects that he took no notice of the dirt, the poorly laid fires, or the ill-dressed meat put before him. Apart from sleeping and eating, the maids did little, once they tired of searching for keys to chests and cabinets, and spinning out slanders on their master. There was small satisfaction to be had in using his absences to rummage his papers, for neither woman knew her letters. It was in pursuit of her calling that the old woman met her death. Too decrepit to bring her eye to the keyhole, she was listening with all her will at the door of her master's study, where he was in conference with a rare visitor, when it was thrown open of a sudden, toppling her on her head. Moaning and tossing her limbs, unable to speak, she was dead within the hour. It is to be hoped that her mumbles and moans were prayers for forgiveness; but 'tis likely she was only attempting to impart to Jane the remarkable news she just overheard, that their master was to be married in a fortnight.

His bride was the daughter of his tailor, who formed a favorable opinion of Marius when he paid his bill on the spot, without questioning a penny. He took him to be a simple, open-handed country squire, just such a man as he would wish for a son-in-law; for a careful inquiry confirmed Marius to be a bachelor of good estate. I do not say that old Mrs. Bye would have approved of the match, but Marius found nothing to carp at. This tailor was no beggarly pricklouse in leather breeches and ragged shirt sitting cross-legged upon the floor; but was instead a contriving haberdasher with journeymen to do the snipping and stitching. He set himself up as Master-Tailor to the wealthier gentlemen of the Green Ribbon, who showed their disdain for the Frenchified Court by appareling themselves in prick-eared gray, whilst they nonetheless satisfied their vanity with choosing the most sumptuous and costly draperies. The tailor talked smoothly in an approved style of factious cant, and fell in with everything his expectative son-in-law said upon the themes of arbitrary government and popery. To oblige her suitor, his daughter sang and played whiggish ballads upon the virginals; and if she stumbled over the words, her voice was sweet and tunable. The tailor's luxurious mode of living, and his daughter's fine clothes, argued his ability to pay the dowry he promised. The grand expectations of the young bride, which her father had fomented, were cruelly dashed when her husband carried her to her new home. It was ill furnished, Mrs. Bye having claimed the best pieces when she took up residence in Hatton Garden some years before; and it was ill tended by a single servant, a slatternly maid of hideous aspect, her one eye red and swollen from weeping her loss. 'Twas honeymoon for but a sennight, before her husband returned to his usual haunts, at Thanet House, the King's Head, and the Amsterdam.[10]

Marius was keeping a station in the lobby of the Commons, hungering for news, upon the very day that the secret correspondence of Lord Treasurer Danby was exposed, wherein he solicited money from the French King in exchange for proroguing Parliament.[11] This revelation, which enraged the Members, to learn they had been thus sold to the enemy, filled Marius with joy. If an angel just then descended upon Cheapside to proclaim the New Jerusalem, he could be no more certain that a great transformation was at hand. He went at once to the King's Head, called for pen and paper, and whipped out a broadside, wherein he denounced King Charles as a betrayer of the nation, worse than his father, and deserving of the same fate. Reading it aloud to the company, he did not receive the expected applause. Some of his auditors left the room before he had concluded his first thundering period; others went off to a side, to make loud disjointed talk among themselves, so that they might say afterwards they had not harkened to the thing. Baffled to a stop, Marius gathered up his paper and left in great confusion. Not knowing what to do, he took his writing to a friend whose opinions, he believed, chimed with his own. He had scarce begun to read his piece, before his host started up in a great rage; and, seizing him by the throat, roared out, Do you think to trepan me with such a barren device as this? As Marius turned his face full upon him, he stayed his hand; for he was himself an author, and in that pale countenance he read the pained vanity of one who is greeted with jibes where he looked for acclaim. He gazed upon him for a long moment, before releasing his hold and speaking more calmly. —I perceive you are in earnest, he said, but you mistake the matter entirely. No more can be aimed at, than to drive Danby from office, for there are many in both Houses who can be persuaded to impeach him, not so much for his treachery in secret dealing with the French, as for pique, at his having stopped their pensions, or blocked them and their friends from getting offices in his control. Marius did but half believe his friend, saying, It was incredible that a free and proud people, and their elected representatives, would stomach that their king should be pensioner to the greatest tyrant in Christendom, one that aimed at their destruction as a nation. —Thou art a child in these matters, said his friend. Those who cry out so violently against the Lord Danby have filled their own pockets with pistoles; and in this they do the French King's bidding, for he is Danby's great enemy. He added that Marius might publish his polemic if he chose; but all that would come of it would be this: that the affecting spectacle of his bleeding head upon a pike, his entrails smoking in the fire, and his tarred quarters fixed over the gates, would distract a giddy populace, so that the King and his Minister would escape any reckoning at all.[12]

I do not say that Marius instantly believed all that his friend told him, for he was a man fixed in his notions, reluctant to revise them. But some part of his speech must have made an impression upon him, for he hasted home to his neglected wife. He gave her now so much of his company that the poor woman almost wished him away again. She found her new husband, who was almost twenty years her senior, to be mopish, sullen, and difficult to please. When she chatted of commonplace stuff, he paid her no heed. When she attempted to engage in political talk, only to please him, he waxed irritable. Despite his ill humors, Marius was not harsh to his wife, nor was he mean in his views. When she asked him for things, for servants, furniture, and apparel for the house, he absently agreed to all that she proposed. A butler, a footman, a cook, and two maids were added to the household. Jane, for all her fawning and wheedling, was degraded to the lowly rank of cook-maid. Moreover, though surly by day, Marius was a proper enough husband by night, and before Lady Day his wife was with child.[13]

However cloyed with his wife's company, Marius was for some time merely content to go to bed, and to wake up in the morning, with his head still firm upon his shoulders.[14] He did not venture far from home, arranging his wife's many purchases through an agent in London, who bargained shrewdly for the things and pocketed up the difference. He attempted to busy himself in the Parliamentary elections, only to find that he was not in great credit with his neighbors, who recollected his father's complaints of his waywardness, to which they added their own disapproval of his management of his estate. After this repulse, he affected indifference, resuming his study of philosophy and history. His contrived quiet was abruptly extinguished when his bookseller in error sent him A True Narrative of the Horrid Plot, by Titus Oates, instead of Killing No Murder, by Colonel Titus.[15] He leafed over it, then scorningly held it out to his wife, demanding to know if it wasn't the most tedious and illiterate stuff, penned by a consummate blockhead, that she ever saw: A proposition whereto she could readily concur. She said that Oates and his Plot were only a nine-day wonder; and the only Papists she knew, were of a peaceable and agreeable disposition, that would never mean to murder people, or burn down their houses.

She found that she had taken the wrong tack, when her husband fetched down his own pamphlets and began to read them to her, to teach her the difference, he said, between a good writer and a bad. He called Oates a hobble-brained, blink-eyed botcher, who had spoiled a fine discovery, one that might have brought down the Duke of York, and his brother with him, if it were rightly managed. Pausing upon this notion, he fell silent. Next he began to pace the room, flapping the book against the furniture, as he abused its author in choice epithets: loutish dunce, dog-pated dolt, treacherous lick-spittle, base practitioner, sodomitical knave, illiterated turnspit, low, sneaking, slubbered hack. The new servants had until then given little attention to the master and his sullens: their finicking mistress being the one that must be pleased. The noise he made on this occasion, and the odd scene he enacted, afforded them much diversion; whereupon, Jane advanced her credit amongst them by retailing all the family history that was at all disfavorable to the master. It was a disappointment to them, a relapse to rustic dullness, when Marius once more began to spend his days, and his nights also, in the City. His perplexed wife did not know whether to lament or rejoice for his absence, inasmuch as his odd freaks and change-able fits rendered him unwholesome company for a woman with child. ✠

CHAPTER 5

His return to caballing and scribbling. His discouragement and illness, with the diagnosis of his physician. Doubts of his patron's fidelity to the Old Cause. A jar about money brings about a calamitous sequel. The servants dismissed, except for Jane. He contributes to the pope-burnings and political feasting of his party. Bedrid with the gout but visited by his fellow-plotters. Betrayals and arrests.

DURING THE long months wherein Marius attempted to occupy himself in the management of his estate and the conversation of his wife, he could not, by such feeble diversions, slack his recollection of the admonishments of his friend, which had frightened, shocked, and offended him by turns. After the first fortnight of quiet, he lost his apprehension, felt at every commotion on the road, or knocking at the door, that the King's Messengers were come to hale him forth to prison.[1] The discouragement he underwent, upon learning that men he admired, had taken the French King's money, was less quick to fade.[2] Were it proposed to him that they had been bribed only to do what they themselves intended, he would have considered it a devilish sophistry. If he finally resolved to put up his disgust at such venality, it was rather due to an unremovable resentment against this friend for mocking his simplicity (which, as it was true, he was unable to forgive). He vowed to prove himself a complete politician upon his return to London, and to the circle of scribblers and plot-mongers under Lord Shaftesbury's management. He could have chosen no better master, if he wished to become a politician; but events will show, if the master had an apt pupil or no.

Lord Shaftesbury received him with smooth and encouraging words. When Marius first whispered the secret of the Plot to the malcontents at the King's Head some nine months agone, the wiser heads judged it to be a sham sponsored by the Court, in order that the King might demand money and soldiers for his defense. It was Shaftesbury who saw that the Plot could be turned against the Duke of York, by virtue of the forgeries and satires spread by Marius, which had sharpened the confused and blundering accusations of Oates, into an attack upon a corrupt and Frenchified Court. The great man praised Marius and graciously gave him instruction, opening up to him the secrets of the politician, and schooling him in policy. While the Parliament was in session, he was unleashed to publish. Under his lord's direction and protection, Marius once again enjoyed the inexpressible delight of viewing his words, if not his name, in print. He poured forth his powers of invention and insult upon the Papists; and if men went to the gallows protesting their innocence, he little noted it, so fierce was he under the impression of his ideas. In this he was not alone, for at this time, any who questioned the testimonies of Oates, Bedloe, and their fellows would be himself accused for a traitor and a secret Papist.[3]

He was at first inclined to shun the King's Head, whilst the humiliation he received there pricked in remembrance; until he began to note that the Green Ribbon men who visited and dined with his patron, did not affect to remember it, and used him with courtesy. He gladly turned to such another outlet for his factionary talent. From their den at the King's Head, the Green Ribbon Party fomented fear and disorder with scandalous papers that were too dangerous for the printers. The genius of Marius to this species of writing was well known, and he was eagerly recruited to the work. Amongst other tricks, he wrote slanderous verses, wherein he showed a new bent for ribaldish levity: thus far the experience of marriage and genteel society had improved him. Smut and slander ever delight in combination, so that these little inventions were passed from pocket to pocket amongst all classes of Londoner. For the grand pope-burning of that year, Marius contributed a dialogue between the Pope and the Devil that was much applauded.[4] In all his busying of his pen in that busy year of Seventy-Nine, I believe it was his only public success.

Ever since the outburst of pique that was provoked by Oates and his book, Marius had been meditating upon a work of his own. He had curbed an impulse to consign the offending book to the kitchen fire, forcing himself to con it over and to fix its claims in his memory. His long-considered response to A True Narrative of the Horrid Plot, by Titus Oates, was to produce a truer narrative of his own. Where Oates had given bare memoranda of names, dates, and places, Marius provided a full account of the plotting: what each man said, or engaged to perform; which he might readily do with apparent fidelity, having been a conspirator himself since the last days of the Rump, and knowing what would be said upon such occasions. He did not omit that constant element of every cabal, the spy who trepanned others into committing themselves, or eavesdropped upon their meetings, or treacherously peeped at their letters. Though he painted the Papists as murderous devils, there were a few touches to suggest that Oates and Bedloe might be something yet worse.

It was the only of his writings whereto he dared affix his name. He did not write in the helter-skelter heat that was usual with him, but labored over his style with great care. His greatest difficulty, occasioning much crossing and rewriting, was a general perplexity as to how to balance the preservation of his head, with the accusations that he wished to make regarding the King, the Duke of York, and the Earl of Danby. Besides which consideration, he had few unbroken hours for this undertaking. His pen was much in demand, and he was many times interrupted by the events of this tumultuous year, each occasioning a bustle of caballing and scribbling. Doubtless he had a hand in producing the seditious papers that were scattered in the streets at the time of the Scottish rebellion, so quickly put down by the Duke of Monmouth.[5] The acquittal of Dr. Wakeman, accused by Oates of plotting to poison the King, provoked Marius to a squib that ridiculed perjured Oates and bribe-taking Scroggs with such impartiality that a reader would have wondered which faction the author followed.[6] (For all who wrote in those days were of one party or the other.) The grave illness of the King that summer threw Shaftesbury's party into a fever of plotting, until the return of the Duke of York damped their plans. On account of all these distractions, it was December before he took his work to a printer, a delay that was fatal to whatever success he might else have attained. For the London populace was sated with revelations of papistic conspiracies, and showed a renewed preference for reading of lamentable murders, unfortunate lovers, miraculous judgments, and monstrous births. The Plot had lost its terrors, and the sentiment of his wife was now that of the general.

Though Marius may be, as he told his wife, a writer much superior to Titus Oates, the latter had the name and fame of being the Discoverer of the Plot and the Preserver of the Nation: a preeminence that he provably owed to the forgeries of Marius, which gave his faction a notable weapon against the Duke of York. In the flood of factional pamphlets that gushed forth from the presses in these days—Accounts, Appeals, Answers, Animadversions, Addresses, Advices, Dialogues, Discourses, Discoveries , The Full and Faithful Account of the Popish Plot, by Marius Bye, went unnoticed and unread. He pleaded with chapmen to vend it; he sent it gratis to coffeehouses, taverns, and inns; he at last resorted to dropping pamphlets in the street and tossing them into windows. His discouragement was such that he neither ate nor drank; thereupon he fell ill of a fever, dangerous at first, that gave place to a lethargy. He was carried home in Lord Shaftesbury's coach, to the wonderment of the neighborhood, to be tended by his neglected wife, who lately augmented his disappointments by bringing forth a daughter. He lay languishing abed for a fortnight, accepting nourishment only at his wife's urging. As he grew stronger, he would sit at his table and toy with his pen, only to blot or tear all that he wrote, before returning despondingly to his bed. A physician summoned from the City, who had viewed such cases before, diagnosed a political melancholy: telling his wife, that her husband would not regain his health, unless he returned to Town, to meddle once more in affairs of state.

Although a return to caballing relieved his melancholy, Marius was yet so affected by the failure of his book, as to show unwonted meekness, and a readiness to accept advice. Lord Shaftesbury comforted him, and agreed with all his complaints of Oates, saying, Pity it is that such a one as yourself, Mr. Bye, do not have the management of the Plot; but even a blunt and notched sword may be sharp enough to draw blood. By such confidences and caresses, Marius was the more firmly attached to his patron. He submitted to write under his guidance, almost, at times, upon his dictation. Marius, I am certain, cared as little for King Monmouth as King James; yet at his lord's urging he dutifully rehearsed the praises of the Protestant Duke.[7] He recovered enough of his former spirit to pen a lively satire upon the Adventures of the Black Box; even so, I do not think he relished the themes that his lord put him to writing.[8] At the King's Head, he might vent his ill humors in sharper libels traducing the government; yet his invention flagged, and he wrote no more of his poetical squibs. Nor could his overweening ambition be satisfied with scribbling papers that were passed about for a week or two before ending in the bog-house.[9]

The pamphleteers who served the faction were not of one make. Many were base Grubstreet hirelings, but some few were men of learning and sincerity, whose works are yet read. (If, reader, you are so dull or rustical as not to know which men I mean, you'll find their books at Mr. Baldwin's shop in Warwick Lane.)[10] Marius could copy the arguments of these English Machiavels in words befitting the ordinary understanding, but could not otherways hope to emulate them, which plucked the feather of his self-conceit.[11] He might now regret having fretted away so many years on his alembics, when he might have taught himself languages and bettered his intelligence. Moreover, as he had proved himself a writer upon the Popish Plot, he now found that he was yoked with Oates and compelled to draw the same load. Although the public might have tired of the horrid Popish Plot, Lord Shaftesbury had not. The acquittal of Dr. Wakeman stimulated this wily lord to set a train in Ireland, that might bring down the Duke of Ormonde, whilst renewing public fear of the Papists as an ever-present danger. His agents were already in Dublin, sifting witnesses and feeing informations.[12] For this long-hatched design, both Marius Bye and Titus Oates had usefulness; whereby my Lord Shaftesbury kept both men dancing attendance, the one led along by glozing, the other, a far more moderate man, by guineas. Marius suffered the jealousy of a lover whenever he witnessed his lord making much of Oates and listening to his impertinences. His queasiness must have been daily augmented by the sight of their two uncouth figures in conference: the one dwarfish, crooked, and diseased; the other framed like an ape, with a huge misshapen muns.[13] A far handsomer man than Oates was another of his patron's confederates: the Duke of Monmouth was now a constant visitor, for whom Marius entertained a hearty contempt that hardened his disgust of rank and privilege. Thanet House thronged with discontentful citizens and courtiers without places.[14] Their talk rang the expected changes upon the words, Liberty and Tyranny; but sounded most upon Property and Monopoly. They were apt to be diverted from talking of Rights and Parliament, to discoursing instead upon the discounts current on tallies, or the expected return upon a stock. Goldsmiths, Turkey merchants, and other wealthy traders found a patron in the great lord, who always had mind of profitable undertakings. So that when Marius came to dinner, he found himself seated below a set of men who talked continually of remittances, discounts, bummery and other such money matters. Marius came tardily to understand that his patron had always several projects in hand, more tending to the advancement of the good Lord Shaftesbury than of the Good Old Cause.

He had thus begun to discover to himself some doubts and discontents regarding his patron, prior to the arrival of the witnesses to the Irish plot. He was sent to them in order to perfect them in the Plot, a request Marius understood to be letting them know of the events in England. He must have wondered at them, not merely on account of their ragged outsides and uncouth accents: for these were such evident, shuffling rogues that the poorest bogtrotter, their countryman, would have chased them from his door. He had scarce begun his discourse, when they interrupted him to say that they needed no such talk, only tell them what they must swear to and be done. Marius said that they must tell the truth as they knew it, and was confounded to be answered by a burst of contemptuous laughter. He had placed himself under the Lord Shaftesbury's tutelage, all in the service of his one true mistress; yet he could but dimly ken his beloved Old Cause, so painted and disguised as she now went.

Under the accumulation of these discouragements, he began to spend more time at home, which was much innovated. His wife sought relief from the dullness of country life in giving elegant entertainments; neglecting the management of the estate, which she noways understood, beyond hiring a gardener to plant a fancy knot of flowers and herbs in the fore-yard, where all might see it. She was the first of all the neighborhood to understand the art of making coffee, and to acquire the peculiar vessels required to serve it; for the neighbors, though they disliked her husband, had begun to visit her, pity her, and copy her. She was a woman who wished to please, and to be pleased, and to have things neat and spruce about her. These were qualities that recommended her to all, save her husband, and the house was continually filled with company.

His wife's popularity might have redeemed his standing with the neighborhood, had Marius only smiled and scraped and offered; had he shown the same form at his own table that he did at my Lord Shaftesbury's. Instead he withdrew from his wife's visitors and kept to his chamber, where he was engaged upon a new project. Having failed as a politician, he hoped to prove himself a philosopher by writing a rebuttal to Sir Robert Filmer's Patriarcha, just then published.[15] He hoped to outgo, or at least equal, the works of Major Wildman, Thomas Hunt, and Samuel Johnson, who were the theorists of the faction.[16] He had first, however, to ground himself in a knowledge of law and history. But though he filled his little room with law books, he spent altogether too much time ruminating, or turning over the pages of his commonplace book, to master these difficult subjects. Over the course of the year he produced a few derivative pamphlets on natural law, the ancient constitution, and the inalienable rights and liberties of an Englishman. None of these writings was ever judged worthy of being burned by the common hangman;[17] but it may be that he thereby raised himself above the level of a Junior Oates within his faction. Though he failed to acquire great learning, his studies strengthened him at coffeehouse chop-logic. He once again took to visiting clubs, and to arguing the merits of annual parliaments or perpetual parliaments, of a venetian republic, or a commonwealth without a single head.

He came home one day wearing a blue ribbon that bore the motto, No Popery, No Slavery; shortly thereafter he astonished his family by announcing that he was travelling to Oxford for the Parliament among the train of gentlemen who were attending the Lord Shaftesbury, and that he might not return for some weeks.[18] His wife was then heavy with child; when she saw him mounted, wearing a sword that had belonged to his father, and carrying a short but villainous flail, she gave a frightened shriek and begged him to do nothing that might make his children orphans. The maids wept and shrieked for company, though they cared not a farthing for their master. After increasing her alarm by their affected grief, they warned the mistress that she would do a mischief to her child, if she did not calm herself. Marius rode hastily away to escape the yowling women.

He returned but ten days later, looking weary and vexed, his horse blown. The family believed the messenger had reached him, who was to let him know that his wife was delivered of a son before her time; until they saw by his surprise, that he knew nothing of the birth. When he took up his son, he looked upon him solemnly before saying, 'Tis wrong to bring a man-child into a world where he is doomed to servitude. His wife was so bewildered by his grim look and ill-boding words, that she was afraid for the child, beseeching he not harm his innocent babe. He stayed home for a month, in consideration of his wife and child, who were both ailing; but he was withal so fretful and morose in his manner, that the poor woman got up betimes from her sick bed, and put on a cheerly look, only to be free of his presence. He needed little prompting to return to his gang of plotters and scribblers. At first he came home every few days; his wife, warned of his arrival, would rise up hastily and pretend to health, not to please her husband, but to encourage his departure. She had not been greatly disappointed by his indifference to his daughter; but it embittered her gentle heart to observe that he showed little fondness for his son, except that he would sometimes take him up and look earnestly into his face a long while.

For nigh three years Marius trod a path between Thanet House, the King's Head, and sundry whiggish coffeehouses, seeking recognition and acclaim; but those who did caress and praise him, made heavy demands upon his purse. He was obliged to take his turn at providing dinners for the Green Ribbon Club; he had joined other cabals also, whereby he was bound to furnish treats and entertainments in the taverns and coffeehouses which they favored. His pen-and-ink offerings to the pope-burnings would not have been accepted without his engagement to furnish the rich trappings needed to deck his representations. Moreover, though Lord Shaftesbury kept a princely table, his purse-strings were otherwise close drawn; so that Marius was obliged to fee printers and hawkers, and to contribute to the publication of other men's work as well, his fine clothes nominating him as able to do so. He had been many times to visit his wife's father, who had as yet paid only an earnest of the portion-money. It proved difficult to engage him upon that troublesome theme, for the instant Marius appeared at his door, he would take him kindly by hand, and begin to talk upon politics, wherein he was always well informed. Then, when he had spent his breath and his budget of news, he would display to Marius a buckle or lace or other finery, which his son might have for nothing, or at a small price, less than was paid for it. In consequence, Marius was always freshly decked in the whiggish mode, although much the poorer for his marriage, from the costs of keeping his wife.

In the weeks following the Parliament at Oxford, his family noticed that Marius seemed more than usually perturbed, and it was not with a concern for the health of his wife and son. There must have been some heavy demands upon his purse, either for guns or treats; for the Whigs, their designs thwarted by the sudden dissolution, were caballing furiously to determine what they should do. He came home one day to take up the household accounts, whereto formerly he gave only an incurious survey. They were in a state of total confusion, such that he could only make out, the rents had been anticipated, and he was in some considerable new debt to several London merchants; for his wife had high notions of the furnishings necessary for a firstborn son. Marius was not a man of a hot or hasty temper, and so he did not task his wife with her excesses at once, and in private. It was at dinner, with servants present, following an innocent remark about her ambitions for their son, that Marius burst out in a violent rage: saying his son would grow up a beggar thanks to her wantonness and her father's double-dealing, for barely a penny of her dowry had as yet been paid him. The poor woman went pale from shame and astonishment: for, as she halt-ingly answered him, she knew not what her father promised or what was yet to pay; he had, for his part, assured his daughter that she was marrying a rich, open-handed country squire, one who would spare no expense for her comfort and content. Marius may have felt a touch of shame when he saw her so affected; but he was not a man to take back his words. He withdrew to his chamber, where he spent the rest of the day, taking only a crust for his supper.

His wife, I wager, passed a wakeful night, for she was up betimes, having determined that she would go herself to her father, to plead with him to pay her husband the money owed him. Her father's response was to bemoan his own plight, saying his customers would not pay because of the uncertainty of public affairs, and he himself was deep in debt. However, she did not surrender as readily as her husband, and at last her insistent pleading, else his desire to be at peace, softened him to the extent that he gave her first thirty guineas, then another ten, swearing a solemn oath that it was all he had, and he did not know when he would have the like sum in his fist again. She had come up riding pillion behind a servant upon a hard-trotting horse. 'Tis a great pity that she did not hire some better conveyance for her return, or at the least make a longer stay and take some nourishment; but she was too troubled and fretful to do so. Her maid was instructed to tell the master that his wife was indisposed and keeping to her chamber. Marius looked out the window when the horse came clattering into the yard. His anger swelled upon discovering he had been deceived, until he saw how weak and fainting she was. She was supported to her bed, where she had just strength to tell him what she had done, and to give him the forty guineas. Marius, thinking she was fallen asleep, left the room: the shrieking of her maid informed him of his error and he came rushing back. The surgeon was sent for, to no purpose unless to give his opinion, that a rupture from her difficult childbirth, which was not fully healed, broke open by the rough gait of the horse. The poor woman must not have known herself to be dying, or her last words to her husband would not have been of the forty guineas: she would have warned him that the nurse must be watched, to prevent her being overcome by drink. This everyone in the house knew, except Marius; but they were overmuch occupied in pretending to grief, and making calculations of their wages in case they were dismissed, to recollect it. Nevertheless, they did not scruple to say, afterward, that their master had killed his wife by his cruelty, and his son by his neglect.

The presence of these chattering, idle servants was a goad to Marius, that kept him from lapsing at once into a black melancholy. Having laid his wife and her infant son to rest in the churchyard, he dismissed them on the sudden, all except Jane, who assumed a doleful face, saying she would be content with twenty shillings for her yearly wage, if she could remain with her dear master. By that bargain she had the advantage of her fellows. They presumed upon their master's grief and abstraction of mind; and thus were taken by surprise, when he required them to open their boxes and pokes, into which they had conveyed many little knickknacks belonging to his wife. The fury in his eye, upon discovering these stolen trinkets, was more terrifying than the constable; so that they were glad to depart with their skin whole, and no wages at all. Jane must have struggled to keep a sorrowful countenance, and not show the spiteful joy she felt at the discomfiture of her fellow servants. Yet it seemed an empty triumph, if she stayed at such wages, to do all the business of housekeeper and cook—and dry-nurse as well to the daughter, who was now about a year and a half of age. Though her appearance could not commend her to a squeamish mistress, Jane had improved herself after passing two or three years in the company of City-bred servants. She could carry herself properly, and she had acquired respectable skill at seething, roasting, and pastry-making. Through close observation of the cook and butler, she had learned cheats and dodges that the old woman never taught her. Yet they were often obliged to go snacks with the other servants in what they filched. This, and her master's heedlessness to household accounts, determined her to stay as solitary servant. She doubtless considered that her master was unlikely to have knowledge of all his late wife's finery and kickshaws. When he again lapsed into his usual abstraction, she might make away with this and that, to sell to peddlers passing on the road. Herein she was disappointed; for the broker who had been engaged to purchase these furnishings was brought to the house to buy them back and cart them off. I am certain it was an agony to Jane, to creep from room to room and listen, as the broker cheapened all the pretty things belonging to her late mistress, saying they were marred or sullied or no longer the fashion. I am likewise certain that Marius knew he was being choused twice over; yet he would not endeavor to bargain, but took what the man offered. As he and the broker passed from room to room, pricing sundry toys and furnishings, Marius may have noticed a disregarded child gazing up at him, and recollected that he had a daughter: for he kept his lady's dressing-box, her napery, a richly figured gown, and other such apparel, which were all laid up in a great trunk; whereof Jane, for all her trials, never found the key. I picture Marius solemnly laying these last remaining vanities to rest: I wonder if he then observed, what all the servants knew, that the linings of some of his wife's best clothes, were cabbages and off-cuttings of his.

I wish that Jane had sometime learned to read and understand accounts, for then I might know why Marius was so troubled for money, that he disfurnished his house and stripped it of movables at the soonest moment following his wife's death. I am sure she snooped and pried to her best ability; but her master was silent and solitary for a great many weeks, keeping to his chamber and rarely leaving the house. Jane regretted the bargain she made with her master, now the fine things of her late mistress had all been sold to the broker or locked away. I think she would have absconded at once in disgust, with no more for her pains than a pewter mug or candlestick, did she not discover that her master had no notion of the cheapness of victuals, drink, and fuel in the countryside; so that she could safely double the prices and pocket up the difference. However, Marius was so sparing in his diet, and indifferent to his comfort, that she gained but a shilling a week at best, and oftentimes no more than a tester. Her disappointments were so great, and her temperament so poor, 'tis cause for marvel that the infant Delia, left to her rough keeping, survived.

With the forty guineas and the money got for his wife's trappings, Marius could pay down his debts, however considerable they may have been, and perhaps they were not great. The butler, at the least, heard him upbraid his wife with her spending on that fateful day; but how much the numbers may have been magnified, as his words were bandied about the household, then repeated, some twelve years later, by Jane to Delia, is to be questioned. The poor woman had been spendthrifty, yet was easily contented with trifles. Marius never offered to carry her to the City except for a few visits to her kin, and she spent much of her brief married life a-breeding, so that her opportunities of spending were limited. For a certainty, Marius wanted money for some purpose, and it is not to be supposed that he would run up large debts of his own, given how prompt he was to pay his tailor's bill. He must have made some further attempts to get his father-in-law to pay the large remainder of his late wife's portion, but I doubt he succeeded in extracting another penny. For now the tailor could counter him by lamenting the loss of his daughter, and hint, or perhaps openly declare, that it was her husband's cruelty and harshness that brought about her death. Yet for all his sartorian deceits, he spoke something nearer to truth than he knew, when he told his daughter that the forty guineas was all he had, or was like to have: for he absconded to Whitefriars at the end of Eighty-Three, brought down by the faction whereto he had dedicated his needle and scissors.[19] He might have written a tailor's chronicle of these turbulent years, only by noting the dates when his whiggish customers ordered new clothes for their treats and cabals; when they first declined to pay him; and when he at last marked their debts as desperate. Those who were new-suited in fanatic gray for the Oxford Parliament would not be requiring more clothes of that cut. After the Tories wrested control of the City from the Whigs in the Summer of Eighty-Two, Leveller green was no longer the wear: Yorkist red was the fashionable hue. Timeservers turned their coats, new-trimmed and pranked after the Court mode. The tailor turned out his journeymen and servants, all but one parish-boy, but he could not recover his losses. He was ruined. Those who owed him the most, went abroad, or crept back to their country estates without paying their debts. A tailor should be the first to discern that the fashion is shifting, and to shift with it. On that account, I believe the man may have been sincere in his siding with the faction, if in little else.[20]

Mice and rats have the cunning to know when a ruined house is in danger of collapse, and to flee to new quarters; and so it was with the Irish witnesses to the Plot, who were the first to desert the faction. They shrewdly perceived that greater rewards might be had by turning on their masters and laying informations against them. Marius Bye might now be glad he had balked at instructing these cozening shams and makeshifts in their perjuries;

for those that did so were brought to trial for suborning the witnesses that were now suborned against them. Nevertheless, whilst the whiggish sheriffs could pack the juries with presbyters and other supporters, none of them suffered harm. There was a great rejoicing in the streets when the Tory attempt to convict Lord Shaftesbury of treason failed. The last great pope-burning took place that year, to which Marius contributed an effigy of Roger L'Estrange, that had a confession of calumnies and lies pinned to its back, and on its breast a placard, "Kiss Me, Pretty Mistress Printer, Or Pay Me."[21] If the great issue of the succession were to be decided by the bustles and brawls of apprentices, watermen and porters, then the rabble shouting "A Monmouth" were superior in number to those crying "A York." In truth, the loyalty of the multitude was purchased with bonfires and ales; there would have been a crowd as great to roar their lusty approval were Lord Tapski brought to the scaffold.[22] Convinced by the clamor of the rascality that his faction was predominant, Marius failed to perceive that it was not Forty-One, but Fifty-Nine that was come again.

Near the end of Eighty-One, the leaders of the two factions began a battle of pies and joints, a contest of rival public feasts.[23] If there was any design behind this curious battle, other than the striving of rich men to outdo one another, it was to win over neutral or wavering men with a treat. Herein the Yorkist party were upon the vantage-ground: for they oftentimes had the King's own venison out of Richmond Park to serve their guests, along with abundant good wine; whereas the presbyters and precisians were sparing of drink, and mostwhat they served was only butcher meats, to the disgrace of their party. The first skirmishes in this war of fare came with some factionary banqueting at Yuletide among the whiggish lords and citizens; but by Eastertide both sides engaged, and the contest was heated. Each party recruited a formidable troop of cooks, confectioners, grocers, fish-mongers, butchers, huntsmen, and wine merchants to their faction, not omitting a band of fiddlers, ballad-singers, and Bow-Church preachers to entertain the company.[24] (Whereof some wore the colors of both sides.) The caterers of the whiggish feasts were strictly enjoined, not to concoct any Frenchified sauces, nor ape the made dishes of Roman nations; but to provide good English Protestant fare, yet withal of a rich and rare quality, in order to display the wealth and pride of their faction. The Tories, which had their quarters in Merchant-Tailors' Hall, gained a notable victory, much sung by their bards, when their enemies were routed from Haberdashers' Hall, leaving behind some rare chines and brave pies, rallying only for a decimated dinner in a whiggish lord's lodgings. Maugre their teeth, the

Whigs persevered in matching every dinner of the Yorkists with an anti-dinner of their own. Now, Marius took no pleasure in gourmandizing or carousing; I am certain he never joined in drinking a health to the Duke of Monmouth without muttering destruction to all the Stuarts under his breath; yet he bought his ticket, or paid a subscription, and partook, at whatever cost to his purse and his constitution, as 'twere a duty to his Cause.

A fit of madness overtook the City at Midsummer of Eighty-Two, as the chief citizens veered as sharply to the Yorkist party, as before, in the panic of the Popish Plot, they had to the Whigs.[25] The Conventiclers were now deemed a greater danger to Property and Security than the Papists. By Michaelmas the trimmers and time-servers had plucked their green ribbons from their hats. The Tory room at the Warder in Lydgate was every night filled, whilst the custom of the King's Head dwindled. The magnificent pope-burnings were no more; the mob must content itself with the modest spectacle of Jack Presbyter, put in a halter and set afire. Two and twenty years before, Marius Bye had been among the last to perceive that the Good Old Cause was doomed; now he had fellows, as there were many prominent citizens and great lords who had dared too much to retreat: for the Duke of York was known to be of an unforgiving spirit. Lord Shaftesbury, who had turned so many times over his long career, could not twist himself into a Yorkist; though even now, no one could read his intention, for it seemed that he was one day for King Monmouth, the next for a commonwealth, as he boasted of having ten thousand brisk boys in Wapping, ready to rise up at a word. Marius was new-infused with his old leaven, and such extravagant talk attached him again to his patron, as in the early days of the Popish Plot: until the great man made tonies and totty-heads of his fellow conspirators, by his sudden and secret flight oversea.[26]

All this while, Marius scarce came home except to shift his clothes or fetch some book or paper. The house was not inviting of a longer stay, stripped of its comforts and occupied by a slatternly maid and a forgotten child who, most days, was as ragged as any beggar and as thin. ('Twas only when Jane had notice of her master's coming that she gave attention to the child.) Jane was as fretful as her master. She had formed grand ambitions from witnessing the superior airs and graces of the servants of her late mistress, and could no longer be satisfied with eating her full and lazing daylong before the fire, which was her greatest happiness in former times. While her master was absent, the money he allowed her scarce yielded any profit at all, even with keeping his daughter half-famished on waterish pap. It was therefore a satisfaction for her, when he began to keep home that winter, as he gave her more money and scarce made any demands, or noticed the disarray of his house and child. He had frequent visitors, so that Jane could resume her old profession of spying; except that she could make little of their strange mumbling talk of lopping points and general points, about executing the conveyance, and the removal of two tables. 'Twas puzzling her master should talk of slaying the stag that would leap o'er the park palings, when he never had a gust for hunting, and at a time, too, when he was so crippled with the gout that he did not leave his chamber.[27]

It was his first severe fit, from which he never found effectual relief, though he consulted several physicians of note; and, after they failed him, a confident charlatan and a wandering herb-woman. The sundry remedies prescribed for him only further weakened his health: So that the fit, which came upon him about Candlemas Day, and might have lasted but a fortnight, or a month at utmost, had him still weak and languishing at Eastertide. He underwent strong scammony purges, cauteries, and bloodlettings; swallowed loathsome potions and unwholesome diets; and applied foul-smelling fomentations and poultices to the affected parts, which sickened him with their vapors. Marius was by nature a lean-bodied man of sparing habits, nor was he of a gouty lineage: his father scarce knew a day of ill health until the end of his life. I therefore consider that it was the feasting of the previous year that brought on his affliction, or brought it up to such severity. As a Whig, he was spared the Frenchified viands of the Tory faction; but nonetheless he partook of rich and highly seasoned dishes, and drank off a great many toasts, upon a stomach that was unused to luxurious feeding. The physicians say that the first few fits of the gout are mild and momentary; so that a man who takes forewarning, and conforms himself to a modest diet and good exercise, may prevent it growing severe for some years. The disease may begin with the dropping of a humor upon a joint, following a sudden shock or injury, and it may at its first appearance be masked by symptoms of the headache, fever, and lassitude. Accordingly, I believe the first paroxysm struck upon the failure of his great work on the Popish Plot, and that he had other spells of undoubted gout, when he would keep to his chamber and withdraw from company. Had he taken a timely warning and reformed his ways, he might have preserved his health; but he would not forsake the Old Cause. For a certainty, nothing that he did, not his incessant scribbling of pamphlets, his writing of scandals, his secret consults, nor his feasting and carousing at banquets, had the slightest power to stave off the destruction of his faction, or the catastrophe that was even then impending. He learned of it by an express, a day or two before it was bruited from one end of the kingdom to the other. A fellow-plotter, visiting in secret on his way to the North, urged him to remove; but he was then too ill to travel or, it may be, too desponding.[28] The King's Messengers did not then come for him, yet there were daily more betrayals and arrests, extending his alarm.

He waked all one night, sorting his books and papers into heaps according to their degree of treasonableness, and burning those that might impeach him (Judge Jeffreys' *scribere est agere* sounding in his ears), before lapsing into melancholic dejection.[29] Morning found Marius yet at his table, his head lowered upon his arms, not in sleep but deep reflection. He raised himself slowly upon his gouty feet, murmuring of dukes and death and bloody insurrections. (He might do so safely for there was no one to hear. Jane was snoring in a trundle bed by the ashes of the kitchen fire. Delia lay quietly awake at her side, the side farther from the fire, huggling her puppet.) He paused at the window. The hedge was ragged with fruit, sparrows chirped in its branches, but he neither saw nor heard. The rattling of a countryman's cart mingled strangely with his thoughts. Forebodings of murderous broils and tumults filled his imaginings. As he sat down again, he slapped his hand upon the table and exclaimed: Monmouth pardoned, Sidney sentenced to a traitor's death. Would it were reversed! Hampden clapped up still, peached by base informers. I fear they've done his business. Pray God I am not traced in this![30] ✠

DEFENSIO INTERJECTA

A vindicatory interlude: the author's apology for the truth of this history.

NOT A FORTNIGHT ago, having in hand a clean manuscript, I met with some gentlemen of my acquaintance at the —— Tavern. I said to them that I would be glad to know their opinion; they, flattered to be thought judges of literature, were content to pay for a treat. We dined first, with a half-dozen bottles of good claret passing up and down the table as I read to them my history. I had come to the end of my fifth chapter, when one of them gave a loud, silly laugh, saying: Why, I have you now. If the maid was asleep and the daughter only an infant of some three or four years, how would you know what your Marius said when there was none to hear him? —What you say may be so, yet how is my story any less a true history for that? Have you never read the great historians of ancient Rome? Do you suppose that Tacitus interrogated the ghosts of Seneca and Nero, so that he might record their private conversations? Or that a writer of shorthand was present at the addresses made by Hannibal and Scipio, so that Livy might later copy them out in full?[1] He was silenced. I hemmed once or twice as preliminary to resuming my tale, when another of the pack took up the scent and began to bark. —But you have done more than invent several speeches, he said. I am willing to believe that this pair of maids devoted themselves to spying and gossiping, and that the maid Jane later passed on their discoveries to the daughter you call Delia, who was so imprudent, and neglectful of her family's reputation, as to retail them to you. But unless we are to suppose that Jane followed her master to Town day after day, so that she might peep into windows and listen at doors, or sneak into taverns, lodgings, and great men's houses, I do not know what authority you can have for the latter scenes of your tale. You set down for a truth, that men do not discourse of their failures; thus we may be assured that your Marius Bye did not relate his disreputable doings during these years to his daughter. Before I could reply, the whole pack raised a cry, calling this and that a fiction or a fable, and exclaiming against me, as imposing a romance upon them, for a true history. —Gentlemen, I said, as I gathered up my pages, as you will not hear me, you must perforce wait upon your bookseller, to learn the further history of Marius Bye and his family.

Courteous and gentle reader, I am assured that you are not such a swill-bellied dolt, as not to understand that the best history is no mere chronicle of names and numbers, but something more akin to the drama and the epic.

Nonetheless, for that there are such men, who moreover set themselves up as critics, I will here attest how diligently I have sought out testimonies and evidences.

A man displays his character in his writings; and, though Delia could repeat passages of her father's pamphlets, I wished to read them whole. I went therefore to the booksellers to ask for the works of M. B. Those few that knew of him said, How now, is that crabbed old rebel yet alive and wielding a pen? We have not heard of him these many years. What I most earnestly wished to read was his pamphlet on the Popish Plot. This work fell at last into my hands by bare-arsed chance. One day I was overtaken by cramps of the stomach, so that I made speed to the nearest jakes, where a blackguard boy was selling waste paper: judging with experienced eye how much he could charge, from the haste and dress of his customer. I glanced at the farthings-worth of paper he put in my hand, whereupon my eye was arrested by the name on a title-page. I called out, Boy, boy, come here! Bring me all the paper you have! The wily brat was mistaking my meaning, mistrusting my intention, and determined to cheat me, all at once; but at last, by threats and bribes, I got him to deliver over his paper, and was able to put together two and twenty sheets of this precious pamphlet, torn and dirtied, but preserved from a final defilement. From studying over these pages, and observing his tricks of expression, I learned much about the author's mind that his daughter was incapable of observing.

My tattling critics were correct in stating that Marius would not have discoursed broadly or continuedly of his doings to his daughter. However, there are other means of tracing and piecing a man's history. In later years, Marius would waste his hours in ruminations, when he would speak aloud his thoughts, more to the spirits of his executed fellows than to his daughter; but she, being accustomed by that time to write down his dictation, listened attentively, and could recollect choice expressions, even without fully understanding their meaning. So that I found I might prompt her memory by my questioning her on particulars. As for an instance, she could tell me that her father said of Sidney, that he was a good Italianate philosopher but a poor man for the business.[2] That Ferguson took up caballing as other men give themselves to dicing and gaming, only he had the judgment to leave off before all was lost.[3] That Essex was trepanned into the plot and likewise had assistance in the slitting of his throat.[4] Of Shaftesbury, he said many contrary things, but this she particularly remembered: that he was not a great little man but the reverse, a little great man, one that wore a tap but would never be drawn.[5] Moreover, Marius had from time to time, as

I shall later rehearse, visitors with whom he spoke freely, never doubting his daughter's loyalty or, it may be, her stupidity. For that my critics gave their censures on her as well, I shall set down a few words in her defense. Jane had a great need to wag her tongue in that lonely house, so that she told her slanderous tales many times over, but never once the same. I am certain that in repeating them to me, Delia selected the story that was least dishonorable to her father, mother, grandparents and uncles. Nor did she, in her innocence, conceive that she was at all sullying her father's name; for she revered him so unquestioningly that she saw no ill in anything. Events will further show, that she is in truth a loyal and heedful daughter, to the pitch of her small abilities.

I do not rely upon the gossiping of females who, by their very natures, must be ignorant of political philosophy. There are many men yet alive who were busy doers in those days of conspiracy and faction, that will discourse freely of others' trespasses, as long as they may depict themselves as moderate men, who sought to free their country from oppression and to achieve the glorious and bloodless revolution that brought our great monarch to his deserved throne. Marius Bye is not entirely forgotten, but variously recalled, as a creature of Lord Shaftesbury, or as a man who sat mumchance scribbling in a corner, yet withal capable of bold speculations, when he hit upon an apt sentence and could not keep it to himself. Not long after Delia first told me her tale, I was plagued with an obstinate chandler who demanded to be paid in full, telling me that he himself owed such and such debts that were demanded of him. I confided my difficulty to a Newgate pettifogger, a shaggy drunkard with a great knowledge of men, who cunningly took what money I had, which the chandler had refused, and applied it to buying one or two of the chandler's tickets, which, as they were desperate, were sold to him cheap; and which he then presented to the chandler, to have my debt forgiven and to shake out a few shillings for himself. In gratitude, I took this conniving law-monger to a tavern in Southwark, where, as I had done the keeper a great kindness in the keeping of a secret, I might drink and eat (though the food is naught) to my heart's content, as well as treat a friend upon occasion, and not be asked to pay. I learned that the man had been among the hot Whigs in his youth. When he was well into his second bottle, he would speak without fear of those turbulent years. But, alas, his recollections were addled by time and drink, and he was more a smell-feast, a hanger-on of the faction, than an active plotter. Of Marius he could say little more than that he had sponsored some fine dinners at the King's Head, and attended a great many more. So that I got little by him other than an enumeration of the dishes served. I can inform the curious reader with good certitude, that Marius Bye laid waste his health by feasting on joles of green sturgeon, salmon in stoffado, oyster chewits, lamprey pies, roast shovelards and heronshaws, lamb-stone pies, baked red deer, and other such costly cates. This rascally sot lamented the loss of a pension when King William took the throne, and I can guess what he did to earn it. Marius is fortunate that this parasite knew him no better, than only to describe his treats, and to insinuate his involvement with Ferguson and other plotters.

Finally, let Marius Bye challenge my account if he dares. It may be that he feels some little resentment at speeches I have put in his mouth, or experiences I have imputed to him; or it may be he is provoked to correct some errant guesses of no great import. Yet let him consider before he hastes to second the accusations of my tattling critics: To refute this my history in sum, he must either admit to being a person of no consequence, or else invite the King's Messengers to his door. Let him reflect a little, and he will perceive that he is a fortunate man to have such a biographer, one who gives such careful minding to his reputation, as to provide him with a role in great events, yet defends his neck from the halter by stopping short of full particulars. Let him also take note that, though I have occasionally made him appear somewhat of the fool, I have paid him some good compliments on the style of his writing, which is a courtesy that a gentleman ought to return. If he decides nonetheless to declare himself, I welcome his revelations. If he was of any consequence in the actions of those times, then many secrets must have passed through his hands and before his eyes: Let him open all. Let him disclose to us the truth of all the shams and villainies that were enacted in those tumultuous years. ✠

CHAPTER 6

Marius Bye in retirement, forgotten by most his faction, his health destroyed. He sends Delia to school, where she learns but little. She is taught thereafter by her father and becomes his amanuensis. A spate of scribbling upon the Good Old Cause is brought to an end when the Prince of Orange is proclaimed King. Marius his opinions, and the jangling of his dinner guests.

PHYSICIANS COMFORT their incurable patients with telling them that the gout is itself a sovereign preventive of fevers, palsy, apoplexy, and other such fatal diseases.[1] Whether that be true or no, it was certainly the case with Marius, that his gout preserved his neck from the hempen cravat, and his swollen great toe was the charm to defend his body from quartering. If not for his affliction, he would have been sufficiently active in plotting assassination and revolt, to be trepanned and betrayed, along with men of greater note. Nonetheless, I question whether his attack of the gout was verily so severe and prolonged as to last the most part of a year. A small child and an ignorant maidservant would be unable to distinguish the groans, the contortions, the close retirement, and the pallor that were due to the gout, from those belonging to fear and conscious guilt. A learned physician, examining him and considering his history, might diagnose a new malady of politic gout; for it seems that his symptoms observed a sympathy with the sufferings of his party. He was thrown into dolorous fits by the defeat of Monmouth, and he lay moaning a-bed throughout the Bloody Assizes, when there were so many men saving themselves by betraying others, he could but expect that one of his former Green Ribbon brothers would point at him and his writings.[2] I wonder when it was that he first experienced the bitterness of knowing he was secure from betrayal, only because he had been forgotten, or else was considered of so little consequence, that no one could hope to preserve his own neck by swearing Marius Bye into a halter. I would give much to know his sentiments, when he at last found out the truth, that his writings had been judged too paltry for infamy.

Besides the gout, he was distempered by splenetic vapors and headache, and was so much an invalid, that he scarce ever left his house; except, if the weather were fair, he would take a few turns in his back-garden, which by his neglect was overgrown with rank weeds. Delia never knew him to give off wearing his cloth shoes and dog-skin hose; for even when he was not under present pain, he feared its return. She says that the only thing that would answer, in relieving his torment, was whipping himself upon the legs with nettles, which his garden produced in abundance.

Thus Marius Bye was as infirm and valetudinary as a man of eighty before he was much past his fortieth year. He had by now accumulated a large and miscellaneous library, including many learned books that he was badly instructed to understand. He had no languages, excepting a little Latin, which he could read but slowly, with much mumbling and consulting of word-books and lexicons. He had no mathematics beyond ciphering, but he bought the works of the new philosophy nonetheless. Such books require hard study, but yet his infirmity frustrated his effort to master any subject. He became instead a sort of word-scraper, a caterpillar of books, a ransacker of learning. Without attending to the argument or the sense of a passage, he would catch at sentences that could be wrested to suit his conceptions, much like an ill-lettered fanatic reading his Bible and finding it the mirror of his own confused mind. His linsey-woolsey philosophy was a patchery of Descartes, Machiavelli, Hobbes, and Spinoza. During the years when L'Estrange tyrannized over the London printers, Marius suspended his pamphlet writing perforce. He could not continue long without a pen in his hand, howsoever; and it was during these years that his commonplace book swelled to many volumes. He again indulged a hobby-horse of inventing utopias, as in his apprentice days long ago.

I attempted to sound Delia concerning her father's religion; for though he belonged to the same faction as the sectarians and enthusiasts, she never knew him to attend any church or conventicle. Her answers were confused and contradictive; in part owing to her ignorance, but also, I am certain, because her father's chance-medley studies led him into many inconsistencies. Undoubtedly he was at first much attracted to the Quakers: I am sure he would relish keeping his hat firm upon his head and asserting his equality to his master or father; but he would fly off in disdain at their mystical mumblings and shakings.[3] He next fell in with the Fifth Monarchy fanatics, for the sake of their talk of violent revolt; yet he was always such an enemy to single-person rule, that he would join forces with Satan to try to shake King Jesus from his throne, should He descend from the heavens to claim it. In his middle years, in the solitude that came of discouragement and gout, reading at hazard and speculating freely, he became a Socinian, a Pyrrhonist, and a Freeseeker: his notions being now remote from those of any sect, and rebellious to all creeds.[4] His daughter heard him oft declare, that what the vulgar take for revealed truths, were only the inventions of priests to cow free spirits into servitude. Though he was thus one of those who proudly elevate Reason above Revelation, his intellect was ill-taught and unruly; and, in his eager desire to carry his point, would stoop to a deceitful sophistry.

There is a story famous in the village, and often related by Jane, that a churchwarden once called upon Marius to upbraid him for his absence from divine service, and to threaten him with the severe penalties then being enforced upon the sectaries. Marius gravely pledged that he would attend church, his gout permitting, if the man could satisfy him upon a few points that troubled his conscience. The churchwarden, who thought himself well able to dispute with errant sectaries, readily agreed: only to find himself immired in quibbles and equivocations, and lured into foolish admissions; whereby he was forced in the end to admit that, according to his own declared principles, the one true religion was Mahometism. He was so addled by this argumentation that he went direct to the vestry and declared himself a Turk, giving great scandal to the godly and merriment to the ale-bench scoffers. Thereafter Marius was left undisturbed.

Although Delia cannot well remember how it happened, it was about this same time that Marius began to take some notice of his daughter. He required Jane to feed and clothe her better, and had her brought upstairs to pass some part of the day with him, where she would play quietly on the floor while he pursued his habitual studies. He taught her her letters, and to repeat after him a peculiar prayer of his own composition. Though his manner was grim, he spoke gently to her at all times; which was, she says, a great change from Jane, whose stormy temper ran to extremes, such that it was sometime kisses and sometime blows, and sometime one after the other. Delia had been left in her keeping for so long, that Jane almost fancied herself the mother. For certain, she had come to view the child as a miniken maid who would in due time perform the work of the house under her direction; so that she murmured and grudged when her master took the child under his abstracted protection.

One day Delia committed an offense wherefore she was well-nigh exiled to the kitchen and to Jane's rough fostering. Marius came into his study to discover that the child had climbed upon his chair, where she had taken hold of a pen and was scrawling upon the pages of his commonplace book. He let out a roar and gave her such a push that she fell groaning to the floor. He then saw that she had not blotted or otherwise spoiled his page. The pen was almost dry, and with it she had only traced over the letters on the page, with a neatness remarkable in a child. He had by now the gout in his hands, so that his writing was irregular and tremulous; but the child had followed his pen's trace, or, where she departed from it, had drawn the letters straight and clean. Marius thereupon perceived that this girl, who hitherto was only an amusement, like a lapdog or a prattling parrot, might yet prove a great solace and convenience to himself. He picked up the child, who was wailing as much for displeasing him as for pain, and comforted her, saying, he was going to send her to a school so that she might learn to write and to be a help to her father.

In the village was a dame's school of good reputation kept by the vicar's wife, who taught the usual subjects, but was capable of giving instruction in handwriting if desired. Marius, however, knew himself to be the object of spying curiosity. He could do nothing to curb Jane's tongue when she went about, relying only upon her ignorance for protection. But the child was at times set waking by the door in order to give admittance to midnight visitors: whereby Marius feared his child's innocent prattle, added to the maid's tale-bearing, might draw unwanted scrutiny. He chose therefore to send his daughter to a school that was some miles farther, run by a gentlewoman called Urith Witherby, who overwent the vicar's wife in offering fine needlecraft, calligraphy, and the French language. Either for the tuition was high, or her pretensions doubted (she was a newcomer to the neighborhood), there was at this time no other pupils in her select academy, which recommended her the more to Marius. He stipulated that he would not have his daughter learn foreign tongues, nor waste her time on fancy needlework; but she was only to be improved in her letters and taught a good Italian hand.

Excepting when she was carried by Jane into the village or to church (and that only now and then), Delia had never been away from home until she was brought to Mrs. Witherby. It was an ill-furnished, cheerless house, not much different from her home, only it was smaller and some deal cleaner. It was occupied by only the mistress and her maid, who were neither of them of an easy or cheerful disposition; which was also not much different from her home. Even Jane's rough nursing had not prepared her for the treatment she received during her first few weeks, howsoever, when poor Delia was pinched and slapped for answering like a dunce with "I do not know" or "I cannot tell"—though she was noways reluctant or slow to learn. Her father had solemnly enjoined she was not to give out information about him; thus she was in great difficulty when her schoolmistress pestered her with questions, as, what did Mr. Bye take for the gout, how long had he been a widower, if he had a favorite dish, and other such matters of no great import. Mrs. Witherby was of a grim, ugly look (she was a tall gaunt woman with ferret-eyes and lantern-jaws), which became truly frightful when she altered her manner to one intended to be soft and coaxing. Then, bending down from her great height, she would stretch her muns into a hideous dog-toothed grin, such that Delia could scarce refrain from shrieking at such a goblin face. (According to Delia, Mrs. Witherby could put her head through the horse-collar and infallibly bring home the prize.)[5] At length the mistress perceived that the child was obstinate on this one subject of her father, but otherwise meek and obedient. The maid, in the meantime, discovered that Delia would fully and ingenuously answer questions about Jane. By shifting their pursuit in that direction, mistress and maid pried out information on the family to satisfy their curiosity. Mrs. Witherby's desk was scantily furnished with books, but those she had were easier and delightfuller than her father's; so that Delia soon improved in her reading, from being allowed to take up whatever books she liked, as long as she kept herself quiet and out of the way. At length the mistress recollected her undertakings to Mr. Bye, and gave Delia her first lessons in join-hand, which she quickly mastered. Noting how neat-fingered the child was, Mrs. Witherby exceeded her instruction and taught her also to sew, whereat (being the granddaughter of a tailor) she rapidly excelled, and could do all the mending of the household. When she went home to her father at Yuletide, he was pleased with her improvement, giving the schoolmistress credit for what was purely the student's diligence and steady application.

She had been a year and a half in Mrs. Witherby's school, when her father made trial of her abilities by dictating a letter. She kept writing so long that he at last called for her to bring the paper to his chair; whereupon he saw that she had filled it with absurd pothooks, dashes and senseless flourishes, and withal formed the characters so that they were scarce legible: the paper looking more like a pattern for an embroidery than a letter. He was so vexed that he blamed the pupil when he ought to have blamed the teacher, until he saw her look of sorrow at having displeased him. It might be that he was reminded at that moment of her poor mother, for he made her a kind of apology, saying, he saw that it was a mistake to send her out to a foolish idle gentlewoman, when he ought himself to tutor her in what he would have her learn. The next day he put before her specimens of different hands, and gave her advice on smoothening her letters to write more quickly. He discovered, to his great joy, that she was not only apt and quick to learn, but showed a knack in nibbing quills and altering the ductus of her strokes, that might enable her to feign different hands. This was a skill possessed by two or three scribes in the pay of the Green Ribbon Club that Marius had been obliged to employ, from a lack of ability to disguise his writing. King James the Second came down upon the whiggish printers and scribblers of his brother's reign with such severity that those who scaped imprisonment were either silenced or fled. Marius had dared do no more, all these years, than grumble and write in his commonplace book. He now expressed his resolution that he would yet fulfill his destiny (for he had never abandoned belief in Lord Shaftesbury's fortune-telling, however disabused he might be in other regards). His daughter was not many weeks at her copybook before she was a complete secretary. She became a necessary furniture of her father's study: pen, ink, paper, Delia; and there was little that he said or wrote during these years to which she was not accessory.

Thus she was pretty well able to write at his dictation, if he spoke slow, by the Spring of Eighty-Eight, when were the first shocks of the kingdom-quake that toppled James the Second from his throne; or, as I should have said, caused him to vacate it; when also Marius Bye and his fellows believed that the confusion in the government might topple the throne itself.[6] Delia's recollections of that year are jumbled together with her own sensations. At first she was put to copying over some of his old tracts with sundry erasures and additions to render them current: her father thereby showing not so much a want of fresh notions, as a steadfast adherence to his Old Cause. The Queen's pregnancy and the miraculous birth of a son stirred him to compose some verses, which his daughter was required to copy over so many times that she can repeat them to this day. They were no better nor worse than other such verses on that fertile subject, which were then being dropped in coffeehouses or passed from hand to hand; yet they nonetheless bore the stamp of his peculiar genius, in being only moderately bawdy, and alluding much to tyrannic power and papistical cheats and juggling.[7] The talk of a Dutch invasion, with the fear of another civil war, raised him to such a fermentation that he watched at the window for intelligencers, sending his maid and daughter into the road to interrogate carters and chapmen for news. Jane was better at this task than Delia, for she could fable her report from slender hints and rumor, without spending any of the small coin supplied to her for inducement. One night they looked out to see the sky strangely reddened, as if the sun had set in the south: Jane was no original in reporting to her master that the Papists had fired the City, for it was the firm belief of all the neighborhood. The next day they learned that the fires that lit up the sky were in truth fueled by the Papists, but all unwillingly. London and Westminster were under the sway of the mob that night, and for some days and nights thereafter. They roughly seized upon notorious

Papists, plundered and pulled down their chapels, convents, and embassies, then burnt their books and furniture in the streets. It was only by the veriest chance—for there was no authority to control them—that they did not fire the town in their recklessness. The bonfires of the London rabble were the beacons to proclaim that King James had fled his palace, and that the kingdom was then without a government.[8]

The road before their house was in a commotion, even as fear kept people from markets and ordinary travel. The King's army had been partly disbanded; soldiers, dismissed without pay, swarmed to the City to join in the riots. Others roamed up and down, begging and pilfering. It needed only for someone to overhear them jowering in a boorish tongue for a terror of the Irish to infect an entire parish. Householders constituted themselves into patrols on watch for Papists and other suspected persons. Thieves and rogues organized themselves as counterfeits, so that any stranger might be seized as a suspected Papist and required to prove his innocence by buying off his captors. The dangers to travelers were as great as at no time since the Great Rebellion. Marius was so far from participating in these fears, that he thought to hire a coach to carry him to Town, that he might be present at these tumultuous events, and witness the fulfillment of the Good Old Cause. Howsoever, Jane, who sometimes made a show of great affection for her master, fell upon her knees, begging him not to leave his poor daughter an orphan, for he would without doubt be murdered by the bands of Irish Papists who, she said, were roaming and marauding along all the roads to the City. One of his visitors then brought news that the citizens were so fearful of the Irish, who were conceived to be a great invading army, that they stood waking all night in their doorways, armed with cowl-staves and cudgels.[9] Marius determined that he would not, after all, venture his valetudinary carcass. He therefore depended upon his visitors to bring him certain news of events, as well as to convey his writings to the printers and coffeehouses.

For Marius had not been forgotten by all his former faction, only by the men of worth and reputation. Among the fanatic portion of the citizenry, there were many who despised King James in their hearts—and in their words also, when there was a safe place to utter them, along with good drink to loosen their tongues. Moreover, Lord Shaftesbury had collected under his protection three or four score bullies, adventurers, and false loons; upon his death these men attached themselves to lesser patrons such as Marius Bye.[10] Providing only they could talk a plausible republican cant, he bestowed on them his hospitality, which was not to be despised by such men as these. He set before them the best he had, and when they asked, he opened his purse.

His house had other conveniences for sectaries, plotters, and rogues, for it stood apart from any neighbor, and at just such a distance from the City as to afford good shelter from pursuit; for such men, coming down on bye-lanes and cow paths, the weedy state of his neglected grounds afforded cover to escape notice all the way to his back door. They were certainly seen by Jane, who might be a danger to them; but they took heed to blunt her malice by calling her comely or tipping her a few coins. From her grumblings to Delia, it seems she suspected that these small vails came from her master's own purse, and suspected likewise that these men were naught. Howsoever, her knowledge of wrongdoing was limited to those sins of the flesh to which she herself inclined; so that her desire to unmask them for rewards, or for better bribes than sixpences, was frustrate. She never caught them in conveying a woman to her master's chamber, which was a discouragement. She hoped they might be housebreakers or highwaymen; but, despite her peeping and lurking, she never overheard them to betray themselves. They were all of them well practiced in disguising their meaning so that they never spoke plain words except in their secretest cabals. Disappointed in her hopes of informing on them, Jane contented herself with her paltry vails, and with what more she could embezzle from her master on these occasions, for he always bespoke a good dinner for his guests. As his one servant was neither trusty nor comely, Marius and his guests would serve themselves; until one day it occurred to him to use his daughter. She was carefully instructed in how to wait at table, carving, passing dishes, and refilling glasses, after the manner he had observed in Lord Shaftesbury's servants. This was a duty she joyfully undertook, for it required that she be furnished with a decent suit of apparel, not to shame him before his guests.

His guests repaid his entertainment according to their kind. Marius was well defended against the undiscerning flattery of the common parasite: being indifferent alike to pickthank praise of his estate or of the excellence of his table or the grace of his daughter. Those who wished an invitation to repeat their visit must needs use blandishments of greater subtlety, by reading his writings and lauding the vigor of his style and the solidity of his arguments; or, if he had managed to slip something into print, reporting that his pamphlets and verses were the talk of the coffeehouses. Marius was as susceptive to such cajolery as a warm-hearted milkmaid to the toying of a well-looked lad. Yet he seemed withal to have a preference for the company of his more quarrelsome guests, who had not one good word for anyone, but would engage in argument upon all questions. It was sport to him to sit at table with a party of men who washed down their meat with a dispute.

It needed only that one of them should state a proposition or an opinion, for another to oppose it with utmost vigor and emphasis. If one man spoke for a general toleration of all Protestant sects, excluding only Romans and Jews, another would be sure to answer, And why not Papists? For extending toleration to them, would take away half the strength of the Tory Party; and for idolatry, superstition, and preaching submission to tyranny, the High Churchmen are full as bad as they. If one said, William of Orange would be a tyrant as absolute as James if he were enabled, another said, Not so, he would make a fair Stadholder of England, or President of a Council. Such being a pattern of their wranglings in Eighty-Eight, when it seemed to Marius and his fellows that England would at last throw off its fetters, or at least new-forge them to be but a trifling restraint on men's liberties.[11]

Marius had no suspicion that the turbulence of this year, which seemed to him to augur a great innovation, was working only to replace one monarch with another. He was reassured regarding the intentions of William of Orange by the presence in his train of Wildman, Ferguson, and others of lesser note that were reputed hot Whigs.[12] If he had but consulted his own recollections of Fifty-Nine, or had he studied the philosophers in his library with greater attention to their argument, he might have understood that his beloved Cause was in ashes, burnt in the bonfires of the mob in their rage after priests and plunder. The men of property desired above all else that there be some authority to keep the rabble in awe. They were very willing to sacrifice a few superfluous civil liberties, whereof they would scarce reckon the loss, in order to secure from harm their hoards of coin and plate.

I wished to know of her father's emotion when the Declaration of Right made William king with only slight limitations of his powers: Delia told me, she could not say, though she is certain he was extreme dejected. She herself was so weary of writing and copying, that when her father quit his dictating, she almost wept for joy, and blessed the new King in her heart, for freeing her from such drudgery. Which, she said, was wicked and undutiful; but it must be considered that she was but nine years of age, and unable to understand much more than that she was now free to play and recreate herself, as she had not been able to do for many months. He still kept his daughter by him for part of the day, and would have her read to him, and copy extracts into his commonplace book. Othertimes he was closeted with his restless thoughts, which broke out at times in moody soliloquies which she did not understand.

His Green Ribbon faction had ceased to be: Those who returned from exile, or regained their liberty, had been seduced by honors and offices, and were now men of the Court, busily repairing their fortunes. The few that had voiced objections to endowing William with all the prerogatives of James, were, it seems, merely crying up their own worth in the competition for places. It was only the republican tag-rags that still came to Marius and talked the old levelling cant; though they turned footpad, cut-throat or coin-clipper, between-whiles, for want of better patrons and employments. Marius, being no respecter of persons, persuaded himself that these were honest men, broken by their dedication to the Cause, and as deserving of consideration as a duke or earl. He longed still to meddle in plots and hungered mightily after news but would subscribe to no newsletters, having an inveterate contempt for writers of that loose and slovenly tribe, since his days of haunting the coffeehouses and observing their methods.[13] He therefore relied upon his remaining visitors, who understood very well what sort of intelligence would prompt their host to order a good dinner and loosen his purse strings. They soothed him by reporting that William's grasp of the scepter was no firmer than Richard Cromwell's had been, that the goldsmiths and City leviathans were reluctant to advance their monies, that most the great politicians and officers of state kept up a secret correspondence with St. Germain, and that the generality were grumbling and regretting their Dutch bargain.[14]

Of the swarm of licking and biting parasites that visited during those years, Delia particularly recalls three: a bleating, tansy-faced Quaker called Henry Jellico, a blustering, runtish, bull-voiced Anabaptist named Sidrach Gryce, and a spruce, gentleman-like fellow of no particular persuasion that I shall call Ned Shift. (Though I could give him the name by which Delia knew him, without violating my resolve to inform on no one, no matter how worthy of the rope; for I am certain that he christened himself along the way to Marius his house, or took a new name whenever he wore the old one into difficulties.) Ned Shift was the one that would call Jane handsome, chuck her under the chin, and otherwise soothe her up to a doting good humor. 'Twas chiefly upon these three men that Marius depended for information and for the hot disputation wherein he yet took a fierce pleasure, when all other delights were lost to illness, despondency, and confinement. They would dispute with him whether William were a worse tyrant than James, and whether it were possible to compound with James, to set him back on the throne as a monarch with more limited sway. In all these debates, Marius maintained that he would have no king, neither Hooknose nor Hatchetface.[15] He was unshakeable in this opinion, even when his friends agreed with him. (For sometimes one or another would declare himself convinced by Marius before the latter had tired of the sport; whereupon Marius would triumphantly present the rebuttal to his professed opinion.) Ned Shift took little part in these debates, except to hum and applaud what he said were good arguments. He did not cease to praise Marius for having pithy words and sound reasoning at his command, until his flattery and coaxing heartened Marius to return to his pamphleteering, whereupon Delia resumed her secretaryship; though now, she says, her father's bouts of dictating were occasioned by the visits of these men and the news they brought him. For Marius was like a blind man led by hand, accepting, of necessity, the what, why and where of his leader. Backed by these men, encouraging him by flattery, and enriching his invention with their argumentation, Marius took up the themes they put before him. On their return visit, which was, Delia says, usually about a fortnight after, Marius would place in their hands the finished work, with money for the printer, and for the hire of agents to have it spread abroad.

Delia is not sure of the monies involved, saying that her father took the men's advice concerning the number of copies, and how it would be put out. She thought it was some three pounds to the printer, for his risk, labor, and paper; and another ten or twenty shillings to the agents, or more if there would be carriers hired to take it beyond the city. I said to her, Your father trusted these men too far. Did he have them bring him copies of the printed work, so he might know they did not play him altogether false? She said that Ned Shift would sometimes tell him, as a token of good success, that inquiries were being made to find the author and printer; which was a sufficient hint, so that he did not want his pamphlets on his hands. —Why, that is as gross a device as I ever heard, I said to Delia. These men pocketed the money and used his precious writings as so much waste paper. I wonder at your father if he was thus fooled for long. —I believe otherwise, she answered me. They were exceeding particular and painstaking about what they would have him undertake; when he would read over his work to them, they would listen attentively, praising this and that, but urging sundry changes, which he would oftentimes be softened to make. It was Ned Shift who was most attentive and encouraging; the other two men, who had seemed friends, left off visiting after her father one day fomented a virulent quarrel between them, regarding Justification and the Spirit. They denounced each other in the scurrilous language of zealots, tossing back and forth such compliments as: Thou art a reprobate; nay, thou art a bawling Ranter; or if the one was a filthy-natured blasphemer, why then t'other was the bloody-mouthed spawn of the burning pit. 'Twas a scene that must have delighted their host, though it subsequently cost him their company.

I asked Delia what it was that her father wrote at these men's urging; she answered me that he wrote much against the war, that it brought only hardship to Englishmen whilst fattening up the Dutch. He wrote of the mounting debt and the great quantities of coin being carried off, some of it going oversea, some into the pockets of officers, purveyors and vituallers, who would rob the spittle to make a profit and who starved the soldiers and poisoned the sailors with offal and offscourings.[16] He was especially bitter, she says, about the land tax, and upon this subject he needed neither prompting nor guidance. His long-standing neglect of his proper affairs had reduced his rents (his tenants having cut his timber and neglected the hedges and ditches). Now, with one farm untenanted and others in arrears, he was unable to pay what was due, without selling a parcel of the estate that his father and grandfather had acquired by their careful husbandry. ✠

CHAPTER 7

A visit from Hull, who is now a great moneyed man. Marius practices economy.
Jane departs to marry the baker's apprentice. The new couple set up a cookshop,
whereby Jane may continue to cozen her old master and his daughter. Delia is given
the key to her mother's chest of finery.

ONE DAY the family took alarm at a sudden loud rapping on the
door. They seldom had visitors of a respectable kind that would
come to them by the front. Mrs. Witherby would call upon
them now and then, saying, she was passing on the road, and
wished to know how her favorite pupil was doing (which was surprising
to Delia, considering the negligence of her instruction); but it could not
be Mrs. Witherby: she did not deliver such a hard knock as this. Marius
could only conceive that the King's Messengers had come for him at last.[1]
Escape was impossible on his gouty stumps: summoning up his courage he
took a station by the hearth to await the event. Jane, too, seemed abashed
and doubtful what to do. It may be that she too was guilty of something
whereof she feared discovery: her master had to bid her twice before she
went to the door. She let out a screech, then stepped back to admit Hull.
She knew him straightaway, despite a marvelous metamorphosis, from a
crooked, lame, crump-shouldered, thin-gutted wretch, reeking of smoke—to
a crooked, lame, crump-shouldered, richly dressed burgess, monstrously
fat about the middle, smelling of musk and ambergris: Leviathan in person,
he might have been. In his glad surprisal, Marius let fall a few words of
welcome, which he regretted as soon as he understood the motive of this visit.

—Cousin, said Hull, I am exceeding happy to have occasion to call upon
you after all these years, and by the luckiest chance in the world. I happened
to employ an agent to look out for a farm for purchase, only to humor a
fancy of my dear wife; and the farm he found for me was your own, Cousin.
You are a shrewd dealer to be ridding yourself of land, Cousin. Land is a
lumpish trade nowadays. Only my wife has a fondness for the neighborhood
from her stay with you, and she told me again and again how she wished to
have a piece of land, and so I was obliged to satisfy her whim-wham. I was
just over to view it. As my agent said, it needs such a deal of improving that
'twill be a long while before I have a good return on my money. You have
got the better bargain, Cousin, but I cannot regret it, for women must be
pleased, else there is no peace.

As he spoke, his eyes kept busy, lighting on this and that, until they
settled upon Delia, who, having outgrown her clothes, was dressed that

day in patchwork, with one old gown providing pieces to eke out another. I'll wager my foolscap that he was conjecturing of her raggy look how soon the whole estate might fall into his hands. —That is your daughter, as I suppose, a well-grown girl. I am sure she is a solace to you. My wife and I have often wished for a daughter, for though they are a heavy charge to get off one's hands, sons are burdenable as well. We have four, and each must get something, some annuity or mortgage or 'prenticeship to give them a start. Jemmy, my eldest, began as a factor to Mr. M——, the Iberian merchant; but shipping being so troublesome by reason of the war, he subscribed to the Bank at the first offering. Now he no longer risks his worth upon a single bottom. He still has a share in a ship that brings him in fifty pipes of canary wine about Martinmas time. Pay us a visit in Gracechurch Street, Cousin, and he will pour you the finest tipple you ever tasted. Francis I placed as clerk to Sir B——, the goldsmith, which cost me a plaguey sum, more than I spent on Jemmy; but he made good use of his opportunity. For, with only a small stock to start, he's dealing in tallies and bills of exchange with more profit than his elder brother though three years behind him in age. For Tobias, Father Boult was determined that he must follow the corn trade, and my wife backed him and you know there's no arguing with women. So I was obliged to put Tobias in that line, but thanks to King William and the war, he has a good thriving concern in corn export. And now I think on 't, the farm might go to Willy, the youngest, who is yet at his hornbook. Though I'll have to find him out something more. I suppose you'll be putting your money into the stocks, Cousin. I recommend to you the Swordblade Company or the Glass Bottle Company. It may be you are thinking of the Bank stocks, but I would advise you to wait a while, as Jemmy says the price is likely to fall.[2] Now, it may be, for I see you are a man of frugal habit, that you have more at your disposal than the price of the farm, and so you may put out your money more advantageously than the stocks. If you have four thousand to dispose of, I can introduce you to a victualling syndicate, where you might treble your money in two years' time, three years at utmost, unless there is a peace made, which no one is presently expecting. The war is plaguey expensive and long, Cousin, and mayhap it has brought misery to some, yet it offers a fine chance for men of daring and good mettle who will take the risk. For I tell you, Cousin, the battlefield is a fertile soil that multiplies one's seed a hundredfold. From there, whilst his host scowled and stared, he fell to praising the government, and commending the King that he had removed most the Tories from their offices and put good dependable Whigs in the best places. The wheel was turned and the Whigs were on top now, and they were all men of substance and credit, not a mean rabble of weavers, porters, costermongers and fanatics as in former times. He named men well known to Marius as former brothers of the Green Ribbon Club, that were, he said, his special friends, and beholding to him, and ever ready to grant him a favor.

Marius said not a word all this while, made speechless, successively, by surprise, astonishment, and rage. It may be that he believed a sullen front and frosty silence would drive out his unwished guest; in which belief he erred, for such men as Hull are never abashed or affronted. Such a man will follow you home through the streets and call through the keyhole before he'll be put down. If there be any readers who doubt my account of him, let them seek out his original on the 'Change and at Jonathan's, and I question not but I will be found to have limned him to a hair.[3]

After Hull at last took his leave, Marius fell into a passion such as Delia had never before witnessed. He raged and ranted mightily, pacing up and down the room on his gouty pins, roaring about turncoat money-takers, City changelings, whiffling knaves, base crouchers and cringers to tyranny, bloody-mouthed leeches of the commonweal. Jane was reminded of the day that her master made such a great noise about the book by Dr. Titus Oates, which in turn reminded her of the time that he raged at his wife over her spending and her unpaid dowry. She would no doubt have continued to tell tales of her master's fits and humors, and thereby enriched my history, if he had not just then called Delia to him, to begin dictating his unshaped thoughts. For just as a fever produces botches and boils, so Marius, when he was put into a heat, would swell with angry pamphlets.

This visit, though lasting but an hour, operated upon the family like a quacksalver's elixir. Marius became of a sudden costive in his purse, stifling the flux of silver: Jane could no longer tell him a tale of the cost of beer and beef and bread, without his strictly questioning her on the disposition of every penny he put in her hands. He was so far suspicious of her, that he enjoined his daughter to accompany her, so that she might inspect tallies and reckonings to determine what was owed. Whereupon Jane declared that she would no more continue where she was so little trusted. She broke out in passionate speeches and discharged abundant tears, with Delia shedding hers in sympathy. Nonetheless, I believe Jane was only hastened to take a course long contemplated, but repeatedly postponed for the sake of the weekly half-crown superadded to her saving. She had long favored the baker's apprentice: squeezing his hand or pinching his arm, as if checking his fatness for the market, and oftentimes giving him a penny for sweetmeats.

The lad was up-grown, or near enough not to scandalize the parish, when Jane directed at him a rapid train of ogles, hints, and provocations, which prompted an offer of marriage to a fresh, plump purse of good silver and a pursy, one-eyed woman of near forty years. The money went to setting up a cookshop where she and her young sprig baked bread and pies for the market. The villagers said she ought to have let her apprentice ripen for another season before she plucked him. Her bridegroom looked yellowish, and (they said) staggered like a sick calf from his long hours of labor at such a pair of hot ovens. But he manfully tugged and toiled, and before six months were out, Jane was with child.

Although at first she broke out in great choler and made some cankered, shrewish speeches at her master's purse-bound innovations, Jane was mindful that she must leave on good terms, if she would have the family's custom for her cookshop. In this way, she continued to squeeze her fingers into her former master's purse; for Delia paid whatever price she named for whatever dish she urged upon her. I'll say in Jane's defense, that though she could have imposed upon Delia with rusty or corrupted meat, she was sufficiently fond of the girl, only to overcharge her for food that was fresh and toothsome. While yet in the honeymoon, Jane would vapor boastingly of the raptures of wedlock. What she said on this fascinating subject was entirely new and perplexing to Delia. It had been her understanding that infants were brought to the mother's bed in warming pans; so that she was little able to credit what Jane told her in contradiction.[4]

At the time of the sale of his land, Hull's agent paid him in guineas, which Marius had carefully inspected, rejecting several as suspicious in color or light in the hand. The agent said, he had no more gold, guineas being hard to get at nowadays, so that the remainder must be made up in silver. Marius haggled fiercely over the price to be set on the guineas; he must have thought he got the better of the argument, for he gave much less heed to inspecting the silver. After telling out the money needed for the land tax, he locked up the remainder; until one day he thought to take out some of the silver for Delia to settle accounts. She was standing before him, holding out her hand for the coin, when he exclaimed, What a damnable cheat! For he just then discovered that three shillings were shrewdly clipped, and two were arrant counterfeits, being only copper whited with arsenic. Though he looked upon the bad coin for a long moody while, he said nothing more, but took out a supply of good silver for Delia to make payment with. She described this trifling scene to me, by way of demonstrating that her father's temper was mild and gentle; she gave it out for his honesty too, for he did not tell her to try to pass the bad coin. However I believe that she, in her simplicity, mistook the matter entirely; that 'twas this occasion which put Marius to think seriously of money; not of gaining and keeping it, as other men do; but of how the King and the moneyed faction might be undermined and betrayed by it. Delia told me that when she returned an hour later, he had the bad coins still before him on his table. He roused himself from his rumination, only to bid her fetch down some books, along with an old volume of his commonplace book. I wish Delia had been more curious, as Jane would have been (were she able to read): she could say of these books only that they contained hard words and strange symbols. I doubt not but these were his books of alchemy, with the journal of his former experiments in that art. I venture to guess, were it not for the gout, Marius would have busied himself again with his alembics, perfecting a method to improve upon the crude forgery that had been passed upon him by Hull's agent. He spent many hours poring over these volumes, dismissing Delia from her usual attendance, saying he would take notes in his own hand.

Marius did wisely in sparing himself the tedium of spelling out his spagyrical recipes to his daughter, who was in a shittle-headed state these days. For it was about this same time that Marius called to mind the chest containing his late wife's finery, whereof he now gave Delia the key. Perhaps he had seen, in following Hull's gaze, how ill his daughter looked in her patched gown; or it may be that he hesitated to release the things while Jane was yet in the house to coax or filch them from the girl. Be that as it may be, the opening of the chest let loose a swarm of vanities, delusions, and troubles. Its contents were much the more dangerous to his daughter's peace of mind than Jane's obscure boasts of chamber-delights. In relating her story to me, Delia was not sparing in her description of the contents of the chest. Indeed she catalogued each particular item as if she were crying it at auction, though not omitting to tell me very honestly its exact condition, and how she employed her needle to remedy its defects: for she was of a tall, spare, lathy figure, and none would fit without much mending. Moreover, the trimmings and fastenings were such as required the assistance of a lady's maid, whereas Delia had no one, not even clumsy one-eyed Jane, to help her dress. It was an undertaking of many weeks: for, being made up of tailor's cabbages, the bodies and skirts of these garments were cunningly trimmed, slashed, and pleated to conceal the seams. For all which particulars and weighty considerations, she gave a complete narration; so that I might swell my book by a quire if I followed her faithfully in her tale; but I would spare my reader, and in truth myself.

When Ned Shift and his fellow guests next came to dinner, when they would flatter their host, and dispute with him, and batten upon Jane's best pies (got for the occasion), Delia perceived that they were surprised at a change in her father. They had often urged upon him the view that such men as Hampden were now become butterbox foot-lickers; and being false to the Good Old Cause purely for gain, were as vile after their fashion as Lord Grey and Lord Howard of Escrick.[5] Yet Marius had resisted these accusations; saying, he would not hastily judge them, nor call them trimmers or timeservers, for he believed them true to the Cause. Now the men whom Hull had praised, and claimed for his friends, Marius denounced as corrupted and suborned, their eyes put out by wealth and offices.[6] He was readily persuaded to write a satire, The Green Ribbon Turned to Gain. He bid Delia note down all that Shift and his fellows said concerning sundry men, who had been commonwealthsmen in Seventy-Nine, but were now courtiers and placemen busily enriching themselves. For a good fortnight, Delia was kept from her sewing by the inditing of this satire. When Shift returned for it, he was well pleased and much applauded the author's wit. For Marius had added to the foundation of what he was told, with many recollected speeches and other particulars, to make these men appear the worse; and though he veiled their names, he mocked their manner and appearance with such taking precision that no one could fail to perceive who was meant. But alas!, Delia's headpiece was at this time so stuffed with stitchery, with tucks and pleats and hemming, that she could give me no account of this satire, nor could she recollect any of his jibing epithets on his former friends. I much would wish a view of this work, esteeming it likely to be both a good specimen of Marius his style, and an unmasking of some double-faced deceits that have been passed upon the public; but it may be that it never reached the printer as he intended it. Though Shift professed himself greatly pleased with this witty pamphlet, and with its jeers and scoffs upon the Whigs, he was disappointed to find that Marius would no longer part as readily with his money; saying, he thought his satire ripe and apt and requiring no money to assist in its bringing forth. Yet I doubt his paper was tossed into a privy, or sold for a half-penny to dunghill rakers. I believe Delia was so far correct in her opinion of this man, that he was a collector of Marius his wit as well as his coin, whereof both were put to other uses than intended; so that the fate of this satire was to be severed into word-cabbages, with the choicest remnants stitched into other men's writings, to suit other themes than Marius dreamt of. ✣

CHAPTER 8

Delia is sent up to London to deliver a manuscript. She falls easy prey to a foppish rake. Her father's furious disavowal and her banishment. She makes for Cambridge, to seek her husband there. A beating, a prayer, and a talking bush.

FTER PRODUCING this satire upon the Williamite Whigs, Marius returned to his alchemical studies, whilst his daughter resumed her stitching, except she was sometimes called to her father's study, when he wished to dictate a few pages. Her own thoughts, all the while, were picking out seams, and what she could tell me of his dictation was only that it was upon the subject of money. He wrote out some pages in his own crabbed hand, she said, which were full of strange words and symbols. Always fearing that his handwriting could be traced, he bid her copy them over. He waited some weeks for his friends to return, that he might entrust them with this manuscript; but they did not come, nor otherwise communicate with him. At last Marius felt the world must no longer be balked of enjoying his latest work; he bid Delia prepare to take it herself to the printer the next morning. She was to furnish a basket with eggs or garden stuff obtained from one of the tenants, in which basket Marius would conceal his manuscript. She was to be ready before cockcrow, so that she might follow after the market-women to the City, only leaving off when she saw St. Paul's, taking one turning and then another, and arriving at last at the hole of a secret printer who pretended to be a chandler. Her father gave her abundance of instructions, calling her back several times throughout the day, either to repeat what he had said or to add some new precaution. The directions to the printer's secret shop were given to her again, as Marius recalled sundry waymarks; forasmuch as he had not been to the City in many years, his recollections were stale and faulty. She was taught what to say to the printer and how much money to give him. Most important of all, she was never to name her father or to give any information about him. To the printer himself she was only to say, 'Twas from the hand of M. B., but not even that if there were others present. Marius well knew that his daughter had no talent of deceit, but would answer questions right honestly: thus he attempted to furnish her in advance with a few essential falsehoods. If anyone were to look in her basket and discover the papers, she must tell a tale that he carefully rehearsed with her: that she was but a simple girl going up with her basket to market; that an old gentleman stopped her in the road and gave her a half-crown to carry a bundle of paper up

to Town, telling her to wait at the dial in Covent Garden for another man, who would give her another half-crown for her pains; that she did not know the gentleman, who came up to her at a crossroad; and that he spoke polite but seemed somewhat crazed in his wits (which last was true enough). Her father said also to her, when she came up to the City gate, she might see the rotted quarters of men displayed there, that had given up their lives for the commonweal and the cause of liberty. And no matter how she was threatened, whether with blows or with prison, she must say nothing more than the tale he taught her: else her dear father might undergo the same terrible fate, which would be due entirely to her frailty. He warned her of spies and trepans, magistrates, soldiers and messengers; but not a word was said of men, of their guiles and snares, or what attempts they might make upon her: to that danger he gave no heed. He gave no thought, moreover, to how a green girl, setting out upon her first visit to London, would choose to array herself; how she would not go in her plain workaday serge, if she had a trunk of out-of-fashion finery for her choosing.

She was up by four to dress herself, having determined, after much consideration, to wear her mother's sky-colored tabby over a cherry-red satin petticoat; which, being short, exposed her thick stockings and cobbled shoes. She completed her attire with a checked headcloth and a straw-hat, the latter adorned with a fresh red ribbon. She then set out with her basket of lettuces, all unwitting of the incongruous picture she presented, being motley clad, half herb-woman and half fine lady. Had her father awoke in time to look out his window and view her, he would have roared with consternation. Yet, though she drew curious eyes, and thereby ruined his plan of concealment (which was of second-hand subtlety, as stale as his daughter's basket of green-stuff), she did not greatly endanger his guilty secret, her appearance exciting wonderment and derision rather than suspicion. From shyness or discretion, Delia kept well to the rear of the basket-women, who did not take note of her until near Islington, where they stopped to sell their stuff to higglers. They stared and barked out ribaldries that she did not understand. She had indeed some consciousness that others had pointed and made remarks as she passed. She was sensible 'twas her finery that attracted their notice, and felt a mingled pride and shame that she had so evidently stirred their envy. Once she reached Red Cross Street, her attention was distracted and her sense staggered by the great din and rush of people; there also her unusual appearance drew less notice in the bustling swarm. She might have been in some danger of being stopped and questioned as a supposed thief, if not for an air of great simplicity which imbued her face and manner, which was not yet extinguished when I made her acquaintance, and is indeed her badge and signature.

The printer's hole was somewhere in the neighborhood of Bridewell, and I marvel that Delia found the way to it; but she said her father was exact as to signs and other marks, which were most of them just as he described. The printer was a mean, blear-eyed man that gave more attention to the coins she counted out, which were to pay both for printing and for the hire of mercury-women, than to the precious manuscript she rendered to him, singular fruit of the many hours Marius spent reviewing his alchemical investigations. In my questioning of Delia, I got from her a recollection that her father wrote words to this effect: that corruption is driven out by corruption, and that kings will be no more when all men are kings; which would seem only ravings, if not for his alchemical lore. I think therefore that Marius devised a superior method of forgery, whether of gold or silver, that a man might undertake at his own fireside. Such a work would be instantly famous; which makes me suspect that, when this scurvy printer looked upon it, he determined to keep the secret for himself; and from his obscure hole he has made a mushroom ascent to keep a coach and six and a lordly style of living. I wish I might have the recipe to make trial: for unless my gracious readers applaud this my history, and clamor at their bookseller's for another work from the pen of D. M., I know not how I'll meet my occasions come quarter day.

Marius gave his daughter no direction for how she was to dispose of her basket of garden-stuff after she delivered his manuscript to the printer. Delia bethought herself that she would sell it so that she might return a few pennies to the poor tenants who supplied it to her. (Though they gave her such refuse as was vendible only among the abject rabble swarming the squalid courts and alleys beyond the walls, just such a place as she now found herself.) She might open her throat to cry, Buy my fine lettuces; but that she was too bashful to attempt, not wishing to become a spectacle (and not knowing that she was one). She was thus considering what to do with her basket of stuff when she was aware of an uproar in the street: a violent quarrel broke out, which drew a jostling crowd of blackguard boys that pushed her forward. She shrieked at a knife held up dripping with gore, and might have fainted, had not a pair of arms caught her and drawn her back to safety. Of what happened next, she gives a wandering account. Her confusion was too great for her to note many particulars; so that I must supply them from a knowledge of men and manners, and I believe my readers will judge I have it correct in the main. What is certain in her recollection, is that the arms that drew her away were still holding her: one was about her waist; the other, toying with her neck and shoulder, displayed a Venice-gold bone-lace turned over a brocaded cuff. She breathed in a rich perfume that was grateful to the sense after the stink of the streets. A warm mouth at her ear was speaking words of reassurance and comfort. A gentleman had saved her from harm, and was leading her to safety. She was trembling violently in horror of a murder; she trembled the more when the gentleman stroked her breast in soothing her; yet she did not cry out or pull away, as he led her to a corner that afforded a momentary privacy.

I doubt this gallant is a man much affected to reflection; he may have figured to himself that the little peacock-colored woodcock he had caught, was a country simpleton, sent by her old mistress, whose discarded frippery she wore, into Town upon some errand, and that she had someway mistook Whitefriars for the New Exchange.[1] He supposed that she would come to her senses and shriek out, and even in a place such as this she might have rescuers; therefore, he performed his intention with very little ceremony. She may have made some little exclamation of surprise, but she did not interfere with his pleasure. This unexpected yielding determined him to make better use of his good fortune. He kissed her and asked her name and called her his darling. Tears stood in her eyes, but she made not a single complaint, and only stammered her name in reply. His arm was about her again, and he led her, somewhat fainty and staggering, into a public house. He said to the people, Will you show us a room and bring a cordial? My wife is taken ill and needs to lie down. If there was laughter at his remark, Delia did not note it, for his words were a certain confirmation of a notion that was forming in her puzzled head: that she was now, like Jane, a married woman.

After they were shown to a chamber and served, her gallant stripped her naked and laid her down upon a dirty bed, gazing at her while he drank off the cordial to recruit the animal spirits for another bout. I do not think such a beau would be found on those streets, at such an early hour, unless he had been all night engaged in the selfsame sport. His condition was that of the householder who goes to market, where he is persuaded into buying a piece of old mutton, for which he pays too much; only to come upon another stall where he might have had fresher meat for less, if he had only waited. Delia was somewhat too lean, and lacking in salt, to make a market, but she was unquestionably a fresh and wholesome morsel. When he had done with her, he gallanted her to the street, putting some money in her hand as he thanked her for her kindness. Delia, catching hold of his sleeve, found her tongue to say, Husband, sure you can't be leaving me. You must come home with me and meet my father. He'll be worried I've been so long away. I hope he'll not be angry I've married without his leave, but 'tis too late to be sorry. At these words, her beau drew back in terror, perceiving that he had been mumped by a cross-biting wench of a most fraudulent innocence, who had her bully lying in wait; that between them they'd strip him to his shirt, and perhaps jail him too. Delia looked down at the silver in her hand, then into her gallant's face with a simplicity no mere whore could counterfeit: —Is it pin money for my use, husband? It is generous of you, as I fear my father is too straitened in his means to give a portion with me. At this her gentleman laughed broad in her face. Recovered from his fright, he told her that his name was Robert Cloudsley and he was a student at the University, to which he must return that very hour by coach; however, he would present himself to her father within a few days, and then take her home to his own family. Delia was satisfied with this answer; staying only to teach him where to find her, she went on her way.

It was a weary trudge homeward, in a mood much altered from her setting out. She mused upon Jane and why she told such lies to no purpose; for there was no joy or rapture in marriage that she could discover. She shed a few tears as she went, more for gaining a husband than losing a maidenhead. When he uncased, she perceived her husband was not so sightly as his trimmings, and it would be happier to be united to his coat or his hat than to his unlaced and breechless person. Looking full upon his face, something flushed with activity, she saw that his eyes were goggly and his skin blotched with pimples. The breath that seemed daintily perfumed whilst he whispered in her ear, was by no means as sweet when he lay panting on top of her. Beside which considerations, she would be sorry to leave her father, even to live with a rich husband in the Town.

It was true enough, as she told her inamorato, that her father would be concerned for her long absence. She had been gone some two or three hours more than her errand required, and he was anxiously looking out the window all this while, fearing she would return in the company of the King's Messengers. When at last he saw her approach in her bedaggled finery, his relief was but small. Her drooping head and imprudent dress tokened the committal of some indiscreet betrayal, so that he was equal parts enraged and frightened before she parted her lips to answer his anxious questions. When he was fully assured that she had obeyed his instructions faithfully, delivering the manuscript to the printer, and betraying no information to anyone, he was well enough appeased, so that he might have refrained from chiding her for her showy apparel or for loitering and gawking; had she not then gone on to excuse her long absence, with telling him, she was just now wedded to a gentleman in an alley near Bridewell, which was avowed before a tapster and his servant, and solemnized again in an upstairs chamber. She began to say, she hoped it was not a fault, to marry so suddenly without her father's knowledge, when he struck a blow to her head that staggered her to the ground. Vile trug, gaudy strumpet, flaunting trull, brazen-faced quean, and other harsh names were flung at her, and he struck at her again with his crutch before she could rise to her feet and escape his gouty reach. Not even his fury at Hull's visit could match the rage now directed at this whore-daughter, that he had tenderly raised up and trained to be his support, who had pulled up her coats and parted her legs at the first asking. He commanded her from his house, saying he would not have her continue there a single hour. She must practice her vile trade on Turnbull Street, or in Shoreditch, or offer herself in the fields, like the filthy drab she was.[2] Delia was mute with astonishment; stumbling from the room, she hastened to obey, running off to her chamber, where, weeping abundantly, she shifted from her tainted apparel, and made up a bundle containing her linens, with a few of the treasures of her mother's chest, with which, even at a moment such as this, she could not bear to part.

When she stood before her father for the last time, her bundle in her arms, he looked much troubled, but said only, Get thee from my sight: thou art a vile, wicked, and undutiful daughter. In truth, he did not wish her to leave, for he could not manage his house without help, and did not relish hiring another Jane. She, poor fool, had not the least inkling that she might continue in her quiet life at home: the only difference being, she would have the words trull, whore, filth, thrown at her for the rest of her days. She had never disobeyed or disputed with him, and she did not now. A few minutes later she was in the road again, not in the least knowing where she should go. She felt the disgrace there would be in turning to Jane for sanctuary; she understood, moreover, that her father would wish her farther away. Although Mrs. Witherby stopped from time to time to visit her favorite pupil, Delia was not so great a fool as to fail to apprehend, that the schoolmistress might speak very different if she oped the door to find Delia a-begging with her bundle. All, therefore, she could think to do with herself, being so utterly friendless, was to walk to the University to seek her husband.[3] She was gone a full mile northward before she chanced to recollect that there were two universities in the kingdom, and her husband, Mr. Cloudsley, had not told her which it was. There was nothing else for it, but to proceed first t'one then t'other, and to look until she found him.

She was not frightened: The dismay she felt at being spurned and insulted, gave place to indignation at the great injustice done to her. She well knew, whatever the other ill names might mean, what a whore or strumpet was. Jane had accused half the women of the parish that were between fifteen and fifty years of age of being such. Whores were women that had more than one husband, whereas she had but one. 'Tis true her wedding was hasty and irregular, not pledged in a church like Jane's: but she had her father's own words to affirm to her, that it was as good a marriage as any. She had been present, about six months before, at a dialogue between her father and his guests, when her father had urged this very thesis. An Anabaptist that was making a defense of gathered churches, put forward a simile instead of an argument, saying, if it be wicked for a man and a woman to live together in the carnal privileges of marriage, without the public solemnity of a ceremony; so it is no less disorderly to claim the privileges of church membership, without the public solemnity of a water baptism. Though Marius attended neither church nor conventicle, he is a man that will argue upon any topic, like a hunter for whom all birds and beasts alike are game. He answered at once, not so; and proceeded to demolish the premised similitude, saying neither church nor minister was needed to solemnize a marriage, that it was a civil contract requiring only witnesses; or it might be a written pledge, a mere letter, without any witness at all. Nor did it require any particular formula, but only a statement of an intention to take each other in marriage. He pursued this point so far, as to the indifferency of the words, that Delia could have no doubt of the validity of her marriage-state: for had not her husband called her wife before the tapster and his boy, and had not she named him her husband in the street, where anyone could hear?

It had been a wearisome day for a young woman so little used to taking exercise (the short while she spent on her back had not been restful): yet her indignation at being wronged renewed her strength and carried her to a proud resolve. She saw as she passed through the village that the people were at supper; later on, a light could be seen at Mrs. Witherby's window; but she did not think of stopping. She went forward until she was out of all knowledge of the country. Only then did she sit down beside the road to eat a crust she put in her pocket at the beginning of the day. She counted over her money, which was only what her husband gave her and a few pennies beside. It was sufficient, she supposed, to purchase food and drink that would get her as far as Cambridge. The moon was near the full, so that she might walk on until she could go no more; her thoughts were too busy to permit her to take a longer rest. She held a sure belief that, whatever her sorrows and struggles might be along the way, she would be reunited with Mr. Cloudsley, and then she would be his faithful, loving wife, notwithstanding his popping eyes, his pimples, and his stinking breath.

She encountered few passengers upon the road; none of them troubled her. She had, whether from late-come prudence or mere haste, put on her workaday attire instead of finery, so that she appeared to be an ordinary country wench, hasting home at a latish hour. The road had left the fields and farms behind, and brought her into an open country, varied here and there with lonely wood, when she was hailed by a man hurrying to overtake her. He greeted her heartily, saying, how glad he was to have a companion on the lonesome way, and that it should be a pretty lass. Although Delia would have much preferred to be alone with her unquiet thoughts, she had no fear of the man, who appeared to be an honest tenant farmer or small yeoman. He asked her name and other such things, to which she answered as little as might be, saying only: she was called Delia, and she was travel-ing at night for haste, on her way from her father's house to her husband. He said to her that she was a tight, trim, dainty girl, that it was dangerous to be on the road by herself, but he would protect her. He leered at her whenever the shadows parted and he might take a better view. Delia felt some misgiving that such things had been said to her not many hours ago; that this idle chat was a bumpkin's rendering of what her gallant whispered her that morning. They had come to a well-grown wood, when he grabbed her about the waist with an arm that was far stronger than her town beau's, saying, as he pulled her towards the trees: Come, sweetheart, this is the right place for us to enjoy some sport. Your husband will be none the wiser, and I'm sure you've served him thus before. Delia's notions of the world were limited; nonetheless, she knew, as before-mentioned, that a respectable woman could have but one husband. She fought with all her little strength, twisting about to scratch his face, and letting out a loud shriek, which there was none to hear. The astonished swain let go of her at once, clapping one hand to his bleeding face, while the other snatched up the heavy stick he let fall in his amorous attempt. —You filthy minx, you conniving hussy, you waggle your tail in the common road and then treat a man thus—take that! And he fell to swinging his stick, belaboring her back and shoulders with good country vigor, until he had tired himself. His lust gave place to a righteous fury, that a loose female, strolling upon the road, should be so hoity-toity as to refuse a good man. He rapped her soundly, calling her the same rude names over again (his stock of epithets being much smaller than her father's), then spurned her with his foot in conclusion.

Her rejected lover was a furlong or two down the road before Delia raised her face from the dirt. She had no heart to go forward. Violated, cast out, and now drubbed senseless: it was the third and crowning misery of the day. She thought she might lie there still, and let the carters drive over her, and so end her misery; then she considered how much more grievous would be the hurt, to be trampled and dragged by horses. She crept from the roadway but had no will to move farther. Staying or going, she felt a great fear of mankind, which was a sore and too-late lessoning. She recollected the prayer that her father had taught her long before, and thought how she had repeated it after him, without ever understanding its meaning until this moment. She put herself upon her knees to speak its truth to the darksome road and the solemn wood:

Creator of all things, of all that swims or flies or goes upon the ground, of the lowly herbs and the lofty trees, of earth and fire, water and air: Look upon us and hear our plea. Beautiful and good are the sheep in their green pastures and the brooks that water the grasses; beautiful and good are the birds of the air and the trees that shelter them. Beautiful and good also are the hawk and the tiger; for though they rend and slay their prey, they are not cruel, and 'tis their necessity that impels them.

But what shall we say of man? He is wolf and tiger to his own kind. He rends their flesh and savors their tears for his sport. Great men wear that on their backs, which would save a hundred families from want. Perfect thy creation, Lord of All. Pull down these tyrant lords, these ruthless masters, that all men may be equal and free.

She had scarce finished her prayer, when near beside her, a voice spoke from within a bush. —What ails the poor fool? She took a hard knock to her noddle, to talk riddle-me-ree to the trees. This miracle was given a natural explanation, and Delia's astonishment somewhat diminished, when the bush stepped out from the gloom and revealed itself to be a smallish woman, shrouded, except for a brown, round face, in a russet cloak. ✠

CHAPTER 9

Delia begins her rambles with Nan Trundle, the chapwoman. That woman's eccentric manner of proceeding. A return to London, where Delia is tricked into breeches and rechristened Jack. A brief stay at the Dog and Bear, with a surprising encounter.

WHAT AILS the poor fool? She took a hard knock to her noddle, to talk riddle-me-ree to the trees. To which question Delia was too bewildered, or knocked on the noddle, to supply an answer. The woman helped her to her feet, then led her off through the trees to a mossy bank where a smothered fire let out a little light. She poked it to a brighter flame so that she might examine the girl's hurts. —Ah, well-a-way, you are nicely taught your lesson. You wonnot be taking midnight rambles with mankind again, unless you like him better. From a large pack she drew forth a handful of herbs and a lump of butter that she kneaded into a salve for Delia's sore flesh. Sleep a-while, she said. I'll wake you when 'tis day. Saying no more, the woman damped down the fire; and, wrapping herself in her cloak, took a seat reclining against her pack. Delia was tongue-tied with wonder and fatigue, such that she could barely stammer out a thank. Her companion, though she spoke but few words, was singing to herself all this while. Delia fell asleep to Hind Horn and awoke to snatches of Robin Hood.[1] The sun was at about 7 o'clock, and a pot was steaming over the fire. They passed a bowl of savory broth between them. The woman said her name was Nan, that she was a petty-trader, coming from London and traveling through all the country thereabouts. She knew every by-road and footpath; so that she could unerringly find the surest and safest way to any place, without taking the North Road through Enfield Chase at midnight.

Thus prompted to give an account of herself, Delia made several fumbling starts and stops, before determining she must tell the whole story of her unhappy day, only suppressing any mention of her father's writings; saying instead that he had sent her up to London on necessary business. A twice-told tale is tedious: yet the responses of Delia's auditor were so curious as to make it fresh; for at every stumbling pause in her narrative, the chapwoman struck in with a fragment of old song:

—When we went into the street, he put some silver in my hand.

—Oh why was your love so easy won.

—And gave me another kiss and made as if to leave. I said, Husband, where are you going?

86

—When will you be back, Lord Lovel. When will you be back to me? The effect of this faburden commentary was to gain Delia's confidence; and without any further prompting she told her whole history, which would have been a short tale of being motherless and friendless, except that it suggested more old songs. Nan was humming hey trolly lolly lo as she put her pack together and prepared to depart. —So you think to go to Cambridge and to find your husband there? Delia said it was so, and it may be her heart sank to recall that her plouky-faced Robert Cloudsley was no Sweet William or Lord Lovel. —I'll be going to Cambridge by-and-by. You may come along with me if you like.

They went but a short way upon the road, before Nan turned into a narrow track running along hedgerows. She stopped at the rear of a gentleman's house, directing Delia to wait beneath the hedge whilst she went to the door with her pack. Upon her return, they were off again through a succession of meandering paths to a succession of houses, most of them goodly places belonging to gentry. At midday they rested in the shade of a great tree, whereupon Nan produced from her pack a loaf of bread, a cheese, and a bottle filled with good brown ale, which Delia supposed, no doubt rightly, she obtained from one of the houses where she stopped. They continued in the same round until nightfall, when they took shelter in a barn belonging to the last of these houses. The next two days followed the pattern set by the first; and throughout Delia was as deficient in thought and observance as a donkey. (I suspect the chapwoman would have loaded her with the pack, were she not too feeble to bear it.) She was rendered stupid by fatigue, so that she sank to the ground in dumb exhaustion whenever the chapwoman made one of her stops. When they went on again, the strong effort needed to keep with her guide (for the chapwoman kept a sharp pace) was a goad that deadened observation. Nevertheless, she was aware that they passed a good many farms and cottages where the chapwoman did not once pause to peddle her wares. Walking or stopping, she was seldom silent for long, seldom without a hey down derry down derry, the greenwood tree, the lark the linnet and the nightingale; yet she spoke little to any purpose, and Delia asked no questions.

The weather, though warm, was showery. Delia supposed they were tending northward, though the sun, when it appeared, was sometimes on one side of them and sometimes on another. On the afternoon of their third day of perambulation, Delia could see spires and smoke in the distance, which she supposed to be the Town and University of Cambridge. When they stopped upon a broad expanse of heath to have their dinner, Delia began to think that it looked to be an overlarge place to search out a strayed husband. She was pondering how much of her silver she should give to her traveling companion, for sharing her food and guiding her so faithfully on her way, when the chapwoman spoke up to say, What have you got in your poke? Taking it from her, she began to rummage its contents, muttering of shillings and pence, as she drew out and examined each item. Poor Delia kept mum from indecision; for though she would be pained to part with her finery, she knew she ought to preserve her money if she could. Having completed her appraisal, Nan passed the bundle back, which allowed the girl to postpone a decision until it was time to part ways. From their stopping place, the road dipped down so that the view of the town was obscured. They were not many miles farther along the way—they were traveling straightway, without the usual divagations—when Delia began to be surprised at the greatness of the town: she had supposed there was but one place of such immensity in all the three kingdoms. She was surprised, moreover, at the multitude of people upon the road and the jumble of poor dwellings, which were little better than rude huts; yet she so trusted the chapwoman's promise to get her to Cambridge that they were within a furlong of the wall before Delia was able to comprehend, that three days of hard walking had only brought them back to London.

She pulled her companion by the arm, to force a pause so that she might catch her breath to say, Why, I thought it was Cambridge and I see now it is London again. You said you was going to Cambridge and I went along with you for that reason, so that I might find my husband there. The chapwoman answered her that they were at Cambridge Heath but a short space afore, and she might have searched for a husband there; but observing that the girl was close to tears, she changed her tune, saying, By-and-by did not mean straightway; that she would go there in truth, by-and-by. Only she must renew her stock of goods before going again on her round. With this answer Delia was little content, but said nothing more, her distress heightened by the squalor surrounding them. Despite her recent adventures, she retained the appearance of an ingenuous country maiden, a semblance that was enhanced by her gaping wonder and confusion to find herself in such a place. Such innocency drew ribald mockery and worse: for, falling behind her conductress at one unwary moment, she was grasped in a disgusting embrace, her helpless protests drawing general laughter. —You would go better in breeches, was Nan's only comment, though she did take her hand after that, to keep the girl close, which was a little protection.

They came up to the City upon Bishop's Gate Street, but before they reached the gate, Nan turned to pass through Houndsditch, where she pulled Delia into an old clothes shop, and, laying out the contents of Delia's bundle, began a vigorous bout of higgling. Delia only sat dumping upon a stool, struggling not to sob aloud with fatigue and discouragement. No bargain was concluded, and the same scene was rehearsed in a second shop, where a smock Delia prized was sold for twelvepence; then she was tugged back to the former shop, where a bargain was made for the rest of the bundle. Delia roused herself from her corner to observe the transaction; whereupon the chapwoman held up a pair of breeches, and a man's coat and waistcoat, and bid her pull them on. To Delia's expostulation of indecency, she answered, How many new husbands, as you call 'em, would you like to have by nightfall? You nearly had another just now, for the man that slabbered and tousled you, would have pulled you into a cellar if he could. The rag-seller brayed with laughter, as Delia, with tearful reluctance, went behind a blanket to shift her clothes, handing her gown and petticoat to Nan as she undressed, for the space was small and dirty.

As she fumbled with the buttonings, a lock of her hair slipt loose. Her hair was long and abundant, not easily concealed beneath a hat. She stepped forth, holding up the stray tress, to demonstrate to Nan the absurdity of attempting to conceal her sex: whereupon she saw that there was now a second man in the shop, leering upon her, who brandished a pair of scissors. She shrieked and pleaded, but 'twas only too evident that she was trapped, and must submit. The barber or periwig-maker, whatever he might be, told her that the fashionable ladies of the West End all wore their hair short, only pinning on false tresses as they pleased. Nan said she made a fine boy; that no one would be the wiser; and that her hair would soon grow back, before she found her lost husband. The rag-seller said many gentlewomen came to him in private for breeches, it being a more convenient attire. Which declarations may have been meant for comforts, though they were made smirkingly. Delia stumbled out of the shop after Nan, who pocketed the money for her hair before she could see it, but she perceived it was a good many shillings, about two pounds. She angrily demanded her money, to which the chapwoman answered, In a while, in a while. Don't be such a fool as to count your money in the street. Finding that Delia could not be as easily put off, this time, the chapwoman drew her into a bousing-ken, where they sat down in a dim corner.

The chapwoman told her not to keep such a coil about her hair and coats. In a very little while she would find how much pleasanter it was to go about in breeches. She herself had worn them when she was of Delia's years, though she was far abler to fend than Delia, who was as helpless as a

new-hatched chick with the shell stuck on its head. When they went into
the street, she must practice a mannish strut, and not mince along with
her legs clapped together, which looked very foolish. And as for giving
her the money, Delia would be as easily bubbled out of it as she was of her
maidenhead; so it were better she herself carried it. Upon Delia's angry
persistence, Nan at last said that since they were partners, she could carry
half of it; whereupon she drew out a handful of money, told it quickly, and
thrust a portion of it at Delia, bidding her put it away before the tapster saw
it. Half placated, half benumbed by strong drink, Delia put away the money
and made no more resistance: understanding full well she'd been shrewdly
cheated, though there was nothing, for the time, she could do to right herself. She must cleave to the chapwoman to have any hope of recovering her
money, or at least getting the use of it. Nan said to her, Delia would not do:
she must have a new name. Sprinkling a few drops of double-double upon
her forehead, she christened her Jack, adding, if he needed more name than
that, he would be Jack Trundle, which was her own name. If he were asked
to give an account of himself, he must say he is her nephew from Ipswich.
She enjoined upon Jack the necessity of forgetting, as far as possible, that
he had ever been other than what his clothes proclaimed him to be; for if
by any fault of words or bearing, he were to reveal himself as she, 'twould
be beating hemp in Bridewell.[2] Which good advice I shall follow myself,
and beardless Jack will be a masculine in my history, until he chooses, or
is compelled, to resume wearing petticoats.

They entered the City at Aldgate, but left the high street to pursue a
winding course along a multitude of back lanes across the City to Ludgate,
stopping at last at a tavern close by Drury Lane. Directing Jack to wait
below, the chapwoman went up the back-stairs as though she belonged to
the house. A few minutes later, she beckoned him into a parlor where a
half-dozen men were gathered, some dressed like gentlemen, others looking rough, but seated at the same table. The gentlemen asked him two or
three questions, whereto he only gaped and stuttered in response; till they
laughed and said to Nan, Your Jack Fool will do well enough, providing his
back is stronger than his head. Nan thereupon took Jack up two more stairs
to a garret chamber, where she made no comment upon his ill performance,
being noways displeased with his stupidity; for she had observed that her
companion told falsehoods badly, and was glad to be spared suspicions or
further questioning. Jack was in truth overtaken by a great amazement, from
which he was not yet recovered: During the time he was left alone at the
foot of the stairs, a gentleman came down them, who pushed him against the

wall and demanded to know what he was doing there. He was too overcome with shame to command his tongue to say, Oh, Mr. Shift, I beg you not to tell my father you have seen me in such improper gear, for it would grieve and anger him sorely. Before he could get out the words, his gabbled plea was cut short with a sound box of the ear and a curse upon fools.

They stayed two nights at the inn, where Jack was obliged to share a bed with the pot-boy, which at first gave him some alarm, until he found it was only a lad some three years younger than himself, who was run so hard backward and forward, from morn to late at night, that he spoke barely a word but fell insensible into the bed. Jack passed half the day lolling and moping before daring to peek without doors, the chapwoman being out and he all alone, unregarded by the people of the place (which is called the Dog and Bear). Venturing forth at last, he found that he was overlooked everywhere, unless he unwisely took the wall or otherwise impeded the way of someone more considerable, when he might earn a shove or a kick; which was preferable by far to a slabbering kiss or unwelcome embrace. He did as Nan bid him, observing men as he went and mimicking their behaviors. He began to feel kindlier toward the chapwoman; so that when she presented him with a pass bearing the Lord Mayor's seal (expertly forged) and a pack to carry the next morning, he shouldered it without grudging. Upon the bridge, she stopped to buy pins, sewing silk, ribbons, inkle and other small wares, choosing only the cheapest and most disregarded stuff, haggling down to farthings; which wares were added to Jack's pack. Even as green a fool as Jack would know that Southwark was not in the way to Cambridge, yet Delia admitted to me that he made no protest nor questioning. (I beg the reader's pardon for brabbling upon names: but she was Delia in a gown again when she told her tale to me, and so I must name her.) She said to me, that ever since the chapwoman first appeared, jump upon saying her prayer, she could not but view her as a heaven-sent deliverer. Her trust staggered when she found that she had been led in circles and then choused of her hair; but now she fully perceived the prudence of going as a Jack, when otherwise every stranger would treat her as his Jill.

I think indeed she (I beg the reader's pardon, I ought to write he, only it would make nonsense of my thought) had additional reasons to follow her guide so unquestioningly. Though she persisted in supposing herself married to Mr. Robert Cloudsley, with an obstinacy worthy of her father and his Old Cause (for wasn't she ready to acknowledge him her husband at any time, despite his plouky face and stinking breath?), it was nonetheless a pleasant thing to strut in breeches, albeit they chafed her tender skin. So it was that she set out from London, in a direction clean contrary to her supposed husband's whereabout, in a state of greater cheerfulness than she had know since she went up to London with her basket of lettuce and sedition. The life of Delia had been drudgery; whereas Jack enjoyed undreamt-of liberty, at least for two good hours, until he began to droop under the heavy pack and the whipping pace set by his conductress. She scolded and abused him, saying, I am sure the pack upon your back is lighter than mine. To which Jack, being irked, made answer, That may be or may not: but I am certain that the silver in your purse is heavier than my share of it. Whereat the chapwoman vented all the fraudulent indignation of her kind, berating the ingratitude of her companion, whom she saved from perishing on the roadside, or becoming a hedge-trull that lifts her coats for bread. If she did indeed creep all the way to Cambridge or London on her own, did she suppose herself capable of bargaining with Houndsditch rogues and wrangling the like sum out of them for her old frippery? Did not she, Nan, share everything that she got along the way, even offering the shelter of half her cloak from the rain and dew? All this speech she delivered without any slackening of her pace, so that her companion lacked breath as well as reasons to return against her. Jack was not man enough to answer, that the value of her services to him was not more than five or six shillings, say it were six; then the men's clothes, being coarse and shabby, and the coins delivered over to him amounted to about seven shilling sixpence; so that, setting the value of the hair at two pounds and the clothes at six shillings (though it was probably greater), there was a difference of one pound four shilling sixpence that was owed beyond any debt of gratitude or claim of fellowship. Jack indeed was so newly out of his coats and into his breeches, still so much the dutiful and compliant child, that he could not endure arousing her displeasure: yielding, he made peace by declaring his gratitude for her kindnesses. The chapwoman was so far pleased with his submission that she allowed a long stop at an alehouse, where they sat at the door and had their dinner, before hurrying on until nightfall.

They departed from the Kent road after passing through Southwark, at first pursuing a winding course along back lanes and footpaths. The chapwoman was seldom quiet for many minutes, singing or sometimes discoursing of herbs and crops, or it may be, only giving voice to her passing thoughts. She never seemed to look for a reply: either she was accustomed to being solitary, or else she held but a mean opinion of her companion's intellectuals, who was in any case too overwearied to return many words. The chapwoman stopped only once to utter her wares, and that was near the end of the day, at the house of a small farmer; where the women looked doubtfully at the chapwoman's goods, and after much bargaining agreed to a purchase, the price being a small sack of meal and some eggs. This hotchpotch, eked out with herbs gathered along the way, made them their supper and their breakfast too. The next day was much the same, except that Jack began to notice how the countryside was changed from what he knew, for it was wilder and less peopled. They were sometimes in deep wooded lanes, and other times upon a high narrow way where they could see all about for miles, into a country of wastes and scattered farms. He could give no coherent account of their travels; for, though his legs were now stronger, he was so wearied and pained by the pack, that his thoughts were only of when they would halt, and not of where they were or whither they were tending. He fretted inwardly at the chapwoman's preference for obscure winding tracks, which seemed only intended to lengthen their way: without, however, daring to complain or question his guide, for he feared the woman's wrath. He was so far out of his ken, that he might have been lost upon the sands of Arabia, for all the hope he had of finding his way back to London on his own.

About mid-morning of the third day, they came to a hilltop that gave a distant view of the sea, which appeared calm and glassy. The chapwoman looked out with evident satisfaction, saying to Jack, We made good speed after all, despite your lagging. It was not the end of their journey, however: they descended the hill and took a muddy way that led, after a good hour's walk, to a mean dwelling that stood apart upon a marshy shore, without any neighbors. Taking his pack from him, Nan told Jack to wait in the road: she would not be many minutes. While she was within what appeared to be a low tippling-house, enjoying little custom, two men came out of it, who by their dress he judged to be a gentleman and his servant. —'Tis the worst meat and drink in Christendom, said the servant. —Call it the worst under the sun, said his master, for I think the Turks treat their slaves better. —I would dearly like to see that knave swinging at the end of the rope, said the servant again, I'd give up a month's wages to watch him dance the Tyburn jig. —That would I, said the gentleman, except that too many good men would hang by him and with him. If they were on the point of saying more, they broke off upon seeing Jack. The gentleman plucked him by the sleeve, demanding to know what he was doing there. —I don't know, was his foolish response, whereupon he was boxed on the ear and demanded of again. He was saved from a beating by the return of Nan, who was accompanied by a squat, bow-legged, clump-gaited man that must have been the master of the house, which the other two were damning and consigning to the devil by way of a noose. He took Jack out of the gentleman's hand, only to squeeze his throat till he was half-strangled, saying to him, You don't like it, do you? Then I bid you remember it, and be true to your friends. Nan observed this moral lesson with an easiness that Jack could not share, saying, 'Tis only my Jack, my dead brother's child. He's but half furnished with a headpiece and does harm to none. —He does talk like a fool, the gentleman allowed. There was a little mumbled talk which Jack did not hear as he was gasping for breath, except that the chapwoman answered, Do you think I cannot mind the weather without a glass? You wonnot be cheating and choking me with your ill fare. The man made fists at her, whereof she took no notice, saying that she would be back betimes, and giving Jack his pack. They stepped away quickly until the road, bending, brought them out of view. —Out of the road, out of the world, said Nan, as she slacked her pace. They then stopped a long while at a good clean alehouse. When they shouldered their packs again, Jack noticed, belatedly, that his was now lighter; when the chapwoman began another of her old songs, he joined in the burden, singing a clear sweet treble above the chapwoman's low throaty tone. The effect was pleasing to their ears, and they went along the way in great good spirits and apparent friendship. ✶

CHAPTER 10

Wandering about the Weald. The chapwoman's story. A soldier's story.

THEY CONTINUED upon the highway a mile or two before the chapwoman left it for a by-road. Jack feared she would strike the same rapid, winding course back to London. Instead she chose to saunter easily from one farm to another, plying her trade as she had not done before, except for their daily bread, on the way to the sea-coast. It was a wild, meagre, little-habited country of small farmers, such as possess no more than a dozen hens, a brace of thin-bellied pigs, and an old despairing cow. Here the chapwoman's faded wares were viewed more favorably; but as the people were without money, they would exchange eggs, butter, and peas for ribbons, pins, and thread-lace. Jack could only suppose that the chapwoman's trade was chiefly in vending such paltry trash, the unwanted offscourings of the City shops, so that it was necessary to journey some two or three days to find a market. He could not, however, figure what the profit might be, of walking so far, only to eat well for a season; and, for their pains, perhaps earn a hock-end of bacon and a fistful of brass farthings to bear away with them. Yet, those pains being but slight, he was too content to rest and make holiday, to be critical of the chapwoman's doings. He scarce called to remembrance that, but a fortnight before, he had been only child and heir to a gentleman of respectable estate, and was now no more than a hedge-bird, a runagate, a vagabond stroller. In truth, he thought his present existence delightful, and gave no thought to past or future. They would idle for much of the day beside a shaded stream, where they would chat or sleep or sing; then walk to a likely farm to barter their wares for food, which they rarely failed to do: such walking about the country being now no hardship, but a diversion and a spur to appetite. Jack proved so quick in learning the chapwoman's songs and singing them after her, that she began to have a better opinion of her companion and to be more conversable than formerly.

They were lingering upon a mossy bank after supping upon cribble bread and butter, and a salad gathered along the way. The spot was too pleasant to abandon for another aimless ramble; the chapwoman proposed they spend the night, the weather being warm and dry. She sang what seemed her favorite song, Robin Hood and the Beggar, though 'twas altered at each rendering, so that Jack was unable to sing it with her. He ventured to ask why the song was never twice the same, to which the chapwoman answered, it was the old

way of singing, before books and paper made all the songs the same; and it
was the way her mother had sung before her. Musing, singing over again a
few lines, she began to give her own history, which may be repeated to the
reader within the space of a few pages; but, in her way of telling, her words
suggesting a song, and the song in turn recalling to mind some event, she
was an hour or two in relating her story. Her mother, she said, knew all the
songs and all the herbs and all the ways about London and the Weald, which
is where she was born. She had a strong, tuneful voice such that she could
make a pleasant living as a ballad singer. They traveled about the country
to fairs and markets when the weather was fine. The winters they would
pass in London, where the people, though much richer, would give less, and
seemed to expect to have their music for nothing. In the spring they would
go out into the countryside to gather herbs for salads and medicines, which
they would sell in the City. But that trade was not now so good as it once
was, for people now wanted to buy drugs from quacksalvers and apothecaries,
which nobody knew what was in them. Her mother had been careful with
her earnings, saving up whatever she could. Fearing footpads and highwaymen, and having no friends in the world but each other (another song came
here), she buried her stores in wastes and overgrown hedgerows and such
like places, where no one ever put spade or mattock or plow to ground. They
would return to these sites from time to time as they were gathering herbs,
the mother carefully instructing her daughter so that they might not be
forgotten. When her voice was grown hoarse from so many years of bawling
out her ballads, she judged she had sufficient money to get a cottage with a
little land, upon which the two of them might shift to feed themselves, and
sometimes carry a basket to the London market. She found such a place
near Dulwich, upon the edge of the great wood, that was very agreeable to
both mother and daughter.[1] Nan was, at this time, a young woman of about
Jack's years, and like Jack, wearing breeches; but thinking she might now
be able to wear a gown and talk to the young men and, it might be, make a
marriage for herself. (Her songs much impaired the progress of her story at
this point.) Her mother directed Nan, with many cautions, to go one direction to dig up half their hoards, whilst she went another. They intended to
meet in two days' time at an alehouse outside Dulwich:

   We carried our coin in pokes that had secret pockets, and we sewed
extra pouches into our clothes. My mother advised me to divide up each
hoard—there were three I was to recover—among these pockets before I
went back into the road. But I was always to carry a good five or six shillings
worth of silver in my purse, so that any footpad would be well satisfied

with his takings, and not expect to find more. I was to carry myself neither too fearful nor too confident in any encounters with strangers. I did as my mother bid me, and performed my part without difficulty, except that it rained hard upon the morning of the day I was to meet her. I thought it might be deemed suspicious to be out in such weather, and feared also that my wet clothes would betray there was money hid in them. So I stayed for the weather, whereby I was late in coming to our meeting-place, which was a place where we were known. The people said they had not seen my mother; I tarried there until the next day, before deciding I would seek her along the ways she was likeliest to take. I asked after her along the way, and was told, We take no account of poor strollers or vagabond females. But my asking such questions brought forth the beadle, who arrested and threatened to whip me. I was then in breeches, as I told you before, and could not chance being stripped of my shirt, so I was obliged to sweeten him with a shilling to regain my freedom. This discouraged me from asking after my mother, and knew not what to do but go up and down the countryside, returning always to the alehouse that was our meeting-place; but each time they told me, she had not been seen, nor heard of. I saw that she dug up the hoard of coin that would have been the last upon her route, with only some eight or nine mile of way left to cover; but I never found her, nor any sign of her. There were several ways she might have taken, and I rambled over all of them. Mayhap she suffered some hurt or was taken sick, and sought shelter along the way. I kept wandering up and down, asking after her when I dared, and returning always to the alehouse in the hope she was come at last. The hostess there urged me to go to the gypsies, saying that the old woman who was their chief had great cunning, and was famous for finding lost things or kenning the thief that took them. She said that she herself would pay the fee, for she was certain that the gypsy-woman could help me.

When it was gone four days without my getting any word of my mother, I agreed to go with her to the gypsy, who was a crooked old crone squat before a fire in a mean hut. She beckoned me to sit down beside her, and looked upon my hand. She shook her head over it, saying, she saw that I was troubled by some secret grief or loss, which I think anyone might know by looking upon my face. She threw some powder into the fire so that it flamed up red and smoky. She closed her eyes and mumbled her gypsy lingo before looking into the fire. —I see a woman dressed in brown, with a sack upon her back. She is bent over and hurrying. She is hurrying because it is raining. There is some place she needs to reach. Do you know the woman? —I might, I answered, what you describe is very common. —She stumbles, her hood falls down and I can see her face. Her hair is mouse-colored, her eye hazel; her face broad and flat with a strawberry on her chin. (The witch then looked at me, but I was still to conceal my fright, for she described my mother exactly.) The gypsy-witch put her powder into the fire again, then said: Now everything is changed. It is dark, dark. I see nothing. No. I see trees, I see the ground. The leaves are heaped up over a shallow mound—a grave, the grave of the woman who stumbled. Thereupon the gypsy came out of her pretended trance. Looking full upon my face, she said, 'Tis in vain to search longer for your mother. Nor will you ever find where she lies under the trees: the spirits will not reveal it. I scrambled up and took to my heels. I heard the alewife calling after me: I paid no heed but got myself away, having all my gear with me; and I hope never to come near her or the gypsy again in all my life.

—I have read marvelous things of gypsies in the books belonging to my schoolmistress, how they can find lost things, or name the person who stole them. But whether their soothsaying is of the devil or not, the books do not agree.

—You are a baby yet, as simple as the day you dropped from your mother's womb. I have been about with my mother to fairs and markets since I could walk. We traveled upon the road with gypsies, sorcerers, jugglers, scryers and such like, and I know their tricks and dodges. The lesser ones have only to tell the maids that they'll have a rich handsome lover, the wives that their husbands will die soon, and the men that they'll inherit an estate or dig up a treasure in their field. The knowing ones make trial with random words, short or tall, dark or fair, gain or loss, until they wind their coney. But though the devil will have them in the end, they are mere coggers and foolmongers.

—But you, as you tell it, told her nothing of yourself. So I do not perceive how she could describe your mother without the aid of the devil or some other spirit; unless it might be that your friend gave her notice of you beforehand.

—There you said a shrewd thing. You are not altogether ninny. But that was not my thinking then. The devil may be sure of her, and most of her ragged kind, without the granting of favors and special knowledge. Such favors he keeps for lords, aldermen, and magistrates. No, she could only know so much by being told so by the villain who robbed my mother and knocked her in the head, then hid the body afterward. The gypsies swarm all about Norwood, and my mother would likely encounter them on her way to the alehouse. Though she knew them to be thievish cheats, she would not fear them as footpads or murderers, or make any strong effort to shun their company.

That is what lay under my cap at the time, that it was some of the gypsies that did the murder. Thereafter, I considered that it might be my seeming friends at the alehouse, the woman and her husband, that had been so kind to me when I was roaming up and down searching after my mother; it might be they were the ones who killed her for her money. She might have been there already, looking out for me during the time that I kept shelter from the rain. It might be she let fall some stray word out of confidence in them, telling them about the cottage we meant to buy. For certain, one of those two women in the hut was a murderer or complice; and I run away for fear they would serve me the same. For a long time afterward, I thought upon my mother much, and dreamt of her at night. I had many idle thoughts of how I might take revenge, or bring about the discovery of the murder. But I knew not how I might compass it.

—What did you do next, once you understood that you would not find your mother?

—I did not at first know what to do with myself. I had money enough to get a husband, if I liked; but I had my mother's fate constantly in mind, and I figured to myself, that a woman may be knocked in the head as well by a husband as a footpad.

—But you changed from breeches to coats for all that.

—A woman may converse with the young men without marrying them, especially if she be wise in herbs. She then rattled out a recipe which she said was infallible; but which Jack, not foreseeing that he might someday require it, heard only imperfectly. It was compounded of a half-dozen dried flowers of wild carrot, a like quantity of sabin leaves and tansy root, and a thimbleful of the seed of cuckoo flower.[2] There was a fifth ingredient that she said was sovereign, which had a peculiar name; but before Jack could put a question, she had another song upon her lips:

They sweetly hugged and kissed a while,
And afterwards they parted.

Jack (as Delia tells me) reflected much upon this conversation, and judged it sufficient to explain why the chapwoman had been so exceeding wary along the way, in avoiding other travelers and preferring to pass the night in hedgerows and barns instead of alehouses, even if good and cheap. Of late, however, her mistrustfulness did not at all appear. Although they chose to sleep without doors that night, they more usually lodged in alehouses, when the chapwoman liked the place well enough to bide the night. Perhaps

she found her companion dull-witted, for she was prone to idle upon a
bench and chat on the weather, the crops, and other such-like themes, to
whosoever happened by. This seemed in the ordinary character of a lazy and
prosperous peddler, only it differed much from her behavior afore, when
she had shunned all contact, except she went up to some particular dwelling
to truck her wares for food. When the chapwoman was minded to move,
she would take the highway for the sake of noting other travelers. Though
she was yet wary of gypsies and hang-dog rogues, she was very ready to
mingle with any honest folks who minded to make answer to her greeting.
These were mostly farmers going to and from market or poor cottagers on
the pad for haymaking, weeding and other such work.

Of the days passed in this dallying fashion, Jack kept no count, supposing
that they would pursue the same easy course until the coming of winter
would force a change. But their summer halcyon ended in less than a fortnight, with a change in the weather, whereupon Nan, urging her companion
along, struck a sharp pace towards the sea-coast, stopping only for a hasty
cold dinner in the afternoon. After another five miles more of brisk walking,
they came upon a large alehouse where two roads met. Here she paused
to drink, then proposed that they would lay there the night; which was
surprising to Jack, as there were still some hours of daylight for travel, and
the place was dirtier than most of its sort. However, when she asked for a
chamber, the host said to her: We have not one bed to spare, or even a heap
of straw in a corner. Look you at this room (which was much disordered).
Can you not guess? A plague of redcoats are quartered on us, to ride up and
down the country after smugglers and Jacobites. Our custom is ruined until
they take themselves elsewhere, and when that will be I know not. To Jack,
who had a hearty dread of soldiers, the host's words were reason enough to
be on their way, though it now began to rain, but Nan answered the man: I
do not mind soldiers, and the boy is weary and all but lame. Cannot charity,
and a half-crown, find us a bed for the night? Jack was on the point of saying that he could, if need be, walk another five mile to better shelter, but
the chapwoman pinched his arm for silence as she haggled the price of the
host's own bed, which she got for another sixpence, and an offer to pay two
rounds of the soldiers' drink. Jack was yet puzzling over the chapwoman's
doings—for he was not fool enough to credit her concern for his weariness,
and he had never known her to spend her coin so freely—when a noisy
stir announced the return of the dragoons from their patrol. They came
clattering in, shouting and cursing and calling for drink. It was a party of
ten men led by a corporal (who went at once upstairs, calling for service).

After they had wet their throats with the house's common ale, Nan called for the host to serve them his best, saying: I was once preserved from a highwayman by a party of troopers and so I will be a friend to redcoats for ever after—a speech that was answered with loud huzzahs. She asked, had they encountered any highwaymen or other villains upon the road. Their tongues loosened by good strong ale, they answered this and all her questions freely; for she wished to know particularly which roads and by-ways they were keeping safe for passengers such as herself. She asked what other parties of brave fellows were on patrol; but of this they could little inform her: only that of their company there were two other patrols, one of them about Dymchurch and the other about the isle of Thanet.

During this dialogue, a young man in a patched and tattered coat crept in from the rain and looked as if he were avoiding the host's eye. Jack, for pity, brought him a cup; he sat still and grim as the redcoats, warmed by the chapwoman's flattery, fell to idle boasting. Their uniforms were fresh, their horses good; and though they had done little more than harry poor strollers and suspected Papists, and break the furniture of the alehouses where they were quartered, they considered themselves heroes and doers of great exploits. One of them said, he was from Bristol, where he had been apprenticed to a nail-maker, but he disliked both the work and his master; so that he was willing enough to follow the drum and take the King's shilling, as 'twas promised he'ld serve at home. His parents urged him to stay with his master, but he did not regret the change, for he fed well and was better clothed than ever before in his life (his parents being overburdened with children and his master miserly). He could not say that he much liked the rotten old barracks at Sheerness. 'Twas tedious to repeat the same maneuvers over and over again all the long months of winter; but the postures for firing his gun, and daily parade and other exercises, were none of them as dull and damping as striking out nails all the day long. But though the camp was tedious, riding up and down the roads after Jacobites and highwaymen was a jolly life. —I wish only, he concluded, that I might meet with someone who could write a letter for my parents, so they might know how well things go for me.

The beggarly stranger was roused from his torpor by this innocent speech, and landing a loud thump upon the table, he got their attention. —There are many such as you in Flanders, that were made the like promises, which were never intended to be kept, except as convenient. Do not think (he said, still addressing the volunteer whose foolish remarks provoked him to speech) that you will feed so well in Flanders. There we got only enough coarse bread, hard cheese, and foisted beer to keep us on our feet; to get even a morsel of flesh, you must pay the sutler. Our promised pay was only a wretched sixpence a day, yet upon one pretense or another, we got not even that, only about two or three pence, irregularly paid. You may suppose that the sutler did not sell his meat so cheap. Upon the marches, many men were so enfeebled by hunger that they lagged far behind and were not seen again, and to good purpose. For the only means to get money for food, was to sneak away from your company, and then offer yourself as a recruit to another that was short of men. If they were expecting a muster, the officers would pay a bounty of ten shillings to new men, so that they might fill out the parade, and collect their own pay. It risked flogging, but 'twas easy enough to do upon a march, if the way went through a wood. Whereupon it was only a matter of changing the lining of a man's coat to shift from one regiment to another, which is what I did when I could endure no more. Thereafter my life was somewhat better, for now I was in a company that was better officered, and I got more of my pay. There also I found a fellow that was from the same part of Gloustershire as I am. I'll tell you some part of his story. He had volunteered, upon a promise of being in the household guard, which he thought would be a better life than that of a day-laborer, which was all he else could expect if he stayed at home. He was a half-year in the army, when he was guilty of some trifling fault of insolence to an officer, whereby he was in dread of a whipping. Instead, he was clapped up in the Tower and put into a party that was being shipped to Flanders. I doubt we would have ten words to say to each other if we never left our own villages; but here 'twas a great comfort that we grew up among the same hills, drawing water from the same stream, and so we kept by each other's side as much as we could.

He died at a place called Steenkirk; I saw him fall.[3] The wounded were put in wagons, and then into barges, only to be left in the streets of Brussels, because the Dutch hospitals took their Dutch soldiers first; the Papist hospitals took their Papist soldiers first; and our King and our generals did not see fit to provide British hospitals. And there they would have perished, the good burghers crossing the street to avoid them, did not the Princess de Vaudemont take pity upon them, sending her own coach to take up the wounded from the streets, and bring them to her palace, where her own physicians, nay, she herself and her ladies, tended them.[4] So that whenever I am angered almost to madness to recall all that I witnessed in that horrid fight, where we English were left to die by the malice of Solms, I think of that lady standing at my bedside and speaking comfort, part in her language and part in mine, while she dressed my wounds with her own white hands.

(Whereupon he held up his strengthless right arm, to display his maimed hand.)

He had the attention of all; as he paused, as if considering his words, a soldier broke in with a question, saying, he heard mention of that fight, as a bloody encounter where the English showed their mettle, and put down many hundreds of the French, and he would be glad to be given an account of it. —I can give you only a soldier's account, all smoke and confusion, a hellish noise of guns, shouting and cursing, and groans of dying men. For what was intended, you must ask the generals. We set out from our camp in good order and readiness, but we had not gone more than a few miles when the way became difficult, a broken ground of gills and streams that was slow and cumbersome to cross. When we got past that marshy ground, we entered a narrow way through a wood, and found that there was a company of our own horse gone before us, that could neither move forward quickly nor give way; and so we were forced to push past them however we could. Our officers said it was Solms who had so foolishly ordered the horse where they could not go. Now we were much disordered and straggled; upon coming out from the wood to a broad expanse of ground, we were drawn up in battle order, though we were yet a mile, at the least, from the enemy camp, which it may be our officers did not know. But being put into a line, we went even slower. By now the French were roused out of their camp and setting up defenses, so that all surprise was lost. They were as ready for us, as we for them. Before us was not level ground, but a hillside divided into enclosures by hawthorns and ditches. My companion said, This was good farmland before war came to't. I looked to the hilltop, where the French were running back and forth, shouting; but I saw many that had their arms at readiness. We were ordered to make a line before a hedge and fire through it, as the lines of the French advanced toward us, keeping at the advance until we were musket to musket firing through the hawthorns. Someway we broke through and then we were between the hedges, so close to the French that we slashed at each other with our hangers. For a time they were giving ground to us, but the Dutch General, Solms, sent no troops to support us, and the numbers of the French kept increasing until we were overcome and forced back. Whether we killed more of the French or they of us, I cannot tell. When the ground is thick-sown with the fallen, writhing in the agony of their wounds, or else stark perished, those left standing are not reckoning the dead by the fashion of their coats. Though I saw my friend drop, I could not spare a glance to see for certain whether he lived or no; or if I did I would be laid out beside him.

The horror of the fight between the hedges was but little compared to the retreat. And though we retreated in good order, the French pressed so close, that the moment when you must turn your back to go to the rear, is a greater terror than fronting the enemy with gun or sword. And that is when I took my worst hurt, a French sword chopping my arm at the shoulder as I turned. I could not go far, but the bad ground saved me from being trampled, for I can just recall that I tumbled into a ditch. The pain threw me into a dead swoon, from which I did not recover until the jolting of the cart renewed my torment. I felt such misery, that I little cared whether I lived or died, if not for the goodness of the Princess, which heartened me. But I was a long time languishing, with a wound that festered and a fierce ague, so that I was moved one place to 'nother and at last put aboard ship for England with many others in like condition. We were lodged in the Tower, which was an odd-seeming hospital; for sure, 'tis no crime to be wounded in battle or in honorable retreat. I regained my health, however, and thought at least I would be pensioned, and able to go back to my home country to live in decent poverty, for that I am not able to work with my right arm made useless. Then, however, I learned that the doctors approved me to return to my battalion in Flanders. I said I could not fire a gun or wield a pike; how then could I serve as a soldier? 'Twas no matter: I must return. I was put aboard a lighter with some thirty other men, some lame or blind in one eye. Blind or halt or maimed, we would serve to swell out the muster so the officers could fill their purses. At Gravesend we disembarked to await the tide, and as we were but poorly guarded, I took my opportunity to be off. I exchanged coats with a poor cottager and made my way back to my home, expecting that my friends would aid me.

Now I must tell you how I came to be in the army. My parents dying young, my uncle apprenticed me to a spurrier, who was a good master and taught me well. There was however not work enough in our town to afford me a good living. Though I might have stayed as his journeyman, I hoped to be a master myself one day. I thought I would travel to seek my advantage. My uncle and my master approved my notion, the one providing me with money to travel, and the other with tools. My master said the best work was done in London. I thought well of my abilities, though I was country-reared; I thought I might make myself a complete man of the craft, if I could find work with a London master.

I was just come to the City, where, finding the posting inn too dear, I was walking up and down looking for an alehouse like those we have in the country, where a man might have a bed good cheap. A man in a cloak who sat at the door, seeing my eye upon such a place, said to me, The ale is good, you need not fear. I answered him, 'Tis lodging for a night or two that I'm seeking. Upon his saying, they could accommodate me in all, I entered and he after me. We drank together, he being friendly and obliging; and I thought there was no hurt in answering his questions, for it might be he could direct me how to proceed, as he seemed very knowing; he said indeed he thought he could help me to good employment. When 'twas time to pay the shot, he took out a shilling and handed it to me, saying, What do you think, is it good coin? The moment he put it in my hand, two men that were seated nearby, rose up and took hold of me. He took up the coin, which I had let drop, and thrust it in my pocket, saying, Now you are the King's man.

I did not understand what he meant, only marveling that these were an odd set of villains, that put money into a man's pocket instead of stealing it out. The tapster looked calmly on, an it were nothing of his concernment; there were no others in the room. I tried to shake them off, and struggling with them, we tumbled out into the street, where I began to shout, Villains, villains, let me go. What do you mean? He said to me again, You took the King's shilling. You are now his man. —I did not take it. You put it in my pocket. —You took it certain, one of the others answered; and in broad day I could see they were dressed as soldiers, which in the gloom I had not noted. —We both saw you take it, and so did the tapster. I continued to struggle and to call out and appeal for rescue, but to no purpose. The people in the street stopped to watch as though it were a play being performed for them, one they had seen before. As there were three of them upon me, they were able to pin and tie my hands, and then they stopped my mouth with a rag; once bound, I was pushed into a hackney coach, and as I was still kicking and twisting to break free, they pinched my nose till I was stifled. Half-smothered, I was carried to a house in Holborn, and put into a room with nine other men, all held there by force. One of them was a Welshman who sat weeping by himself, blubbering out his tale, that he was a gentleman of good family, and his friends would ransom him if they knew. For the most part, they were friendless young men like myself that were strangers to London, lately arrived and seeking work. Two were lured to the house upon a pretense of being hired as servants. Another was forcibly seized in the street, upon a pretense of being a deserter. Most were decoyed as I was, being made to drink, then beguiled into handling a shilling. There were several parties of these man-thieves at work all about the City, as it answered their purpose better than beating the drum from town to town for rustic simpletons to pledge away their liberty. If we had all combined and acted in concert—for there were some fifty or sixty prisoners held in the house, guarded, at some hours, only by two soldiers at the door—we might have accomplished our own rescue. But each man thought his case the worse, and sat privately lamenting. Some said that this was only some peculiar error or excess, which would be set right when we were brought before a judge to make an attestation.[5] But 'twas not so. The great men of the City and Court connive or wink at this manifest abuse and allow it to continue. It is, after all, better that a few friendless men should suffer, than that the King should lack soldiers for his army. The Welshman was able to put up a ransom of thirty shillings—to free him from his enlistment, it was pretended. The rest of us were sold to the captains that came to inspect us and bid for us like cattle at market. You may guess we were carefully guarded until they got us aboard ship and to the camp in Flanders. Whipping was the gentle method employed to teach us the postures. There were sermons preached before us, to say that we were fighting to keep the Papists out of England, so that the fires of Smithfield should never be relit.[6] But the good Princess de Vaudemont is a French Papist, and the officers who enrich themselves and keep us half starved are Protestant and English. Nor was I treated with charity or kindness by my friends upon my return, as you will now hear.

To take up my tale where I left it off, from Gravesend I made my way home on foot. Along the way, I met with some good people, themselves poor and pinched, that pitied me and shared their bread. In any case, I was used to march long hours on an empty belly; I had no longer a heavy burden of arms to carry, or anything in my possession more than the outworn coat upon my back. My friends were thunderstruck to see me return to them in such condition. When I told my story, they expressed their amazement that such things could happen, as my being forcibly pressed for a soldier, which they said was utterly contrary to the law of the land. It would be another matter, they said, if it was a strolling beggar, or a thief destined for the gallows, or a spendthrift languishing in prison—it was only fitting and proper if rascals, reprobates, and sturdy beggars were pressed into service by land or sea; but it was unheard of that an honest, unoffending person should be so misused. I soon conceived, from their choice of words, that they doubted that part of my story. They suspected instead that I fell into wicked ways while in London, and was obliged to enlist to save myself. They did not make any such accusations outright, but some such notion was present in their thinking. The nearest they came to compassionate my losses, was only to say, How pitiful it was, that a lad of such good promise, on whose education such pains were taken, should be brought so low. When I was forced to ask them what they could do for me, they shook their heads alas, and told me how bad the harvest had been, and how high the taxes, and it was not in their power to do much. My uncle said, I was clearly predestinate to ill fortune; and at last told out five pounds to give me, saying, he could do no more, having his own children to help, and the whole parish suffering such reverses on account of the poor harvest. He let me understand, that in exchange for the purse of silver he put in my hand, I should betake myself to the road, and not think of staying, or returning again. None of my old acquaintance gave me any better reception. They said, they had misfortunes and reverses of their own, owing to the poor harvest, and that there were many others, resident in the parish, requiring charity, which were more deserving than a returned prodigal. They seemed to consider that my disasters might be infectious, and it were better for all, if such an ill-omened wanderer should take himself off.

I went forth from the town in a bitter frame of spirit, and in such a rage, that I minded to throw my uncle's silver into the river in contempt—and it might be, myself as well; only I was at that moment in too great a fury to perish tamely. Upon my way, however, I encountered a poor Kentish drover and his dog, driving home the Welsh beasts bought for his master, and I offered him the money. He was astonished, but refused it, saying, it was none of his; and if it were ill-gotten and I remorseful, then I ought to return it. I was as astonished by his virtuous refusal, as he by my offering it. Not to prolong my tale, we fell in together, and shared in all, though that all was very little. There were a great many poor bodies on that long march, driving their beasts or seeking harvest work, and sharing quarters for the nights. There were many occasions for me to repeat my tale; and upon one such, a Welshman asked the name of the Welsh gentleman that was a prisoner with me. I did not know it, but I described the man; whereupon the fellow said, Why, that was Mr. Gwynfor Davies, that lives near Chepstow and owns an iron-works and a great woodland in the Wye Valley. I described him to a tittle. I was glad to have such a confirmation of my history, though it was only my friends that doubted me. I asked, Was it possible this gentleman might show me some kindness, if I sought him out, since I was certain he would remember me. I was told, He is a proud, haughty man, liker to summon the constable and have you whipped, for resentment that you was witness to his humiliation.

The drover who was my companion has a cottage in Romney Marsh, which he invited me to share with him. I am sure I have listened to many a sermon praising humility and contented poverty; I thought that this was such a humble, contented man, and I might learn from him how to accept my unhappy lot. But though he was honest, he was not proof against temptation. My uncle's five pounds was a great sum of money to him, who had never had the free spending of more than a shilling. He had a sottish weakness for drink that he had not been able to indulge more than once in a quarter, before I placed this money before him. Having offered the whole to him, I could not object to his spending a half-share of it as he pleased. So that he squandered away, in six month's time, a sum that might have kept us for two years, if well managed. At last, coming home from the alehouse on a dark night, he got a fall that broke his leg. I tended his master's herd until he was sound enough to halt after them upon a stick, and then I gave him half my remaining store of money and took my leave. Though 'twas not by my will or intent, he is the worse for making my acquaintance, or at least from having the use of my uncle's money. I am not yet reduced to begging, while I can get a little work in the fields, though 'tis mostly the work of women and children, and for like wages. What I'll do to subsist myself this winter I cannot guess, unless someone was to hire me as a herdsman.

Jack, who had refilled his cup, brought him bread and cheese, which he received with evident hunger and thankfulness, then departed without further words. His account of the battle had been heard with great attention; but there grew a murmuring against him, from a resentment of the gibes and taunts he threw out. They said, he was but a foot-soldier, and they dragoons, not subject to the like injuries or hardships; and while the Papists at home were daily plotting to bring back their king, they would not be sent oversea. Moreover, he talked like a plotter himself, and if their officer were not upstairs drinking or sleeping, he might have found himself in ill straits for some of the things he said, against the King and the true church, and praising the kindness of Papists.

Nan had evidently tired of the company of the soldiers, for she said to the host that she would go up to the room he promised them. He however answered that he agreed only to let them have the use of his bed this night, that his wife and daughter had need of the room in the meantime. Upon this refusal, Nan showed much indignation and made an outcry that it was a cheat and a shame. She promised to pay so much for the use of his chamber, without seeing it, though it might be nasty and small, only because the boy was overweary and in need of rest; and now he intended to keep them out of it, despite what was pledged. The redcoats generously took up her cause and made an uproar on her behalf, mingled with curses and threats, and a readiness to hurl furniture about the room. The host took the chapwoman aside to plead with her, saying his daughter was a pretty innocent of fourteen years, and he would not for any money expose her to the soldiers, especially in their drink as they now were. The chapwoman answering, she must look after her own, and he after his; that the boy was the child of her only brother, and as dear to her as his daughter to him. With an air of great injury and resentment, she said that as he was so hard, and faithless to their bargain, they would leave; but he must relinquish any claim to be paid for more than the food and drink that she and the boy had consumed. To this he was forced to agree; and, the rain having stopped, they resumed their way. ✶

CHAPTER 11

*A friendly dialogue concerning the Old Times and the Old Cause. The chap-
woman guides a man called Major Boyle to the house of Sir John Herewige, a
Papist baronet. Jack is taken on as a servant. He waits upon his master at table
and overhears a great deal of grumbling talk. An amorous maid, a deceitful priest,
and a sudden departure.*

THE READER will readily suppose that the chapwoman's anger, as well as her tender solicitude for her brother's child, vanished as soon as she stepped forth from the alehouse. Jack had given over any attempt to account for the caprices of his companion, and was occupied instead with meditating on the soldier's story. He remarked to her that, though he greatly pitied the man, he must blame his bitter and unforgiving frame of mind; not so much because he considered it unwarranted, but because it must inevitably deprive him of friends and other help. —Surely those soldiers would have had the generosity to make a collection for him, Jack said, if not for his taunts and gibes at them as volunteers. To which the chapwoman replied, Pshaw, do not speak of the generosity of dragoons. Such men are the refuse of the countryside. Only fools and knaves would pawn their liberty for the sake of riding upon a tit in a new cloth coat. If such as they are shipped off to Flanders, the country is saved the trouble of hanging them. These sentiments were clean contrary to what the chapwoman spoke but an hour before, so that Jack was dumbfound for a moment, before continuing. —However dreadful and deadly the battle had been, it was his account of how he was waylaid and held prisoner, then sold to the best bidder, that was most shocking to me. If his account were true, and it was too circumstantial to admit of much doubt, certainly it is the greatest abuse, and worst act of tyranny, that was ever known in this country. The French King himself, though he claim absolute powers over his subjects, can be guilty of no worse. The chapwoman answered, Such abuses were brought over with the Dutch, and were not known before among Englishmen. —I have heard such things said by others (Jack made answer, being careful not to name his father). I have heard it declared for a truth, that there will be no peace, as long as the moneyed men of London can reap vast profits by loaning money to the King, and by supplying the soldiers and sailors with bad provisions. The citizens grow rich by the impoverishment of the country; country gentlemen and yeomen being forced to sell up their land to pay the tax, though the only men who can afford to buy their land, are these same moneyed men of the City. Moreover, it is not true that the war is fought to preserve us from Papist tyranny; for our army fights together with Papists as well as against them, which the soldier's history also shows us: the Princess who tended the wounded soldiers being, as I take it, the lady of one of the allied princes and generals.

The chapwoman attended to this little speech, as Jack repeated faithfully the opinions of his father, with greater regard than she ordinarily showed him. —Jack, she said, you are sometimes a ninny, but I hope you would never play the knave. (Jack startled at these words, recalling, a little late, that his father's supposals might be dangerous to utter.) Nay, I mean, you would be true to your friends, and you would never betray their secrets, would you? (Jack declared solemnly that he would never be guilty of such a wrong.) Then, I believe, from what you have now said, that I may trust you further than I have beforetime. And I consider that it might be safer to confide in your sincerity, than to risk that you might blab names and places or give out accounts of what you might happen to witness. (Jack repeated his declaration of fidelity.)

You must know that I am not a common peddler, but a confidential messenger for a select party—they are all gentlemen of estate and some are sons of lords—that hold such things as you speak of, that want to restore England to what it ought to be, and bring to an end this Dutch tyranny. I convey letters and secret papers from place to place, under the pretense of vending ribbons and pins and such like trash. I know the by-roads and footpaths all about London and over much of Kent, so that I can slip past every road where there might be officers stopping travelers and searching their baggage. The packs we carry have a false bottom, 'tis where the papers are concealed, but 'tis better to avoid the test. So you may understand now, why I pretended to a fondness for soldiers, only that I might learn which roads are watched and which are not. Besides carrying letters and packets of papers, I am employed at other times to lead men from place to place by concealed ways, their faces and names being known, so that it is dangerous for them to ride upon the high road. Tomorrow we must return to Farmer Grigg, old Wry-legged Bill—you know the man I mean—he that gave your neck a squeeze.

Jack was not pleased with this last news. He begged that he might be spared the re-encounter, and join her again afterward. —No, she said, 'Twould excite a fear that you was gone to seek an officer to betray them. You need not fear the man. All that is necessary, seeing as he moves slow on his stump-foot, is to keep your eye upon him and stay beyond his reach. This was not greatly reassuring to Jack, though Nan added, she thought Grigg would do him no further harm, beyond that lessoning, and they would not stay long, only to meet the men he smuggled over, and then depart. The men they were to guide to safety, would be as anxious to be out of his clutches and upon the road as Jack. Jack asked, What are these men, and what sort of papers and letters do you carry? The chapwoman answered, I do not know, nor do I wish to know. 'Tis to my good fortune that I never learned to read, and can pretend to ignorance. Hab or nab, it may be the difference between a whipping and a hanging if I was catched. What I know for certain, is that the cause is to restore England to the English, and to bring back the good old times before Dutch William and his dirty war.

—My father often speaks of the Good Old Cause, said Jack, no doubt considering that one confidence deserves another.

—Then he thinks like us, and I did well to confide in you; for you would not betray us, and your father too.

—That I would never do. My father trusted me with his secrets, and with carrying his papers, so you may be sure I'll be faithful and true.

After this conversation, the two continued along the way in perfect harmony and agreement, the chapwoman singing her songs, and Jack wondering upon the singular chance that had brought him among people of his father's party; which seemed the more remarkable, as his father had often lamented that there was scarce a dozen men left in England who were true to the Cause. Whereupon, he called to mind that he saw Ned Shift at the Dog and Bear, which made it certain he was among his father's friends. Although Jack harbored a resentment that his father had been unkind to his child, and overhasty in judging her, he was nonetheless heartened to discover that he had chanced to fall in among people whereof his father would approve.

They passed the night in a small, neat alehouse, the chapwoman being as unwilling as the boy to arrive beforehand at their stop; so that an hour's walk brought them to the place early the next morning. The party they were to escort was only a solitary traveler, a tall, dark, fierce-looking man whose name was given out to be Major Boyle. He looked unfavorably upon the woman and the boy, saying, he had done greater service than to merit such a paltry escort. He scowled mightily when it was explained to him that they must travel afoot in order to avoid the patrols; but upon setting forward, he struck a quick striding pace like a true Kentish long-tail.[1]

The chapwoman said that they need only walk as far as a certain house, where they would be supplied with horses for finishing the journey. However, when they reached that house, which was some fifteen mile inland, the

gentleman there was embarrassed in his manner of welcoming them, saying, he feared he could not accommodate them as he would wish. He said,
'twas unfortunate Major Boyle had come to him so, upon the pad, in the
company of a female stroller. —Nay, good woman, do not take offense.
I say it only because I cannot trust all my servants, and I am sure their
tongues will wag and all the parish will hear of it, if I seat you at my table
or otherwise provide the hospitality I am sure you deserve. Boyle said to
him, The tattle-talk of a country parish is of no account. I would be horsed
and gone at daybreak, long before any possible inquiry into my presence.
Moreover, it is an easy matter to contrive a tale to explain my case; as for
example, I was beset by highwaymen and my horse taken, and consequently
I had no choice but to use my legs. Their host (or rather, the gentleman that
was so fearful of being their host) would not be persuaded, saying, there
would be suspicions excited against himself, so that he might no longer
dare to aid the gentlemen that came to him in secret from over the water.
The proposal was, that they must spend the night sleeping upon straw, as
vagrants who had slipped into an outbuilding; however, there would be a
trusted servant appointed to bring them food and drink and whatever else
they required. Boyle looked ugly and menacing at this proposal; but as he
could hardly compel, by fist or sword, courtesy from a backward host, he
might do nothing but scowl.

Their reluctant host made some amends for his discourtesy by providing
abundant meat and drink from his own table, conveyed by his manservant.
The claret was of such quality that, as Boyle pleasantly said, it might be it
traveled in the same bottom as he himself. He was now less grim, though
far from jovial, by the irresistible effects of good food and drink; so that
Jack ventured to ask, was he an officer, and had he been at Steenkirk? He
said, he knew of that fight, and 'twas a brave one, fought gallantly on both
sides. The boy replied, he was told it was a terrible slaughtering of men,
that accomplished nothing.

—Those that die in a fight, die quickly, unlike those that lie abed whim-
pering with a dropsy, a palsy, or a pleurisy; but they are all dead just alike.

—Some soldiers are recruited by compulsion, and 'tis none of their choice
to bear arms. Is it not very hard upon them, and a great wrong, that they
must either kill other men or be themselves killed?

—If a man falls into a turbulent sea, he must swim or drown. I do not
pity men that meanly despair, or struggle feebly till they sink beneath the
waves. It was not entirely of my seeking that I became a soldier. A younger
son of a younger son must do something. I applied myself to soldiering as

my trade, as a blacksmith might apply himself to his hammer and tongs, or a weaver to his loom: so that I raised myself up from an ensign, to a position of trust and authority.

Jack hoped, at these words, that Boyle would proceed to give his history, which he was sure would be a lively relation; but the man was not inclined to waste many words upon a hobbledehoy and a blear-eyed hoyden, that, having gorged and guzzled to excess, was slipping into a drowse. It must have been the spirit of his father rising up in him, that Jack did not give over, but continued to dispute.

—It was still of your choice, even it was a choice among some very few options. But I have heard there are men of honest station, who have been seized upon shallow pretexts, and compelled to take up arms and serve.

—That does not greatly surprise me. There are many sorts of compulsions. A child is compelled by his father, a servant by his master, a subject by his king; and why should a subject not be obliged to serve his king in war? It was every man's duty to bear arms for his lord in former times.

—It is by reason of their dependency, and owing to their youth or poverty, that the child and the servant must obey. And it is always with an expectation that the commands be just and lawful, and within their power to fulfill.

—It is not for the child or servant, or for the soldier, to quibble and question his superior. Orders must be obeyed.

—But surely an order that offends the laws of God or man ought never be obeyed. Suppose that you were commanded to cut the throat of this harmless, helpless woman sleeping here beside us—would you commit such a crime?

—Helpless she may be, but that she is harmless I very much doubt. Men are by their nature corrupt and under the sway of their appetites, which corruption may only be contained from breaking loose by good government. Every man has a superior set above him to keep him in his right course, and above the King there is God. I may not presume to dispute a command given by my superior, any more than I am permitted to doubt the wisdom and justice of God in Heaven.

—Not all men are wicked, and none are created so. There is that divine spark within them that keeps them honest, unless something perverts them from their natural bent. They should enjoy their liberty, and be at their own command, as long as they are peaceable and honest. Except they commit some wrong, their liberty is their birthright and cannot, or should not, be taken from them.

—This liberty whereof you speak, belongs only to propertied men, to elder sons of elder sons. You might as well propose that all men should share in wealth equally, for that is the only way they could be equal in freedom from command.

—So I do propose, said Jack, answering just as his father would. But Boyle, though he was amazed, and much diverted, to find such faculty of discourse in a rascally boy, only laughed at him: You are yet a child. When you are a man, you will think differently of the matter. The last word belonged to Jack, though he spoke it only whisperingly: That day will never come.

Pity 'tis that Boyle would not engage in further debate, for the boy was full ready to defend his proposition. After the flight of Lord Shaftesbury and the defeat of the whiggish party, during the years when Marius Bye could find little to occupy his pen, except dreaming of commonwealths, he devised a republic wherein the privileges of elder brothers, the cheats of brokers and badgers, and all attempts at anticipating markets were strictly forbidden; the relations of fathers and masters, with their children, apprentices, and servants, were exactly regulated; new agrarian laws were passed in order to break up great estates and restore the commons; to the end that, within a few generations, the wealth of the nation would be redistributed in such a fashion, that never again should any starve of want, or be reduced to beggary, except by their own demerit. These propositions he argued with his visitors many times over, until Jack had them by heart. Thus this homebred Hobbes, that acquired his philosophy in the camp and upon the field, might have been hard pressed to gain the victory.[2]

In the morning, Boyle again tried to impel his host to have him horsed, saying his business was urgent; but that gentleman replied, he was by no means so well provided with horse, nor did he have at that moment a trusted guide to take him forward. Nan said to Boyle, 'twould be only six mile more, to reach a house where she was certain they would have a better welcome. Jack had little faith in the chapwoman's assurances, and so he was agreeably surprised to find that this time she spoke truth. Their host, when they reached him about mid-day, was an open and agreeable baronet named Sir John Herewige. He greeted Nan kindly, saying he was glad to see she had brought him another guest, and he even took notice of Jack, asking if the boy was her kindred. He had been then at his dinner, which he broke off to welcome them; giving direction that Nan and Jack should have a dish with his servants, before he sat down again at his table, with Boyle beside him. The next morning saw Boyle mounted and upon his way. The chapwoman was in no such hurry to depart from a place where the beds were good, the food abundant, and the cost nothing. It happened to be a Sunday, when Sir John and some of his family attended mass in his private chapel, while the rest of his household went to the village church; for he required his servants to be good members of one communion or the other, without imposing his own; nor could it be seen that he favored his Papist over his Protestant servants, except in hiring. Sir John kept open house upon Sundays; but upon any day of the week those belonging to the parish could stop at his buttery and be refreshed. For the gentry there was always a bottle from his cellar. His hospitality won him such liking that his religious and political principles were winked at by most. It was generally believed that he was a man too good natured, and altogether too fond of his ease and of his table, to involve himself in plotting; which belonged rather to hungry-looked knaves, than to an open-handed baronet like Sir John Herewige.

Nan and Jack were seated with the servants and the small farmers in the buttery, which was a vast space, as good as the hall of many a country gentleman, when Sir John entered with his glass in hand and proposed his usual toast, To the King Over the Water. His kind eye lingered upon Jack, which prompted the boy to answer with a pledge he learned at his father's table. Confusion to Butterboxes and Timeservers, he cried, holding up his cup, whereupon Sir John laughed so heartily that he went into a fit of the hiccup, and left the room to seek relief. Jack was half-afraid he had committed a fault; on this point, however, he was reassured the next day, when Nan was preparing to depart. Sir John said to her that if she left Jack with him, he would make him his footboy. Nan, after a moment of surprise, began to deny him, saying that the boy was the son of her only brother, that she dearly loved, and she could not forgo his company. The baronet remonstrated to her, that 'twould be greatly to the boy's advantage to have such a place, and if she cared for him, she should rejoice to see him raised up from a stroller on the highway, at all too great a risk of being whipped from parish to parish. Nan began to blubber, saying, it might be truth, but the boy was all the kin or friend that she had in the world, and it was a very hard thing, to be asked to part with him. Jack was so moved by her tears that he was at the point of promising never to leave her, not for a world of riches. However, Sir John took up a cue she gave him concerning the loss to her of a second back to carry her goods; and, reaching out his purse, which was always well-supplied, he put two half-guineas in her hand, saying he hoped 'twould make amends for that part of her loss. It was certainly more than she would have dared ask; so that it would have been evident to a keener-eyed observer than Jack, how greatly the weight of broad coin put in her hand overbalanced the chapwoman's affection for her only friend. Nonetheless, she had the cunning to continue her show, saying, she was convinced, by his generosity to her, that he would be a kind master to her dear Jack. To the boy she said, she hoped he would not forget his poor Nan Trundle. Whereupon, as Jack was about to profess his affection and loyalty, which might have been a long-drawn speech, she said she could not stay another moment, lest her grief and misgivings overcame her. She set off at such a quick pace, no one could doubt she had a great anxiety to be away: fearing the baronet might repent of his freak, or Jack might lay claim to the money she got in Houndsditch for Delia's hair and clothes.

There was an almost fresh suit of livery in the house that needed only a few stitches to fit him perfectly. (It was made for a boy Sir John hired the previous winter in London, who mumped and moped at being brought to live in the country, until he ran away in the company of three silver spoons.) When Jack viewed himself in his livery (which was encrusted with an superabundance of buttons and trimmings), he was enchanted at his transformation from a dusty ragamuffin to a charming footboy: his waist was slender, his limbs long and delicate, and his face bore a mild, good-natured look, which gave his new master some confidence that this boy, at least, would not make away with his plate. He was in truth an ornamental and superfluous addition to a household that was supplied already with an excessive number of servants. His master was at first puzzled how to task him, his virtues being of a negative kind: he was not lazy, impertinent, glut-tonous, or disobedient; yet he was bashful, ticklish, and awkward, especially in dressing his master. At length it appeared that Jack was adept in serving at table, his manner and carriage being notably graceful, nothing like what would be supposed to belong to the companion of a female stroller. For that trifling duty he was principally employed, in addition to fetching and carrying. He was, withal, so willing and wishing to please, that his master was for the most part extreme indulgent toward him, and his footing in the family was something between that of a poor relation and a spaniel.

Sir John, who delighted in good cheer, could not relish his dinner unless there were guests to share it. The Grumbletonians of the parish—which were three small squires and two substantial yeomen—often made up a party. There were also, though residing more distantly and frequenting his table less often, some of the Romish religion that were always made welcome, which included a physician from Tunbridge Wells, a wealthy brewer retired from business, with his son, a gentleman-grazier, and a hop-dresser. Lastly, there was a species of back-door visitor, not unlike those who frequented the house of Marius Bye in his more prosperous days, that came and went at unseasonable hours, sometimes afoot and sometimes ahorseback. Sitting over their bottle, which was frequently renewed, the parish malcontents complained of the moneyed men that were driving the war for their own profit; of the shortage of good coin, which was owing, they said, to the Hogan-Mogans that were clipping English silver for profit. They said, the greater the tax, the greater the thievery. They spoke of the dishonest dealings of the King's Ministers and Councilors, who would be sent to the Tower or to Tyburn tree, if all were known. The Papists said, when they made a party at Sir John's table: That the great men of the Court and Council could be turned against William in a moment, upon the slightest encouragement; that his throne was tickle and he would soon take a tumble, if a bullet did not find him first. Moreover, the bad and scanty coin was working like a mine, to blow up his government. None of this talk was surprising to Jack, nor greatly differing from what had been said at his father's more frugal table (for, as might be supposed, Sir John was a lavishing host). The toasts that were proposed to the king over the water confused him, but the squeezing of oranges brought him to conclude, that they were only pledging their wish to send King William back to his homeland. I believe Jack was under too great impression of his master's kindness, joviality, and good cheer to be at all critical of the sentiments expressed at his table.[3]

His notion that he was among his father's party was strengthened when Ned Shift came upon a Yuletide visit. As Jack was serving, he perceived Shift had his eye upon him more than once; until he at last asked Sir John, where he got his sightly ganymede. Sir John answered that he was nephew to the chapwoman that carried letters between the sea-coast and the City. Shift then said, the boy carried himself too well, and his manner was too refined, for someone gadding about the country in the company of a gross drab. Jack had been uneasy under the man's scrutiny, and was not less so upon hearing these words; which, though they were not addressed to him, prompted a response. He said that the chapwoman had been kind to him when he was homeless and friendless; that neither a good heart nor a good demeanor were bought with gold. His father, though poor, was a book-learned man, who taught him himself, and also sent him to a school. Though this commentary was somewhat pert, it was delivered with a blush and a bashful stammer, so it did not offend; but ended any further inquiry into his breeding, at least at that time. Shift went, upon this occasion, by another name. He was as smooth and flattering to Sir John as to Marius Bye, though upon different themes, praising his host for his manly virtues, his gentility, his generosity, and his fidelity to a great cause. The two of them discoursed of men and means, rather than words and reasons. Sir John asserted that he could raise, arm, and horse, at a moment's notice, a gallant troop consisting of the servants of his household and the twenty-odd countrymen he treated in his buttery, certain they would be loyal to him to the death, in exchange for all the good food and drink that went down their gullets. To prove his boast, he conducted his visitor (Jack lighting their way) to a locked storeroom containing a number of great chests, whereof several were then opened to reveal a gleaming stock of helmets, cuirasses, sabres, horse-pistols, and carbines; sufficient, Sir John said, to furnish his men. Shift left, after a stay of five days, with a great deal more money than he had ever drawn from Marius Bye: Jack believes it was about thirty pounds, which was to be spent to raise a secret army and keep it in readiness. Jack thought much of his father as he waited on his master's table; he wondered if Mr. Shift yet visited him, to give him news of all the efforts going forward for the overthrow of the King.

Shift was not the only person to take notice of Jack's graceful bearing. There was in the family a pretty chambermaid of about his years, named Sally, who was besotted with love the moment she saw him in his livery. As he was a shy, backward lad and her passions were warm, she became an urgent suitor for his affection, seeking him out seven times a day, bringing him fairings and sweetmeats, fastening kisses on his blushing cheek. Poor Jack was greatly troubled how to manage her advances, knowing full well that however innocent Sally might be, if he accepted her clips and busses and hugs without any restraint, she would inevitably discover that he was not what he appeared. When bashfulness would no longer serve to withstand her amorous addresses, he told her he was pledged to another, but she would always be for him a friend and sister; which answer sent her away in tears, but only for an hour; then she was back again with questions and complaints: Wanting to know, who was this true love of his, and was she prettier than his Sally? And even if she was, she could not love him half as much. These various and diverting scenes could not be so private but that they were known and discussed by their fellow servants. Jack was condemned by all the females for his cold heart; whereas the men mocked him for a capon, saying, he kept his nutmegs in a box, to protect them from grinding and rubbing.

Among his household store of idle, gossipy servants, poor relations, and other parasites, Sir John kept a Sir John, a tame mass-priest for his chapel. This Romish black-coat was so unpresuming, and so trusting in the baronet's protection, that he rarely left the house and kept much to his chamber, where he would take his dinner whenever the baronet was entertaining the local

Grumbletonians. He could only with great urging be prevailed upon to visit the sick, and then would only venture his safety in the baronet's coach, with the curtains drawn. (Those of his religion, who desired to receive the sacrament from his consecrated hands, were obliged to come to him; which was no great hardship, as they would receive a good dinner from the kitchen of the baronet.) His dress and carriage were so discreet that he appeared to be an upper servant or else some humble kin of the baronet; so that, although it was generally known that Sir John kept a priest, few could describe him who were not themselves loyal members of that church. He had a very great fear that Seventy-Eight might come again; for, as he said to Jack, the infamous Titus Oates had been granted a pension by the Dutch usurper; and, his whipping forgotten, was again holding forth in London coffeehouses.[4] This timorous reverend took notice of Jack from his first entering the family, seeking to gain him as a convert to Rome. The baronet, though he himself did not tamper with the consciences of his servants, did not object to the priest's doing so, as it was his calling. The good father was as perplexed in his catechizing as Sally in her courtship; for Jack was utterly ignorant upon many points, yet able to catch unexpectedly at others and answer like a philosopher, such that it was utterly beyond the capacity of this mass-mumbler to counter him.

It was about six months since Jack joined the family, that Sir Priest was taken ill and unable to do his office that Sunday. The baronet paid a kindly visit to his bedside, and offered to send for the apothecary. The priest answered, he thought he would be well in a day or two, without any physic; but asked as a small boon, that Jack would bring him his dinner, and give him a little of his company; to which the baronet readily agreed. At the appointed time, Jack came bearing a dish of meat, which he put down beside the bed and was about to leave, thinking the priest asleep. A faint voice said, Jack, do not leave, I want your company. Is the door shut? For the cold air might prove fatal to me. Now open the curtain so I may see you. The poor man looked to be in a fever, his color high, his eyes haggard, and his skin sweating; so that Jack was much surprised when he said he was very chill, and would Jack get into the bed with him for a moment, to warm it. Jack, not knowing how to refuse a sick, trembling man, complied; only to be seized in a tight grip, and to have a hot breath at his ear, calling him a darling pigsney, a tasty sprig, a pretty fawn, with other words Jack never heard before. He was too surprised to cry out, and 'twould be to little vantage, for there was none to hear. The priest was holding him down and fumbling with his clothes, when Jack, struggling to regain his feet, clapped his knee hard into the man's privy parts, which allowed the frightened boy to make his escape. He could only suppose that the priest had discerned his sex, and meant to use him as his wife; though certain of the man's endearments confused him greatly, and made him wonder if the priest knew the difference between male and female. In all events, he perceived that he must straightway leave the house, before the priest shared his discovery with the master or the other servants. He went just as he was, his eyes full of tears, to tell Sir John that it was necessary for him to depart instantly: that he would ask no wages, nor keep his livery; but would depart as poor as he had been, before the kindest and best of masters had taken him up.

It may be supposed that the baronet was more than a little astonished by this urgent and tearful speech; but to the boy's departure he made no objection. For in truth, he was a useless mouth in a house already too well supplied with such. Whenever Sir John's steward was urging the baronet to have respect to his overburdened estate, he would instance Jack as a frivolous expense. Jack's onion-eyed dejection as he sought this interview did not escape notice: there must have been ears at the door, and tongues to carry the news to Sally, the lovesick chambermaid. She fell weeping into the boy's arms, saying, she would wander the world with him, if only he would have her. Jack was sadly troubled and perplexed to find that someone should bear such love to him upon a false surmise. He wished he could whisper in her ear the truth, but did not dare. When, a few minutes later, he came out from his chamber in his rusty old clothes, she gave a little cry and ran off. The spying servants concluded she was cured of her infatuation by his sudden uncasing and transformation into a poor stroller. But it was not so: she went away only to make an urgent bargain, sacrificing, it may be, a good portion of her wages, to get him a substantial cloak to keep him warm; for it was about a fortnight before Lady Day, and the weather still cold.

As Jack was shifting into his old coat and breeches, and gathering together his few possessions, his master sent for him. Jack hoped—Delia could not say in more particular what it was that he hoped, except he hoped that something might transpire, whereby he might stay. However, the motive of sending for him was only to carry letters to London, where he said he was intending, and for this Sir John tipped him four shillings, only to have Jack seize his hand and kiss it, weeping, saying again that he was the best and kindest of masters. The baronet could be reasonably certain that this boy at least would not make away with his plate. He did not suspect that when Jack set out upon the road, which he did at once, he in truth carried away something that did not belong to him.

It was a pamphlet he found upon a table, which he had idly taken up, only to discover that it was a work of his father's inditing that he recollected very well. Howsoever, although many portions were unaltered, at least in substance, there were whole passages interpolated, which he was sure were foreign, that seemed to change the meaning of the whole. His father had in the past complained of timorous printers who expunged passages they thought dangerous; so that Jack could only suppose the knavish printer rewrote what he doubted, and wrested its meaning in his ignorance. But he was not considering of the pamphlet, as he began a long trudging journey, but lamenting the cruel fate that took him from his dear master; for Sir John Herewige had been kinder to him than his father, or Jane, or Mrs. Witherby the schoolmistress, or Nan the chapwoman. ✠

The author reminds the reader that this is a true history, not a romance. Jack returns to the Dog and Bear Tavern. A dangerous questioning by Shift resolved in laughter. Jack is hired as a drawer. His conversations with Tom Found, his fellow servant. Plots, cabals, and public rioting. Mrs. Peatfoote seeks consolation. Jack seeks new employment.

MONG THE letters Sir John entrusted to him, was one to be delivered to his lady, who was on a protracted visit to her daughter, residing near Bromley, where she was brought to bed of her first child late in the year, and was yet weak and languishing. Although the house was out of the road by a few miles, it afforded Jack a place to pass the night, a pallet-bed being provided for him in the kitchen.

—What's this? Sir John has a wife? I never expected that. Why does this fool of an author only now bring her into his story?

—Sir, I have not seen fit to mention her before, for the reason just stated: she was away these many months, first to take the waters at Tunbridge Wells, and then upon this visit to her daughter's house, in expectation of the birth. Nor was her absence an occasion for remark. Sir John and his lady use each other civilly at all times; which is rendered easier by one or the other making long stops away from home: the lady visiting her kin, and Sir John going frequently to London upon his private business.

—Still, I think you might have mentioned her sooner, to avoid misunderstanding. I certainly thought there would be a wedding to conclude your little comedy.

—Oh, but consider, sir, I am scarce to blame if my readers take a false scent and bay at the wrong tree. I told you in my commencement that this is a true history, not a fable or romance; that I have only altered names and some few particulars, in recording the story Delia related to me. In all things else, my history is true to life. That you may be assured I do not trifle with you, I shall let you know, further, that Lady Mary Herewige enjoyed very good health when Jack delivered her husband's letter, and is presumed to be in good health down to this present day, as far as Delia is informed. If the baronetess has since then caught a dangerous cold, or had her coach overturn, or eat too many green plums, 'tis more than either of us know.

The other letters entrusted to Jack were to be left with Mrs. Peatfoote, the hostess of the Dog and Bear, where Jack and the chapwoman lodged upon his first being put in breeches. As Jack hoped to find the chapwoman there, this was very convenient; for, though he knew she could be deceitful in making her bargains, he could not but trust there was some truth in the professions of affection she made to him on parting; and he plainly recalled that she said to him, never to forget his Nan Trundle. Upon entering the tavern, the first person he encountered was Ned Shift, who took the letter addressed to him in a negligent manner, then asked Jack why he was out of his livery. Upon Jack's saying he parted from his master, Shift turned mistrustful. Laying hold of Jack and pulling him close, he demanded to know why an idle useless boy, such as he, would leave such a comfortable place, when he could never hope to have another like it: unless he had some other intention in coming to London, than delivering a few paltry letters.

Jack gaped and stuttered and looked, no doubt, very shame-faced and guilt-ful. He thought there was nothing else for it, but to tell Mr. Shift all, revealing himself as Delia, and pleading for his aid in effecting a reconciliation with her father. —This past Sunday, Jack began falteringly, the mass-priest was sick and kept to his bed, but asked that I be the one to bring him his dinner. When I went to his chamber, he said he was exceeding chill, and asked me to get into his bed to warm him. —Hah, hah, hah! The foul old boy-lecher! Did he make you his catamite? Did he butter your buns? Did he anoint you in your mouth or in your bum? Jack's look of squeamish enlightenment was a further occasion of mirth. At last the boy found words to say, he had not understood the man's intent, but was so greatly startled that he struck him a hard blow between the legs in the struggle to escape him. Then, fearful for what the consequences might be, he went at once to his master and begged to be dismissed. Shift roared with laughter until he could scarce catch his breath. I think it fortunate there was no one else in the room to whom the story could be repeated, or Jack would have had some opprobrious byword fastened on him, which he could never shake off as long as he wore breeches. Instead, when his laughter was spent, Shift said to him, As you have given me such an occasion for mirth, I shall do you a good turn. Whereupon, he called for the hostess, saying to her, This boy is very graceful and discreet, and knows how to serve gentlemen. He would be a better servant for you than the clumsy sot you presently employ as a drawer, and no doubt cheaper to keep. Upon this recommendation, Mrs. Peatfoote was persuaded to take him on. He was sent out in company with Tom Found, the pot-boy, to a nearby salesman, where he was to be provided with good clothes, towards settling the man's score. His new mistress was well pleased with his appearance, the drawer was turned out, and Jack was put to serving the gentlemen upstairs; which was presumed to be a place of greater honor than that belonging to Tom, who filled cans for the neighborhood that came in at the street door, and fetched jugs to the daily customers. When the two boys had a breathing-space to sit together on the bench, they would dispute which had the worse service: the one bearing great jugs of small beer to thirsty journeymen, the other running up and down the stairs at the whims of gentlemen that desired a fresh bottle or clean glass, or some dainty snap to be fetched from a cookshop or confectioner. If the contest were judged by which boy fell into exhausted sleep first, then it was Tom who had the harder service, for he lay as one of the dead in their shared bed; whereas Jack would lie awake for a time, reflecting upon his singular fortune, and lamenting afresh that he had so foolishly parted from his kind master; for he understood from what Shift said to him, that it was the priest who had reason to fear discovery and play mum.

The gentlemen that frequented the upper rooms of the Dog and Bear were not all deserving of that name. There were two parlors on the first floor, and four small rooms on the second that were furnished as bedchambers, though used for drinking and caballing. Each room seemed to be reserved for a particular knot of malcontents, though there was congress among them. Shift kept a station in the back parlor, which he occupied as a casual clerk's office, for he was often surrounded by heaps of papers and printed pamphlets. The party that met there was large but discreet; for though Shift remained friendly to Jack (and could scarce refrain from smirking), little was said while he remained in the room: excepting on one occasion, when they were all well-soused, he overheard them dividing up rich places that would soon be vacant, and pronouncing hangings and beheadings upon current office-holders. The party in the front parlor was of a different character, such that Mrs. Peatfoote would oftentimes attempt to persuade the parties to exchange chambers, but was unable to effect it. For the front parlor was occupied by a gang of roisterers, damme-men, and cashiered officers from King James his army, that would make such a racket it could be heard in the street. Jack was oftentimes sent to close the window but only got kicked for his pains. His mistress would then wheeze up the stairs and beg the gentlemen to have a care for the reputation of her house, which was a notion to stir great mirth among these drunken revelers, who were not moved by her pleas, nor abashed by her threats; for they all wore a sword, and some were armed with pistols; and at any rate they were sufficient in number to dare a reluctant tipstaff to do his worse, and the devil take him. But this was by no means a daily annoyance, for oftentimes there would be men in their midst that would keep them under better rule. Sir John Herewige and other gentlemen would have a drink with them and settle their score, which might otherwise go unpaid. Major Boyle also appeared among them, and when he was present they were better settled. None of these swaggerers had any constant employment or more than some small annuity to keep himself. They were sometimes tasked as messengers, and sent flying to the north upon errands to disloyal lords and gentlemen of that far country; but most were so addicted to soaking and gaming that they could not be relied upon. They called each other captain or major, either because they had once been such, or else boasted of a secret commission and a sworn company of men in readiness to rise upon a signal. (Which men were as credible as Lord Shaftesbury's brisk boys of foregone days, and might be the self-same, if they could battle on crutches. Howbeit, I am reminded as well of that lord's saying to Marius Bye, that even a blunt sword may draw blood; for 'twas no doubt upon that basis that these swaggerers were patronized and abetted by more circumspect plotters.)

In going in and out of these sundry chambers, Jack must certainly have overheard a vast deal of treacherous talk; yet I was unable to draw many particulars from Delia, nor could she give an exact description of any of these men. In truth, Jack was much afraid of the roistering officers, who used him roughly upon occasion; whereas the plotters who assembled in the other chambers, were cautious in speaking before him, sometimes taking the drink from his hands at the door, or bidding him leave it there and depart. What he did hear was mostly conspiratorial cant, to which he could assign little meaning. Nonetheless, I think it a great pity he was not more curious and enterprising, for I am certain a multitude of plots were laid in those upper chambers, which might be now succeeding. But alas, Jack had not Jane's facility for espial, but only did as he was bid and sat wearily upon the bench whenever he was not wanted. Consequently, what Delia could relate of these men was little to the purpose, though she was tediously full of particulars concerning Mrs. Peatfoote and Tom Found.

Although both boys were worked hard, Mrs. Peatfoote was indulgent toward Jack and prone to give Tom the heavier duties; which might have caused some jealousy, but Jack would make amends by going snacks on any small spills or vails he got. Tom was moved by his fellow's generosity, as well as by envy, to say to him one day: 'Tis true you carry yourself very genteel, what makes the tip-merry gentlemen more generous. But I am gentle by birth. You must know, my name is not Tom Found, which I am called only for being a foundling. My true name is secret. It was by the negligence or wickedness of my nurse that I was left on the parish. I trust that my parents have not despaired, and search for me yet, and that they will come for me if they can but get news of me. An' if you doubt me, I have certain proof, which is the needlework that swaddled me. I know not whether 'twas my mother or her maids that worked it, but 'tis the token for my parents to know me, and I keep it always with me. With that he reached into his shirt to extract a short length of coarse linen, that was worked in red with a clumsy brede-stitch. Jack might have replied, his own name was concealed and he too was of better family than he seemed; yet it was prudent to say as little as might be, and he was glad not to be asked to give his history. He only replied, he wished his friend might enjoy such a happy discovery and change to a more prosperous condition. In the course of another such conversation, he was less discreet, and heedlessly risked betraying himself. Tom had begun a discourse on the subject of women's privities, concerning which he was but ill-informed. Jack unwisely corrected him, thereby revealing an intimate understanding of women that was beyond his years, especially considering that, in all other instances, it was Tom who was more knowing. To explain himself, he could only say that he had a twin sister, who confided in him and he in her. She married suddenly, which infuriated their father into banning her the house and he has not seen her since; yet he hoped, in spite of spite, to rejoin her one day.

It was troubling to Jack that he could be sincere with no one, but must invent falsehoods, and shun all confidence; yet he well knew that 'twas better to be kicked in the breeches by the drunken officers than to come among them in gown and petticoat. Thus, he was far from content in his present service, but knew not how to remedy its defects. He found an opportunity to creep humbly to Sir John Herewige, and to say how happy he had been in his service, and regretted leaving it, which was upon a false surmise; but that gentleman showed no inclination to take him up again. Jack was disappointed as well in his hopes of reencountering the chapwoman, having understood that the Dog and Bear was a post office for the plotters, where she was obliged to make frequent stops. She, however, having knowledge that he was now attached to the tavern as a drawer, made such running visits that he had no notice of it until after her departure. Having asked his fellow Tom to give him word, he was able to surprise her on the next occasion, saying to her, Why, Nan, you are in such haste to go without a word to me. Did you not tell me, never to forget my Nan Trundle? And have you so quickly forgot your Jack Trundle? Being thus penned and obliged to excuse herself, Nan began to cry, saying, Oh Jack, I have suffered such hardships since we last met that I go in fear everywhere. For upon the road near Southwark, I was beset by footpads who took all that I had and beat me sore. —What, answered

Jack, was there no gallant company of redcoats to rescue you this occasion?
You do me wrong in telling such a tale. For I did not intend to upbraid you,
or to demand the money that is mine. Though now I am reminded of it, I
think you ought to pay me, for I am sure you have it in one of your pockets,
or stitched into your clothes, or concealed in the lining of your wallet. The
chapwoman let out a screech at the unmannerly boy presuming to handle
her so roughly (which in truth he had not done). The ringing of a bell, and
a call of Jack, Jack!, relieved them from playing out a scene that could yield
advantage to neither. He had spoke truth to the chapwoman; he was ready
to forget past ills in his eagerness to be away. Without her, Jack could not
conceive of how else to maintain himself; and if he left his current employment, he feared he might fall into something worse.

The Dog and Bear bore no very good character, though 'twas said in its
vindication, that it served wholesome drink and 'twas not a bawdy-house. The
swaggering officers were a great nuisance. Whenever they were outrageous,
Mrs. Peatfoote was obliged to make humble apologies to her neighbors (one
of them being a godly joiner named Wedge that was a steward and informer
of the Reforming Society), saying she was a widow with only two boys to
help her, and she had no power but her pleas to get them into better order.[1]
In truth, as she acknowledged to the boys, she did not in the least wish these
officers to take their custom elsewhere; for they drew in better customers
after them, in the form of gentlemen who relished their bold talk. Moreover,
there were four treason taverns in London, each frequented by a gang of
plotters and grumblers: Mrs. Peatfoote would humor any number of bullies,
cutthroats, and cannibals before she'ld risk that the Old King's Head, the
Fountain, or the Blue Posts should get their custom away from her. She was
disadvantaged in that her trade was only supplying drink and letting rooms;
whereas these other traitor-nests profited by harboring highwaymen and
receiving their goods, or more commonly by providing women. She lamented
her ill fortune in having an informer for the Society so near her door, for
she was certain her neighbor, the sanctified joiner, would have her before
a magistrate, if a strange woman so much as showed herself at a window.

When the officers were troublesome, it was in being loud and boisterous,
so that people in the street and in the next houses could plainly hear their
blasphemies and pitcher-oaths. This was an annoyance that did not threaten
the peace, for which their hostess offered humble words in appeasement.
So things went, until a certain day that was an anniversary sacred to their
cause, when they drank themselves into a dangerous pitch of fervor, then
carried their riot into the street, stopping passengers and demanding that

they declare their allegiance, whether to the Dutch usurper, or to the Rump, or to their rightful king. Mrs. Peatfoote ran out beseeching them to have a care, but in the confusion she was knocked down, which so staggered her that Tom and Jack had to bear her into the house. Soldiers were called forth in sufficient number to block the street and effect a good many arrests, that went first to the Compter and from thence to Newgate. Mrs. Peatfoote lay moaning in bed when her neighbors came to congratulate her, whether innocently or of malice, upon being rid of such pests, which was no consolation to her. She well knew that her house would be a suspect place, so that both the prudent conspirators and the Grumbletonians would take alarm and seek new quarters. So it was: the next two weeks the rooms above lay empty, and the only custom was from the neighbors, which would provide a living too low to keep both boys, and she was obliged by the parish to keep Tom for another two year. This Jack understood from Tom; accordingly, when his mistress bid him come to her, he expected to be turned out of his place. She began by asking, how old was he? It might have been wiser to deduct two years, but Jack answered truthfully that he was sixteen this past November.[2] —As old as that, said Mrs. Peatfoote, and she stroked his cheek tenderly, so that the tears started in his eyes at the thought of leaving a mistress who was grown so kind. —As old as that, and your cheek so soft, I marvel at that. And so slender in the waist, too. I think, Jack, you have not been feeding well enough, is that it? I believe Jack would have blubbered at her motherly regard, if not for a suspicion that his mistress was petting and eyeing him very much as Jane had handled the baker's boy. Mrs. Peatfoote had one hand upon his neck while the fingers of the other toyed and probed and pinched, to test where he was well grown, and where a mite too thin: now it was his arm, now his neck, now upon his waist, then his thigh, then back to his waist but a little lower, and again upon his thigh, only higher. Jack blushed and wriggled, which his mistress took as a cheering sign that he was riper than would appear. Mrs. Peatfoote was a plump, bouncing widow of about thirty years, who had lain single in her cold bed for the two years since Mr. Peatfoote was put below ground in his; which she would not have endured two weeks, if she could figure to herself how she might get a husband without gaining a master. She admired a sweating porter more than a perfumed fopling, and she was by no means as enamored of Jack as were poor lovesick Sally and Sir John the mass-priest. But what she chiefly desired was a sound, safe bedfellow who would be atop her for a bout or two by night, but beneath her all the rest of the day; and she had been wondering whether Jack could suit her requirements. She was much inflamed by his blushing and wriggling, and I believe she would have haled him to her bed for a trial of his ability, had she not been interrupted just then by Ned Shift, come to offer consolation on her mischance. Jack rushed from the room in shamefaced flight, for the widow's inching grope was moments from making a discovery.

Jack, having packed his gear, was exchanging farewells with Tom Found, and getting his fellow's counsel on seeking a new place, when Shift came upon him. As I doubt the widow confided in her visitor, he must have witnessed enough of the scene he broke in upon to interpret it, for he was smirking broadly: —Hah, hah, hah, you are a finicking boy, you are mighty squeamish in your feeding. You wonnot have the fish and you wonnot have the fowl. To scorn an amorous mass-priest is one thing, but you are a green fool to naysay a lusty, lively widow that is only twice your years. But you may wash your blubbered face and come along with me. I'll do you another good turn and help you to a new master. I assure you he'll not put covetous hands upon you, unless for a baptism. Though Jack resented the man's smirking, this was an offer that might not be refused. He therefore bid a last farewell to Tom Found (who was, as he said to him, his only friend) and went along with Shift. He was led but a short distance to one of the dogholes that lie crammed together in the narrow courts festering the environs of St. Clement Danes. They entered a shop that seemed to belong to a poorish ironmonger or botcher; Jack was left wondering, with many misgivings and much distrust of his guide, how the person keeping such a place could be in need of a servant, or able to maintain one. Upon Shift's rapping the counter, a voice from the rear of the shop bellowed out: Who's there? I'm coming. The diminutive, gorbellied man who then came forward, wearing a blue apron over his clothes, was his father's old friend, Sidrach Gryce.

—I have brought you a boy, said Shift, that will suit you better than that crew of blackguards you employ, who look so ill-intentioned that people will cry "Stop, thief!" just upon suspicion. This one has a face as guileless as a newborn babe; if he has a fault, 'tis that his face is a true index to his character. However, if you instruct him carefully in his duties, I believe he'll be as true as any you are like to find fit for your purpose. I'll tell you what I know of him. Whereupon, to Jack's shame and confusion, Shift gave a full account of his time in Sir John Herewige's house, with the attempt upon him by the priest, not sparing any particulars, and concluded by saying: The boy chastely considered that he must himself be to blame, and departed at once from the best place he was ever like to get. He next became a drawer in an alehouse near Covent Garden, where he continued some months, until his lecherous mistress desired to initiate him into manhood. I trust she meant to put him on top, or else he would snap like a twig under her bulk, or melt to a puddle from her heat. Having narrowly escaped the toils of a ramping, all-devouring widow, he flies to you for sanctuary. Before Sir John took him up, he was carrying a pack for the chapwoman that conveys secret letters and outlawed men for the Select Number; therefore I judge him of sufficient character and fidelity to serve you.

Gryce heard Shift's lively narration as solemnly as a sermon, remarking very gravely to Jack: You did well to reject the blandishments of Rome, and the lures of a wicked woman. Although your years are oftentimes an age of wantonness, you have shown yourself to be of a pure, clean, upright spirit. If you continue as you have begun, you may hope to be accepted by godly brethren who will guide your steps in the paths of righteousness. Which speech Jack hardly knew how to answer, being further nonplussed by observing that Shift had thrust his handkerchief between his teeth, like a fop, in order to choke back a laugh. Jack stammered some few words, thanking him for his kindness and hoping to be always deserving of it. Shift departed, his handkerchief still between his teeth, leaving Jack with his new master. He expected to be instructed in his duties but was only put in charge of the shop for the afternoon. There was a paper pinned to the counter giving the price of sundry wares. If anyone asked for his master, he was to say only that his master was out and he did not know when he would return. So far from standing at the door and calling "What d'ye lack," he was told to stay within and not show himself. After repeating his injunctions, to answer no questions and remain within, Gryce went up the stairs and gave Jack the charge of his shop; which, as there was nothing in it worth more than a groat, I think he might safely do. The reader may consider how low were Jack's spirits at this juncture, how he regretted the meanness of his place, and wished that he had never left his kind master, Sir John, or never parted from Nan Trundle; or that he was yet an ink-spotted girl, taking down the dictation of her gouty father. He wished, moreover, that he had not departed from his too-kind Mistress Peatfoote in such a great hurry that morning, for he had missed his dinner and was now mighty hungry. (My reader, haply, is so fortunate in his state and condition, that he does not know what it is to be alone in a bare, poor room, with a lean belly aching to be filled; but I know these sensations too well, and feel my stomach tighten in sympathy with Jack's.)

Jack was not left to his lonesome meditations for long. He had been there about an hour, when a rough man came into the shop and demanded to see his master, who Jack denied as he was instructed to do. The visitor was not to be so easily put off, however, and answered angrily: You little lying whoreson rogue. I know he's lurking within, or else close by. Tell me where he is or 'twill go hard with you. Jack, though beginning to tremble, answered, Indeed, no, he is gone out. The man shook his fist in his face and said, I know I have not mistook the shop. Your master is a dwarfish, big-bellied man with a thundering voice, is he not? Jack said, I know not. I know nothing of him. I was only hired and put in this place this very day. For however frightened Jack might be, and it required but little to unnerve him, Marius Bye had taught his child well; if Gryce crept down the stairs to listen, as I suspect he did, I think he took a better opinion of the boy than the recommendation of Shift could give him. The man discharged further insults and upbraidings, but left without violence. A half-hour later, a more gentlemanlike visitor entered, in search of a hinge of a certain make. He was very pleasant to the boy as he rummaged helplessly in search of the item, asking him a variety of innocent questions, as to his name, his age, and was he happy in his place, and what manner of man his master was. To all which, beyond giving his name as Jack (which he could not well avoid doing), he answered, I know not, sir, or I cannot say, sir. The gentleman did not grow angry at his foolish answers; though the hinge could not be found, he purchased two dozen dog-nails, and in payment gave Jack a shilling, saying he might chop up the change for being such a civil, handsome lad. Adding, if he would like a pleasanter place, he could come along with him this minute, and he would be made a footboy in a fine house in Bread Street. Jack was not such a green fool, not to mistrust a man that was so unaccountably friendly to him. He declined to leave without giving any notice, saying, would the gentleman let him know the name, so as he might consider of it. But the gentleman took offense, saying, if he were that ungrateful not to leap at such an offer, it would be withdrawn, and upon Jack's further denial, he departed in a high, angry manner.

After these two encounters, Jack was inclined to suspect that his loyalty had been tested by accomplices of his new master: and yet there was but the one steep narrow stair, which Gryce had climbed to the first floor, so that it was impossible someone should come or leave without Jack noting it. Near the end of the day, there was a commotion on the street: not as great, certainly, as the riot of the officers that brought out the guard; but sufficient to draw everyone within earshot to a window or door. Jack, however, kept within, as he was bid to do by Gryce. A short while later he was called to come up the stair, into a room something jumbled in its furnishings, though they were of a quality befitting a much better dwelling. There was a bed with good curtains, a substantial wardrobe, and a table too large for the room, with three chairs to it, his new master seated at the middle. He said to him: Jack, I am your master in this world, who you must obey in all things, and strive to satisfy. But who is your one master, both in this life and the life to come, to whom you owe supreme loyalty and obedience? I am sure Jack looked stupid at this, for he expected only to be given instructions for shutting up the shop. He rallied his wits to answer, The Lord Jesus Christ, our Savior. Gryce proceeded to catechize the boy, concerning baptism, grace, election, and salvation, for a full hour by St. Clement's bell. Poor Jack was graveled by questions that would not puzzle a workhouse boy. But as he knew nothing of orthodoxy, and was as ignorant of the Book of Common Prayer as he was of the Quran, he oftentimes hit upon an answer that was acceptable to the old Catharan. 'Twas the only solace in a perplexing and troublesome day that they supped at a good eating-house where he was allowed to eat his fill. It was not until the next morning that he was given a task, though 'twas only to carry a packet, which was closely wrapped and sealed, to a cheesemonger on Leadenhall Street. I am certain there was a spy set at his tail, to report whether he loitered or spoke to anyone along the way, which he had been strictly enjoined not to do. Upon his return, there was another packet of similar appearance awaiting him, except the seals were not properly affixed; which Jack indicating to his master, he answered, Never mind, never mind. Take it as it is, for 'tis needed. They again ate heartily at a chop-house; and in the afternoon his master again catechized him. Jack, perceiving it was *cuius regio, eius religio*, answered as he thought his new master would wish.[3] It was only after the third bout of catechizing, by which time Jack could exactly expound absolute election and reprobation, that Gryce decided to retain him. His first act was to carry the boy to sundry clothes-dealers, where he got him three suits of clothes: a livery, something smirched on close view, and a wig to be worn with it; leather breeches and apron, like an artisan's apprentice; and also some handsomer riggings, such as would belong to a prosperous trader's child. These bargainings naturally catched the boy's attention: he observed that Gryce did not expend a tenth part of the words that the chapwoman would consider necessary to the haggling; yet when he paid over his money, it was accepted frowningly; so it seemed he had his own method of cheapening goods. Jack was much puzzled to understand what his master's trade might be; he knew only that it must be some secret undertaking relating to the same Old Cause, which his father, the chapwoman, and Sir John Herewige all endeavored to fulfill. ✣

CHAPTER 13

Jack is introduced to Izaak Bushrod and required to swear a solemn oath. He falls in with a button-maker of great ability. A project to multiply the wealth of the nation.

AT **GRYCE'S** bidding, Jack put on the leather breeches and apron for his daily apparel, so that he was to all appearances an iron-monger's boy, except the flock-bed he slept in, and the dinners he eat, were a vast deal better than the common lot. He was tending the shop as instructed by his master, when in popped the gentle-man who offered him a place in Bread Street and then waxed angry upon his refusal. This time he nodded civilly at the boy as he said: The wheels are loose on the carriage. 'Twill give way soon. Whereupon, instead of rummaging the shop for spindles or pins, Jack replied, Yes, sir, will you come up the stairs to my master, sir?, as he had been instructed to do, upon hearing any such expression regarding wheels coming off. Gryce stood to meet his visitor, then said, Jack, stay. This is Mr. Izaak Bushrod, who is come to induct you into our society. (Jack could not guess the meaning of his master's words, unless he was about to be dipped in the Thames, and thereby be made a member of their conventicle, whether he would or no.) It is no slight thing, to swear your faith in a solemn undertaking, and then to fail your companions and violate an oath. Howsoever praised or rewarded in this world, such treachery can only merit endless torment in the eternity hereafter. You understand that, Jack?

Jack answered this ominous speech by saying that he understood it very well, and therefore could not swear an oath unless he understood what he was to engage to do, lest it be beyond his abilities or for some ill intention. Why, said Gryce, surely you comprehend that we serve the cause of England, and are banded together to drive the Dutch invader from our land. Jack said, he had indeed given his word to the chapwoman and some others, never to betray his friends; yet he had been told as well, by an officer come over the sea, that it was necessary to obey all commands, even if it was to murder an innocent; this he would never engage to do, nor to perform any evil part, however good the cause. Gryce scowled, declaring, in his best kill-cow manner, I did not think a boy, who is scarce able to distinguish prevenient from irresistible grace, would bandy words with me regarding the righteousness of my commands. Whereupon Jack at once replied, 'Tis only that I would know what it is I swear to do before I swear it. (I believe, and so does Delia, that Gryce was not yet willing to trust Jack so far as to explain his business to him.) It was at this point that Bushrod interposed, saying, If the lad is squeamish about swearing before he knows the undertaking, 'tis a token he can be trusted. A mere rogue would have no regard to swearing and forswearing as the wind shifts. As Gryce yet looked sullen, Bushrod undertook to open up to Jack the business whereto he was entered.

Bushrod took from his purse two coins, which he held out to Jack saying, What think you of these shillings? Are they good coin or naught? Jack shrank away, crying out in dismay, I wonnot touch 'em, I wonnot take 'em up. I'll sooner cut off the hand that touched the money, than be forced to take up arms and be a soldier! 'Tis a mean, murderous, skulking business! Bushrod gave out a roar of laughter; Gryce so far forgot that he was one of the Saints, as to smirk as broad as any sinner. When their merriment was spent, Bushrod assured the boy that there was no danger in touching the shillings, that they were not about to trepan him into being a soldier. He was only to examine them, and note their quality, for a reason that would shortly be given. Jack did as he was bid and inspected the coins: One was of good Queen Elizabeth's reign, her image worn and all but effaced by its passage through countless hands, till-boxes, purses, and pockets; though 'twas as yet but lightly touched by the clipper's shears. The other piece bore the image of Charles the Second, its border regular and properly edged. Pressed to give his opinion, Jack said, They both seem good coin to my eye, the one being an ordinary shilling, though better than many; the other is a rare good coin, as fine as it was just come from the Mint, which no one would choose to spend whilst he had worse to serve the purpose.[1] Bushrod said, Look again at the image of the king on the coin you admire. 'Tis an uncommonly good likeness of the man. Upon this hint, Jack gave a second look, whereupon he saw that the figure was strangely altered: the nose was sunken with disease and the mouth turned up in a lecherous smile. His look of surprise gave the men further amusement, Bushrod remarking to him, Both coins are freshly minted, and, as you perceive, 'tis work as fine as they do in the Tower.[2] Your master and I are agents to put these good coins out to the public, where they are sorely needed. For poor men, lacking money, can get no credit, and shopkeepers, burdened with debt, break and run away, or else commit some desperate act.

—This is no murder, said Gryce, in his rough, ranting manner. This is preserving men from self-murder or other wickedness they might commit for lack of good coin, the Dutch tyrant having sent all our good money oversea, to pay for his war.

—Men seldom feel much gratitude to the coiner, upon discovering that they have been passed false money.

—As you have seen for yourself, such coin will pass very readily. If a man should scrutinize it so nearly as to have some doubt, he will only resolve to spend it at once, instead of putting it away like a miser. Why should a usurper have sole authority to declare what coin is lawful? Or how is it just or right that a gang of moneyed men in Parliament may declare bank paper to be as good as gold, which is an arrant, rascally cheat?[3]

—It is no murder, certainly. But is it not a species of theft, to pass false coin?

—Our trade is to make and vend good coin. Those we sell it to know full well 'tis of our own making. If a chandler sells a man a candle that happen to set a house afire, he is not thereby guilty of arson. There is no sin in coining, no more than there is in any man pursuing his craft or his calling, or selling his goods to those who want 'em. The coining of money is nowhere condemned in the Bible. No earthly creature can declare it wrong, if God has not. 'Tis the mark of a tyrant to claim a monopoly over any property or work of man's hands.

This argument, though exceeding specious, resembled propositions that his father would put forward. Accordingly, Jack made no further question, professing himself satisfied and ready to pledge his faith. Gryce, taking up his Bible, then told Jack the oath he was to repeat: I swear upon the Holy Word of our Savior, by whose grace, and by whose grace only, I hope to be saved: that I will never blow, squeak or peach my fellow, or otherwise provide informations against any of our gang, whether it be out of a wicked greed for reward, or a craven terror of death, or any other motive whatsoever. I do also acknowledge and admit, that treachery and oath-breaking are the gravest of sins, whereof th'Almighty grants no forgiveness.

Jack perceived the flawed theology in Gryce's conjuration, but restrained his itch to object, meekly repeating the words after him. I am surprised he was so bold as to question his choleric master as far as he did. As I pieced together Delia's rambling tale, I noted that the longer he was in breeches, the more Jack gained assurance and displayed a certain quarrelsomeness, at least (like his father) in words. I wonder how such a transformation should come to pass: whether it might be due to the frictions of the garment upon the skin, which thicken, congeal, and coarsen the animal spirits, which then transmit their occult qualities to the brain; so that the meek, soft, and pliable person in coats, becomes a bold, forward, contentious being when breeched. I must note that this operation obtains also in reverse: for Delia is by no means shrewish or froward when she is in the habiliment belonging to her sex.

The oath being sworn, Gryce took the Bible from his hands, which he put reverently upon his table. He then opened the door of the wardrobe, saying, with his usual violence: Get in. Do not make question. Do as I say. Get in. (Jack could only suppose there was to be a further test of his pliancy, by being locked within a wardrobe for some hours.) Once he was inside, Gryce reached over his head to release a latch; which caused the back of the wardrobe to swing open, giving entry into a room of the same proportions as the one behind him, and similar in its furnishings. He stepped through another wardrobe to enter, being prodded to do so by Gryce and Bushrod. A man with spectacles upon his nose was seated at a table next the window. He looked up sourly to say: Such distractions are a great hindrance to my work; Bushrod responding, We are heartily sorry for the disturbance. But we have a new boy that we consider will be useful, whose fidelity is now pledged to our cause. —We have boys enough already, and they are of no use to me. They are all of 'em lazy botchers.

Jack, who was close enough to spy the work upon his table, cried, Was it you who made that masterful coin? This simple remark was sufficient to provoke a faint, crooked smile. —What coin was it? Oh, that one, of the poxed Charles. I'll show you some others that are as good or better. He put down his spectacles (whereupon Jack knew him to be the gruff, threatening man that came to the shop seeking his master), and opened a little cabinet full of coins, which were each wrapped up as carefully as a fine lady's jewels. He took them out, one by one, to display to Jack's admiration, calling his attention to sundry particulars. Gryce, perceiving his softened mood, said, We intended to use the boy as a runner, but you may have him if you choose. Which remark only provoked him to put away his coins, saying, he would have no more boys; he wished they would let him in peace to carry on his work. Whereupon Gryce and Bushrod conducted Jack down the stair, the building corresponding in all particulars to its neighbor. There was a small workshop in the fore, where a boy pretended to making buttons; in the rear and in the cellar were four more boys, that were engaged in striking and finishing a heap of coin. Bushrod amiably explained the process to Jack, though he used such hard, mouth-filling words that Jack understood more by observation. The boys paused to stare and mock at Jack by way of welcome, which provoked Gryce to bluster at them to muzzle their mouths and do their jobs. This excursion completed Jack's initiation into the business. There was a second concealed passage in the cellar, which they took to return to the adjoining tenement; from there they departed to eat a good dinner.

The boys employed by the coiners answered well to Shift's description of them: for they were the very refuse of mankind, being recruited from the ashes of the glass-houses, or found lying upon the filth under stalls and bulks.[4] They might be supposed to have been generated or concocted from the combustive heat of their filthy beds, they could give so little account of themselves, beyond an uncertain recollection of some wretched doghole swarming with starveling brats. Those that outlived their brutal abandonment were not to be pitied, for they themselves were without pity or tenderness: knowing full well that they were despised, shunned, and destinate to the rope. Paid in coin of their own making, they applied themselves to every vice obtainable. Their youth might preserve them from the gallows for the moment, and they cared not a whit for tomorrow. They seemed to Jack the very confirmation of Gryce's dogmas, for it was scarce possible to imagine a crew more certainly reprobate and doomed to eternal torment. They seemed to think so themselves, without caring, considering the afterlife a jest. Certainly their master never troubled to catechize them as he did Jack. One among them, who was called George Have-Face, knew the whore that was his mother and sometimes carried her a purse of bad shillings; which seemed to Jack to mark him as not altogether lost to grace. They were all of them named John or Tom or Jack, with one or two being George or Bill; what other name they owned was only some byword with which they christened one another. Jack was forced to answer to Jack Puny, there being already two Jacks before him, Jack Shuffle-Up and Jack Brawny.

Aside from pretending to tend the shop, Jack's daily business was to carry new-minted coin to customers, whereof the greatest share went to Bushrod, who lived just off the Strand. He had at the window a sign, bidding all who wished to know their fortune, and secure good health, to mount the stair; for his public trade was as an astrological physician. He knew no more of astrology than he read in Lilly, no more of medicine than he read in Culpeper.[5] However, he wore a great bushy wig and spoke with much assurance, larding his speech with hard words that would gravel a learned gownsman to define, as they were of his own coining, being mere gabble coated in a Latin wash to help them pass. To give himself the greater credence, he sold an almanac bearing his name, which was only a thieving compilation made by some poor hack he employed. With his dog-Latin, his pompous bearing, and his almanac, he got himself some custom. Though there were a certain number of gouty, pursy, poxy persons who went up the stairs, by far the greatest traffic was of those seeking a cure for a chronic leanness of the purse. These visitors I am sure were liker to be satisfied by their consultation with the doctor. In regard to this common ill he possessed an infallible panacea: namely, a chest containing a hundred plausible shillings, that could be had for just four marks of good money; which medicine the patient might take *ad libitum* until his distressful condition was cured. All that the neighborhood noted of Bushrod, from the clutter of people coming and going, was that he seemed to be a popular and successful practitioner. I wager he gained some patients merely from the fine impression produced by the concourse of people coming and going from his chambers. Jack went to him in sundry guises, sometimes as a lackey, othertimes as a shopkeeper's boy or a youth of good family, no one being like to note his appearance with any attention.

When he had been with his new master for a fortnight, he ventured to ask leave to visit his friend Tom Found at the Dog and Bear, but met with a furious refusal, being told: Look not back to Sodom.[6] He thought it hard, and he thought it strange, that he should be held in check, whereas the blackguard boys of the mint were let loose each night to roam the town with a pocketful of false money. It was a particular grievance that every Sunday, when Jack Shuffle-Up and his rope-ripe fellows might do as they pleased, Jack Puny was carried by Gryce to a conventicle in Tower Hamlet, to abide many tedious hours of snuffling sermons.

It was his membership in this conventicle that occasioned Gryce's rise from a beggarly botcher to a prosperous moneyer (which I am sure he took as a signal proof of grace and righteousness). His first attempt at coining was to cast a few shillings at his fireside, which were of lead plated with silver. When he showed the coins to one of the brethren, a button-maker named Blank, his work met with censure: it being enjoined upon him for a truth, that coins must be made by a stamp or punch, not molded upon a coin, which causes them to be too small and light. Humbly accepting the rebuke, Gryce asked his brother for instruction. Upon discovering that the button-maker had a rare skill for such work (which he had never before attempted), Gryce said to him, Brother, do not light your candle and put it under a basket. Do not hide your talent in the earth, if you would enter the joy of your master. As every man hath received a special gift, let him minister the same to another. In plain words, let us be partners, and share alike, and we both shall be rich men. Blank, who enjoyed only a poorish living by his craft, fell in with this proposal and applied himself to cutting punches for coins. In a praiseworthy spirit of emulation, Gryce sweated to concoct a plausible metal that was an alloy of silver, copper, and tin. The two of them worked side by side to stamp and dress the coins. They had not been many weeks at their labor before they were producing coins of such quality that their money was never rejected, even by those who doubted it. Now that he could get a shillingsworth of meat for a groatsworth of silver, Gryce grew monstrously fat and ceased visiting Marius Bye. They exchanged coin for clippings with some of their brother snufflers, Bushrod being one among that elect few. However, they boggled at offering their work for sale to the reprobate many: knowing full well, that though God has not forbidden coining, Pharaoh has. When the reward was set of forty pounds for informing upon a coiner, they thought they must draw in their horns and cease to trade.[7]

They expressed their fears to Bushrod when he came to them for coin, who answered them thus: Brothers, you have taken the staff by the wrong end. Your safety and your best concealment is to put yourself in the midst of a throng of coiners and clippers. You must enlarge your venture, thereby setting yourselves at a farther remove from discovery. Vend your coin to strangers, and let it be coined and carried to them by hirelings. I'll show my truth by joining with you, for I assure you I can vend a vast deal more coin than I have thus far got from you.

Gryce was easier to persuade than Blank. His fellows harried him with parables and plagued him with scriptures: Our merchandise is profitable—let not our lamp go out at night. We have planted a vineyard and must hire laborers if we would enjoy the fruit. Moreover, if any provide not for his own and those of his house, he is worse than an infidel. The button-maker was won over at last, by it being proposed that he might then sit all day at his table cutting new stamps, without the sweat of coining. In graving his stamps, he discovered a joy that was absent from button-making, from meat, drink, women, sermons, and all things else. Within a short while he attained to a mastery of the craft. The piles were cut with considerable elegance, but it was in graving the trussells that he showed his genius. The man must have been a Leveller without knowing it: he took such evident delight in degrading the royal image. For by some subtle stroke, he would give James the First a goatish expression, or put a sneer upon the thick lips of Charles the First. Even when he was tasked with making punches for coins of Elizabeth's reign, which must necessarily appear much worn, he could impart a leer to the eye and lip, a debauched look to the hollow cheek, that made her look the quean. (Delia says she would infallibly know his coin, if one came to her hand, by the degenerate features of the effigy.)

Jack was the hireling that ran the greatest risk of arrest as he was sent trotting from one end of town to the other, carrying messages, coin, and clippings. 'Tis true he was often accompanied by Jack Brawny or George

Have-Face, who would oftentimes be wearing a forged porter's badge and bearing the heavier load. But the blackguards were, from their green days of filching from stalls, quick to take alarm and scamper, and thus were not easily surprised unawares. Jack, by comparison, was yet an innocent, with little comprehension of the risk he ran, which was of being either hanged, drawn, and quartered as a Jack, or burned at the stake as a Jill.[8] His father spoke of that terrible sentence as one imposed upon men of great merit and virtue who sought to liberate their country from tyranny; which made it seem remote from an inconsiderable boy whose employment was only in bearing packets from one place t'another. He was in truth under a continual fear and dread, but it was in regard to the blackguard boys, whose villainy was too manifest, and of his master, for he saw that the boys, who feared nothing, held him in some awe.

It was now about a year since the coiners took the advice of Bushrod to seek safety in numbers. Gryce began by collecting ragged waifs and strays he found skulking in alleys or lurking under bulks at night. I know not how he made his selection, though I wager a guess he chose those that were less ragged and starved, upon a consideration that they were more adept at roguery than their fellows. I doubt an honest master could have taught them his trade, but they were eager to be introduced to the mystery of making money. They stripped to their shirts to perform their sweaty labors, which restrained their ability to thieve. Moreover, they were paid each week in the worst coin of their making; though nothing could make them honest, this latter measure had some force to render them diligent. There were at present twelve boys who worked in shifts at coining, watching the street, and accompanying Jack when he was sent out. Much of the new coin went direct to Bushrod. He then parceled it out among a host of buyers, mostly taverners and traders, who paid him in whatever good coin they could cull from their receipts, which they exchanged advantageously and at little risk. The good coin was carried by Jack and his fellows to a pawnbroker, who put it out to be clipped; the light money returned to him could be forced on his customers when they brought him their pitiful pawns.

It seemed a very prosperous concern, but the profit had not grown proportionate to the enterprise. Despite their many precautions, the coiners had been traced; so that they were obliged to pay out gratuities and bribes to thief-takers, venal catchpoles, and other corrupt officers. They were certain it was one of the dear-beloved of the conventicle that had harkened to Satan and betrayed them for gain; which accusation they made before the elders, only to be rebuked: it being answered, their business was but too generally known, by their putting false coin in the collection when the rest of the brethren put in clipped. The two conventiclers they particularly suspected each met with a judgment. One was grievously assaulted by footpads when he was out late by night; the other suffered a dreadful fire from which he and his wife escaped with only the clothes on their backs. These two calamities were so evidently the act of all-seeing Justice, that the coiners supposed there would be no further discoveries to nick and pluck at their profits. However, about six weeks after Jack was inducted into their confederacy, another extortioner rose up, that was not so easily managed. This was not some beggarly tipstaff who could be fobbed off with a monthly purse of sham coin: but a rival gang of clippers and coiners possessing an exact knowledge of their concern, shown in their manner of making themselves known. They surprised the night-watch, a boy called Foul Tom for his uncleanliness, who they left bound and gagged before the door, a paper pinned to his breast. Jack was awakened by a noise; after looking out and spying Foul Tom, he alarmed his master. Gryce in turn roused Blank, and they read over the paper together. In it, the coiners were complimented for the merit of their work and welcomed into the guild of expert moneyers; as an initiation fee they were to contribute a guinea stamp. Upon its acceptance they would be afforded protection, *durante bene placito.*[9]

Gryce was pacing the room, whipped up by alternating bouts of rage and fear, his usual roaring voice stricken to a hoarse, rattling whisper. Blank, meanwhile, sat staring at the paper, making no response to his fellow's diverse passions, until at last he said: A guinea stamp, I've never attempted a guinea. The paper don't say what reign it should be. I suppose then I may choose. What guineas do we have? Bring them. I want to see them. By which ill-sorting speech, it seemed that the button-maker was in a state of excitement at the novelty of the work and the greater scope afforded to his art by a coin of such size and magnificence. There might, at this juncture, have been a violent falling out of thieves, if fear were not predominate in Gryce's frenzy, so that he did not dare pick a quarrel with the man who must satisfy their oppressor. He happily had another object to vent his fury upon, and fell to kicking Foul Tom, who lay still neatly trussed upon the floor. The other blackguard boys had begun by now to sneak in from their lodgings. What Gryce said to them Jack did not hear, as he had been sent on to Bushrod with a copy of the paper and a request for guineas. A week was allowed to them to produce the stamp; which would have presented no difficulty, if Blank did not squander two days in fingering the guineas brought to him and making various sketches. An old Charles the Second guinea offered a fair pursuit for his genius, but his designs partook more of satire than imitation. In the event he settled upon cutting the twin effigies of the William and Mary coin, which afforded him less freedom to meddle and distort. When it was done, he considered it a work so perfect, he did not want to part with it; and it was only upon being told that their new masters would doubtless want more stamps that he was persuaded to relinquish it.

At seven in the evening, the stamp was to be carried by an unaccompanied bearer to Covent Garden and handed to a man that would be wearing a yellow ribbon in his hat at a station near the dial. Jack was given the task of carrying the stamp to the assignation; George Have-Face and Jack Brawny were instructed to walk with him as far as the square. Four more black-guards were deployed about the square in advance of the hour, to watch for a man wearing a yellow ribbon: whereupon, they were confounded to find a half-dozen of men with their hats so trimmed. Jack did not get that far. When he and his companions stepped out from the alleys into the back-side of St. Clement's, they encountered two coaches stopped in the lane, a veiled lady in rich mourning being handed down from the second by a thin-shanked groom. Jack's companions paused to stare at her; Have-Face was making a lewd remark about offering consolation, when the lady pointed a snapper at him, while the groom leveled a pistol at Jack Brawny. Our Jack was seized and pulled into the other coach, where he was at once blindfolded and his hands bound; but as he did not cry out, or otherwise resist, he was not gagged. Much though he was afeared they would do him a mischief, he was chiefly concerned that the hands which searched him for the stamp might make a discovery that outslipt both the amorous Mrs. Peatfoote and the mass-priest. The coach went a distance of about a mile, making a half-dozen turns, before it stopped in a quiet court; whereupon Jack was plucked out by his pinioned arms, dragged over a threshold into an entry, down an echoing passage and into a room. There was a long-drawn mumbling of several voices before one spoke to him, asking him about his master and the business of coining, to which questions he would give no answer. He was slapped and kicked for his better encouragement; but, though trembling violently and beginning to weep, he steadfastly refused to answer. Though he knew his master to be a wicked man, he had nonethe-less passed his word to him. Moreover, he did not know who it was that had him nicked and was now interrogating him: it might be other coiners, it might be the Messengers, it might be the King's Counselors; so that he feared speaking words that might someway betray his father or his friends. Whatever they were, his youth and evident terror softened them; for another voice said, 'Tis of no consequence. We already know the answers. I only marvel that his master has one loyal servant, for I am sure all the others would unburden in a trice. The blows then ceased, and after only a rough shaking he was given a message to his master: That he not attempt any more callow tricks with spies, footpads, or fire-setters. Those he now had to deal with, could call forth twenty good men to drub his beggarly boys; and moreover possessed mighty friends that would, at a word, rub 'em to the Whit, where their shitten coin would buy 'em a moldy crust and a cup of puddle-water to wash it down.[10]

Jack was haled back to the coach; and, his bonds loosened, pushed out near Covent Garden at about nine o'clock. Upon his return to the mint, he was summoned upstairs to his master's chamber, where he found Gryce, Blank, and Bushrod seated at the table, with the blackguard boys ranged behind them. Blank looked sour at being kept from his bed; Bushrod wore his usual front of spurious benevolence; Gryce looked daggers at him, whilst the blackguards smirked, their eyes gleaming with malign joy. Jack belatedly perceived that Have-Face and Brawny, having preceded him home, had served up a tale that made him answerable. Had he been better practiced in villainy (for he was certainly in a good school), he would have been prepared against such an obvious fetch. As it was, he had no time to compose his startled thoughts before his master began to hector him. It being demanded, what he could say in his defense, being accounted a base, black-souled traitor, Jack began to tell his tale, but was denounced for a perfidious liar before he had uttered a dozen words; and again demanded, and again silenced before he could get out more than a few words. The only questions he was permitted to answer were those asked by the other two of his judges: Blank wanting only to know what became of the stamp, lapsing into sleepy indifference thereafter; Bushrod asking if his captors made any remarks to him, but here his answer only provoked Gryce to still greater fury.

Jack had been fuddled in his wits, stammering like a guilty felon, upon being confronted by a tribunal of villains sitting in judgment on him. His indignation at last got the better of his fear, so that he made a stronger effort to defend himself. It was the grossest injustice, he said, to be accused of being false and of violating his oath, when he had taken a goodly number of hard blows for his refusal to answer such questions as his master's name, the names of his confederates, and the quantity of coin turned out each day. —Your guilt shows in your face, Gryce roared, and also on your hat. Which remark, which seemed belonging to Bedlam, nonplussed poor Jack, until it occurred to him to whip off his hat and look upon it; whereupon he saw it was now trimmed with a yellow ribbon. —Why, this signifies nothing, Jack said. The rogues put it on me while my eyes were scarfed. —They have marked you as their own, cried Gryce, and so hath Satan. But the Lord despiseth the lying lips of snitches and sneaks. These he burns with unquenchable fire. As with Foul Tom, so it will be with you.

It was not until this moment that Jack perceived his master's menacing strain to portend more than a sound cudgelling. It came to him of a sudden, that he had not seen Tom since his disgrace, though the blows he took when surprised, and the subsequent kicks of his enraged master, would not keep him abed for a week. He began to tremble in earnest, and was that close to falling in a swoon, as he could not well mark what was said. He could recall that Gryce next appealed to his fellows for confirmation: Blank saying in effect that he cared not, he might choke as many boys as he pleased; Bushrod however soothed and temporized, saying, for certain, the affair was sadly mishandled. Nonetheless, he doubted this boy was more at fault than t'other two. He himself had an enterprise afoot that required an assistant. Let the boy be given to him in loan to make trial of his abilities. The blackguards let out a roar of disappointment when Gryce gave his assent for Bushrod to take the boy, who could not keep from tottering and quaking as he went.

His new master provided him with blankets to make a bed upon the floor, and he fell at once into a deep exhausted slumber, though not without awaking in a start from dreams so terrible that he feared to sleep again. Delia said, it was the recollection of the blackguards howling with disappointment at his reprieve that filled Jack with dread more than anything else. They were a very prevision of hell, being liker to fiends denied the pleasure of tormenting a sinner, than to human creatures. Jack pondered much on the experiences of this day. He knew his master to be a false, canting hypocrite; but he had nonetheless a trust that he was not a frank villain, from being a former friend and companion to his father. He recollected with some bitterness the seeming rage with which Gryce had proclaimed that coining is no murder. He now perceived that the man kept the blackguards in reasonable good order by commiting a murderous tithing at any hint of disloyalty; which, considering their lively pleasure at Jack's trial, kept them loyal and diligent as much for sport as fear.[11] Jack could take some satisfaction in reflecting that his master's unjust fury prevented him from making a discovery that would have been materially useful to him. No one thought to ask, if he had, despite his bonds and blindfold, discovered any clue concerning the identity of the man-thieves. Had he been asked such a question, he might well have chosen to answer candidly, that in truth he had. Whilst he was being interrogated, another man came briefly into the room, only to say, in a finical tone, My dears, I perceive you are in conference. We shall put off supper until you are at liberty. It was a voice he had heard once before, holding forth at some considerable length regarding his dear sons and their sharpness at making money in new-fangled ways. So that he might have informed Gryce with all confidence that his bloodsucking rivals were the brothers Hull, a goldsmith-banker and an overseas trader, who lived with their father in Gracechurch Street. ✠

CHAPTER 14

A profitable visit to Sturbridge Fair. Some unexpected encounters there, and upon the road thereafter.

I**N SEPTEMBER,** after the last sheath is gathered and the fallen corn gleaned, Hodge and Nell hang up their hooks and rakes to rejoice: wetting their dusty throats and lifting their feet in hobnailed jig, they frolic and frisk. When all the parish, from squire to cottager, have sat down to their harvest supper and got themselves home again, reeling ripe, bursting with beef, plum pudding, and ale; when they have done rejoicing, when they have slept their fill: Now the silver in their purses sets up a jingling clamor like a string of merry bells. Spend! Spend! is the tune it peals, summoning all but a few grum misers to market and fair. Now it is that the peddlers, mountebanks, sorcerers, jugglers, strolling players, pickpockets, and all-cause rogues of England rise up out of their lurking places to set to their labors. For 'tis the prime season for plucking innocents of their coin. From every shire's end they set forth; and, though there is no fair so mean that they would scorn to visit it, the greatest rogues wend to the greatest of fairs, Sturbridge.[1]

I would not flatter Bushrod with an imputation of greatness: but a bold, aspiring rogue he was in truth, with a new project in hand that he wished to attempt upon a large, miscellaneous, and foolish public, such as cannot be better found than at a fair. Having observed that he must share the title and custom of astrological physician with other charlatans of the Town; observing, moreover, that the people were at once infinitely gullible and easily jaded: he wished to renew his line of trade with some taking novelty. It occurred to him to revive the old country practice of scrying, especially as he saw how eagerly people ran off to the fields every summer to consult the gypsies and have their fortunes read. It is a business requiring no stock beyond a basin of water or a beryl-stone, along with a child of seeming innocence to serve as scryer. He had already considered that Jack, though a trifle old for the role, might suit his purpose; but he would no doubt need to offer Gryce some concession in exchange for him. That man's murderous rage at the boy falling so pat to his purpose, I wager he had some role in fomenting it during Jack's absence.

He opened his business to Jack by asking, Are you a virgin? I think it a token of the ill company he had kept since he left home, that Jack was quick to a frontless equivocation, answering, I have never had sinful congress with any

147

female. Bushrod, having no very high opinion of his new servant's intellect, anticipated some difficulty in teaching him his part of the fortune-telling cheat, though 'twas only to listen intently to the coney's replies to questions, then profess to see the people and things he described in the crystal. He was thus much surprised when Jack succeeded to perfection upon the first trial. He might have felt some misgivings over entrusting his business to a boy able to conceal so much smooth cunning behind a guileless countenance, had he not then discovered that the boy was performing his part in entire sincerity. If a draper complained of the theft of a remnant, and had moreover an unruly apprentice with red hair, who was often drunk and suspected of keeping a woman, Jack would view the scene enacted in the crystal, the stolen cloth carried by the Judas-colored boy to his simpering Jezebel. If a rich citizen's wife was missing a ring or other pretty toy, Jack would perceive it being put into the pocket of the thin-chested maid with a squint, whom the mistress regretted hiring without a character. Foreseeing, without any need of a crystal, that this would prove a profitable enterprise, his new master acquired a finer show-stone, set on a white-metal base, to better justify his fee; some new clothes were got for Jack; hand-bills were made up to bruit the expansion of his many exemplary services to the sickly and the superstitious. When all was in readiness, Dr. Izaak Bushrod, Astrological Physician and Speculary Adeptus, reserved two seats on the coach to Cambridge.

Sturbridge Fair was then at its height: Tom Hobnail and Nell Homespun jostled elbows with Squire Rackrent and Mistress Gad-About. Factors traded in great heaps of hops, wool, and cloth by exchanging their paper. Their wives, sons, and daughters frolicked from booth to booth, where they might find every conceivable amusement, from buns to bumfiddles. Every Jack and every Jill might suit their fancy, for there were players, jugglers, fiddlers, toy-men, whores, and gingerbread-sellers for all. Rag, tag and bob-tail, reeling from many a pot of nappy good ale, dropped in untidy heaps about the field. 'Twas a scene of universal jollity and roguery. Bushrod had taken a share of a booth held by a fellow charlatan, his intent being to rehearse his new imposture abroad before preferring it to the more discerning audience of the metropolis.

Now, it is a certain truth that the fair-complexioned lack the second-sight; wherefore his master would not have Jack play his part in his own character, but first blacked his hair and embrowned his skin. He intended to pass the boy as an exiled princeling of Arabia, for which purpose, he rigged him in a trumpery robe: but the boy proved to be too impenetrably stupid (which is to say, too honest) to personate such a figure. He next proposed him to be the visionary seventh son of a famous family of cunning-men in the Vale of Eden. Again he could not well act his part, his speech being too refined. He would dutifully commit to memory and repeat any gabble that Bushrod rehearsed with him; but when he viewed the shadows in the crystal he spoke in his own character. His master at length perceived that the boy was a sincere idiot, and must be let to do the business with a lamentable lack of varnish, sham, and subterfuge.

Jack wished to believe that some benevolent spirit inspired him to see visions in the crystal, in order to expose and punish evil-doing; yet he was obliged to consider, that if there were anything in it, other than the work-ings of his own fantasy, 'twas the promptings of the devil, as no good spirit would keep company with such a one as his master. He thought the busi-ness wickeder than coining. It seemed no great injustice, if a evil-inclined apprentice were wrongfully accused of theft, but it troubled him that a servant should be dismissed with a bad character, only because her mistress had taken a dislike to her. His conscience was granted a holiday at the Fair, where people came to his master's booth only to hear some good fortune foretold to them. Surely no one was wronged if he foresaw weddings to spinsters, buried hoards to yeomen, or unexpected legacies to artisans and shopkeepers. It was holiday in truth, his master keeping shop for only a few hours each day, so that Jack was let loose to ramble. He saw lions, dwarves, and giants; he saw a two-headed dog and a five-legged sheep; he saw rope dancers, conjurors, puppet shows, and drolls; he saw Nan the chapwoman strolling with an open pack of ballads upon her shoulder; he saw Sir John Herewige and Major Boyle looking at horses in the company of two of the rioting officers from the Dog and Bear.

—Why, Jack, I hardly knew you, said the chapwoman. You look a very Egyptian, were it not for your hazel eye. I told you I was going to Cambridge by-and-by, and so it is. You know I would not lie to you, Jack. I must away; I hope you are well. With that the chapwoman made off into the crowd before he could stop her, no doubt expecting to be worried with demands of money. Jack did in truth wish to raise that vexing topic. His purse was heavy with coin, but 'twas all false; which he shrank from passing, un-less it were for the arrantest cheats: so that he sated himself with viewing monsters and hocus-pocus shows, only that he might have the change to buy a honest pennyworth of gingerbread. His master whiled away the hours more productively, in censuring the performances of other charlatans and thumbing the offerings of the booksellers in Cooks Row, so that he might augment his stock of hard words to gabble in his talk. He was possessed of such brazen self-conceit as to talk dog-Latin with the scholars, only to gage how far he could impose upon them.

By the last days of the Fair, Bushrod had brought the performance of his scryer to a tolerable degree of polish, in foreseeing patrons and benefices for poor collegians and awarding handsome rich husbands to wishful young women; which were very pleasant fortunes to be had for mere sixpenny. When, therefore, a two-shilling sixpence customer—to wit, a featly dressed gentleman with an open face—entered their booth, the Speculary Adeptus had reasonable certitude that the far-sighted Cumbrian rustic would discern his desires, whether for a profitably concluded lawsuit, a good match for his daughter, or a good sale of his cattle. Turning his eye upon the boy, however, he saw that the poor idiot was in a fit of trembling, which the magus smoothly excused as a token of some great destiny that the boy descried in the gentleman's features. Jack was in a state of great confusion for shame of what Sir John might say upon viewing him in his degraded state; until he saw that that his beloved master did not know him. He kept his head bowed, his eyes fixed upon the crystal, as the magus jabbered his fustian cant and attempted to draw out the gentleman into circumstancing his concerns. Howsoever, Sir John had wit enough not to expose himself so baldly, and would go little beyond saying that he was engaged in a great enterprise, along with many others, and wished to know how 'twould come out. 'Tis a tricky prospect even for a seasoned cheat to gloze such a close-mouthed customer: Bushrod was casting about for what to say to him, when Jack began to read forth a vision from the beryl-stone. The boy was in a ferment of sympathy, regret, and vivid recollection, which together had power to animate the dull crystal with visions of men and deeds. He saw a room stored with armaments, which were being passed out to a score of men. He saw a stable of horse made ready by grooms. He saw parties of armed horsemen upon the road. He saw a battle; but it was only a skirmish, the enemy laying down their arms to flee or join forces. When they reached the City, there was again a fight; but the citizens themselves rose up to aid their deliverers and take down the chains. The City was won with scarce a drop of blood shed. The King and his Court took a panicked flight, and all of London, nay, all of England, celebrated their delivery from tyranny. The boy would doubtless have next foreseen the meeting of a Parliament that pledged to end all single-person rule, but was prevented. Sir John rose up in full satisfaction and threw down a purse of guineas, saying, 'twas only a token, for he would reward the magus and his boy as they deserved when it all came to pass.

I picture Bushrod transfixed with astonishment: 'twas a state as near to divine awe and belief as he ever came in his life (for I think his presence in the conventicle was only to gain fluency in religious cant to support his projects). Yet the devil was at no risk of losing him, for the next minute Jack sighed forth his sorrowing reflection, saying, I was footboy to this gentleman for half a year, but I am now so altered in my appearance that he knew me not. 'Twas a vast deal more than he should have admitted. He was obliged, when his master insisted upon knowing it, to give out Sir John's name and estate. Upon other questions he feigned ignorance or forgetfulness, his memory not improving even when Bushrod held up one, then two, of Sir John's guineas. Jack persevered that he made a few random guesses, from knowing the gentleman to interest himself in military affairs, and believing that he aimed to be made an officer in the army. Though this explanation only glancingly conformed to the scenes he viewed in the crystal, 'twas as good a lie as Jack could muster to his service. When Bushrod affected indifference and ceased to interrogate him, he thought all was well. That is, at least, what Delia said to me; nonetheless, I consider that Bushrod, being a smooth and practiced cheat of many years' standing, found other ways to worm him, prying out a good many particulars regarding Sir John and his acquaintance, without the boy in the least perceiving how far he betrayed his former master. He had only to wind about on different tacks (as Mrs. Witherby and her maid had formerly done), by asking Jack how he liked serving in a country house with a large family, or whether the gentleman kept a good table and was charitable to his neighbors: to which triflings he would not refuse an answer.

Bushrod gave up his share of the booth, though the fair still had two days to run, and there were yet sheep patient to be shorn of their sixpences. He ambled through the flock of fools in the guise of an idle gentleman; for he left off wearing his great bushy wig and otherwise altered his appearance so that he was scarce knowable as the Speculary Adeptus of yesterday. Jack, being provided with a strong soap to scrub his lying countenance, was emboldened to ask if he was done being a scryer; Bushrod answered, for the moment he was; but there might be other employments for him upon their return to the town. Although, now that he knew Jack had been in service to a baronet, he would take a better view of his comportment, and consider how he might settle him; he knew a gentleman in a fine house in Bread Street that was casting about for a boy to wait on him. Bushrod must have forgotten that he had already flattered Jack with the same promise, and it was not a whit more persuasive upon repetition. Jack apprehended that the

man had some new villainy in view, to which he would be accessory; and if
he were not compliable, he might well be delivered over to the blackguard
boys. It was now, when he was fifty miles from St. Clement Danes, that
he ought to slip away to safety. However, upon the pretense of judging his
demeanor, Bushrod kept the boy close to him for most of the day, so that he
accompanied him as he made another visit to the booksellers, to cheapen the
wares they were engaged in packing up. I question if the man read anything
beyond a news-sheet, unless it were the almanac that went under his name;
but he doubtless considered that a few weighty volumes in his consulting
chamber would lend their authority to his medical and astrological advices.
Though the reputable sellers were not disposed to accept his haggling, they
came upon a student peddling his musty books on the outskirts of the Fair,
who was no doubt ready to entertain any offer, judging from his willingness
to endure Bushrod's ignorance.

—Hem, Aristotle, he said, picking up a volume. Politica. That's politics. I
think if that great man knew of our politics nowadays, he would be much
astounded. He would need to write another volume, hah?

—Certainly, sir. It is Bruni's translation, together with LeFèvre's commentary, a very good aid to understanding. As you see, 'tis a good copy, not
much scribbled.

—Exert-ta-to Ana-to-my-ka de Mo-tu Cord-us et Sanguin-is in Animal-
a-bus.[2] Now that, I consider, is a good volume to add to my bibliothecaria.
I am a physician, sir, with a practice in the Town.

—Yes, sir, it is an important work on the circulation of the blood, very
necessary for a physician. The book is old, I had it from another student,
and the mice have been at it. I do not ask much for it.

—Now that I cogitate 'pon it, I consider a Galen would be of greater use
to me. I do not do blood-lettings; that is the calling of a barber-surgeon.
Do you have a Galen?

—No, sir. But if you are wanting works of natural philosophy, here is
Newton's Principia. The book is almost new: you can see that only the
first pages are cut.

—Ah, that is the book that says the stars exert their occult powers upon
mortals more by ponderability than by levity.

—I find, sir, you understand it as well as any man I know.

The student's forbearance was rewarded when Bushrod decided upon the
purchase of two bulky Latin tomes, which were given to Jack to carry. Passing
on through the fair, they found themselves behind Sir John Herewige and
Major Boyle. They were near enough to catch some part of their conversation.

Boyle was expostulating with his companion on the foolishness of visiting fortune-tellers, with the baronet returning just as warmly that he uttered not a word of their business but the scryer saw it all in his crystal. Jack thought to himself, 'twould be a ticklish thing, if either man were to wheel about and know him. Bushrod must have made a similar reflection, for he whispered to Jack that as the books were heavy, he should take them to their lodging, and await his return. Released from his attendance, Jack took to his legs, scouring the fair for a view of the chapwoman. This time he resolved to seize her by the arm so that she might not escape before he made his declaration: which was, that he would never demand money of her, if she would only take him up again as her companion upon the road. Though he scampered back and forth, and merited the curses he got for jostling his way, he could not find her. He could contrive no other plan of escaping his present master, unless he were to walk home to his father, obtaining a suit of women's clothes along the way, so that he might metamorphose into a repentant Delia, who would throw herself weeping at her father's feet. He had imagined just such a scene many times before, but no crystal could show him what would next ensue. Sometimes he envisioned Marius in his choler, spurning his daughter and striking at her with his stick; sometimes he descried a cold, reluctant Marius permitting his daughter to stay and keep his house for him as a servant. There must be some truth to scrying, for at no time did Jack perceive a scene wherein the father embraced his prodigal daughter, then sent to Jane for her best veal pie. Moreover, if it were necessary to be repenting on his knees, he did not know why he should not keep his breeches, and first beg Sir John to take him back; if he was rejected, at least he would not be struck, and it would save him a long journey on foot to be at the same result. He was still pondering which submission were likelier of good success, when he came unexpectedly upon his master, who said to him: I do not like you should wander about, when I gave you strict instruction. Come, I intend to return to London straightway, by coach, if I may command two places. Otherwise I'll get horses of the carrier, but in any case I must return as quick as I may.

They took their places in the coach the next morning; the only solace in it for Jack was that he was not required to ride in the boot, as he was upon the trip down. The next passengers to take their seats were a family named Bounce, husband, wife, and daughter, that took a holiday jaunt and were loaded down with fairings, which were jumbled on the floor next to Jack's legs, he being evidently an inferior person who might not complain. The last traveller to take his place was a young man with a large bundle—or, considering that it contained his all, a small bundle. There was an exchange of seats by which Jack was so closely pinned, he was wondering if the boot were truly worse. The driver had whipped up his horses and gained the road, when Bushrod addressed a remark to the newcomer: Well, Mr. Cloudsley, so you have sold your books and abandoned your studies? Jack gaped and stared. It was the student that was peddling his books at the Fair, to whom he had given little notice, being preoccupied in looking about for the chapwoman. I wonder that it did not occur to him, when he was pondering his scanty options, to seek out Delia's husband at the university; I wager he was too comfortable in his breeches to wish to take them off for such a purpose or such a person. But this was not the man; or, if it was, he was marvelously improved in appearance. Bushrod's remark prompted Mr. Bounce to utter his observations upon the wayward conduct of young men; Mrs. Bounce and Miss Bounce interposed their questions; so that the young man's best course to escape their pestering was to tell his story:

I do not leave of my own accord or by my fault but because of a plot set to disgrace and ruin me. You must first know something of my family. My father held a decent living in Norfolk, but he died of a fever when I was still an infant at the breast. My mother refused all offers of marriage and devoted her slender means to my education. Her greatest hope for my advancement was to interest her brother, a wealthy London trader, in my welfare. She wrote him many a long letter to which he returned only short ones. My schoolmaster and some of the gentlemen of the parish obtained a sizarship for me.[3] This at last won a little regard of my uncle, and it then became a question of what profession he would choose for me. Whether I would be a divine to pray for his soul, or a physician to treat his paltry ailments, or a lawyer to manage his suits at law. If I were to have my choice, I would study law or physic, and find my way in the world however I might; but I would not for the world's wealth disappoint my mother, and she would not offend my uncle, or cross him in his whimsies, for fear of his leaving his money elsewhere.

My uncle is a bachelor of about fifty years, with no other relations except one other nephew, who has the advantage of living in London and bearing the same name. I became acquainted with my uncle and cousin when I was invited to visit for the fortnight before my matriculation. My uncle's conversation was upon the course of study he would have me undertake; and as I carried myself with modesty and listened to his advice, I think I gained his approval. My cousin Bevil Maynard must have thought so too. He kept up a decorous character before my uncle, but his conversation was of a different sort in private, for he boasted much of his wenching and whoring, and of how many foolish young women he had beguiled and abandoned. He wished me to join in his nocturnal round of dissipation, but I declined, being disgusted by his hypocrisy and not trusting his professed friendship. He, however, seemed to take no notice of my coldness, and promised to visit me at my college. I hoped his promise would be forgotten, but he came at last to amuse himself at the Fair. He was acquainted with two pensioners of another college, so that I was not overburdened with his company. I accepted his offer of a treat at a tavern in the town, which was a breach of the college rules, though one so common that 'twould not be noticed. His friends showed me more courtesy than I was accustomed to as a sizar (for usually I was serving such men, not sitting at the same table). It was a lively gathering and the bottle passed up and down the table a good many times—too many times, truly, for my head was too weak for such jollity, and the last I remember of the occasion was their laughter when I attempted to stand up.

Thus I spent the night out of the college, which was a serious infraction; but I hoped, as it was my first offense, 'twould be forgiven. I was later that day called before my tutor and the master of the college, whereupon I found I was accused of a great deal worse than the transgressions I owned. 'Twas said I swore and uttered blasphemies, and bawled out obscenities, while disordered with drink. I said, I had been at a entertainment with some gentlemen, and one or two had been very jovial and a little loose in their conversation, but I had not been guilty of any grossness in word or deed. (Maynard, my cousin, had been the great offender in this regard.) I named the pensioners as my evidences that I was guilty of no greater impropriety than being made drowsy by unaccustomed indulgence. I was then informed that they were my accusers. I was so confounded by this, I knew not how to answer, except to say, It was not so; the gentlemen were mistaken. I could hardly hope that my word would be valued above theirs. I perceived that my cousin was behind it, and his two friends gave out their story to oblige him, and perhaps it was sport to them, to ruin a poor sizar.

Now, it may be, that my trespasses, real and pretended, might be forgiven if I humbled myself; but now a new accuser came forward, a serving woman at the inn, who said I surprised her in a passage, and, putting one hand on her mouth to silence her, took disgusting liberties. I was filled with indignation and accused the woman of being bribed to make her base accusation. I only harmed myself by doing so, for her tears, her faltering words, and her trembling reluctance to come near me, declared her honesty. Too late,

I understood that, while I was overcome with drink, my cousin put on my clothes and went forth to commit outrages, knowing they would be brought home to me. I forgot to tell you that my cousin and I look something alike, being of the same height and similar in feature; so that he might pass himself for me if the light were dim. To be brief, my denials only made my guilt blacker and I was expelled at once from my college. I took a chamber in a poor eating-house outside the town, wanting a few days to consider what friends I might interest in my defense, or to give me counsel. It was at this time that I received a letter from my mother, which began by saying how sorrowful she was, to learn that I had forgotten all the precepts of a good Christian life and was fallen into sinful and infamous ways. The paper dropped from my hand in my surprise and anger: I wondered who had ridden by post to Norfolk to give my mother the news of my expulsion. 'Twas not beyond my cousin's malice though certainly 'twas beyond his vigor. When I took up the letter again, I found that another catalog of crimes, this time committed in London, had been laid at my door. While I was upon my visit to my uncle, my cousin was behaving riotously in Covent Garden bawdy-houses, gaming dens, and other low places, all the while taking my name as his. I think he went beyond his usual depravity for the pleasure of polluting my reputation. A poor foolish girl, with whom he went through a sham marriage, presented herself and her big belly at my uncle's door, pleading to speak to her husband, Robin Cloudsley. My uncle, then making inquiries, uncovered other instances of vice and depravity attached to my name, whereof he did nothing spare my mother, though she would not repeat them to me, assuming I knew all too well my own guilt. I at once dispatched a letter to my mother declaring my innocence and exposing my cousin's treachery. I trust she will believe me; but knowing that I have been sent down from my college will be another discouragement for her to bear, and her health is not good. I stayed only to sell what possessions I could to get money to travel. I am determined to go to my uncle and to seek an interview to clear myself: however prejudiced he be against me, he cannot with conscience refuse to hear me. I can only hope my candor will persuade him, for I have no other advocate to plead for me. If he will not credit my honesty, then I must support myself by my pen—a poor living in truth, but all I am fit for.

His story commanded rapt attention: 'twas a disappointment he was so brief, for they wished to know more of his cousin's lechery. Now they broke out in a cackle of commentary and advice. Mrs. Bounce urged that he go straightway to his mother; which would mean a deal more than he could put in a letter; for in a letter one may say what one will, but a mother will read truth or falsehood in her child's face better than any words. Bounce and Bushrod were of the contrary opinion, that he must cope his uncle before he was too settled in his prejudice; but they differed on how he should present himself, whether he ought to be humble or bold. When there was a pause in the talk, Jack offered as his opinion, that the young man attempt to find the big-bellied woman who claimed him for a husband. Surely she took a better view of her supposed spouse than the poor serving-woman had of her assailer; moreover, the cousin likely went about London in his own dress, so that the difference between the two might be easily discovered. The young man thanked Jack for his counsel, saying, he would attempt it; but he did not know how the woman was to be found. His mother's letter said his uncle had treated her with disgust, dismissing her with a little money and declaring he would lodge her in Bridewell if she showed herself again. Bushrod objected, 'Twould serve no purpose to find her. The uncle would suppose they conspired in their tale. And so the talk went on until they stopped to bait the horses and to snap a hasty dinner; which had the fortunate effect of putting the chatterers into a drooping dog-sleep when they resumed their journey. Jack and Robin Cloudsley were wakeful and silent, each with much matter to ponder.

The next day, Jack put himself next the window where he might spy out his village and his home. He fancied he might perceive whether he would be welcome from the appearance of the house; he hoped he might chance to see Jane or her husband going in the street, or his father seated at his window. They passed the spot where the amorous rustic beat Delia to the ground. They passed the seat where Delia paused to eat her scant supper. Jack took a peep of Mrs. Witherby's house, and thought it looked a trifle derelict. His heart leapt as they rolled through the village, and though they were yet a mile from home, he lifted the window. A noise of complaints required him to close it. He could only peep through the pinholes of the blind for a glimpse. The horses, knowing the stable to be not many miles farther, went without whipping, passing the lonely house at a clattering quick pace. His feeble efforts to extricate himself had come to nothing. Jack supposed he would again be dabbed with atramentum and put to telling fortunes; but in truth Bushrod intended to dip him in far blacker deeds. ✠

CHAPTER 15

A betrayal balked. Jack becomes Delia and attempts to return to her father. Failing in that, she takes service in the house of Sir Maynard, the uncle of her suppositive husband. A lesson, learned too late, concerning the deceits of romance authors.

JACK, SAID Bushrod, would you do your country a signal service, and, it may be, earn a great reward for doing so? Jack, much astonished at such an unexpected overture, made careful answer, saying, he would serve his country any way he might, without expecting a reward; providing only he was not made a soldier and sent to Flanders to fight—or a sailor sent to sea. His master gave an affected little laugh, saying, 'twould be no hard thing at all he had to do and without danger, if he was discreet in his dealings. —You would not deliver your country into the bloody hands of a tyrant, would you, Jack? Or connive at murderous broils which might be prevented? Jack only shook his head, speechless in wondering how the Good Old Cause of his father, and of his beloved master, should have such scandalous rogues as Bushrod among its supporters. —Why then, Jack, here is how things stand. 'Tis grossly apparent that your quondam master is in a conspiracy against the government, and has been buying up arms and horse for an insurrection. I am willing to believe you have been too innocent, or too blindly loyal, to perceive that you are obliged to lay an information, or else be guilty of misprision of treason, which is a felony, Jack, and very serious.

Jack was alarmed, and frightened, but not quite out of his wits. He little respected the threat made against himself, but was much concerned that he had betrayed his master, and perhaps his father as well: so that he was casting about for how to save them. —I have heard it said, Jack answered, that there are two witnesses required to prove a treason. Whatever I might have chanced overhear, which was only some talk at the table where I was serving, I do not think it matters what grumbling gentlemen say over their wine. —That will not do, Jack, for now there are two of us that heard what was said at the Fair, which pointed squarely at an armed rising being plotted, a great enterprise involving many men. Sir John was so pleased with your scrying, that he threw down a purse of ten quid, and later, we found him talking to another man about it. Who is that man, Jack? I believe you know.

Jack attempted to whiffle off the question, but Bushrod dropped his benevolent manner and turned threatening, so that Jack at last acknowledged: They call him Boyle, but I do not think it his real name. What you and I

158

heard, may be judged suspicious, but it comes to very little, except that Sir John enjoyed the fantasy I spun out from the show-stone, and thought it worth mentioning to his companion. —Do not persist in playing the fool, said Bushrod in heat. What was said was treasonous. 'Tis only a matter of putting some of your words in his mouth to catch him, or else you are caught yourself. There will be evidence enough to be found, for I am sure you did not invent a chamber stocked with chests of arms. Jack, being deep in the game, decided to risk all upon a final throw of the dice. —There is another way, he said, to catch a good many men more that are guilty of worse than Sir John, who only talked large and gave money and good cheer to those that battened off him. They gather at a tavern hard by Drury Lane where they grumble and hatch plots. I have seen Boyle there many times, and also a man called Ned Shift, who carries treasonous papers with him. I know the pot-boy there and I believe he can give evidence that will catch them and others, if I speak to him and tell him, as you told me, that it is his duty to lay informations on them. —Why, do you think I cannot see what you are about? You and the pot-boy mean to take all the reward money for yourselves. —No, sir, for the pot-boy knows nothing of Sir John, but can add his evidences to catch Boyle and Shift and some others, for whatever plot there might be, if it is more than loose talk, then they are all in the combination. Jack was compelled to provide further particulars concerning the two men and Tom Found before Bushrod agreed to his proposal. He walked him, arm in arm, to the Dog and Bear; then waited for him in the street, where he fell in conversation with Wedge the joiner, gathering in much scandal concerning the tavern and its custom (it was once again full of loud, riotous swaggerers). This is the neighbor before mentioned, that is a steward of a Reforming Society, who inveterately informed upon tinkers and porters, but kept a wishful, censorious eye on the flashy gentlemen of the Dog and Bear.

Jack's one notion was to get free of Bushrod so that he might dispatch some warning to Sir John, then take to his heels however he might. Upon entering the tavern, much beyond his hopes, he saw the chapwoman exchanging some talk with Mrs. Peatfoote. He saw Boyle and Shift at a table looking over some letters. Nan said to him, Why, Jack, you are your old self again. When I saw you at Sturbridge you was painted to pass for a Egyptian. Have you given over telling fortunes to dupes and culls? —Hah, hah, hah, cried Shift. So he was playing a gypsy at Sturbridge Fair? That is making a fool's progress from wearing livery and waiting on a baronet's table. This boy (said he to the major) was a servant to Sir John Herewige, and the story of how he came to leave his service is a very amusing one. He looked so lovesome in his livery that he caught the eye of Sir John's mass-priest, who feigned illness and asked for the boy to bring him his victuals, then caught him in his arms and attempted his virtue.

As Shift was rattling along with his story, Boyle got out of his chair and made a motion to Mrs. Peatfoote, which she understood very well, to bar the door. It was something, Delia says, about the slow, deliberate way he stalked toward Jack, and the sternness of his eye—giving no heed to Shift's tale beyond the first words—that gave him the alarm. He rushed for the back-door, throwing over a bench as he went; he turned this way and that through the back lanes and kept a hot pace for a good half-mile, when he was forced to a halt for want of wind. His first reflection was to marvel at his own folly. He had come to confess to a foolish error and to make amends with a timely warning of danger. There he had found his friend the chap-woman, who could vouch for his good character, and Shift, who would at least attest him to be an ignorant noddy incapable of designs. Yet his wild panic ruined all. So he reasoned to himself, without, however, dispelling his terror at the menace he read in Boyle's eye and manner. He recalled his father's much-repeated warnings to Delia, and his evident fear that she might be prevailed upon to peach her parent. Jack knew already that Boyle would not budge at murder, and might well consider that the only means to be sure of Jack's loyalty, would be to put him out of the way. The chapwoman might perhaps say, 'twas a sad thing and a pity, or words to that effect, whilst Shift would not care at all. In sum, Jack determined that his feet had been wiser than his head, and preserved the latter from a knock.

He was however yet in danger. There was but one place to hide, and that was inside a petticoat and gown. He had run through many winding lanes and alleys; discovering he was in the neighborhood of St. Clement Danes, where he might encounter the blackguard boys, he set out again, now in the direction of Whitefriars, where there were many pawnshops stocked with women's apparel, though of a poorish sort. He paused at first one, and then another; but the clothes were so beggarly smirched that he shuddered at the thought of putting them next his skin. In the third shop he tried, there was a woman at the counter tearfully bargaining over the sale of two silk handkerchiefs, which no doubt were stolen, yet the woman appeared so desperate poor that Jack pitied her. Looking on as she was cheated by a decrepit old man, who ought better be preparing his soul for judgment, Jack resolved to pass his false money; which sop to his sleepy conscience permitted him to select the best apparel that the shop offered. He was much surprised when the old man refused his money. —Fah, said the old cuff, I know where these shillings come from and I can get a guinea's worth for two crowns. —At the price you demand for your apparel, you are getting them for less from me. If I do not question your price, then you should not question my coin, for 'tis good enough nowadays. —I wonnot take 'em, I tell you. I have enough of these shillings already. They are getting a stink and soon they will not pass at all. Come, what else have you to offer? A watch, a ring, a bit of old gold? It then occurred to Jack that he might pawn one of his mother's trinkets (which he had kept carefully hidden all this while in a pouch within his clothes). He brought forth a pair of gilt scissors, —What will you give for this in pawn? 'Tis a keepsake from my mother, and I would not sell it outright. The old man held the pretty little toy to the light and examined its ornaments with great attention. —Thief!, he shrilled, Thief! How came you by this? I gave it to my daughter, my poor dead daughter, gone these many years. —Why you lying old villain, do you think to chouse me of my things so easily? Give it back. I'll go somewhere else for the clothes. But the old man held the scissors tight in his shaky claw as he continued to shriek, Thief, Thief, 'tis my daughter's. I gave it her on her birthday the year before she was married. A constable, someone call for a constable! Jack's only recourse was to snatch up the clothes and make off before the old man's cries brought out the neighbors.

In a dirty corner (much like to the one where Delia was wed to her sup-posed husband, the supposed Robin Cloudsley), Jack paused to shift his clothes and to emerge, once again, as Delia—a Delia who dropped a few tears, wiped with the corner of a passably fresh apron, acquired at a too exorbitant price: for at a fair valuation, the little gilt scissors would have purchased two suits of such clothes. She was in a state of helpless fury at having such a trick played upon her by a palsied, lying, old villain: when it then occurred to her that he might have been speaking truth. All that she knew of her grandfather—beyond the oft-repeated complaints of a dowry unpaid—was that he broke and ran away to Alsatia some twelve years ago. The more she considered of it, the more likely it seemed: had she lost a scissors, only to recover, by it, her venerable grandsire? She might step back at once to the shop to say: It is I, Delia Bye, dear grandfather! My mother's little scissors has joined us two, who might never else have met. See, here is the thimble that matches it. Then, he might embrace her, weeping with joy, and they would share in all things and live happily together. She had read of just such happy rencounters in the penny romances belonging to Mrs. Witherby; but those were tales of lost princesses and their royal sires, not pawnbrokers that dealt in stolen goods, and hoydens that went ramping about the Town in breeches. She was, in balance, both ashamed to show herself and doubtful of her welcome. I think her reluctance wise, for 'tis but too probable that Grand-dad Snip would prefer keeping a gilt scissors to gaining a penniless granddaughter—and if he had the opportunity, he would snatch the thimble from her too.

It was now necessary to consider whither to betake herself and how to subsist. Her dress, which was decent though plain, suggested she might offer herself as a maidservant, which business she understood well enough from her time in Sir John's household. However, she resolved that she would first present herself to her father, and beg that he give audience to her tale. She would tell him, first, that she had not committed any willful sin or uncleanliness, but had been surprised and overcome by a gentleman that assailed her innocence by force and deceit; that she had, since that time, taken service in the house of a gentleman who served the Old Cause as fervently as her father; that she knew of preparations now being made for an uprising against the tyrant-king, to send him over the water. Moreover, she still retained the pamphlet Jack found in Sir John's house, that was so strangely altered by the printer. Although this latter information was news that would vex him, she hoped it would be a witness to her fidelity that she had so carefully preserved the pamphlet for his view. If her father proved unrelenting, then it was only another humiliation and a weary trudge back to the city.

When she came to the house, she was surprised to find it much altered. The yard was swept clean, the door and shutters were freshly painted, and there were curtains upon some of the windows. She could only suppose that a superior sort of Jane was now in her father's service. She knew not whether 'twere better to knock or open the door; but being of a timid nature, she knocked. She was startled so by the ill-favored woman who threw it open to frown upon her, that she was a moment in finding her tongue. —Oh Mrs. Witherby, how kind of you to visit my father. I have been absent from home many months. I hope he is well. I am anxious to —Whore! roared the woman, Strumpet! Wicked hedge-trull, get you gone! —Mrs. Witherby, it is Delia, I am come home to my father. —My name is Mrs. Urith Bye. You are a vile wretch, and you'll be whipped at the cart's tail if you are not gone this minute. Whereupon, to give weight to her threat, the woman took up a broom that stood at the door and attempted to belabor the bewildered girl's shoulders, so that she was forced to retreat to the gate. —Father, Father, she cried, looking up at his window. —Father, it is Delia, let me in! A pale face appeared at the window, which she could scarce make out for her tears, then turned aside. Delia stumbled back to the road weeping. She wept for disappointment and vexation, but chiefly for her poor father, whose plight must have been dire indeed, to make such a marriage.

Twilight surprised her upon the road, and as she was now fearful to be abroad at night, she was compelled to spend some of her good coin to get her supper and a bed in Islington. She called for paper and ink—called twice before she got more than a snub—and took up the pen, intending a letter to her father: though how she would get it past the harpy at the door, she did not know. She took up the pen, she put it down in perplexity and discouragement; the manservant, passing through the parlor, made sneering observation. She took up the pen again; but now it was to write a letter from her father, which gave a character for the girl Delia, who had been his servant for more than a year, during which time, she had tended him faithfully and honestly, without ever returning a pert word, or failing in her duties: all which was certainly true. She never before attempted to copy her father's hand or his manner, but she found she could do so passably well, without any waste of paper. Next she invented a similar letter from Sir John; which was, by comparison, a difficult composition. Her conscience made no difficulties in regard to forging a letter, provided only that it contained no falsehood. Herein she was aided by the slovenliness of Sir John's hand: so that whenever she could not avoid a reference to gender or kind, she concealed it in a scrawl or a careless drop of ink.

The maidservant of the place had served in London, and, being of a sociable disposition, a tuppence was sufficient to open her lips to impart an abundance of sound advice. 'Twas deuce well spent, for upon reaching the City, Delia went direct to the alehouse she told her of, where servants congregate to gossip, grumble, and read advertisements of places. Looking over the registry, her eye was drawn to one that sought a chambermaid of modest demeanor and good character for a house in Langbourn, which was where the true Robin Cloudsley said his uncle lived.[1] Under the pestering inquiry of the two female Bounces, he had given a description of the house; which, when she came to view the place, corresponded exactly. Delia could not but believe such a coincidence was providential, and an evident presage that her wanderings would end in a reunion with her errant husband, the plouky-faced, pop-eyed Bevil Maynard. If her hand trembled in applying at the door, if her heart throbbed with greater violence than the timid stroke she gave to the knocker, 'twas because she was overwrought with awe of the severe, but just, Providence by which she was come full circle

to her fate. Although her bashful, tremulous air stamped her as possessing the qualities demanded in the advertisement of place, the butler, who
served as house-steward, looked at her very doubtfully before beginning
a discouraging speech:

The master (he said to her) is a bachelor gentleman of mature years, so
you must understand that you will have no perquisites of clothes. Moreover,
Sir Maynard—he was knighted by King James—does not allow vails to
housemaids, so you get nothing by your place beyond your wages, which will
be five pound, or five pound ten shilling as you happen to please. By happen
to please, my meaning is, as you happen to please me; for the master cannot
abide women, especially young ones. You are not to speak to him, unless
he asks a question of you, and then you must answer as brief as possible.
Although it is necessary for you to be in them to clean and make the bed
and do suchlike work, the master much dislikes females in his bedchamber,
his parlor, or his study, or in any room he happens to occupy. He is willing
to endure the wives of his friends for society sake, but he will not tolerate
female servants in his way. So you must keep yourself informed of his
whereabout in the house as you do your work, and you must leave any room
at once when he comes in. In addition to Sir Maynard's chambers, there are
also two bedchambers kept ready for guests, with a back parlor, and also two
rooms that belong to the master's nephew, young Mr. Maynard. The gentleman has lodgings in the Town, but comes to dinner often and sometimes
stays the night. He do nothing share his uncle's aversion to females; and I
advise you for safety sake to take heed of being alone with him.

Although Delia thought these conditions very strange, she was willing
to abide by them, being so strongly convinced that she had been guided to
the house by Providence, when it was only her own foolish curiosity, to
see if the house were the same. For the circumstances were so disagreeable
to any woman able to find a better place, that the family was perpetually
seeking a fresh maid to replace one who had just left in a passion or in
disgrace. Having agreed to the terms, she was introduced to her fellow
servants, which were a footman-valet, a second footman, a man-cook, a
coachman, two boys, and a housemaid. The last-mentioned was a creature
so stout and strengthy, and withal so hairy in the face, that 'twas a wonder
she did not pass herself for a man to improve her wages. The house was
very grand to be kept up by only two women servants, the deficiency being
met by a laundry maid and a drudge that boarded elsewhere. Delia feared
she might be required to share a bed with the viraginian housemaid, and
was relieved to discover that there were two garrets for maidservants, so

that she might sleep alone. She said her prayers very humbly and contritely that night, and pondered what was to come. She perceived that she was a sinful, fallible creature; that it had been wrong to gad about the countryside in breeches; and that marriage to Mr. Bevil Maynard would be the rod to correct her of her faults. She asked for forgiveness, and she laid her plan, in accordance with a favorite volume of Mrs. Witherby's bookshelf, which recorded how the heroine disguised herself in order to win the love of the man that deceived and abandoned her, which book she took to be a true history and infallible guide.

The butler, whose name is Biggs, is formal and severe in his usage, in imitation of his master, with whom he has been some twenty years. He kept the underservants in good order by his presence, but the moment he was out of the way, they were full of lewdness and tattle concerning the master and his nephew, who they called the old'un and the young'un. They told Delia that the young'un would leave no woman alone: that he would even attempt the amazon, were he not afraid of her arm. The last chambermaid left with a big belly and bitter tears. The one before that, attempted to go before the magistrate with a complaint of rape, but being threatened with the workhouse, had desisted. The old'un, as the butler told her, so distrusted females, especially if they were at all well-favored, that any Abigail who complained of his nephew was judged to be a Delilah. Her fellow servants carried themselves towards Delia with mocking commiseration, as though she were a condemned prisoner in hold. She was so inescapably marked out for the whorehouse or the workhouse that the two skip-kennels (who aped the young'un as the butler did the old'un) seemed to consider that they were entitled to a taste before the flesh was spoiled. Their impudent gallantries became so lewd and vexatious that Delia took to concealing a bodkin in her dress, and to using it too, before she could bring them to some decency.

She had not been many days in the house before young Bevil Maynard came to dinner. Though he behaved himself with propriety before his uncle, he found occasion to follow her down a passage and, with scarcely a word to her, attempt to thrust his hand into her dress. She shrieked and brandished her bodkin before she recovered herself and ran away. 'Twas wrong, she acknowledged it, and she asked divine forgiveness. Being thus taken by surprise, she could not contain her disgust at his spotty face and his bloodshot goggle-eyes. She had not fancied his appearance upon their first encounter; now that she could compare him to his cousin Robin Cloudsley (whom she had regarded, closely and clandestinely, over many hours of a jolting ride), 'twas so much the harder to humble her flesh and force her complaisance. She could not do it without much prayer and reflection. Upon the next occasion he assailed her, he was able to grope her and plant a foul kiss upon her mouth before she squeaked and shied away from his embrace; which was, no doubt, encouragement enough. When he next came to dinner, he expressed an intention to stay the night.

'Twas past midnight: Delia's sleep had been but light and fitful, when she heard a stealthy step upon the stair, followed by the creak of the hinge. Albeit the open shutter let in a cloudy moonlight, her visitor stumbled over a box and let out a faint oath. Finding his way to her bed, he put a precautionary hand upon her mouth; but as she did not struggle or cry out, he removed it, so that he might have both hands for undoing his breeches. He wasted few words of compliment or gallantry: only making an occasional soft cry of encouragement as he topped her, such as a man might give to his horse on a gallop. I doubt Delia is familiar with the French proverb, in the dark all cats are gray, but nonetheless she regulated her behavior upon that principle. She did not flinch from embraces that would have disgusted by day. The gentleman must have fortified himself beforehand with oysters and other provocative cates, for he did not tire as readily as before, and it seemed a long while to Delia until he dropped to her side and fell into a doze. He was upon her twice again in the course of the night, which she patiently endured. By the gray light of dawn, he put himself in his breeches and was in some haste to leave before the other servants would be rising from their beds. Nonetheless, he did not neglect his gentlemanly devoirs, first patting her cheek as he thanked her for her kindness, then putting a half-guinea on the pillow. (Had she been a little fuller in her flesh, and livelier in disposition, she might have earned two.) Delia seized his hand as he turned to depart. Holding up the coin, she said, Is it pin money for my use, husband? Do you not know me yet? It is I, your Delia: who you wedded in a by-lane of Alsatia and pronounced to be your wife before a tippler and his boy. Delia, that was called harsh names and thrust out of doors by her father because of you. Delia, that was grievously cudgeled and left bruised and bleeding in the road, only for fidelity to you. Delia, that wandered all about England in search of you; and with whom you are now at last reunited.

I shall do the goggle-eyed gentleman the justice to say, I wager he had not the slightest recollection of his Delia, nor any notion that he had lain with such a woman before. Though he had a hearty appetite, that would not scorn a twopenny hedge-trull if she lay in his way, he would not willingly couple with a madwoman. Either 'twas lunacy or else a poorly laid trap, and he was no woodcock. —You cracked and crazed bitch! I am not so easily caught as that. You speak a word to my uncle and you'll find yourself in Bridewell, or Bedlam, I care not which. Despite his resolute words, delivered in a furious whisper, he skipped down the stair as soft as possible. His feeble head was pothered and perturbed; he had not courage sufficient to outface the woman should she grow frenzied. Taking alarm, he departed from the house at an hour when no one had ever seen him stir from his bed, leaving behind a scrawl for his uncle, excusing himself with a pretense of urgent business in the Town.

Deeply astonished, his twice-forsaken mistress was left gathering her thoughts at such an unlooked-for conclusion to the tender scene. She had fully expected he would fall upon his knees, beseech forgiveness, and humbly ask her hand in lawful marriage. Else she would never have endured such a wakeful night; during which, she told me solemnly, she once felt a fluttering sensation that might have been pleasurable, had not the moonlight happened just then to fall upon his face. Her first notions were an angry resentment of Providence, but 'twas only an instant before she repented, and confessed to herself, it was her own prideful folly that brought her to this humiliation—that, and the lying romance she read in the former Mrs. Witherby's school, which professed to be The Famous and Delightful History of the Beautiful Diaphanta and the Unfaithful Prince Florinto. She holds to this day a resentful grudge against its author; giving as her opinion, that such works should be repressed and their authors pilloried for imposing falsehoods upon their trustful readers. And yet, mingled with the shame of having been whore to Mr. Maynard for a night, was a feeling of release and reprieve that she would not, after all, be his lawful wedded wife for ever and ay. Her head in a great turmoil of vexation and shame, she made herself as fresh as she could, and smoothed her countenance before stepping from her garret: for, above all else, she wanted none in the house to suspect her of having submitted to such loathed embraces. —That was a prudent fear, I said to her, yet Heaven sees all, and judges all. —That, she said, I would never deny. Yet Heaven knows my heart was free of all base desire of pleasure or gain. For there was no pleasure in it, but only mortification. As for the ten shillings sixpence, truly, I would as soon turn dunghill-raker, or cry mackerel in the streets, as suffer the ropy kisses of that pimpled coxcomb.

If any of the servants peeped at Delia as she went about her morning duties, they would notice that she seemed lumpish and out of sorts, for her carriage was naturally quick and graceful. She wore a frowning look and was muttering to herself. 'Twas not her prayers. She was saying to herself, again and again: Wild carrot, tansy, savin, with a thimbleful of cuckoo flower its seed, brewed together in a tea. Yet there was another thing in't she said was sovereign. Did it begin with a V? Vervain? Valerian? No. Or was it a W? Wallwort? White bryony? No, 'twas not that neither. Thus she mumbled and fretted and cudgeled her noddle without being any the nearer to recalling the chapwoman's recipe. She told the butler she was feeling sickish, as indeed she must have appeared, and wished to go to an apothecary to have a medicine made up for her. So she purposed to do, hoping an infusion of the four herbs, supplemented by wishes and prayers, would be efficacious. However, upon a sudden resolve, her wardrobe being scanty, she stopped to buy a hood, which she pulled low about her face. With this slender disguise, she thought she might venture to approach the Dog and Bear. The hour was one when Tom Found would be carrying jugs of ale to daily customers. Delia hoped to find him upon his rounds and to ask him if Nan Trundle were at the tavern just now. If he happened to notice her uncommon resemblance to his former fellow, why then she could admit to being Jack's sister and beg his secrecy. She thought he would be faithful; of the chapwoman's constancy she had some doubt. All the same, she had about twelve shillings of good money, and twenty shillings of bad, with which to purchase her silence and her recipe. I do not think her plan wise: she might have asked a Covent Garden apothecary for wild carrot, tansy, cuckoo flower, and savin, with whatever else was good for women's complaints, without any risk at all, except of being poisoned.

When she came up within a few doors of the tavern, she was surprised to find it deserted, and that at an hour when there would usually be a brace or two of idlers at the door, and a noise of boastful talk from the front parlor. Seeing the joiner outside his shop, she dared to say, she had been upon this street many times before and never known it to be so quiet; which was enough to spark a discourse, in which others joined in. She learned that the Messengers, assisted by a troop of the guard, had descended upon the place that same morning. They seized everyone within, even the mistress and her servants, and carried them to the Compter. Delia had not, until that moment, considered that naming Tom Found to Bushrod might bring trouble to him. She stayed in the street a little while, listening to what more she might learn, which was very little beyond rumor, and then went away; too alarmed and concerned to undertake her own necessary business with an apothecary. ✠

CHAPTER 16

Delia attempts to write to her father to warn him but is prevented. Sir Maynard,
his suspicions aroused, questions her closely.

**WOLF THAT** is balked of a lamb will seize a hen; a dog that
cannot get a bone will gnaw upon a stick: Bushrod, having
failed to take Jacobites for want of a second witness, delivered
up a brace of coiners, Gryce and Blank, for forty pounds each.
(I believe he had it in his head from the beginning that, being catched for
vending bad coin, he would save himself by exposing them, along with as
many of the blackguard boys as were worth the taking.)[1] Gryce saved himself
by informing upon Ned Shift, who he said was deep in Jacobite plotting.
Shift, being nabbed, squeaked Sir John Herewige, Major Boyle, and some
others. Wedge, the joiner, being late to join the pack and take up the cry,
was denied the best bits of the carcass; yet his informations were sufficient
for issuing an order that everyone at the treason-talking tavern be taken
up, including Mrs. Peatfoote and Tom Found.

The next day Delia took her first opportunity to slip from the house. Mrs.
Peatfoote had been released that morning, due to the intercession of Ned
Shift, who said that the woman was honest, having many times reproved
her guests for their unruly behavior and blasphemous oaths; and that she
could not be expected to know what was whispered among the knots of men
meeting in her upper chambers. Tom Found was let go a short while after,
having imparted the little that he knew, which was but a few words let fall
while he was waiting on a party. Delia came up as the boy and his mistress
were relating their news for the second or third time to a cluster of neighbors
and inquisitive passers-by. Mrs. Peatfoote said, there were more warrants
out for those named by Mr. Shift, whom she called an honest gentleman
and a kind one, for sparing her; for he might easily have contrived a tale to
the effect that she often sat down with her guests and heard things; which
would then compel her to give informations of her own, to save herself.
Major Boyle was wanted, she said, but had not been seen in a sennight, and
had perhaps taken alarm and fled. She and the boy had been asked many a
question concerning Sir John Herewige, a very kind and generous gentleman. He was evidently in danger from an informer; she hoped it was not
Mr. Shift. The King's Messengers might be at his house this hour, searching
for arms and treasonous papers. She named the persons who were taken
up out of her house, which were five officers, two unlucky gentlemen that

happened to be in their company, and a pretended chapwoman that carried messages for the plotters. The boy Jack who was formerly her drawer was among those wanted. Here Tom interposed, saying he was certain Jack was innocent and had only overheard a little talk, as he had. The mistress said, Jack was a false-fronted, slippery sort of boy, which caused her to misdoubt him, and to turn him out.

Delia cared very little for her own (or rather Jack's) danger, but she was sorely troubled to learn that Sir John was in difficulties. It was apparent that Bushrod had laid an information, alleging he had a store of arms in his house and an excessive number of good horse in his stable. It might be that Major Boyle had the generosity to send him warning, though she doubted it. She was concerned as well for the chapwoman, and hoped it was not another charge to be laid against her own conscience, for leading Bushrod to the tavern. She could not, having brought others into peril, give much heed to her own frets and cares. Upon her moping return, the butler gave her a severe rating for absenting herself from the house without leave. —Oh, sir, she said, dissolving into tears, I am sorry for it, truly; but some of my friends are in great distress and I don't know how to help them. —I take no account of your tears or your excuses, answered Biggs, for I am beginning to perceive you are a designing minx. Yesterday you said you was ill and needed a medicine from the apothecary, which is only a few steps to go. You come back a full hour later with a new hood upon your head, which you did not have upon going out, and I am sure you did not get it from a druggist. My eye is on you. If you absent yourself again, I'll turn you out of your place.

There was no answer she could return to this rebuke, and it was a some-thing superadded to her dejection to feel that she had earned it. Her misery and sorrow were such, that she could liken it only to the day when she was ravished in an alley by a pimply fop, banished from home by her outraged father, and, after setting forth on a long weary trudge, soundly thrashed by a rejected swain. That had been a black day; and yet, things were now worse for her. Then she had been surprised and assailed; now she had whored herself. Then her father had been hasty and unkind; now she herself had betrayed the good Sir John, whom she esteemed as a father. It needed but a third calamity to turn the scale. Upon this ill-boding train of reflection, she began to consider that she had not reckoned up the current disaster in full. Mrs. Peatfoote reported that Ned Shift was laying informations on a number of men. It might be supposed he had treasonable papers in his possession whereof he needed to account, and 'twas presumable he might name her father as their author. Although she herself might be affrighted by the gorgon at the door, the King's Messengers would not be. Being thus surprised, her father might have papers on his desk that would bear out the accusation; she must therefore get a timely notice to him. A letter from Delia would be torn up unread; but it was an easy task to disguise her hand and to represent the warning as from an unnamed well-willer.

The master was entertaining company at dinner; the butler and footmen would be occupied in service, and the boys in the kitchen with the cook. 'Twas an opportunity too good to be neglected. She sneaked to the master's study, sat down at the desk and began her letter. She was so concentrated upon her task, that her first knowledge of anyone entering the room, was a burst of angry words and a hard clap to her head that cast her from the chair. Sir Maynard, wanting a book to answer some contested point, had come into his private chamber to discover a housemaid seated at his desk, making bold with his pen and paper as though they were public commodities. He snatched up the paper she was wasting, expecting an illiterate scribble to a lover, to discover, to his supreme astonishment, written in a fine italic hand, a letter that began:

Reverend Sir, Your free and noble spirit hath often prompted you to open up your thoughts in well-penned arguments for the benefit of the commonweal; and to put your country before the safety of your own self. Certain men, that are now under arrest for their disturbances to peace and liberty, may seek to preserve themselves by delating you under a false and malicious construction of your words.

—What the devil, he exclaimed. What can this mean? What maidservant ever penned such a letter since the beginning of the world! Delia, trembling upon her knees, stammered out an apology. She was writing to her father, who is a learned man that wrote some pamphlets critical of the government, but none that advocated sedition or violence. Among the conspirators that were lately seized at a tavern near Drury Lane, was one who many times visited her father and carried his writings to the printer. Though her father had no knowledge of their plots, she feared his former friend might inform upon him. Some of his writings might be misconstrued; she fears he may be taken up on a charge of misprision of treason.

A common servant able to use such words! Then again, if her father is a learned man, she is not a common servant. Her eyes glistening with tears held his for a long moment, until his inveterate suspicion of females was aroused. Drawing back, he asked (for her hair had fallen down with the force of the blow), What happened to your hair, have you been ill? Delia gave a jumbled and hesitating tale, that it had been sold, for money.

She had no money. Her father—her friends—she was separated from her friends—and now without money—so she sought and found employment in his household. Stunned by the force of the master's blow, Delia had too little wit or guile or presence of mind to fill out her tale beyond disjointed phrases; fortunately so, for Sir Maynard understood it altogether different. He took that her father was a nonjuror and a Jacobite, who wrote some incautious words in defense of that cause; which caused him to relent in his harshness to the girl. For, though he adhered to a moderate whiggishness for the sake of his interest, he preserved in his heart a secret allegiance to the king who granted him his knighthood. Were it safe and expedient to pledge fealty to King James or his heirs, he would do so very gladly.

Sir Maynard dismissed her with an appearance of severity; nonetheless, he let her have the unfinished letter, along with a pen, a bottle of ink, and a few spare sheets. Having finished her letter, she gave it with a sixpence to the trustworthier of the two boys; beyond that she could do no more but pray. She was yet in the butler's ill graces and unable to budge from the house except to church. The arrests of a knot of plotters made a buzz in the town for a day or two. The net had taken a pack of ex-Jacobite officers that were notorious swaggerers of no importance; some frightened gentlemen that promptly swore allegiance and begged clemency; and a mass-priest that belonged to Sir John Herewige. The orders to search his house had been hasty and ill-written; when the searchers pulled the priest from his lair, they thought they had performed what was wanted, and did not trouble the baronet any further. That same day he received an abusive scribble from Boyle, which said nothing clearly but made biting allusion to gypsies and their cullies. Sir John got together as much money and plate as he could carry; then, as soon as it was night, saddled his best horse and made off at a furious pace to the house of Farmer Grigg, where he gave up his horse and thirty guineas in exchange for an uneasy passage in an open shallop. In all the talk of the town, no one could say in certainty what the plotters intended. Some said they meant to assassinate the King at the Newmarket races. Others, that they would poison him when he went on his progress to Oxford. A third rumor had it that they planned to spirit away a certain large, jostling, obsequious prelate, as it would embarrass and annoy the King, to be made to pay a ransom for his detested ex-chaplain.[2] 'Twas but a few anxious days more before Delia heard news to reassure her that Sir John had escaped oversea. She wondered what was become of the chapwoman; but as there were no further arrests, she presumed her father was secure from harm.

Her thoughts were full of unquietness, as her position in the household was not a happy one. Young Mr. Maynard came back to the house for his usual dinner with his uncle. Though he avoided Delia as steadfastly as she did him, it was still uncomfortable for her. His presence in the house raised a train of doleful reflections and regret. Moreover, Sir Maynard seemed to regret his leniency to her (though the clap he delivered to her head was not a gentle one). He several times came into a room where she was at work and looked sourly at her; but when she offered to withdraw, told her to continue at her task. With a frowning look, he would put questions that were difficult to answer honestly in a way that would bring trouble upon no one. His first question was, why did she write to her father in so formal a style? To this she had a ready reply: Her father was lately remarried, and her new stepmother hostile to her, though she had shown her much pretended regard before the marriage. She feared the letter would be torn in pieces, unread, if she did not disguise her hand and write as 'twere from an anonymous well-willer. With this truthful reply, she could account for being out in the world upon her own, which might otherwise be difficult of explanation. Upon another occasion, he asked, did she have no other clothes but those upon her back? She answered that she did not. She had owned many pretty things which she inherited from her mother, but they had all been sold or pawned for money to subsist, though she'd been sadly cheated in the bargain. Her master then said to her, You must ask Mr. Biggs for an advance on your wages; if he charge you interest on it, I'll see that the sum will be made up on quarter day.

This was something Delia dared not undertake; she hoped it would be forgotten, but it was not. The next day, the master came upon her at her work again and asked, did she get some of her wages from Mr. Biggs? Delia was obliged to say that she feared to ask it, for she was in disgrace with the butler and she could not blame him for it. She absented herself from the house twice, upon an urgent wish to get news of the plotters and their informations, which she feared would implicate her father. Mr. Biggs, catching her at it, had conceived an ill opinion of her. Sir Maynard frowned mightily and went out the room. An hour later she was summoned by Biggs, who likewise frowned coldly upon her (he did everything in imitation of the master). Nonetheless, he advanced her twenty-five shillings and told her to go out at once and get her apparel that was fitting for a maidservant in a fine house as she fortuned to have her place. Delia, who delighted in good clothes, had never had such a sum in her fist to buy whatever pleased her. Yet it was with only a somber joy that she went about to the ready-made shops and got herself two cambric shifts, a striped tabby gown, a flowered taffety, an alamode silk scarf, a good petticoat trimmed in lutestring, two pair cotton stocking, one pair silk, and new roses and ties for her shoes. Having accepted the money, she could not now throw up her place, which she had been greatly tempted to do: partly from her anxiety to know what was become of the chapwoman, but chiefly to avoid the sight of Mr. Maynard. 'Twas no great solace to believe she looked handsome in her new clothes, if 'twould bring a renewal of his odious embraces.

When she appeared in her new clothes, her master seemed approving; he then, however, began to ask a great many fresh questions concerning her parentage and her upbringing. Delia feared there was something more in it; she mistrusted being carried into revelations concerning her father that might be dangerous. Her master got from her answers to the effect that her family had a middling good estate in the county of ——; that her father was the youngest of three sons, not expected to inherit, and so not instructed in farming or management of an estate, being always more inclinable to books and writing. That her mother was the daughter of a fashionable tailor and that she died when Delia was a small child. That Delia had been sent to a gentlewoman's school to learn to write and to improve in her reading so that she might assist her father, who was gouty. That her father had been compelled to sell part of his estate to pay the land taxes. That her new mother-in-law was her former schoolmistress, and that she would not permit Delia to visit her father. Sir Maynard was not done with his questions, when Delia cried, Please, sir, I must say no more. I fear that my father is yet in danger, though innocent. I must say nothing that might expose him. Her master, much surprised, said, he had no such intention. He was more in sympathy with her father's politics than otherwise, though truly it was not safe to belong to his party. Delia was very little reassured; she could not conceive of a motive for her master's curiosity, or for the seriousness with which he put his questions and attended to her answers.

Sir Maynard was not always a woman-hater; he had upon a time been as partial to the sex as his nephew. When he was a man of about five and twenty years, newly come into an inheritance, and with a thriving business interest, he seduced the beautiful, fresh daughter of a bankrupt trader. He was so dotingly fond that he installed his mistress in fine lodgings, indulged her in every luxury, and would have devoted his wealth to her gratification, had she not poxed him. His cure was long and painful; he was thence forward the avowed enemy of all simpering daughters, all tittering maidservants, all lecherous wives and mistresses of other men. A quiet, modest girl, reared by a bookish country gentleman, one that was never taught to dance or sing or play upon an instrument, was as unlike his faithless Jenny as she might be. Her carriage was remarkably graceful but free of affectation: she had not the least touch of coquetry to her character.

It needs no great ceremony or delicacy for a wealthy gentleman to propose marriage to his servant girl, nor was Delia foolishly coy in accepting. A license was obtained; they went out separately to the church; so that the first notice of anything extraordinary was their coming through the door together. The butler might have thought that Sir Maynard catched her upon a ramble, and was leading her home for chastisement, except he had her upon his arm. His first words were these: Biggs, you see here your new mistress. She is now Lady Maynard. The poor man managed to bow and mumble a few words, before he tottered into the kitchen and gave out the dismal news. The boy who had put a turd on her pillow began to howl; he had been hired from the workhouse and now he would be turned out in the street. None pitied him, for they had all played pranks or delivered snubs that would now be avenged. The footmen, Jeremy and Nat, looked blank upon one another. Though the livery was of a sober fashion, they liked their places, and now they would lose 'em, and perhaps leave without a character too. Biggs was sunk in melancholy: 'twas far too late to bite back those offending words, a designing minx. He had served his master for too many years to fear the loss of his post; but 'twould be a sad thing to serve under a mistress who detested him. Only the man-cook was unafflicted with regret, for he could get a new place at will; Sir Maynard had ordered a fine dinner for two, which he was just then busily preparing.

It was served up very clumsily, with a clattering of covers, and a good dish dropped and chipped. The master frowned and waxed testy, until his wife said to him, Sir Maynard, shall we dismiss them from waiting on the table? I always served my father's table when he had guests to dinner, and why should I not serve my husband now? This was agreed to: Sir Maynard was charmed to observe how skillfully his wife carved, how gracefully she handed dishes and refilled his glass. After the table was cleared away, Sir Maynard went to his study to write his news to his friends. Lady Maynard took this opportunity to summon the servants. They came shuffling before her like so many prisoners in the dock. 'Twas only a question of who she would turn out instanter, and who should stay until their places were filled. She addressed herself first to the offending boy, whose face was red with tears. —Will, stop up your sniveling. You will scrub the front parlor fireplace and polish the grate till it shines, and then you'll be forgiven. Jeremy and

Nat, if you ever offer rudeness to any of my maids, you will be dismissed at once without a character. I am willing to extend a pardon to you, because I consider you had a very ill model before you in the behavior of Mr. Maynard. I wish to let my husband understand his nephew's depravity, and I hope some of you can aid me in making a discovery.

They were now her friends and very ready to offer suggestions. Jeremy said, he thought he could find the last chambermaid but one, who said she was forced, but had not been believed by the master. Delia answered him, I consider that Sir Maynard is not yet so free of his old prejudices but that he would doubt her unattested word, and believe rather that she consented, and afterwards regretted it. If his nephew has made himself notorious as a lecher, a rakehell, or a gambler, then that will shake his belief in him. 'Tis almost certainly the case that Mr. Maynard keeps his residence in the Town so he may more easily engage in debauchery without his uncle hearing of it. I think it very likely that he commits his depravities under a false name. He lives upon Hanover Street, does he not? There is a joiner keeping shop a little distance from there, named Wedge, that spies for the Manners Society at that end of town.[3] If Mr. Maynard has made his face notorious, under his own name or a false one, this fellow will know it, or will know how to get the information. (There was then almost a quarrel among the menservants, as to which would have the glory of the undertaking, until Delia put an end to further debate by selecting Nat, who is a tall, well-favored fellow of good address.) —Such men as this joiner do nothing without being fee'd; if he gets a shilling for a poor woman crying cherries on the Sabbath or a silk-weaver overheard swearing, I judge half a guinea sufficient for informing privately on a gentleman. Mr. Biggs, would you advance Nat the money? I'll make up the sum out of my own purse at the end of the quarter. Mr. Biggs, I wish you to know that I bear no ill will towards you for any harsh expressions you may have used to me. For the appearances were such, that your suspicions were very natural. These last words were uttered with such candor and dignity that the old fellow was instantly attached to his new mistress; and, in imitation of his master, fell in love with her upon the spot.

The footmen clubbed together a description of Mr. Maynard, which they brought for review to their mistress. —It was, she said to me, the only thing concerning that gentleman that ever caused me to smile. She made a fresh draft wherein she struck out parts and corrected the style; the original was so pat as a character that she kept it. 'Twas evident that Mr. Maynard had ingratiated himself with none of the family except his uncle:

Infarmation wanted consarning the doins of a young gennelman of twenty yeers. Is beleeved to go about under a false name. Dresses mighty rich flashy and smart tho his linins but indefrent clene. Effecks a gold watch he allways pullin out to shew. No sword as he wuld be affrighted at sight of it tho it be his own. Of middel hight, summit soft in the belly tho scraggy inis arms and legs. Face yelowe an plouky. Black goggle eyes shottin red with drinkin & unwholsum howres. Unhansum manner of spittin. Very affrontin tordes enny he consider beneeth him. Gives small vales no matter how offin he come to the house and all thats done for him.

The joiner, upon being given the revised character, said that he believed the man was a notorious offender, and he could find witnesses to it, though they would want fees of their own. Nat, who was entrusted to undertake such bargaining, made a compact with the man. He was to bring his witnesses to Sir Maynard's house next Saturday about noon, when they would be able to confront the man before his uncle, who has as yet no knowledge of his ill doings.

Mr. Maynard by now was in receipt of a note from his uncle, which announced his marriage to the only child of a gentleman of respectable estate in the country of ——, and invited his nephew to dinner a Saturday, that he might become acquainted with his aunt. The nephew must have been much disturbed by this news, for an aunt is a vast deal worse than a cousin, especially if she happen to be young and broody. He could not conceive how his uncle would have occasion to meet such a creature, for he only entertained the wives and female relations of his friends from necessity. She might be some such relation that was brought to the house, and someway ingratiated herself. It seemed likeliest (upon reading over the letter) that she was a mature women of his uncle's years, and very rich, or soon to be so, when her ancient father died. I do not know, of course, that Mr. Maynard reasoned thus to himself, for he was but slenderly supplied with brain; but he did have two days to consider it, and I believe he would indulge himself in the most easeful and soothing conclusion. I wager he dressed with extraordinary care for this introduction, even (if it may be believed) to the extent of cleaning his teeth and bespeaking a fresh shirt of his laundress.

Coming at the appointed time, he was directed to Sir Maynard's study, where he found his uncle in conference with three plainly dressed citizens. He was excusing himself to leave, when one of them cried, —'Tis the man, that is, 'tis the gentleman I spoke of, that was indecent to a girl of twelve years, and when the bailiff went to arrest him, he had his bully beat him.

—I know him as well, said another of the men. He was carried to the Poultry Compter, as drunk as a drowned mouse, after he broke into a respectable woman's house, which he mistook for a brothel, and insulted the mistress and her maid; but before he could be brought before a magistrate, he corrupted the officer and made his escape.[4] Wedge then said, Sir Maynard, as I told you, I might bring you more testimonies concerning his riotous behavior in bagnios and other low dens, he being but too well known in such places; only I do not think you would wish to admit the witnesses to your house. —I would not, answered that gentleman. However, I thank you all for coming to me. I knew none of this. (Upon this hint, the footman that had his ear at the door, scampered away on stocking feet, while his fellow showed the men out.)

When Sir Maynard came to dinner a short while later, he looked pale and angry so that his wife asked, was he feeling ill? Or did something occur to disturb him? He answered that he had been credibly informed, within the hour, that his nephew was guilty of vicious and depraved practices, such as were scarce fit to be spoken of, certainly not to his wife. He had forbidden him the house. He was glad they did not meet, for the mere idea that a man of such bestial appetites should touch his wife's hand, or salute her cheek, disgusted him. (Delia herself shuddered at the thought.) To put her husband in better temper, she asked, did he have no other family but this one nephew? Yes, he said, a widowed sister with an only son, in Norfolk. As he seemed pensive, she did not trouble him with further questions, knowing that there would have been one servant, at the least, posted ear to door; though by the time she had the opportunity of hearing an account, 'twould no doubt be altered and amplified by the surmise and commentary of their fellow servants. Although, indeed, Jeremy and Nat made a long-drawn relation, the pith of it was this: The master taxed his nephew with bringing the family name into disrepute; whereto the noddy replied, 'Tis false, sir! I always used my cousin Cloudsley's name! ✠

CHAPTER 17

The conclusion of this history, with the fates of many persons in it. A final view of Marius Bye.

A SPLENDID COACH and six, passing out of the City at Ludgate, slowed to a foot pace in the crowded passage round St. Clements Dane, then turned up Drury Lane and stopped before a nearby tavern. A boy that was drowsing upon the bench is called over to the coach. The lady within says to him, Tom, can you guess who I am? I am sister to Jack, who was server beside you. Jack is gone away; before he went, he got from me a pledge that I would be a friend to you. Tom, would you like to be my footboy? Tom scuttled within-doors to say three words of farewell to Mrs. Peatfoote, bundled up his gear, then came flying back. The coach proceeded from High Holbourn to Gray's Inn Lane, turning towards Highgate. Tom gaped at his new mistress, who was young, well-favored, and richly dressed. She was, moreover, kind and affable; so that he was soon recovered from his awe, and able to answer the questions she put to him; for she promised her brother that she would send him an account of his friends as soon as she was able. (She cautioned him that he must not speak of Jack to any of the family, as Jack had been wrongly accused of plotting; but must say only that he got his place by a friend that recommended him to it.)

The first of his news, though of the least concern, was that Mrs. Peatfoote was lately married to Ned Shift, who showed his willingness to be ruled by the distaff in promising to take her name (his own being worn into infamy); that they minded to sell the tavern, whereupon Tom would be without a place. Here he began to blubber, saying, he had lost hope of finding his parents, but it was a blessing beyond his prayers to be taken up by a beautiful lady that was so kind and good. —You will have a handsome livery to wear, Tom, and when you are grown to a man, we'll make a footman of you; for I know from my brother's account of you that you are honest, faithful, and diligent. Now wipe away your tears and tell me what you know of the others that were peached and clapped up.

Tom said Mrs. Peatfoote sent him to Newgate with meat and drink for those that were nabbed out of her house. The officers were lying in easy circumstance on the master's side.[1] They were supplied with money by some unknown benefactor (it could not be Sir John Herewige, as he was fled), and were in their usual case of boastful drunkenness. One of them said to him, they expected to be given the liberty of the prison within a few days' time, whereupon they might take a long stroll. (I am informed that they subsequently strolled as far as Yorkshire, where they found patronage and encouragement to further plotting.) The chapwoman he found on the common side. She took what he brought her so eagerly (though it was only broken meats and dribbles that the officers left behind) that he thought she must not have eaten that day. Mrs. Peatfoote's charity, however, was not as interested in the chapwoman as in the officers; he was not sent to her again, and consequently could give no further word of her. Delia said, she was much surprised by his account; for she understood from Jack that the woman had a good store of money on her person, it must have amounted to two or three pounds at the least, some of it properly his own; moreover, her trade of carrying messages was profitable. Tom said, it may be she was robbed, or had it all extorted from her, as there's no knowing what such knaves as catchpoles and turnkeys might do with a woman that was only a stroller and without friends. His mistress answered, it might be so, though privately she doubted. She knew Nan had money concealed in the linings of her clothes with such cunning and care, that she must be stripped as naked as she was born before 'twould all be taken. She said to Tom, she would send him tomorrow with a basket of food and drink to comfort the poor woman; only it must not be said where he got it, for she would not be troubled with questions regarding her brother, which was a secret between the two of them.

They went a mile or so farther upon the North Road before Delia bid the coachman slow down, and stop before the next house. Nat jumped down to run to the door, only to have Mrs. Urith Bye, wondering very much to have such a coach draw up before her house, meet him half-way. Nat said, My Lady Maynard is come upon a visit. As he went to open the coach, he was crowded by Mrs. Bye, very obsequious in her manner, and unable to curb her curiosity. Delia says, when she looked into the coach and saw who it was, her goblin face was so convulsed with rage and envy, 'twas fortunate Tom Found was screened from seeing her, else he might have feared his new mistress was a fairy creature, in league with demons to hale him off to hell. The woman took a leap backwards and would have toppled if Nat did not catch her by the shoulder; then she fled back into the house. —'Tis my stepmother, who cast me out from my home, said Delia to the astonished footman. I think she is much surprised to see me prospering. ('Twas an admission that could do her no harm, for all her servants would thereby know she was a gentlewoman by birth, with a very disagreeable stepmother

to vindicate her for being on her own and going into service.) Unwilling
to prolong an unpleasant encounter, she directed the coach to return home.

Early the next day, Delia dispatched Tom to Newgate with a basket of
food and drink for the chapwoman. When he was gone a great while longer
than she would have supposed necessary, she felt a little alarm, imagining
him returning in the company of the King's Messengers, come to arrest that
fell traitor, Jack Trundle. At last he reappeared, wearing a downcast look;
she took him to her closet to learn how his errand succeeded. He said, The
chapwoman has just died, which I know will grieve Jack, but milady will
best know how to tell him the story. There was a delivery since I was last
there, and the prison was less crowded than before, but still very foul and
swarming with wretches and rascals of every sort.[2] I found the poor woman
stretched on a filthy pavement. She seemed to be moaning, as though she
were in pain; but when I come close I perceived she was singing to herself.
She didn't know me and was very listless; when I offered the food she only
looked at it. I then showed the bottle of ale that was in the basket, and that
she gave an eager look. She beckoned me to hold it for her. Having wetted
her throat with two or three long pulls at the bottle, she began to talk but
'twas little to the purpose, only stuff such as, —They wonnot get it from
me, I'll die afore I let 'em have it. I said to her, Goody Trundle, there are
so many informations laid already, it little matters what more you say. Sir
John Herewige and Major Boyle are fled. Why not say what you can to save
yourself? But she only talked the same riddle-me-ree, and I began to think
her gone mad and unable to understand her case.

Some idlers come forward as I was urging her to eat and drink. I suppose
they was hoping for a bit from the basket, there being some very thin-
gutted beggars among 'em, poor creatures. One said to me, You have taken
the staff by the wrong end. She means she wonnot pay the money that the
turnkeys want for food and drink. For she was very loud about it when she
first come in; being told that a pot of small beer and a two-penny loaf could
be had for eight pence, she roared she'ld not be robbed. The officer only
scoffed at her haggling—she'ld not go above a groat—saying, she'ld pay up
gladly when she was a-hungry and athirst; but as you see she's well-nigh
famined, though I wager she has money on her. —Don't ye know, woman,
he said to her, that the keeper gets all if you perish? Another man, that
seemed a sort of hedge-preacher, said, 'Tis self-murder, woman, don't ye
know you'll roast in hell for it, same as you took a knife t'your own throat?
Someone told him to be quiet, the woman was touched in the head and
'twas a devilish suggestion. Another said, She needs some gruel to eat, she's

too sickly for the victuals you give her. Upon this good advice, I went in search of an officer to bespeak some broth or pottage for her. As I took the basket with me, the most part went away again; but the pretended saint was still huffing her concerning self-slaughter and damnation. I came back not many minutes later, bearing a pen'orth of barley-pap that cost ten pence, a keeper trailing after, to see what else he might gain by me.

I see the chapwoman now made lively by the ale, I fear 'twas too strong for her. She was on her feet, swaying back and forth, propped up by the hedge-preacher, who I think was as mad as she, and done very ill in talking to her of death and damnation, for her look now was wild and staring. Setting eyes on the turnkey that was following me, she reached out a purse and flung her money into the yard, crying, You swindling, sharking devil, I said you'ld never get it from me and you see! Now it was Bedlam come to Newgate in the moil of people fighting for a share of the money. She was fumbling at her pockets to get out more, when some villains seized hold of her and began to pull off her clothes. There was nothing in her gown, but it was rent to shreds all the same. When they took her coats off her, which were quilted and heavy of coin, the rabble-rout was clawing each other for a share. All this happening so quick, there was no preventing them. They knocked her about until she was bleeding hard at the nose, and they did not let until they stripped her of her stays. I took the napkin from the basket to stop the blood, but then I saw her face was stark and blank. The keeper said, She is no more, the poor mad fool. There was nothing else I could do there. I left the keeper some money to bury her, and I gave out the food in my basket to some poor prisoners that was not among the rioters. Delia had much ado to compose her countenance so that her footboy might not perceive how affected she was by his tale. —You did very well, Tom. Now go down-stair and let Mr Biggs know that I would have you measured for your livery. I must think what to write to my brother.

Even alone in her closet, Delia did not feel at liberty to indulge her tears. There was no one to whom she dared confide; her only recourse to relieve her feelings was to take up a pen and begin a letter to her dear brother Jack. 'Twas a curious composition, full of wire-drawn sorrowings: She told Jack her many regrets. She said, the chapwoman had performed such a signal kindness to her when she was homeless, that she regretted any hard words that fell between them, or any complaints about money. She wished she could have got aid to her sooner, though how that might be, Jack knew as well as she, 'twas next door to impossible. She wished she had sent Tom Found with small beer and sops, which might have been reviving. She wished a score of things that were done, could be undone. She knew it was Nan's stubbornness in getting the better of every bargain that was her undoing; which made her yet more regretful that there had been quarrels between them about money; the woman could not help what was her nature, no more than the leopard can change his spots. When she had exhausted her thoughts upon this subject, she wrote more cheerfully. She hoped her brother was pleased to learn that she had taken on Tom Found, whom she hoped to employ to fetch out what had happened to other of their friends:

Sir John Herewige's household broke up when he fled, as he proved to be deeply in debt, above all to his own steward. I am sure you will not have forgotten Sally, who spent her wages to get you a warm cloak for your journey to London. I am at a loss for the moment how to get word of her. For you must know, Jack, that a poor body in breeches may go about freely, without anyone taking notice of him, but the same is not true of a rich knight's lady. There are always servants about, listening for every word, and I may not go anywhere without at least one footman. If I can find Sally, I'll be sure to help her to a good place, or otherwise repay her generosity to you. I wish it were possible to hire her as my woman, but I could not tell her the tale I told Tom Found, and expect to be believed. I have lately taken a maid who seems a good honest girl. If I find she is reliable, I'll send her with some finery to sell at a loss to the old man in Alsatia. For though he is a villainous cheat and sharper, he is still our grand-daddy. Moreover, if he put the scissors for sale, I hope to buy it back.

Jack, I know that we shall never again meet. I fear also that I shall never again see my father. When Sir Maynard learned that I had taken the coach there, he said to me very gravely, he hoped I would not do so again; if my father had engaged himself upon the Jacobite side, even if it were only writing in support of the Stuart title, it would be dangerous to admit an acquaintance with him. He himself wished King James should have his rights, but it was not safe to say so outside these walls, and 'twould be ruinous to his interests in the City and the Court. He would not forbid me to write to my father, but I must not send any letters by post, as it is but too probable our correspondence would be opened. I stuck in my answer to him, and my speechlessness he attributed to my devotion to my father. At last I managed to say, it had been a mistake to attempt the visit, my stepmother being so much my enemy, and it would not be repeated.

Jack, I am sure it was foolish to be so long in the dark regarding the aim of the conspiracy; but I believed, as I had been lessoned, that men would not risk their all, only to replace one tyrant with another. Though 'twas perplexing to hear Sir John's guests toast the king over the water, there was Ned Shift making one of their number, which seemed confirmation that their cause was the Old Cause. If our father, with all his learning, could not perceive the double-dealing of Shift, who was serving both sides, but himself foremost, it could not be expected that his child's eyes should see farther. Moreover, I know that you wished most heartily to believe that Nan Trundle and kind Sir John were of the same party as our dear father, so that you might continue to be faithful to him, even in exile.

My husband was also testy with me that I hired another boy in service when we had two already; saying, I might have as many women about me as I pleased, but liveried boys were a vanity, not worth their feeding. To which I could answer little, except that I knew Tom Found to be loyal, discreet, and diligent, and I could safely employ him to carry messages to my father. I had in readiness some news that I knew would transform his humor from spleen to joy. I said to him next, that I was with child. My husband being very solicitous of my health, I shall now be under greater restriction, and, in all probability, may not stir abroad except upon warm, fine days. The paper is full. Jack, adieu! from your affectionate sister, Delia.

In due course (or somewhat less, for he came a fortnight before he was looked for) Lady Maynard presented her husband with an heir. The family resemblance was so manifest as to refute any tittle-tattle. A few good-natured jests were broke upon Sir Maynard, saying he showed a quick disposition and keen ability in a business he had long neglected.

Lady Maynard has occasioned a reconciliation between her husband and his nephew, Robin Cloudsley; to which Sir Maynard was very willing to consent, providing only that no one expected him to acknowledge that he had been deceived, or that he had wronged his nephew. Mr. Cloudsley occupies the rooms that formerly belonged to his cousin; he also keeps a chamber in Gray's Inn, where he has launched into the study of law. He is much in the confidence of his aunt, and performs many little services for her: I do not know all, for sometimes Lady Maynard keeps her own counsel. It was about this same time that I became acquainted with her, and ingratiated myself by helping her to knowledge of some of her friends and former associates. I was able to tell her that Bushrod also informed upon the brothers Hull; for plainly 'twas he that betrayed Blank and Gryce to their rivals. Nonetheless, it was no idle boast of their father, that he had powerful friends: for not only did his sons come to no harm, but Bushrod was impelled to transport himself to the New World. Whereabout he settled I could not discover. He is such a nimble talker of religious cant that, whether he elected to be a Puritan of Boston or a Quaker of Philadelphia, I make no question but he is prospering. Gryce also found the city grown too hot for him. He has taken a neat little box in Middlesex, where he busies himself in growing wall-fruit. Of Blank I could get no tidings; it seemed probable that he made one among the bountiful harvest of clippers and coiners that hang like apples upon Tyburn tree. One day, having in hand a fresh purse of guineas from her husband, Delia took up one to examine it. The metal appeared to be good; or, if it were false, 'twould require a master goldsmith to discern the cheat. 'Twas the pile that drew her attention, for there were certain little strokes that seemed to be of his hand; only when she studied the effigy she was less certain. On balance, she thought it might be his work. Certainly, it would be in the power of the Hulls and their friends to save him; or, his talent being manifest, the Master of the Mint might have claimed him for employment. If such be the case, it is a fitting punishment that Blank should be compelled to cut flattering portraits of a king he despises.

The Dog and Bear being sold, Mr. and Mrs. Peatfoote took the lease of an inn in Southwark, close by the Kent Road, in a parish where the neighbors are not disquieted to observe that Mrs. Peatfoote has hired three maids to see to a small number of rooms, or that their guests arrive at strange hours with their horses in a lather. I wager Mr. Ned Peatfoote, having noted the profit to be made by informing, means to develop a discreet side business as a thief-taker.

News of Sally was obtained by means of a letter writ by Mr. Cloudsley, addressed to the minister of the parish; which letter stated that a cousin in London had left the young woman a modest legacy, only it was as yet unpaid, for no one knew where the woman was to be found. The minister returned an account of her. It seems that the breakup of Herewige's household sent more servants in flight than the neighborhood could well support. Pretty Sally fell spoils to a yeoman who required little leisure to repent of his amorous haste. He regretted taking as wife a woman that had no money and no housewifery beyond making a bed and sweeping a room. He vented his ill humor upon her in words and blows. Unless she is a weak fool, the legacy should work some improvement in her husband's disposition; for it is settled upon her, to be paid into her own hands.

Delia was yet uneasy for her father, left to the tendance of his termagant wife, and wished very earnestly to know how he fared. At last she hit upon the device of writing a letter which purported to be from a printer that knew him by reputation. Mr. Cloudsley, who is a well-informed gentleman (why should I not call him Robin, as we are friends?), helped her with inditing it:

Honored Sir, The power of your pen and the cogency of your arguments in
service of the Old Cause are yet remembered. As you live in retirement (for
I am told that you languish of the gout), it may be you are as yet little aware
that, by revolution of the times, there is risen up a new generation of men
that proudly style themselves republicans. Some congregate at the Grecian in
Devereux Court, where they hold discourse of the virtues of mixed government,
of tolerance, and the rights of men. Rumor speaks also of a knot of bold spirits,
men of the old levelling stamp, that would have no king at all. Their enemies
name them the Calves-Head Club, but what they style themselves I know not.
Another set, which calls itself the College, boasts men of considerable learning
as its members. They are encouraged by Lord Ashley, who wishes to redeem
the fame of his grandfather.[3] *The works of Harrington, Milton, Neville,*
and Sidney are again being read. Moreover, the past few years have seen the
appearance of pamphlets attributed to Ludlow, though whether they be truly
his work or no, may be doubted.[4] *Sir, the times being so propitious, why should*
not the persuasive arguments, that appeared under the letters M. B., be again
published and ventilated in the coffeehouses of London? I would esteem it an
honor, as well as a service to a great cause, if you would loan a copy of one of
your works for reprinting, upon whatever reasonable terms you should ask
of me. The messenger who puts this letter in your hands may be trusted. He
is instructed to stay for a reply, and to expect no vail.

Hoping that you are in good health and spirits and able to oblige, I am your
humble servant, ——

When the letter was complete, Delia dispatched it by Tom, with careful
instructions, repeated twice or thrice over. He was to go in his own clothes,
out of livery. Upon arriving at the house, he was to insist upon putting his
letter into the gentleman's hands, and staying for a response. Moreover, he
was not to answer questions, saying only that he was sent by the printer
with instructions to deliver whatever papers or books were entrusted to him.

As Tom could ride (though not well), he was absent only some two or
three hours, though the time seemed very long to Delia. He said that the
woman who came to the door viewed him with suspicion; but upon his
insistence, let him proceed up the stairs: —The gentleman seemed older
than what I would expect, being milady's father. He was seated in an easy
chair, with one foot upon a stool. He wore a plain black coat with his own
gray hair hanging down about his face. His eye was very keen upon me, like
a magistrate's. He took the letter and read it through with a look of great
surprise. He asked me a deal of questions, but I answered just as milady
instructed me to do. He read it over again and sat awhile in thought, every

now and again looking up at me with that keen look, to read something in my face. At last, he seemed to come to a resolve. Getting up surprising quick from his chair, he began to hop about the chamber on his crutch, gathering a heap of paper out of a cabinet. I would have offered to help the gentleman, only something in his look told me to be still. Then he sat down at his desk and wrote a paper, then he give it all to me in a bundle and told me to be exceeding careful of 'em. 'Tis well I took a satchel with me, or I never would have managed it and the horse both.

Though Lady Maynard was glad to get word of her father, she regarded the manuscript Tom delivered to her with dismay. ('Twas in her hand but out of her memory; she supposed it a forgotten work of that busy year, Eighty-Eight.) —I am undone by my own device, she said. I wished only to find some trick to evade my stepmother so that I might learn of my father's health, and also give him encouragement he would value. I don't know what to do with this paper, which my father, by his letter, expects to see in print. 'Twas suggested to her, that she might follow the example of Ned Shift, with a harmless fib to the effect that the authorities were searching for the author. She answered, No, I would never suppress a work of my father's inditing. Yet I would not for a hundred pounds that Sir Maynard should find such papers in his house. I said to her then, that I knew a poor beggarly printer that would print off one or two copies for a small sum, ten or twelve shillings. She said, it was just the thing to answer, and gave me the manuscript to bear away with me. Then she perceived that Tom had something more to say concerning his visit.

—There was something that puzzled me, milady. Upon the day I rode with you in the coach, and your stepmother come out of the house, I did not get a full look at that lady's face.

—You were fortunate in that, Tom.

—Yes, milady, I believe it. Though I saw enough of her to know she is a tall, thin, bony woman.

—That is right, Tom.

—But she that let me in, and saw me out again, was a square-built, foggy woman with one eye knocked out of her head.

—Jane! Jane! It could only be Jane! Why in heaven would she be there? What could have happened to her husband? Tom, you did not see my stepmother at all?

—No, milady, it seemed there was only the two of 'em in that big house, though I cannot be certain of that.

As 'twas evident Lady Maynard would enjoy no peace until she had bottomed this mystery, and as there were yet some hours remaining to the day, Robin and I said that we would set out at once to discover what news we might learn concerning her stepmother. It needed only that we stop at the nearest alehouse, where we made mention of the house and asked to whom it belonged, to draw out a complete history of the family. We were told that it belonged to a brain-sick, scribbling gentleman, who let a good estate go to ruin by neglect. That he had not been known to leave his house for many a year. He had a daughter that he used as a servant until she run away from him the year afore. He then got a hideous squintifego wife, but not half a year after, had the luck to escape her grip. For one day, wanting his dinner, he came down the stair to find her stark upon the floor. The surgeon judged she was cut down by catarrh or apoplexy; but 'twas said abroad, she must have looked into her glass unguardedly. (I think 'tis probable that it followed hard upon her encounter of Delia as a knight's lady, which cast her into a violent frenzy, for the dates seem to fall pat together.) The new widower, being lame with the gout, needed someone in the house, and it happened just at this same time, that his old maidservant, who had left him to marry, needed some place to hide her ugly head, bruised and scarred from the pillory.

It seems that Jane was not long content with the modest income she gained from selling her pies, so that she began to corrupt them with inferior meats, relying upon her skilled hand in seasoning them to conceal the cheat. When she managed to do so without anyone remarking it, she was emboldened to attempt further debasements; until, a family that dined upon a kidney pie becoming gravely ill, it was traced to her. The assayers who seized a batch of her pies, and searched her kitchen, reported they scarce knew what was in them. They thought it was cat's-meat and butcher's offal, though it might also be the sweepings of her floor, for all they knew. Only 'twas certain it was not mutton or kidney or beef, or whatever wholesome food she claimed them to be. Brought before the sessions, she was fined twenty pounds and sentenced to stand two hours in the pillory upon three successive market-days.[5] When she was put in the pillory for the first occasion, she drew a mob that pelted her with rotten vegetables, turds, bones, dead rats, and whatever else they judged fitting, as constituting a probable ingredient in her mixtures. She began to howl and writhe in terror that they would knock out her one eye, the constable making no effort to restrain the mob, other than telling one man to put down a stone. She was released at the end of her time to be carried home fainting. There it was discovered that her husband (whether from shame or opportunity) was fled. The moment his wife's neck was in the wooden yoke he broke away, taking with him their infant son, the money-box of the cookshop, and what else of value he could hoist upon his back. The vicar, coming the next day to salve her bruises with a sermon, found her moaning, still spotted with filth, upon the floor. She would not eat or drink or wash herself clean of dirt, saying, she wished to die rather than abide the repetition of such torment. Seeming truly remorseful, or at the least properly terrified, she was discharged from the rest of her punishment, upon a solemn promise that she would never again prepare food for market. All this happening within a fortnight of the death of Mrs. Urith Bye, and being without other means of supporting herself, Jane crept to her old master to beg her old place. She is greatly altered in her character. When she is sent to get two shilling sixpence of shoulder of mutton, she returns with two shilling sixpence worth of shoulder of mutton. I doubt she rakes more than one or two farthings a week from the household money, which qualifies her as a servant of exemplary honesty. She is thus the only person in this history who was detected in wrong-doing, punished for it, and subsequently underwent a reformation.

I carried Marius his manuscript to the printer that I spoke of to Delia. Though the man was eager for the work, he did but a mean job, his types being broken and worn, and the paper scarce good enough to wrap sausages. Delia looked upon it and said, 'Twill serve; for though I would like to gratify my father, 'twould make another sad quandary if he sent Mr. Printer more manuscripts. Thereupon it occurred to her that she might afford him some pleasure by penning a reply. As it was Grubstreet work, not fit for a lady's pen, I said that she might consign the task to me. I began it by writing: There has lately crept from its muck, where it lay hidden these many years, an old scribbling worm, a republican reptile of old Oliver's day, long thought dead and doomed to eternal perdition. A packet of lies and cunning policy, lately issued out a mean printer's hole, which goes, for shame, without a name, is undoubtedly the work of a revolted traitor known only as M. B. 'Tis most miserably printed, which I take as a good omen that there are few left who dare promulgate such filthy diatribes against the rights and good governance of kings. As this viperous worm has nonetheless a pleasing tongue, able to charm the unwary with his wit and smooth style, I thought it fit to give an answer. In what remained, I did not, in truth, direct many words to abolishing his arguments, but only loaded the author with vituperation for one and a half sheets of paper. I called him a king-queller dipped in blood and poison, a despiteous scoffer and contemner of the church as established by law, an infamous freethinking infidel, a cankered rebeller against all authority, an impious engine of destruction, a fell and rancorous foe of rank and distinction. When Lady Maynard read it over, she was greatly pleased and thanked me mightily. —'Tis done to perfection, she said, 'tis exactly meet. My father will be delighted. I do not know that there is any greater happiness he could wish, unless it were to have his works burnt by the common hangman. I have some little qualm that 'twill provoke him to find a scribe to take down a counter-reply; but even so there would be no great harm in it, there being such a rage of factious scribbling nowadays, that 'twould not be noticed.

When Tom Found brought to him the printed piece and its reply, it took as expected. Marius drew down his muns in a sour look at how ill his own work was printed, and might have vented his disappointment upon the messenger, except his attention was next drawn to the reply, which (it being my own work) I took care to have decently printed. Tom said, his eyes grew large and his mouth turned up in what was almost a smile. He all but capered upon his crutch when he got up to call Jane to let the boy out. Since then his mistress has sent Tom to the house for news. Jane is glad to get a shilling in exchange for gossiping of her master, without asking who it is that seeks information on him. She reports that he is much improved in health, that he can go about the house without his crutch, and even walks back and forth in his garden upon a fair, warm day. He never mentions his daughter to Jane, nor wonders what has become of her. ✠

Epilogue

Lady Delia Maynard is writing at the little table in her closet. Tom Found sits patiently beside her, waiting for her to finish and send him on his errand. He passes the time (he has sat there a full hour already) in gazing upon his sleeve and the buttons of his coat in silent admiration of his livery. —There are only a few lines to go, Tom, and then you will take it to the place I told you of, says his mistress, without looking up from the paper, for she is writing down the words as she speaks them.

Yes, reader, it is I, Delia, who has given you this history. It was necessary to work a deception upon you, and disguise myself as Jack Hack o' Grub Street; for I well knew you would sooner credit the words of a pair of patched breeches inhabiting a garret, than of a silk mantua in an elegant closet.

Though I have juggled with you concerning particulars of no great import, I have nonetheless given you a true account of our times, as I promised I would do. For the undertaker of a history ought to outgo mere chroniclers and mechanic scribes, and aim to be a superior sort of scryer, one able to perceive the truth concealed beneath a veil of cant, subterfuge, and double-dealing.

I told you in my apology, that Delia would yet prove herself to be a faithful daughter, and I consider that I have done so, in setting out the tenets of my father whilst feigning to contemn them. Though he be forgotten and his writings lost, his cause survives. A great and high conception, once it is gone forth in apt and speaking words, cannot perish. It may be belied or dishonored by the turnings of men that are too weak or venal to be true to it; yet always it persists, like a spark of smothered fire, that will one day flame up to purge the dross of three nations.

—Here, Tom, is your bundle. Now skip to the printer. Be sure you say nothing if he question you: only that the person who gave you the packet to carry to him, awaits a reply. ✠

Explanatory Notes

Notes were prepared by students enrolled in Honors English 409, "Origins of the English Novel," Fall Semester of 2019 at Fudler State University. (See Introduction, xxxvi–xxxvii). Cross-references within the notes take the form of chapter number followed by a period and then by the note number.

Publisher's Note: The title page shown on page 1 is a reconstruction based upon the description provided by Dr. Angus Burdock in the foreword to his 1975 edition.

Dedication

1 The author writes a mock dedication to a nonexistent patron as a way of signaling to the reader that she is writing in a new genre. The mock dedication and the mock first chapter that follows it are literary devices that were imitated by men writers in the eighteenth century, like Lawrence Sterne. [H. S. P.]

2 *Ex improviso* is Latin meaning unexpectedly or suddenly. [C. P.]

3 Gaius Maecenas was a famous patron of the arts in ancient Rome. [T. D.]

4 "God's oons" is a curse meaning "by God's wounds." Cursing was a sin against the Fourth Commandment. The Society for the Reformation of Manners used paid informers to bring cases of immorality or profanity before the London and Middlesex magistrates. In general, they left well-to-do people alone and only prosecuted poor people for things like cursing or working on Sundays. They also went after prostitutes but not their customers. [M. K.]

Exordium Scandali

1 *Exordium Scandali* means "stumbling introduction," or "a beginning that causes a stumble." The word translated as stumbling can also mean a trap. The author sets up many traps for the reader over the course of the novel. [C. P.]

2 The people named here were all involved in the Rye House Plot to assassinate King Charles II and the Duke of York. They were sentenced or pardoned in late November of 1683. The author is indicating that the narrative will include political events in the recent past, which was not something done in earlier prose fiction, although it was done in satire and comedy. [C. H.]

3 The author begins by writing in an old-fashioned style that is formal and abstract. This older style romanticizes people and places by giving them exotic names and high social status. The style has to be abandoned because it fails to represent real individuals and contemporary events. The author is contrasting the old way of writing prose fiction with her new style. [H. S. P.]

4 The author is very specific about places. The North Road mentioned here is probably the Great North Road, which went from London all the way to Scotland. There was also an Old North Road that followed a different route out of London. Marius Bye probably lived somewhere between Holloway and Highgate on the Great North Road. [H. S. P.]

Chapter 1

1 Roundhead was the nickname used by contemporaries for the Parliamentary or Puritan party that was fighting against the Royalists and King Charles I. Saying he was a republican meant that he was opposed to monarchy altogether and in favor of representative government. This is known as the Old Cause or the Good Old Cause. [P. S.]

2 The Great Rebellion is the English Civil War. The Battle of Edgehill took place on October 23, 1642. This was the first real battle of the war, which wasn't finally concluded until the Battle of Worcester on September 3, 1651. [C. P.]

3 Turnham Green was a village west of London, about eight or ten miles from the Bye residence which was north of London. The Battle of Turnham Green took place on November 13, 1642, so this gives the birth date for Marius Bye. John Hampden led a famous regiment during the war. His men wore green uniforms and chanted Psalms from the Bible during their marches. The Hampden who went to prison because of the Rye House Plot was his grandson. Moabites were enemies of Israel. Psalm 60 says, "Moab is my washpot." [T. D.]

4 Robert Devereux, 3rd Earl of Essex, was a general on the Parliamentary side. His title went extinct. He is not related to another Earl of Essex, Arthur Capel, who was one of the Rye House plotters and is mentioned later in the novel. Capel was the 1st Earl of Essex in his family line. [T. D.]

5 The king was executed by order of the Rump Parliament on January 30, 1649, when Marius was seven years old. [E. H.]

6 Oliver Cromwell was Lord Protector of England from 1653 until 1658 when he died. The ejectors were appointed to examine teachers and church ministers and expel those who were not qualified or held views that were not approved of. [T. D.]

7 The *Book of Common Prayer* was the prayer book preferred by Royalists. It was not supposed to be used at this time. A colloquy here means a written dialogue. Those of Corderius and Erasmus were written for schoolchildren, though Erasmus later expanded his to appeal to a wider audience. [P. S.]

8 This is the court of Charles II, who lived abroad under the protection of different European rulers. [T. D.]

9 A corn-chandler was a middleman who sold grain and hops for bread and beer making. They were disliked by many people because it was considered immoral to try to profit from food shortages, which is what they did. Queenhithe was a quay on the Thames that handled river traffic from the west, including shipments of grain. [M. K.]

10 The early Quakers were very radical in their beliefs and behavior. They would often disrupt church services. They would also strip off their clothes, which they called "going naked for a sign." [P. S.]

11 Oliver Cromwell died September 3, 1658. As part of the funeral observances, a wax effigy was put on display in Somerset House, a royal palace, dressed as a king with crown and scepter. His son Richard Cromwell succeeded him as Lord Protector, until he was forced to resign eight months later. [H. F.]

12 The government was bankrupt and it was harder and harder to get people to pay their taxes. Finding money to pay the soldiers was the biggest problem. The lack of government stability frightened the rich and the ruling class. However, Marius and other radicals believed they were on the verge of achieving the Good Old Cause, which was democracy and equal rights, at least for men. [P. S.]

13 Coleman Street and the Church of Allhallows the Great were both known for attracting people like Marius who took radical views in religion and politics. [C. H.]

14 The name of their group comes from the rallying cry of apprentices in a riot, "Prentices, Clubs, Clubs!" Fifth Monarchists believed the millennium was about to begin, when Jesus would descend from heaven to rule over England in person. They were feared and disliked even more than the Quakers because they advocated violence to overthrow the government and establish the rule of King Jesus. A Ranting Quaker is one influenced by the Ranters, who believed there is no such thing as sin, or heaven and hell. [M. K.]

15 The year is 1659, specifically the twelve-month period from May 1659, when Richard Cromwell was forced to resign, to May 1660, when Charles II was declared king. During this time, the government changed several times but no one group could keep power or maintain law and order. The Rump Parliament consisted of the most radical members of the Long Parliament, elected in 1640. Once in power, the Rump failed to make any meaningful reforms, disappointing radicals like Marius Bye, and alienating other groups as well. A clash with army leadership resulted in a military junto seizing power in October. This set off a struggle within the army that almost led to another civil war. In Scotland General Monck declared his support for the Rump and began to march his army towards London. In response, General Lambert led his troops northward to oppose him but his soldiers deserted. Monck was able to restore the Rump, and afterwards to force the Rump to readmit the surviving members of the Long Parliament, who then voted for new elections. Unlike Marius, most people at the time understood that new elections would bring in conservatives who would vote to restore the monarchy as the only solution to the chaos. [E. H.]

16 To take up indentures means to successfully finish an apprenticeship. The master returns the contract (called the indentures) as proof that the period of service was completed. [H. F.]

17 Rabshekeh is mentioned several times in the Bible. He was seen as a blasphemer who used insulting language to the Israelites, telling them to drink piss and eat shit. [T. H.]

Chapter 2

1 The Levellers were a radical group during the English Civil War who believed in equality. Although they were defeated, the word Leveller became a negative label for anyone with radical ideas, like calling someone a Socialist or Communist.

Marius is called a Leveller many times in the novel. For Fifth Monarchy men, see note 1.14. [P. S.]

2 Gray's Inn is one of the Inns of Court, which was in an area west of the City. It was the center for lawyers and legal studies. [H. S. P.]

3 In 1659, the Royalists, led by George Booth, planned an uprising for Lammas Day, meaning August 1. However, the government found out about the plan and sent troops to arrest conspirators at their rendezvous points. One of these was at Tunbridge Wells, about thirty miles from London. Sevenoaks is about two-thirds of the way there. The incident is known as Booth's Uprising. [B. C.]

4 The government was proceeding against participants in Booth's Uprising with sequestrations, that is, seizing and selling off their property. This was both a punishment and a way to get money to pay the army. The soldiers were owed a lot of back pay, which is mentioned in the novel. [B. C.]

5 On or around November 1, 1659, London-based troops were mobilized and marched north to encounter General Monck's army (see note 2.6). [E. H.]

6 General Monck was leading an army down from Scotland to oppose the army leaders who expelled the Rump Parliament. In November General Lambert led his troops northward to oppose him, but his soldiers deserted for lack of pay and poor morale. Lacking both military and popular support, the army council (here called the Nine Colonels) surrendered the government to the Rump on December 24. Monck and his army entered London by the North Road on February 3, 1660. No one knew Monck's intentions, beyond replacing the unpopular army junto with the unpopular Rump Parliament. It was given that name because it was the butt-end or remnant of the Long Parliament, which had been purged of conservative members in 1648. On February 11, Monck sided with the City of London in a dispute, a move celebrated by Londoners with bonfires. Monck afterwards forced the Rump to readmit the excluded members. This led to the restoration of monarchy a few months later. [B. C.]

7 Christopher Hatton (1605–1670), 1st Baron Hatton, was a leading Royalist who accompanied Charles II in exile. James Butler (1610–1688), Marquis of Ormonde, was a member of Charles II's privy council in exile. He was raised to a dukedom after the Restoration. He later served as Lord Lieutenant of Ireland. Sir Phineas Dyce has not been traced. [H. S. P.]

8 The Long Parliament was in existence from November 3, 1640, until March 16, 1660. [H. F.]

9 Scrap paper was the only kind of toilet paper people had in those days, so old books and pamphlets ended up at the latrine ("privy-house") or outhouse. [T. H.]

10 John Lambert escaped from the Tower of London on April 10, 1660, where he had been a prisoner since early March. His escape came close to triggering another crisis, since many soldiers and republicans rallied to him and to the Good Old Cause. He called a muster for Easter Sunday, April 22, at Edgehill, but his small army was attacked by Colonel Ingoldsby and easily defeated. Ingoldsby won a pardon and other rewards for turning on his former comrade. On his way back to the Tower Lambert was made to stand under the gallows at Tyburn Field. [B. C.]

11 The Declaration of Breda, a proclamation by Charles II promising a general pardon, was made public on May 1, 1660. The king landed at Dover on May 25 and entered London with much pageantry and partying on May 29, 1660. [E. H.]

12 In October of 1660, the men mentioned in this paragraph were executed for their roles in the trial and execution of King Charles I, the father of the restored King Charles II. Deborah's father, John Milton, was nearly charged with the same crime because he had written books defending the king's execution. Major-General Thomas Harrison was a Fifth Monarchist as well as an army leader and a member of Parliament (MP). It is not surprising that his fellow Fifth Monarchists believed him to be especially important. John Carew was also a Fifth Monarchist and an MP. Thomas Scot or Scott was a believer in the Good Old Cause. Hugh Peters was a preacher of fiery sermons against monarchy and bishops. Contemporaries described how calmly and courageously Harrison and Carew suffered their gruesome deaths.

The sentence was for treason which was punished in a horrible way. First, the person was dragged on a sledge to the place of execution. Hanging was the next step, but while the person was still alive, he was cut down and disemboweled, and his entrails burned before his eyes. Then he was beheaded and his body cut into quarters. The body parts were boiled in tar to preserve them, then hung over the City gates as a warning to others. The heads of traitors were usually mounted on poles at the Southwark end of London Bridge for the same reason. This punishment was specifically for men. The punishment for women convicted of treason was even worse, because they were sentenced to be burned alive at the stake. [P. S.]

13 In the biblical Book of Revelation, the two witnesses are killed by the Beast but are resurrected or reincarnated in some way. Their resurrection triggers terror and destruction but is followed by the Second Coming of Christ. Then as now, many devout Christians believed that the Last Days were approaching. The Fifth Monarchists believed that political action, including the violent overthrow of a sinful government, was necessary to achieve the millennium, when King Jesus would rule the land. [H. F.]

14 This rebellion by a group of Fifth Monarchists is known as the Venner Rebellion after the name of their leader. It began on Epiphany Sunday, January 6, 1661. Although it was a small group, the authorities were taken by surprise and it was several days before they were defeated. The executions (mentioned at the end of the paragraph) took place on January 19 and 21. [H. F.]

15 The book mentioned here is *A Chronicle of the Kings of England* by Sir Richard Baker. The original only went to the end of the reign of King James I in the year 1625. It was updated and continued to the year 1661 by Edward Phillips, who was Deborah Milton's first cousin. Deborah was only eight years old at the time of the Venner Rebellion, so she would have to consult history books or chronicles to write about these and earlier events. If she and Edward Phillips were still friendly while she was working on her novel, he might have provided her with information. [H. S. P.]

16 Saying "Forty-One is come again" was a way of expressing fears that another civil war was coming like the "Great Rebellion." Conservatives used the fear of civil war to bolster support for the status quo. [M. K.]

17 Marius got his allowance on the quarter days, when bills and payments generally fell due. They were Lady Day (March 25), Midsummer Day (June 24), Michaelmas (September 29) and Christmas (December 25). This will be mentioned again. [C. H.]

18 The radical thinkers of this time believed that inequality was introduced with the Norman Conquest, and society was freer and more equal in earlier times.

19 Scrap paper was reused for many purposes, including toilet paper and wrapping packages. [T. D.]

20 The Great Plague of London lasted from 1665 to 1666. It was the last major outbreak of bubonic plague in England. About 100,000 people died, a quarter of London's population. Other towns were also affected but not as badly. The first cases were in St. Giles in the Field, west of the City near Westminster, but by May there were fatalities within the City Walls and people began to be alarmed. The wealthier people began to pack up and leave. The biggest exodus was in July. The poor weren't able to do that and also died in greater numbers because of overcrowding and unsanitary living conditions. [M. K.]

21 Lammas Day is August 1. Henry Danvers was a Baptist preacher who sympathized with the views of the Fifth Monarchists and was a radical and a plotter much like Marius Bye. He was arrested for his activities in early August of 1665 but was rescued by a mob of sympathizers on his way to the Tower. He was involved in many of the same plots and political activities as Marius was in the 1680s, but he is not mentioned again after this chapter. [C. H.]

22 Each parish of London was responsible for publishing a weekly list of deaths and causes of death among its residents. These were known as the Bills of Mortality. Although these lists were very inaccurate, they were the only information people had to estimate where the plague was worse and whether it was increasing or decreasing. Shoreditch and the Minories were poor areas in East London. Cripplegate was a gate in the north part of London Wall but was also the name for the area just outside it. Deborah Milton grew up in this area. [H. S. P.]

23 Sarum is another name for Salisbury. The King and his court first went to Hampton Court. They moved to Salisbury in early August because it was relatively free from the plague. Parliament was summoned to meet in Oxford that October in order to escape the plague in London and Westminster. In late September the royal court traveled to Oxford and took up residence in the university. The town was barely large enough to provide lodgings for everyone who needed to attend Parliament, so there was no room for hangers-on like Roger Bye. [P. S.]

24 Mr. Bye probably went in and out by Aldersgate this time because it led more directly to Cheapside. Cripplegate was probably more convenient for most trips since Red Cross Street passed through it and went directly north. The City inside

the Walls was very small, only about one square mile, so all these places were close
together. There were two places called St. Giles. Here St. Giles Church in Cripplegate
is meant. This was the parish where Deborah Milton grew up. All these places had
special meaning for her. [T. D.]

25 No one knew for sure what Mr. Bye died of. The doctor said it was lethargy,
which could mean a lot of things, possibly stroke. Smoke and different fragrances
were believed to protect against the plague. Earlier we were told that Marius carried
wormwood, a strong-smelling weed, when he walked through the plague-stricken
City. Rosen is the fragrant resin of pine trees. The fatal tokens were the spots and
sores that broke out on the bodies of people infected with the plague. [P. S.]

Chapter 3

1 The Great Fire of London began early a.m. on Sunday, September 2, 1666, and
continued until September 5. It destroyed most of the old medieval City within
the walls, including St. Paul's Cathedral. The cause was a stray spark from a baker's
oven in Pudding Lane, East London. Fires were not at all unusual in a crowded city
full of wooden buildings with thatched roofs, so at first no one was too worried.
Firefighting equipment was primitive, and the usual approach to firefighting was to
pull down all the neighboring buildings. A failure to take this step early on allowed
the fire to get out of control. Strong winds helped it to spread. People in its path
did little except grab their possessions in a panic. [H. S. P.]

2 The fire was approaching Queenhithe, where the corn-chandler had his warehouse, about mid-morning on Monday. At the same time, it was spreading west on
Cannon Street and north on Gracechurch Street. Elbow Lane, where the family
lived, was a small street located north and east of Queenhithe dock. The fire could
have reached both buildings around the same time. However, if the two men had
not been arguing and haggling, they could have saved more of their belongings.
Deborah Milton's father owned a house in nearby Bread Street which also burned
to the ground on this day. Lighters were small barges used to transport goods short
distances, like between a wharf and a ship too large to dock. Bargemen, porters
and carters were all very poor, and the fire gave them the chance to make a huge
amount of money. [H. S. P.]

3 Papist was the most commonly used name for a Roman Catholic. English
Protestants were united in hating and distrusting Catholics. It was felt that Catholics
put loyalty to the Pope before their loyalty to King and Country. They were suspected of plotting to overthrow the government so they could restore Roman
Catholicism as the state religion. Even the people who were in favor of religious
toleration did not want to extend toleration to Catholics. The false idea that Catholics
started it was even inscribed on the Monument to the Great Fire. [M. K.]

4 Ware, Hertfordshire, is on the Great North Road. [T. D.]

5 Roger L'Estrange (1616–1704) was Licenser and Surveyor of the Press, an office
that gave him authority to seize anti-government publications. He had authority to

search the premises of printers and booksellers. L'Estrange also wrote propaganda for the government, including attacks on Deborah Milton's father that mocked him for being blind. He was first appointed in 1662 and given additional powers the next year. When the Licensing of the Press Act lapsed in 1679 his position as state censor came to an end. However, he was soon given new authority to seize books and arrest people for seditious publications. He also continued to be very active as a pro-government writer. L'Estrange was so determined about eliminating dissent that people called him "Towser," which was a name for a large aggressive dog. He will be mentioned again as someone Marius particularly disliked and feared. [P. S.]

6 "The College" is Gresham College, which hosted public lectures on scientific topics. Alchemy was the quest to change or transmute base metals into gold by discovering a secret formula called the "philosopher's stone." It was still considered a legitimate field of research, one that interested Isaac Newton and Robert Boyle, along with many of their contemporaries. [E. H.]

7 The Good Old Cause was establishing a republican form of government, without a king or a protector as the head of state. See also note 1.12. [C. P.]

Chapter 4

1 In June of 1667, during the second Anglo-Dutch war, the Dutch navy sailed up the Thames and the Medway to Chatham, where they burned a number of ships and towed away the flagship of the English fleet, the HMS Royal Charles. A comparison to Oliver Cromwell's much more successful military exploits was often made at this time. [B. C.]

2 "Old Rowley" was a nickname for King Charles, Rowley being the name of his stallion, which alluded to his sexual exploits with his many mistresses. Charles had no legitimate heir so the next in line to the throne was his younger brother, James, the Duke of York. James married Mary of Modena in September of 1673. He secretly converted to Roman Catholicism in January of 1669, which was not known for certain until 1673. The French king is Louis XIV, known as the Sun King. He sought to dominate Europe and to undermine or eliminate the Protestants. Charles II was personally allied to him, against the wishes of the English people. [B. C.]

3 They are objecting to conservatives who wanted to see an increase in the power and authority of the monarchy and the established church. A high-flying churchman was one who claimed supreme authority for the established church and denied religious liberty to others. [A. C.]

4 Marius becomes involved in politics again after joining the Green Ribbon Club, which met at the King's Head Tavern in Fleet Street, located between the City of London and Westminster. It was founded around the year 1675. It was important as a center for left-wing opposition politics from 1679 to 1682. This club was the beginning of the Whig Party in English politics. They got their name from a practice of wearing a green ribbon in their hats. Men wore big hats decorated with feathers and ribbons, so this would not have been as odd or conspicuous then as now. [T. H.]

5 The Popish Plot was a fictional conspiracy invented by Titus Oates in 1678. He claimed that the Roman Catholics were actively plotting to assassinate King Charles so that his Catholic brother, James, Duke of York, would succeed to the throne. The last Catholic monarch of England was Mary I, known as Bloody Mary because she persecuted the Protestants and put hundreds of them to death by being burned at the stake. Oates claimed to have infiltrated the Jesuits in order to spy on them, and in doing so he discovered an elaborate assassination plot involving many Catholic noblemen as well as Jesuits. Oates confided his claims to Dr. Israel Tonge, an anti-Catholic clergyman who was also an amateur chemist. He is known to have confided in another chemist named Kirby, but here we learn he also told Marius Bye about the Plot. On August 13, 1678, Kirby warned the king of a Catholic assassination plot. Charles was skeptical, especially after he caught Oates in a lie. At first these accusations were kept secret while the king's council investigated. Word leaked out all the same, so that it was necessary to inform Parliament when it met in October. Things escalated from there. [A. C.]

6 In Greek mythology, King Midas had long hairy ears (which was a punishment inflicted on him by the god Apollo for "being an ass"), which he attempted to conceal from everyone but his barber. The barber found it too hard to keep such a juicy secret to himself. He dug a hole in some reeds and whispered it to the hole, but afterwards the reeds repeated "ass's ears" whenever the wind blew. [T. H.]

7 The murder of Sir Edmund Berry Godfrey, a London magistrate, is a crime that has never been solved. It was a major factor in getting people to believe in the Popish Plot. On September 28, 1678, Oates went to Godfrey in order to have his testimony officially sworn before a magistrate. However, Godfrey was friends with one of the Catholics accused of treason by Oates, a man named Coleman who was a secretary to the Duke and Duchess of York. Godfrey went to Coleman to warn him. Around this same time, Godfrey was reported as making strange remarks suggesting he feared for his life. He was last seen alive on October 12, 1678. His body was discovered in a field on October 17. He had been strangled and impaled on his own sword. Oates claimed Godfrey had been murdered by Catholic conspirators to conceal what he knew about them. The huge reward offered for the discovery of his murderers motivated a con artist named William Bedloe to invent more lies and accusations against Catholics. More informers came forward, all of them liars after reward money. [B. C.]

8 As public hysteria grew, it was also claimed that the Catholics were planning to set fire to London and to massacre the Protestants. So many people believed in the truth of the Popish Plot that it was dangerous to disagree with them, forcing the skeptics to keep quiet, at least at first. Others, such as the Earl of Shaftesbury (see note 4.9) may not have believed Oates but they saw how his claims could be used to undermine the Duke of York and strengthen the opposition to his succession. Marius seems to have been somewhere in between. He believed Oates' claims but he also saw much more clearly than Oates how they could be used against the king and his brother. Many of Oates' accusations were confused and contradictory. His main motive seems to have been the hope of a reward (which he got).

People were ready to believe in the Popish Plot because of their fears that James, when he succeeded to the throne, would prove to be another Bloody Mary by persecuting Protestants. Ironically, the lies told by Oates and other false informers led to the executions of about thirty-five innocent people, including Archbishop Oliver Plunkett of Ireland, who was later canonized. Others were held in prison for a long time on trumped-up charges.

The narrator takes a distant, skeptical tone in discussing the Popish Plot. There is a lot here that is ironic and it doesn't mean that Deborah Milton hated Catholics. She must have had many Catholic friends and acquaintants during her long residence in Ireland. [A. C.]

9 Anthony Ashley Cooper (1621–1683), 1st Earl of Shaftesbury, was an important English politician and founder of the Whig party. His political career goes all the way back to 1640 and the Long Parliament. He was known for changing sides repeatedly so that many people did not trust him. He was mocked for his appearance, being sickly and very short ("little great man") and having a silver tube in his side to drain an abscess ("Lord Tapski"). All the same, he was a clever politician and effective public speaker. He used the Popish Plot to try to force passage of legislation excluding the Duke of York from the succession. [B. C.]

10 Thanet House in Aldersgate Street was the London residence of the Earl of Shaftesbury. The King's Head Tavern on Fleet Street was home to the Green Ribbon Club, a radical Whig club (see note 4.4 for details). The Amsterdam coffeehouse in Bartholomew Lane was another meeting place for the Whigs. [C. H.]

11 Thomas Osborne, Earl of Danby, was Lord High Treasurer. He wanted to establish an alliance with the Dutch Republic to control French expansion. Contrary to his principles, he was a reluctant go-between in a secret agreement between King Charles II and Louis XIV of France in which Charles agreed to a pro-French policy in exchange for a pension. Danby had many enemies, including Ralph Montagu, who had copies of this correspondence negotiating the king's pension. On December 19, 1678, the correspondence in which Danby bargained with the French king was read aloud in Parliament. True to the principle that "the king can do no wrong," Danby was impeached and sent to the Tower, even though the letters bore an endorsement written by the king. Several well-known Whigs were also on the French payroll, including Sir Algernon Sidney. [B. C.]

12 The punishment for traitors (see note 2.12). [C. P.]

13 Lady Day is March 25 (see note 2.17 for quarter days). [C. H.]

14 Marius is afraid that some of the men at the King's Head who heard him read his manifesto will betray him to the authorities. However, this didn't happen. [T. H.]

15 Oates' account of the Popish Plot, *A True Narrative of the Horrid Plot*, was published in April of 1679. Although very dull and boring, just an account of names, dates and places, it sold a lot of copies because people were obsessed with fears of

Catholic conspiracy. *Killing No Murder* is a much older book. Published under a pseudonym in 1657, it advocated the assassination of Lord Protector Cromwell. After the Restoration, Colonel Silius Titus claimed to be the author and was rewarded by Charles II. The fact that Marius wanted to read it shows he hadn't given up thoughts of overthrowing the monarchy by assassination or other means. [T. H.]

Chapter 5

1 The King's Messengers had several duties. Besides being couriers who carried important dispatches, they served writs and summonses and had the power to make arrests of persons suspected of treason or other crimes against the state. [C. H.]

2 Several well-known Whig politicians, whose names would be familiar to Marius, received secret gifts of money from the French. Sir Algernon Sidney was the most important recipient of these payments. [T. D.]

3 William Bedloe (1650–1680) followed the lead of Titus Oates and made his own accusations of Roman Catholic plots against the life of the king. He was a known con man of very low credibility. However, he was still allowed to testify and he contributed to the conviction and execution of innocent people. He got a big share of a £500 reward by making up evidence in the murder of Justice Godfrey (see note 4.7 for more information on Godfrey). [T. H.]

4 The pope-burnings were anti-Catholic pageants held on the anniversary of Queen Elizabeth's accession to the throne, November 17. The main event was burning a dressed-up dummy of the pope on a bonfire. The pope-burnings held during these years, 1679 to 1681, were very elaborate and expensive productions. The pope was accompanied by devils, cardinals, Jesuits, friars and nuns, all dummies put in elaborate costumes. There was also a figure representing Sir Edmond Bury Godfrey (see note 4.7). Satire on Roger L'Estrange (see note 3.5) was included in some of these pageants. Sometimes he was represented in human shape and sometimes as the dog Towser. The Roman Catholic dummies were tossed on an enormous bonfire at the end of the procession, which went all through the City and was witnessed by practically the entire population. The grand finale was at Temple Bar near the King's Head Tavern, because the Green Ribbon Club sponsored the event. [A. C.]

5 The Scottish rebellion was a brief insurrection by Scottish Presbyterians who were persecuted by the Episcopalian establishment. It was put down by government forces led by the Duke of Monmouth in the Battle of Bothwell Bridge, which took place on June 22, 1679. [T. D.]

6 Oates accused Sir George Wakeman, the Queen's personal physician, of participating in a plot to poison the King. Reading between the lines, this was an accusation against Queen Catherine of Braganza, who was disliked and distrusted for being a devout Catholic. Lord Chief Justice William Scroggs presided over most of the Popish Plot trials. In previous trials he showed an obvious bias against the accused Catholics by downplaying flaws and discrepancies in the evidence against them. At Wakeman's trial, held July 18, 1679, Scroggs was much more skeptical, making

comments on the poor quality of the evidence and saying he would be reluctant to shed innocent blood. The jury took the hint and found Wakeman innocent. Afterwards the Portuguese ambassador visited Scroggs to thank him for the verdict, which protected the honor of the Portuguese-born queen. This visit gave rise to the widespread belief that Scroggs had been bribed with a bag of Portuguese doubloons. [H. S. P.]

7 James, Duke of Monmouth, was the eldest of Charles II's many illegitimate children. He was also the King's favorite child, given many honors and high offices despite his mother's low social status. At least some of the Whig party sought to persuade the King to declare him heir to the throne, displacing the Catholic Duke of York from the succession. He was handsome and brave but stupid, and very popular with the people. [M. K.]

8 The pro-Monmouth party circulated a rumor that Monmouth, the "Protestant Duke," was in fact legitimate due to a secret marriage between Charles and Lucy Walter, his mother. His parents' marriage certificate was said to be locked up in a mysterious black box to keep people from finding out the truth. [M. K.]

9 Bog-house is a name given to a public toilet or outhouse. Toilet paper hadn't been invented yet, so people had to use scraps of waste paper instead. This is one of several times the narrator says Marius Bye's writings were put to this use, as a way of emphasizing his failure as a writer. [T. H.]

10 Baldwin was an actual bookseller with a shop on Warwick Lane. The writers the author has in mind, whose works are sold there, probably include John Locke, Sir Algernon Sidney and Samuel Johnson the pamphleteer (see note 5.16). [E. H.]

11 Calling someone a Machiavel is usually derogatory, implying the person is a schemer or plotter. However, Machiavelli's writings were actually a source for republican theories of government. This is one of the places where the narrator's opinion of Marius Bye and his ideas is deliberately unclear or concealed. [M. K.]

12 The Irish witnesses began to arrive in May of 1680. They were recruited by agents working for the Earl of Shaftesbury to revive public interest in the Popish Plot and extend its usefulness as a weapon against the Duke of York's party. James Butler, Duke of Ormonde, was Lord Lieutenant of Ireland. The Whigs viewed him with suspicion because he granted Irish Catholics a certain degree of toleration. If they could show he was "soft" on Catholic plotters they could force him out of office and replace him with one of their own. Although the new witnesses to what was called "the Irish Plot" were disreputable men, English Protestants had such a great fear and hatred of the Irish that their accusations were believed. These paid informers later showed just how untrustworthy they were by turning on the Whigs and giving testimony against them. [P. S.]

13 Oates' strange appearance was commented on at the time, and caricatured in political cartoons. For Shaftesbury's appearance, see note 4.9. [T. D.]

14 Thanet House was the London residence of the Earl of Shaftesbury. [T. D.]

15 Sir Robert Filmer's *Patriarcha* was a political treatise arguing that monarchy was the ideal form of government and was ordained by God, the king being God's representative on earth. Although written earlier, it was first published in 1680. There were several rebuttals to this treatise from the Whig faction. [C. H.]

16 John Wildman was a plotter and radical politician with a long career, though much of it was spent in prison. Many of his writings were anonymous. Thomas Hunt was most famous for a 1681 "Postscript" to an earlier work that attacked the notion of the divine right of kings. Samuel Johnson was best known for his pamphlet *Julian the Apostate*, written in 1682. It attacked the Duke of York under cover of describing the reign of the Emperor Julian. Both Hunt and Johnson defended the people's right to resist unjust or oppressive governments, something Filmer had denied. [C. H.]

17 Book burning was a frequent occurrence during this time period. The authorities would issue orders that specific books must be seized and burned by the common hangman. The author's father, John Milton, had his books burned by the common hangman in 1660. There was a book burning at Oxford University in 1683, which included works by Thomas Hobbes, John Milton, Thomas Hunt and Samuel Johnson (see note 5.16). It might have been considered a Who's Who of important left-wing writers, so Marius Bye would be disappointed at not being included. [P. S.]

18 The Oxford Parliament met for only one week, March 21–28, 1681. The king called for Parliament to meet in Oxford, not Westminster, due to fears that the Whigs would stir up Londoners in their support. Being suspicious about the king's intentions, many of the Whig lords and MPs traveled to Oxford with well-armed attendants. Shaftesbury was accompanied by an armed escort in which Marius participated. The Whigs dominated Parliament and hoped to use the "power of the purse" to force King Charles to exclude his Catholic brother from the succession. What the Whigs did not know is that Charles had negotiated a new subsidy from Louis XIV that would enable him to rule without Parliament. This was the last Parliament to meet during Charles' reign. Its dissolution marked the failure of the first Whig party and a shift in power to the Tory loyalists. Some Whigs promptly switched sides. The more radical Whigs, like Marius, began to plot to achieve their objective by force. [B. C.]

19 Whitefriars was a sanctuary where petty criminals and debtors (who would otherwise be imprisoned until they could pay their debts) lived to escape the law. It was also called Alsatia, and was located just west of the City, between the river and Fleet Street. [H. F.]

20 The power shift from Whig to Tory loyalist is described here in terms of the failed business of Marius' father-in-law, who depended upon the Whigs as his customer base. After the Oxford Parliament, his customers wouldn't be coming for new clothes in the whiggish style. His Whig customers either skipped town or became turncoats in a literal and figurative way. Deborah Milton is writing from her own experiences like a modern novelist would. Her father often complained about the fact that he was never paid the dowry he was promised by his wife's father. Also, the tailor's business failure might reflect what happened to Deborah and her husband's textile business in Dublin but too little is known about her life to be sure. [C. H.]

21 In July of 1681, Lord Shaftesbury was arrested and charged with high treason, mostly on the evidence of the Irish witnesses who had been bribed to turn against the Whigs (see note 5.12). The case first went to a grand jury selected by a Whig sheriff, who packed the jury with Whigs. On November 24, they gave a verdict of "Ignoramus," meaning that there was no case against him. See note 5.4 on the pope-burnings and note 3.5 on Roger L'Estrange, the Surveyor of the Press and Tory pamphleteer. He was accused of accepting bribes and sexual favors. [P. S.]

22 "Lord Tapski" was an insulting name given to Shaftesbury by his enemies (see note 4.9 for his life). [T. H.]

23 After the dissolution of the Oxford Parliament, the Whig faction had no public forum. Their public feasts, which began in March of 1682 and were attended by subscription, gave an opportunity to display their power and wealth, and to do some campaigning for the upcoming election of the London sheriffs. Some of these were deliberately planned as "anti-dinners," featuring the Duke of Monmouth as chief guest, in order to counter a series of Tory celebrations honoring the Duke of York. The "Protestant treat" planned for Haberdashers' Hall on April 21 (mentioned further on in this paragraph) was forbidden by the king as an unlawful assembly. There were also many private dinner parties held by the Whig leaders, some of which Marius may have attended. [A. C.]

24 Bow Church in Cheapside was often the venue for political or topical sermons that were composed to please a patron or party. [A. C.]

25 Two Tories loyal to the King and the Duke of York were elected sheriffs of London in June of 1682. Their election, plus a growing Tory majority in the London government, undercut the London base of Whig power. [E. H.]

26 The new Tory sheriffs took office in September of 1682. It was almost certain that the Earl of Shaftesbury would face fresh charges of treason, which would now result in trial and conviction. Shaftesbury went into hiding and began to plot more actively. However, he could not persuade other Whig leaders, such as Algernon Sidney and Lord Russell, to join in an armed revolt that was doomed to fail. In mid-November he escaped to Holland for sanctuary, where he died on January 21, 1683. Tony and totty-head are slang terms for a fool or simpleton, with a pun on Anthony which was Shaftesbury's first name. [A. C.]

27 What Jane overheard was a code used by the conspirators to talk about assassinating the king and his brother. They never spoke plainly if there was any danger of being overheard. Marius was involved in the Rye House Plot even though his gout, discussed in the next paragraph, kept him confined to his house. [C. H.]

28 The catastrophe was the discovery of the Rye House Plot in June of 1683. Arrests were made in late June and July, including Sir Algernon Sidney, William Lord Russell, John Hampden, and Arthur Capel, Earl of Essex. Some of the conspirators escaped to Holland, including John Locke, the famous philosopher, who left England at the end of August. [E. H.]

29 "Scribere est agere" is Latin meaning "to write is to act." This is what Judge Jeffreys ruled in deciding that Sidney's manuscript writings on political theory could be used as a second witness to prove his treasonable intentions. Normally two witnesses were required to prove someone guilty of treason. Sidney was found guilty based solely on the testimony of Lord Howard, a conspirator who turned state's evidence, plus the fact that Sidney had written a rebuttal to Filmer (see note 5.15) although it was never published. His trial took place on November 7, 1683. [A. C.]

30 The action of this last paragraph must take place soon after November 26, 1683, which was the day that the Duke of Monmouth was pardoned and Sir Algernon Sidney was sentenced to a traitor's death. This paragraph repeats the "False Start" or "Exordium Scandali" at the very beginning. After the narrator broke off and decided to tell the story "some other way" "without the gilt adornments," it took five chapters just to get to the same starting point. This is because the novel pays more attention to the individual's life history and psychology than older forms of fiction, such as fable or romance. [T. H.]

Defensio Interjecta

1 Unlike modern historians, the historians of ancient Rome would invent speeches and dialogue to dramatize and enliven their histories. The narrator is saying, if they could do it, why not me? [T. H.]

2 See notes 5.29–30 for Sir Algernon Sidney. [T. D.]

3 Robert Ferguson was known as "Ferguson the Plotter" because he was continually involved in schemes to overthrow the government. Marius would have known him well. He accompanied Shaftesbury on his flight to Holland in late 1682, returning after Shaftesbury's death. He next became a leading conspirator in the Rye House Plot, though he managed to escape to Holland in time. He took part in the Monmouth Rebellion in June of 1685, again escaping in time. He returned to England with William of Orange's invasion in 1688. Although he started out as a supporter and propaganda writer for the new king, he later became involved in Jacobite plots against William to restore the exiled James II to the throne. [A. C.]

4 Arthur Capel, Earl of Essex, was arrested on July 9, 1683, for suspected involvement in the Rye House Plot and imprisoned in the Tower. He was found dead by apparent suicide four days later. Due to a number of suspicious circumstances, many people believed he was in fact murdered under orders of the Duke of York. In saying that Essex was trepanned into the plot, Marius meant that he was lured into incriminating himself by informers and wasn't in fact actively plotting. [E. H.]

5 See note 4.9 for Shaftesbury's appearance. [T. D.]

Chapter 6

1 It was a common belief at the time that having gout protected the sufferer from other possibly fatal diseases. [H. S. P.]

2 The Bloody Assizes were the 1685 treason trials in the west of England that followed the failure of the Monmouth Rebellion, which was an attempt to overthrow King James II. The trials were conducted by Lord Chief Justice George Jeffreys, forever after known as the "Hanging Judge." Nearly 1300 people were tried between August 26 and September 23, 1685. About eight hundred were sentenced to transportation; in effect, they were sold into slavery for a profit that went to the Court. Over three hundred were executed. Their heads and quarters were put on display throughout the western part of England. [T. H.]

3 The early Quakers believed in equality so much that they addressed everybody familiarly with "thou" and "thee" and would not take off their hats as a sign of respect, not even to the king. [C. H.]

4 Many Whigs were Protestant Nonconformists, such as Baptists or Presbyterians, who did not attend the Church of England but met for services in private meetings or conventicles. We are told that Marius never became a member of any religious group because he questioned everything and could never agree with anyone else's beliefs. A Socinian doesn't believe in the divinity of Jesus or in the Trinity. This was considered a dangerous heresy; however, Deborah Milton's father held the same beliefs as Marius. A Pyrrhonist is a skeptic. Freeseeker isn't in the dictionary or in Wikipedia but it probably means the same thing as Freethinker, which is someone who doubts traditional Christian beliefs. [H. S. P.]

5 Grinning through a horse-collar was a popular game at fairs. A prize was awarded to the person who could make the most hideous face. [E. H.]

6 King James II ruled from 1685 until late 1688 when he was deposed by William of Orange. As a king he proved to be just what the Whigs always feared. He favored Roman Catholics and gave them positions in the government and the military that they weren't legally entitled to hold. Most Tories still believed in the divine right of kings. Unjust or tyrannical kings were a punishment from God that had to be endured. James was not expected to live a long life and the next in line to the throne was his elder daughter Mary, a Protestant married to William of Orange. Everything changed after the Catholic Queen Mary of Modena unexpectedly gave birth to a son after fifteen years of marriage. The prospect of a Catholic heir caused a group of Protestant nobles to write secretly to William of Orange, asking him to intervene to protect religious liberty and force James to summon Parliament. Accompanied by a party of Whig exiles and a small army, William invaded England on November 5, 1688. James responded with indecision and then panic, attempting to flee the country on December 11. A second attempt on December 23 was successful and he escaped to France. James was given a pension and a palace at Saint-Germain-en-Laye by Louis XIV. [B. C.]

7 The standard Protestant response to the birth of a Catholic heir to the throne on June 10, 1688, was to doubt the child's legitimacy. The most common claim was that somebody else's baby had been smuggled into the queen's bed, concealed in a warming pan. It was also rumored that he was in fact the offspring of a hook-up between the queen and a priest who was one of the king's advisors. [E. H.]

8 The flight of King James on December 11 left the country without a government and triggered several days of anti-Catholic rioting and looting. Early on the morning of December 13, this was followed by rumors of an Irish invasion to burn down the City and massacre the Protestants. There were in fact Irish Catholic soldiers in King James' army, but they were more often victims than offenders in the violence and lawlessness of this brief period. In the confusion, some units of James' army were disbanded without pay, adding to the turmoil and unrest. [E. H.]

9 The Irish Fright was a mass panic that happened in response to rumors of an Irish Catholic army that was massacring Protestants. An alarm claiming that the Irish were cutting people's throats was spread throughout London and its suburbs in the early a.m. hours of December 13, 1688. [A. C.]

10 A false loon was a worthless person or rogue. Shaftesbury collected all sorts of followers, and bragged that he had ten thousand "brisk boys" ready to rise up at his command. [P. S.]

11 1688 is the year of the so-called Glorious Revolution. See note 6.6. [C. P.]

12 William's Declaration stated that calling a Parliament and protecting religious liberty were the motives for his intervention. After the flight of James, it became obvious that he aimed at the throne. To restore order, the Tory and Whig factions worked out a compromise that recognized William and Mary as joint sovereigns and asserted that James had abdicated the throne by his flight. For Ferguson, see Defensio Interjecta, note 3. Major John Wildman was another republican plotter, mentioned earlier in the book as a Whig writer (see note 5.16). [C. P.]

13 There were no newspapers at this time, except the government-sponsored, twice-weekly *London Gazette*. Instead, country dwellers who wanted to get the news from London would subscribe to hand-written newsletters, which were of varying quality and often biased. [H. S. P.]

14 St. Germain was the court of King James in exile (see note 6.6). For Richard Cromwell, see note 1.11. [H. F.]

15 King William was a small man with a very large nose so he was called Little Hooknose by his enemies. Hatchetface must be King James. It was not at all clear that William would manage to retain power and he was never popular with the people or the aristocracy. James still had many Tory sympathizers. Some of the Whigs even began to negotiate with him for a restoration to a more limited monarchy. [C. H.]

16 Marius wrote about the major issues that made King William's government unpopular. He immediately involved England in the longest and most expensive war in the country's history, the Nine Years' War (1688–97) against Louis XIV of France. Trade was badly disrupted by the war at the same time that huge sums were needed to maintain the army in the Netherlands. Meeting the army's expenses required sending massive amounts of silver and gold abroad in payment, shrinking the domestic money supply which was already inadequate. The war also caused a great expansion in bureaucracy and in the cost of government, which led to an increase in corruption, especially among the people responsible for provisions for the army and navy. Taxes went up to pay for the war, with the largest burden falling on landowners in the form of a land tax. The early 1990s were marked by several bad harvests, causing tenants to default and leaving landowners unable to pay the tax without selling off parts of their estates, as Marius had to do. Despite all these problems, most of the Whigs were happy with William's government. They called it "the Glorious Revolution." In continuing to attack the government, Marius is siding with the Tories and Jacobites without realizing it. [A. C.]

Chapter 7
1 See note 5.1 for the King's Messengers. [C. H.]
2 Hull and his sons are getting rich thanks to "the Financial Revolution of the 1690s," which consisted of various money management innovations that were modeled on Dutch practice and introduced to help pay for the war. The Bank of England came into being as a result of the pressure of the Nine Years' War on the existing system of trade and investment. The war required more money than could be raised by taxes and short-term loans, which is how the government was funded in the past. The Bank was founded in 1694 in order to provide immediate funds for the war. Up until this time, banking was a small, high-risk business of individual goldsmith-bankers, like the one who paid Marius his allowance and held a deposit from his father. In addition to being publically traded and funded, the great innovation of the Bank was to issue paper money, called bank notes, which soon exceeded the coin and bullion on deposit. Joint-stock companies were recent innovations that became very popular in the 1690s although many of them failed and people lost their money. The Swordblade Company and the Glass Bottle Company were actual joint-stock companies. Although many people were very happy to invest their money in the new Bank and in the joint stocks, other people were very troubled by these developments, seeing them as cheats to trick people into paying out their good hard cash for mere paper. [M. K.]
3 Speculating in stocks was a new way of making money that was disapproved of and called stockjobbing. The stock market was very informal, with brokers doing business in Jonathan's and Garraway's coffeehouses in Exchange Alley, close to the Royal Exchange (called the 'Change). [H. S. P.]
4 The meaning here is that nobody ever bothered to explain the basics of sex and reproduction to Delia. She got her ideas from the rumors questioning the legitimacy of the Catholic heir to the throne (see note 6.7), which probably came up in the poem her father made her copy over and over. [T. H.]
5 John Hampden was a true Whig who did join William's government, and was the first to call it the "Glorious Revolution." However, he became discontented with

a lack of progress. He also had to live down the fact that he made a humiliating plea to save his life during King James' rule. He became increasingly depressed and finally committed suicide in December of 1696. Lord Grey of Werke was a close associate of the Duke of Monmouth who was captured after the Battle of Sedgemoor and condemned for high treason. He saved his life and was restored to full royal favor after giving testimony against his associates, eventually achieving an earldom. Lord Howard of Escrick was one of the Rye House conspirators. He made a full confession to save his own life, testifying against Sir Algernon Sidney and Lord Russell. He was greatly disliked. [B. C.]

6 "Their eyes put out" is a expression for hinting that someone has been bribed not to see something or object to something. [E. H.]

Chapter 8

1 Alsatia is another name for Whitefriars, which was a region between Fleet Street and the river, to the west of Bridewell. It was a debtor's sanctuary and a high crime area. The New Exchange was an upscale shopping emporium on the Strand. [H. F.]

2 Turnbull Street and Shoreditch were areas associated with prostitution and crime. There were still fields close to London where poor people could go to have sex. [H. F.]

3 People would walk long distances in the seventeenth century because there weren't many good ways to get around, especially if they were poor. If Delia is walking north on the Great North Road, she probably intends to turn at Royston (a distance of about thirty-five miles from her home) to take the Old North Road to Cambridge (twelve miles farther). However, she doesn't get nearly that far. [T. H.]

Chapter 9

1 Hind Horn is a traditional ballad, a love story with a happy ending. There were many different Robin Hood ballads. [C. P.]

2 Bridewell was a prison or "house of correction" for offenders serving short-term sentences, who often were put away without a trial. The inmates were whipped and put to hard labor (such as beating hemp), which was supposed to reform them. Most of the inmates were petty thieves and prostitutes. [H. F.]

Chapter 10

1 Dulwich, now part of South London, was then a small village in rural Surrey. The Great Wood is the Great North Wood (shortened to Norwood), which at one time extended for many miles. It is all built over now. The gypsies camped in Norwood Common, where Londoners would come to have their fortunes told, which is mentioned later. [C. P.]

2 Wild carrot (*Daucus carota,* also called Queen Anne's lace) was used to induce miscarriage or to prevent conception. Tansy (*Tanacetum vulgare*) has similar properties in large doses, though it also treated rheumatism, intestinal worms, and many other complaints. Savin is a species of juniper (*Juniperus sabina*), also used to terminate a pregnancy. Cuckoo flower (*Cardamine pratensis*) must have similar properties, or the chapwoman wouldn't have included it in her recipe. [P. S.]

3 The Battle of Steenkirk took place on August 3, 1692. It was intended as a surprise attack upon the French camp near the village of Steenkirk (or Steenkerque). However, the terrain between the Allied and the French camps proved to be full of ravines, forcing a very slow pace of march. A vanguard of Scottish and British troops did advance close to the French encampment before the enemy discovered them. But the main army was slowed down by the difficult terrain, as well as by a serious error committed by Count Solms, a Dutch general resented by the English he commanded. Solms ordered a unit of cavalry to move forward, though the terrain was not suitable for horses. As a result, the route was blocked by cavalry and the foot soldiers were unable to pass without breaking their formation. Because of these mistakes, only a few Allied battalions of British and Danish soldiers were in position when the battle began around mid-day. The attack was aimed at the right flank of the French camp, and the Allies were initially successful in pushing back those lines. Then the French general, Luxembourg, succeeded in massing his entire army against the British and Danish troops. The Scottish General Mackay was ordered to advance, despite the refusal of Solms to send in more troops to support him. He was killed at the head of his regiment. Five British regiments were completely destroyed. Only about 15,000 soldiers were put in the field against a vast army of French, and of these, over 8,000 were killed or wounded. French losses may have been almost as great, but the outcome was considered to be a disastrous failure for the Allies. [B. C.]

4 The Princess of Vaudemont was married to Charles Henri de Lorraine, Prince of Vaudemont, who was a commander in the Allied Army. [C. P.]

5 As an attempted reform of such abuses, officers were required to bring their recruits before a Justice of the Peace to attest that they were really volunteering for service. This restriction was bypassed by bringing illegally conscripted men before a corrupt JP, who would issue a certificate of attestation without a hearing. [B. C.]

6 West Smithfield was a meat market and sometimes a place of execution in addition to Tyburn. During the reign of Mary I (1553–58), a Roman Catholic, nearly three hundred Protestants were executed as heretics by being burnt at the stake there. The "Fires of Smithfield" became a shorthand way of expressing people's fear that another persecution would result if the Roman Catholics recovered control of the government. [A. C.]

Chapter 11

1 Long-tail is a humorous name for a person from Kent. They walked really fast. [T. H.]

2 Thomas Hobbes (1588–1679) was an English philosopher known for his book, *Leviathan* (1651), which argued for rule by an absolute monarch as the only way to keep the naturally corrupt and selfish behavior of people in check. [C. H.]

3 Squeezing an orange was a way of expressing their hatred for William of Orange. However, unlike Marius Bye, these men wished to replace him with King James II, not with a republican form of government. Some Jacobites were in fact former Whigs (members of Marius' own party) who were unhappy with William's rule and believed a better government could be achieved by bringing back King James with limitations on his power. Other Jacobites (probably including Sir John Herewige) simply believed James was the rightful king, without any restriction. [H. F.]

4 Oates was viciously flogged and imprisoned by order of King James II, but released from prison and given a pension after William took the throne. [M. K.]

Chapter 12

1 For the Reforming Society, see Dedication, note 4. [M. K.]

2 Delia was probably born in 1679 because that's the date of Titus Oates' book, which really exists, so she turned sixteen in 1695. This probably means the current year is 1696. However, it could be the author didn't mean for readers to take the numbers literally, or bother to add them up. [H. S. P.]

3 *Cuius regio, eius religio* is Latin that literally translates as "whose realm, their religion." The meaning is that a ruler can dictate the religion of his subjects. Here it is the master dictating the religion of a servant. [E. H.]

Chapter 13

1 The money supply for everyday business was all silver coins, mostly sixpences and shillings, plus some low-value copper coins. The large denomination gold coins (guineas, worth 20–23 shillings each) were used for savings and major transactions, such as the sale of Marius' farm. Most of the silver money in circulation resembled the first shilling. These coins were very worn and old, dating back to Elizabeth's reign (1558–1603) or even older. These irregular hand-struck coins were easily tampered with by clipping, which was done using a strong shears to take small bits of metal off the edge. They were also easily counterfeited. Better quality coins were introduced in the 1660s. The second shilling resembles one of these coins. These had a milled edge to resist clipping and make counterfeiting more difficult. However, their superior quality caused them to be hoarded or else shipped abroad to be exchanged for gold. [B. C.]

2 The Tower of London was the site of the Royal Mint. The coin shows the king with a deformed nose, a sign of advanced syphilis. [A. C.]

3 There were many problems with the money supply at this time, including coin-clipping and counterfeiting. Since all the money was made of precious metals, there was never enough of it in circulation, so sellers had to give customers credit and wait to get paid. These were long-standing problems, but they were made much worse by the war and by a price differential between silver and gold. In England at this time silver was undervalued in relation to gold, compared to the prices on the continent. This meant unscrupulous merchants could make large profits simply by

melting down silver coins into bullion that they used to buy gold abroad, selling the gold at home to get more silver coin, then repeating the process indefinitely. After the revolution of 1688, still more of the better quality coin was sent abroad in order to pay and provision the army, increasing the problems at home.

The shortage of money meant that people were more inclined to accept low-quality coins, whether clipped or counterfeited. Clipping was an easy operation that required only a sturdy pair of shears to remove shreds of metal from the rims of the old, irregular hand-struck coins. Many individuals would routinely clip any good money that came into their hands. Rings of clippers could operate on a larger scale by buying or borrowing heavier coin from chapmen, alehouse keepers and other traders. Ultimately, a wide cross-section of society was involved in the clipping industry. There was an underground market for the clippings, which were usually bought by goldsmiths. Melted down into bullion, the silver could be used to manufacture plate, to make better-quality counterfeits, or to buy gold on the continental markets. By 1694 the quality of the silver coin had deteriorated so much that the average coin was almost 50% underweight. This occasioned an economic collapse, because no one trusted the coin anymore, and sellers were unwilling to set a price until they saw the coin offered in exchange.

Finally, after much debate, the government decided to call in the old money and issue a new, more tamper-proof coinage according to the old standard. The "Great Recoinage" took place between 1696 and 1698. This was a slow process that caused a drastic contraction of the money supply, resulting in hardships that fell mainly upon the poor. The recoinage was managed in a way that benefited the affluent classes, who were allowed to pay their taxes in the clipped money during the transition. The poor were stuck with money that had lost half its value, since it could only be passed by weight, not on its face value. The social unrest resulting from the bad state of the old money and the hardships of the recoinage were exploited by the Jacobites in an attempt to destabilize William's government. [A. C.]

4 There were many homeless people in London, including abandoned children. There were no shelters for them except what they could find, such as lying on the warm ashes thrown out of the glass factories, or under the projecting fronts (bulks) or stalls of the shops. [M. K.]

5 William Lilly (1602–1681) was the most important astrologer of his day. His annual almanac was a bestseller. He wrote many other books besides, including one called *Christian Astrology* that is still read today. Nicholas Culpeper (1616–1654) practised herbal medicine and astrology. He was famous for publishing self-help medical guides in English instead of Latin which was usual. [C. P.]

6 The reference is to the Book of Genesis, chapter 19, and the fate of Lot's wife. She disobeyed the angel and looked back at the burning cities of Sodom and Gomorrah, which are symbols of evil, and because of that she was turned into a pillar of salt. [H. F.]

7 A law passed in 1694 set a reward of £40 for information leading to the conviction of a coiner or coin-clipper. The law also offered a reprieve for a coiner or clipper who gave information on two others. [E. H.]

8 Counterfeiting and coin-clipping were both considered forms of treason, and subject to an extreme version of the death penalty, which was different for men versus women convicted of these crimes (see note 2.12). In the 1690s, many male coin-clippers and forgers were sentenced to be hanged, disembowelled and quartered, whereas women found guilty were sentenced to be bound at the stake and burned alive. In practice, the extreme cruelty of these punishments was often reduced. The men were hanged until dead, and the women were strangled before being set on fire. [P. S.]

9 *Durante bene placito* means "while it is pleasing" or "during good pleasure." The phrase was most often used to indicate that the tenure of a judge or other official was at the king's will (*durante bene placito regis*) and not based upon time or merit. [C. P.]

10 "Rub them to the Whit" was slang for putting someone in Newgate Prison, where the food was very bad and expensive (see note 17.1). [C. P.]

11 Tithing here means the military tactic of executing every tenth person as a punishment, or to inspire terror and submission. [T. H.]

Chapter 14

1 Sturbridge (or Stourbridge) Fair was held annually outside Cambridge for six hundred years. The dates varied over the centuries, but it mostly ran from late August until the end of September. [H. F.]

2 Bushrod is attempting to pronounce the Latin title of William Harvey's work on the circulation of the blood, which is "Exercitatio Anatomica de Motu Cordis et Sanguinis in Animalibus," first published in 1628. An English translation appeared in 1653, but the student is too poor to be able to afford up-to-date textbooks. [H. F.]

3 A sizarship is a scholarship for a student at one of the colleges in Cambridge University. Sizars had to do various jobs, like waiting on tables, to help pay their way. [H. F.]

Chapter 15

1 Langbourn was one of the wealthiest wards in the city and also one of the smallest. [A. C.]

Chapter 16

1 Under the law, a person charged with a crime against the king's money could get a pardon by providing information against two other clippers or coiners. [T. D.]

2 In the fall of 1695, King William went on a progress to help rally support for his government in the upcoming Parliamentary elections. He was at the Newmarket races in October. The prelate who was going to be kidnapped for a ransom is Gilbert Burnet, Bishop of Salisbury. Here it seems that the year is 1695; however, some other details suggest the year is 1696 (see note 12.2). [H. S. P.]

3 See Dedication note 4 for the Society for the Reformation of Manners. [M. K.]
4 The Poultry Compter was one of two sheriff's prisons in the City of London. It was used as an overnight holding cell. [H. F.]

Chapter 17

1 Newgate Prison was a for-profit venture, and the prison officers raked in money anyway they could. Wealthy people could stay on the master's side, if they could afford the high cost, where they had servants and good meals. The common side was for poor people. People imprisoned for debt or petty theft were mingled together with murderers and rapists. The prisoners in the common side were supposed to get a daily allowance of bread and water. However, it wasn't adequate and often it was stolen by other prisoners or just not supplied. There were very few guards so escape was not difficult, especially if bribes were paid. Prisoners were sometimes given "the liberty," which meant they could go out during the daytime. In general, Newgate Prison was notorious as a "hellhole," being corrupt, overcrowded and filthy, with many people dying of disease before they could come to trial. [M. K.]
2 A delivery, or jail-delivery, refers to the process of emptying a jail by bringing its prisoners to trial. [C. H.]
3 Lord Ashley was the grandson of the first Earl of Shaftesbury. He succeeded to the title in 1699. He was educated by the philosopher John Locke, who presided over a whiggish club of theorists called "the College." The Grecian club was similar. The Calves-Head Republicans were more radical, like Marius Bye himself. They met every January 30 to celebrate the execution of Charles I, who was considered to be a martyr by the rest of the country. [C. P.]
4 Edmund Ludlow (1617–1692) was an English republican whose name would be famous and illustrious to Marius Bye as an upholder of the Old Cause. He lived in exile during the reigns of Charles II and James II. He returned briefly in 1688, expecting that the reign of William and Mary would be more hospitable. However, a speech was made in the House of Commons demanding his arrest, so he fled abroad again, and died in exile. Between 1691 and 1693 four Whig pamphlets were published under his name, though they were clearly not his. John Phillips (Deborah Milton's cousin) and John Toland (her father's biographer) were both suspected of being the real author. [C. P.]
5 The sessions was the periodical sitting of a court of justices of the peace. Here probably the quarter-sessions is meant. [C. P.]

Glossary

Entries were prepared by students enrolled in Honors English 409, "Origins of the English Novel," Fall Semester of 2019 at Fudler State University. (See Introduction, xxxvi–xxxvii.)

Abigail: a female servant

abusion: a verbal insult; abusive language

ad libitum: at will, as one pleases

ague: a high fever, an illness with recurrent fever

alamode/ala mode: a glossy silk fabric; fashionable

alembic: a pair of connected vessels used for distilling

All-Hallows: November 1

animadversion: hostile criticism or blame

apology: a justification or defense

arrant: manifest, obvious, unmitigated

atramentum: Latin for ink or black dye

Aurora: the dawn

badger: a produce dealer; a trader in grain or produce; a hawker or peddler

bagnio: a bathhouse used for sex or prostitution

bait (v): to give food and water to a horse on a journey

bedaggled: dirtied on the hem or bottom of a garment

Bedlam: London asylum for the mentally ill; any scene of mad confusion or uproar

besom: a broom

black-coat: a clergyman or parson

bodkin: a long pin used by women to hold hair in place; a dagger

bog-house: a toilet or outhouse

bogtrotter: an Irish countryman

boot: an outside compartment on a coach

botcher: a mender of clothes, shoes or other items; a bungler, an incompetent person

bottom: a ship or boat

bousing-ken: an alehouse

box: a small country house

brabble (v): to quibble, to dispute

Bridewell: London prison for minor offenses

brogger: a dealer or broker

broody: able to bear offspring, fertile

bruit: to report widely, to make famous

bubble (v): to cheat or hoodwink

bulk: a framework projecting in front of a shop; a stall for selling goods

bumfiddle: a bass-viol (cello) or its player; buttocks, a woman's genitals

bummery: money loans made upon the security of a ship cargo

burden: the refrain of a song

Butterbox: a Dutchman

by and by: immediately, at once; before long, soon

byword: a nickname, often scornful

cabal: a secret meeting of plotters

caballing: plotting

cabbage: cloth remnants kept by the tailor but charged to the client

Candlemas: February 2

cannibal: a ruthless, destructive or savage person

capon: a castrated rooster; a eunuch

carbine: a long-barreled pistol used by cavalry

carman: a carter or carrier

cassock: a soldier's cloak or coat

catamite: a boy or young man who is a passive sexual partner to an older man

catchpole: a bailiff, a sheriff's officer

Catharan: a Puritan

cautery: a caustic drug or other cauterizing treatment believed to heal by burning

censure (v): to judge or give an opinion

216

chance-medley: of mixed character, being partly by chance and partly deliberate

chandler: a retailer of candles, groceries and other basics

changeling: a turncoat, someone who changes allegiance

chapwoman: a female hawker or peddler of small wares

character: a description of a person's qualities; a testimonial or reference from a previous employer

chemical: of or relating to alchemy

chewit: a spiced dish of minced meat or fish

chine: a cut of meat that includes part of the animal's backbone, such as sirloin

chop-logic: specious reasoning in an argument

chouse (v): to dupe, cheat or trick

chum: a college roommate; a close friend

clap up (v): to imprison

closet: a private inner room in a house

coats: petticoats; the skirts of a woman's dress, or those of a young child

cog (v): to handle dice in a way that controls their fall

cogger: a swindler, deceiver or cheater

coil, keep a: make a fuss, keep up a disturbance

coin-clipper: someone who illegally pares down coins to sell the silver while passing the underweight coin at face value

collect: a collection

Commonwealthsman: a republican; someone seeking to replace monarchy with elective government

compeer: a companion, an equal

complice: an accomplice

compound (v): negotiate by mutual concessions

compter: a sheriff's jail, often used as an overnight lockup

con (v): to study, to memorize

coney: a rabbit; a person who is easily tricked or swindled

contriving: scheming, inventive

conventicle: a clandestine or illegal meeting, especially of religious Nonconformists

conventicler: someone who attends conventicles; insulting term for a Nonconformist in religion

coppice-wood: a thicket of small trees maintained for cutting as firewood or other uses

corn: wheat or other types of grain

corn-chandler: a dealer in wheat, barley, hops, etc.

costive: constipated

country: a county or district

cowl-staves: stout poles used to carry tubs or other burdens by two bearers

coxcomb: a vain or conceited person

cozen (v): to cheat or deceive

cozening: cheating, fraudulent

cravat, hempen: see *hempen cravat*

cribble bread: whole-grain bread

cross-bite (v): to bite the biter; to cheat in return, to outwit; to fool or deceive

crown: a coin worth 5 shillings, or the sum of 5 shillings as a unit of counting

crump-shouldered: crooked or deformed in the shoulders

crust: stale bread; a small meal or snack

cry (v): to shout or exclaim; to sell goods as a street hawker

cuff: a miserly old man

cuirass: armor for the chest and back

cully: someone easily fooled or cheated

dame's school: an elementary school run by a woman

damme-man: a profane person, prone to swearing

desperate: hopeless; of a debt: bad, uncollectable

deuce: twopence

diaphoretic: a medicine to cause sweating

distaff: female (figurative use)

dobbin: an old horse, a farm horse

doghole: a place unfit for human habitation

double-double: strong beer

dower: the portion of an estate (usually one-third) allowed by law to the widow

drab: a dirty or untidy woman; a prostitute

drapery: cloth, textile fabrics

drawer: a server in a tavern, a tapster

dressed: cooked or otherwise prepared for eating; clothed

dressing-box: a box with compartments for holding toiletries

droll: a puppet-show; a short comedy or farce

dry-nurse: a childcare provider

ductus: the technique of making strokes with a pen

dumping: to be in the dumps, to be sad or melancholy

Egyptian: a gypsy

enthusiast: a Baptist, Quaker or other sectarian, as opposed to a member of the official Church of England

eruptive: bursting out from restraint

faburden: the refrain of a song; the bass part in a multi-part song

factionary: relating to a faction

factious: relating to a dispute between factions; partisan

factor: a business agent or broker

fairing: a present or souvenir from a fair; a gift from a lover

false loon: see *loon, false*

family: the residents of a household, including servants

fanatic: derogatory name for a Non-conformist; used broadly for the Whig party

farandine: a silk-wool blend fabric

farthing: a copper or brass coin worth one-quarter of a penny

featly: properly, neatly or elegantly

feltmaker: someone who makes felt cloth or hats

fetch: a contrivance or trick

fireball: a bag of gunpowder and other combustible materials, intended to cause fire or explosion

foggy: fat, flabby or bloated

foist (v): to palm false dice

foisted: musty, spoiled

fomentation: wet cloths soaked in vinegar or medicated waters and applied to the body as a treatment

foolscap: a fool's or dunce's cap; a large sheet of writing paper

footpad: a highwayman who robs on foot

fopling: a vain person, overly concerned with dress and appearance

form: good manners, proper etiquette

frontless: unblushing, shameless

fustian: ranting or bombastic language

ganymede: a boy who serves wine; a handsome youth like Ganymede of Greek myth; a young male prostitute

garbage: the entrails or organs of an animal used for food

garden-stuff: see *green-stuff*

generality: the multitude; the people in general

glass-house: a glassworks, a place where glass is made

gloze (v): to flatter or deceive with smooth talk

glozing: flattery

gorbellied: having a big belly, fat around the middle

grave (v): to engrave

green-stuff: see *garden-stuff*

groat: an old coin worth 4 pence; a small amount or trivial value

Grubstreet: referring to London hack writers or writers for hire; poor quality

grum: gloomy, surly

Grumbletonian: a person in the "Country" or opposition party, usually a conservative Tory, who objected to the current government's policies

guinea: a gold coin normally worth 20 shillings but rising in value as high as 30 shillings during the 1690s

hab or nab: hit or miss; however it may turn out, anyhow

hack: a drudge; a writer for hire, a dull, unoriginal writer

halter: a noose

hang-dog: low, degraded or sneaky

harry (v): to harrass

hedge-bird: a vagrant

hempen cravat: a noose

heronshaw: a young heron

higgler: a middleman or itinerant dealer in poultry and other provisions

hobby-horse: a favorite pastime, hobby

hobbledehoy: an adolescent; a clumsy or awkward youth

Hogan-Mogan: a Dutchman

hop-dresser: a hop-grower

horse-meat: hay or other food for horses

horse-pistols: a pair of long pistols, kept in a holster laid over the pommel of a saddle

hotchpotch: a thick soup of barley, peas and vegetables, with or without meat

hoyden: an ill-mannered or boisterous girl or woman

huff (v): to bully or bluster

impertinent: irrelevant; inappropriate

inamorato: a lover

information(s): formal charges made by an informer, in order to establish a claim to a reward

ingenuous: high-minded; naive

Jack: a fellow, a John Doe; a Jacobite

Jacobite: a supporter of James II who viewed William III as a usurper

jakes: a latrine or toilet

jangling: noisy argument; a din of voices or other noise

jar: a dispute or quarrel

Jill: a lower-class girl; a prostitute

jobber: a middleman; a salesman or trader

joiner: a skilled carpenter who constructs wood furniture

joint: a large cut of bone-in meat

jole: a fish head, served as a cut or dish

jowering: speaking with a growling tone; speaking in an Irish brogue

juggle (v): amuse with tricks; cheat, deceive

ken (v): to recognize

kickshaw: an elegant knickknack; a fancy menu item

kill-cow: bullying or threatening

knock in the head: kill by a blow to the head; put to death quickly

lamb-stone: the testicle of a lamb

lathy: very thin

Leveller: a person who would eliminate or "level" all distinctions of rank and power; a republican or "hot Whig"

leviathan: a whale or sea monster; someone with vast wealth or power; the Leviathan: the devil

lighter: a flat-bottomed barge

linsey-woolsey: a fabric made of a blend of wool and linen; a medley of confused or inconsistent ideas

long-drawn: lengthy, drawn out

loon, false: a rogue, a worthless person

made dish: an elaborate, difficult to prepare food

makeshift: a schemer, a rogue or a shifty person

man-thief: kidnapper

mantua: a style of loose gown worn by women, fashionable in the late 17th century

mark: two-thirds of a pound sterling (20 shillings), equal to 13 shillings 4 pence

maugre their teeth: despite their efforts

meat: solid food; animal flesh as food

mechanic: a manual laborer; a craftsman or artisan

mercury-woman: a woman who sells or

distributes pamphlets or news-sheets

Messenger: a royal officer whose duties included arrest of state prisoners

miniken: dainty, diminutive

moil: turmoil

moneyer: a coin maker; a banker or capitalist

moonish: changeable, inconstant

mostwhat: for the most part; almost all

mum: a German style of spiced wheat beer

mumchance: mute or tongue-tied; a dice game

mump (v): to cheat or outwit

muns: the jaws; the face

napery: underclothes

nappy: of ale: strong with a foaming head

neat-fingered: dexterous, having fine motor skills

neuter: a person taking a neutral or undecided position

nib (v): to mend or sharpen a quill pen

nick (v): to steal or cheat; to catch or apprehend

noddy: a fool or simpleton

nonjuror: a clergyman who refused the oath of allegiance to William III

nutmegs: testicles

offscourings: rubbish, dregs

pad, upon/on the: on the road; tramping or traveling as a vagrant

papist: a Roman Catholic; relating to Roman Catholicism

papistic/papistical: of or relating to the Roman Catholic Church

paramour: a lover, a sex partner

passenger: a traveler on foot

peach (v): betray or inform on

pen'orth: a penny's worth

periwig: an elaborate wig, worn by men and women at this time

perquisites: perks, additional gains (such as a servant's right to old clothes)

pettifogger: a low-level lawyer

pickthank: flattering

pile: the reverse side of a coin, or the die used to make the impression

pipe: a large cask

pistole: a gold coin; the louis d'or coin

place: a job or situation; a high office in the government

placeman: someone rewarded with a public office in exchange for political support; a yes-man

plouky: covered with pimples, having a spotty complexion

poke: a bag, pouch or bundle

popish: of or relating to the Roman Catholic church

postures: the steps for wielding a weapon in battle, taught in a military drill

pothook: a curved or hooked penstroke

poultice: an herbal or medicinal paste applied to the skin as a remedy for injury or illness

pound: the sum of 20 shillings

powder: any of various prepared substances used in alchemy and magic

pox (v): to infect with syphilis

pranked: decorated; dressed up, dressed in a showy or fashionable style

prate (v): to talk foolishly, boastfully or at length

Precisian: a person strict in religious observance, a Puritan

prelate: a high-ranking clergyman

Presbyters: a Presbyterian

prick-eared: puritanical; sanctimonious, hypocritical

pricklouse: a tailor

primogeniture: the right of an eldest son to inherit an estate to the exclusion of his siblings

prints: printed sheets or other printed publications

privities: genitals

puppet: a doll

pursy: fat

quarterage: a quarterly payment

quean: an impudent woman; a prostitute

quid: a guinea coin, worth about 20 shillings

rabble (v): to attack as a mob

rag-seller: a second-hand clothes dealer

rakehell: an immoral person, a rake

rascality: the mob or rabble

reeling ripe: very drunk

renegado: a rebel or traitor; an ex-soldier of the Commonwealth army

ribaldish: sexually suggestive, a bit lewd

romish: of or relating to the Roman Catholic church

ropy: sticky, slobbering

roundhead: a member of the Parliamentary party in the English civil war; someone with republican, antimonarchical or puritan beliefs

Rump: the Parliament that was purged of conservative members in 1648

runagate: a vagabond, a wanderer

rusty: of meat: rancid; of clothes: faded or shabby

sad: serious; certain, true or genuine; sorrowful

sad-colored: having a dark, somber or neutral color

sadly: seriously, in earnest; deeply, fully, completely

salesman: a seller of ready-made clothes

sartorian: sartorial, of or belonging to a tailor

scammony: a strong herbal laxative

scryer: a crystal-gazer, someone who sees images in water or crystal

sennight: a week

serge: a durable woolen fabric; a garment made of serge

shallop: a large heavy boat fitted with a mast

shilling: an English coin worth 12 pence or the sum of 12 pence

shittle-headed: fickle, flighty or wavering

shovelard: a spoonbill

show-stone: a crystal ball

sightly: pleasing to the sight; handsome, beautiful

simplicity: foolishness; sincerity, guilelessness, naivete

Sir John: a priest

skip-kennel: a footman, footboy or lackey

slubbered: hastily put together, done carelessly; dirty, sullied

smirched: stained or dirtied

snacks, to go: to divide the profits

snap: a snack or light meal

snapper: a short pistol

snip: a tailor

snuffler: someone who speaks through the nose or talks religious cant

snuffling: speaking with a nasal twang (supposed to be characteristic of religious hypocrites and sectarians)

sops: bread steeped in liquid

spagyrical: alchemical

spavined: lamed by inflammation in the joint

spill: a small gift of money, a tip

spurrier: a maker of spurs, bits and other small ironware or wrought iron

squeak (v): inform on, betray

squib: a witty sarcasm; a lampoon

squintifego: squinting, or with eyes not aligned in gaze

spittle, rob the: make a profit by despicable means

stationer: a bookseller; a publisher

stays: a woman's quilted bodice or corset, lined with whalebone

stoffado: stuffing

straightway: immediately, at once

stroller: an itinerant peddler or beggar

strolling: wandering, itinerant

stuff: fabric or specifically a woolen fabric; supplies or provisions; property; materials

subsist (v): to support oneself

sutler: a seller of provisions to soldiers

sweetmeats: candy, cookies, etc.

tag-rag: riff-raff, a despised person

tansy-faced: with a yellow complexion

tester: sixpence, a half-shilling

thief-taker: someone who collects bounties by informing on or capturing criminals

ticket: a promise to pay; a debit account; a note of goods received on credit

tip-merry: jovial from drinking

tipple: alcoholic drink

tipstaff: a constable, bailiff or sheriff's officer

tit: a small horse, a nag

tithing: donation of one-tenth of one's income to a church; the death or destruction of one person in ten

Tory: the political faction supporting the succession of James, Duke of York; later on, those presumed to prefer the exiled James II to William III

toss: a state of agitation or distress

tousle (v): to handle rudely or roughly

toy: an ornamental object; a knickknack or trinket

traduce (v): to slander or censure

train: a group, series or sequence; a trick, stratagem or artifice

train-band: a militia, a company of citizen soldiers

treat: a dinner or other entertainment provided at the host's expense

trepan (v): to entrap, betray or double-cross someone

trepanner/trepan: someone who entraps or swindles others; an agent provocateur

trimmer: one who switches political parties to serve personal interests

trug: a prostitute

trull: a prostitute

trumpery: showy but poor quality

trussell: the die for the upper side of a coin

tub-preacher: a dissenting minister who stood on a tub for a pulpit

tuppence: twopence

Turkey merchant: a person trading in goods from the Middle East

turnkey: a jailer

turnspit: a person whose job is to turn a roasting spit; a low contemptible person

Tyburn tree: the gallows

uncase (v): to undress

utter (v): to expose for sale or barter, to sell; to pass or circulate false money

vail: a tip or gratuity given to a servant by a guest or visitor

vapor (v): to talk in a vague, wordy way; to brag or bluster

vesicatory: an ointment that causes therapeutic blistering

viraginian: having the qualities of a virago, a masculine-appearing woman

virginals: a keyboard instrument related to the harpsichord

wall, take the: take the inside portion of a walkway, away from the dirt of the street

wall-fruit: fruit of trees that are grown on trellises against a wall

wantonness: recklessness; unruliness; extravagance or self-indulgence; sexual promiscuity

wastes: undeveloped land

Weald: a geologically distinctive region of southeast England, formerly wooded and undeveloped

well-willer: well-wisher

whiffle (v): to speak or answer evasively

whiffling: inconstant, evasive or shifty

Whig: the political faction that opposed the succession of James, Duke of York, and advocated for constitutional rather than absolute monarchy

Whit: Newgate prison

widow's third: see *dower*

wire-drawn: drawn out to great length; over-refined, contrived

woodcock: a dupe, a simpleton

wry-legged: crooked or otherwise deformed in the legs

Neuters and Changelings: Gender Politics in *Marius & Delia*

Janet Spurway

GENDER TENSIONS and misdirection are embedded in the narrative of *Marius & Delia* from its opening lines forward. The narrator, who adopts the tone of an aggressively male loyalist, effectively declares the subject of his true history to be Marius Bye. Although his daughter is to be the primary source for this history, the narrator derogates her intelligence and significance: "she was scarce able ... to comprehend much of what she witnessed" and "was but an inconsiderable actor in the events she related" (7–8). At the conclusion of the text, the revealed deceit of the authorial presence pushes the reader to acknowledge the fluidity of political and gender identities evident throughout the narrative. People switch sides. They also switch genders. Delia passes successfully as Jack as long as she keeps her breeches. Others fail to perceive her sex at the same time as she fails to perceive their political orientations. Within the text, no one can reliably distinguish republican from Jacobite, male from female. Deceit multiplies in its two primary forms, cross-dressing and double-crossing, until the epilogue presents a final reveal of duplicity that perversely undermines the truth claims made by the authorial voice.

Among Marius Bye's earliest works was a biography of the parliamentary general John Lambert, published during a short-lived insurgence against the impending restoration of the Stuarts. It was successful in straddling the market, being "eagerly taken up by enthusiasts and neuters alike" even though it was uncompromising—decidedly not neutral/neuter—in its factional republican rhetoric, which was "rounded with blood-and-thunder threatenings of ruin to Cavaliers and changelings" (18). *Cavalier* and *enthusiast* are of course stock epithets for, respectively, Stuart loyalists and the Parliamentary/Presbyterian party. They are in opposition not only to each other but to the other two categories of neuters and changelings. As figurative labels, *neuters* and *changelings* convey a context-dependent implication of persons who are neither this nor that, who slip out of the expected binary opposition. Here they denote those who either lack political convictions or abandon them for motives of self-interest. Nonetheless, the other significations of the words spill out into the narrative. The categories of neuter and changeling, broadly defined, go a long way towards bridging the text's seemingly disparate themes, which can be distilled to a series of challenges to discerning political and gender identities.

The storyline of *Marius & Delia* is a conventional one that was ancient before the novel emerged as a recognizable genre. A youthful protagonist moves through society, confronting various challenges and setbacks, until the fiction concludes happily in marriage and the formation of a new family. Those challenges include sexual or romantic encounters that are threatening, unsanctioned, deceitful or otherwise ill-advised. The heroine of D. M.'s narrative has at least nine such encounters, which are all unwelcome and often coercive: even the innocent, lovesick Sally cannot keep her hands to herself.[1] Delia experiences several episodes of *éclaircissement* over the course of the narrative, and she is arguably more shrewd, more streetwise, at the conclusion than at the outset of the fiction. Nonetheless, this is not a coming-of-age narrative in which the protagonist undergoes lessons in amatory discernment and emotional maturity that prepare for an emotionally satisfying union. Delia's marriage to Sir Bevil Maynard is devoid of sensual, emotional or psychological content. It is equivalent to a winning lottery ticket, discovered in one's pocket just as ruin and disgrace threaten. The picaresque and satiric elements of the narrative might be read as conditioning the anti-romantic, put-tab-A-into-slot-B presentation of human sexual relations, including marriage. I argue instead that the relationship obtains in reverse, that the satiric/picaresque mode serves to facilitate a focus on externalities, a shrugging indifference to internal states of being. When, upon occasion, the narratorial voice probes the thoughts and assumptions of various characters, it is only to demonstrate how foolishly they misjudge in interpreting the words, dress and behavior of others. Externalities are valorized over internalities but are nonetheless deceptive, untrustworthy, and thereby devalued as vehicles of meaning. Words are generally untrustworthy, and the narrative abounds in figures who go by multiple aliases (including those invented for them by the narrator, to preserve them from the gallows). Among the principal name-changers, Delia/Jack exemplifies the cross-dressing deceits of gender, Ned Shift the double-dealing shiftiness of political intrigue. Only the narrative's cryptic anti-hero, Marius Bye, refuses to adjust his principles to his self-interest.

Marius discovers politics at age sixteen. Confronted simultaneously with a half-naked woman and a subversive speech, he is riveted by the speech. His excitement at this sudden exposure to radical ideas is marked by unsteady limbs, sparkling eyes and trembling lips—bodily symptoms which his master understandably mistakes for sexual arousal. Sexual interest arrives late in life, and he does not marry until he is thirty-six. He is depicted (except for his episodes of feverish political activity) as sullen, melancholy, cold, secretive. In the one-sex theory (shall we call it the epicene episteme?), at this time still arguably the dominant mode for conceptualizing sex difference, it is the superior heat of the male which causes the external genitals to develop, suggesting a potential cause-and-effect correlation between Marius' frigid, morose temperament and his disinterest in women.[2] Either he lacks sufficient warmth to promote sexual functioning or that heat is diverted to political and literary striving. The perverse diversion of libido to political plotting does not forward his literary career, given that his failure to achieve popular success as a pamphleteer is attributed to his lacking "a knack for bawdry" (20). His marriage is passively undertaken and the seduction used upon him is political discourse: his prospective father-in-law talks "in an approved style of factious cant" and his future wife charms him by performing whiggish ballads (36). Thereafter Marius discovers, belatedly, his biological self. Although surly to his wife by day, he does the duties of a husband by night. His mid-life sexual awakening, in conjunction with his association with a more aristocratic (presumably rakish) class of men, combine to address his earlier deficiency and he displays "a new bent for ribaldish levity" in slanderous verses that enjoyed private circulation "passed from pocket to pocket amongst all classes of Londoner" (41).

Nonetheless, physical intimacy with his wife is confined to periods of political and literary inactivity. While Marius is caballing and scribbling in the city, his wife is left alone to amuse herself. His penis thus functions as a surrogate pen during periods of political and intellectual frustration. His daughter is conceived during his first period of voluntary political exile, roughly December 1678 to May 1679. His premature son, born at the time of the Oxford Parliament, March 1681, was presumably conceived when he began to spend more time at home, discouraged to find that his faction viewed him merely as a "Junior Oates" (44–45). The elision of pen and penis has a lengthy literary history, operating as a masculine trope that disqualifies or disables women writers.[3] If the relationship is reversed, if a penis is merely a substitute pen, then writing is not a sex-linked activity, despite societal gendering. Sent to the school of a "foolish idle gentlewoman," Delia is taught to write in a hand so excessively feminized that it looked "like a pattern for an embroidery" (63). Nonetheless, she easily masters the masculine scripts her father puts before her as models and later astonishes her future husband with her ability to write in a fine italic hand. Her gender-stereotype-defying accomplishments within the fiction including penning the narrative itself. *Marius & Delia* communicates skepticism regarding the magnitude of sexual difference beyond the biological essentials. Men have penises, women have babies, but all other markers of sex difference appear weak and unstable. Clothes make the man, or the woman, in a novel that presents readers with a sartorial and performative theory of gender.

Like father, like daughter. Delia is described in terms that imply androgynous qualities. Her mother's clothes require considerable alteration before they will fit her "tall, spare, lathy figure" (75). When Jane boasts to her of the raptures of sexual union, Delia is uninterested and incompletely comprehending—or not until after her rape, which she assumes to be an informal equivalent to wedlock. Her rapist, pleasantly surprised by her docility, views her as a "fresh and wholesome morsel," only too lean and lacking in salt (lust) (80). Delia, in turn, finds him physically repulsive: "it would be happier to be united to his coat or his hat than to his unlaced and breechless person" (81). The two footmen of his uncle's household later confirm that young Bevil Maynard is physically unattractive; here, however, the reader is apt to wonder if Delia is repelled by her first view of a naked male. It was her genuine attraction to a Venice-gold bone-lace turned over a brocaded cuff that distracted her into passive submission. Such a love of finery might be read as a stereotypical feminine trait, vanity in dressing, yet it is clearly gender-neutral in the text. Maynard "dresses mighty rich flashy and smart" (177), in the words of the footmen, but male vanity is not exclusive to fops. The dragoons encountered at the inn are scornfully characterized by the chapwoman as having enlisted "for the sake of riding upon a tit in a new cloth coat" (110). Tom Found finds patience to sit idly for an hour "in silent admiration of his livery" (191). As a more telling instance of the neutrality of dress and of interest in it, Delia's delight in clothes is fully gratified by the suit of livery s/he receives in Sir John's household. Unlike the gowns she inherits from her mother, it needs "only a few stitches to fit him perfectly" (117).

The text's use of pronouns is itself a remarkable signal of gender fluidity. Although I cannot claim to have made an exhaustive survey, early modern texts with cross-dressed females and a third-person narration generally insist upon the stability of gender identity. However the cross-dressed woman may appear to the world, she is always a she. Moreover, the tension of sustaining a cross-gender performance is foregrounded in the narrative. In contrast, although Delia regrets being put to lies and evasions, she otherwise feels it is "a very pleasant thing to strut in breeches" (92), and apparently is able to pass herself as male without conscious effort, once she learns to mimic a mannish gait and "not mince along with her legs clapped together" (90). She is persuaded to accept masculine dress as a protection against sexual assault, only to be subsequently assaulted twice, first by a man and then by a woman, both preying upon a servant. Rape is thus presented as a victimization of low-status individuals rather than exclusively female ones. The sexual perils of Delia/ Jack emphasize her/his androgynous appeal while simultaneously undermining a sense of biological determination. Anyone can be coerced into sex, if powerless.

"Dost thou think, though I am caparisoned like a man, I have a doublet and hose in my disposition?" asks Shakespeare's Rosalind—the correct answer being obviously no. Although there has been a critical fashion for perceiving all cross-dressing in early modern fiction and drama as essentially transgressive, the conventions of fictional cross-dressing ultimately function to reassert gender norms.[4] The Shakespearean heroine succeeds in talking the talk, but inevitably the person in the doublet and hose proves to be too tender- or faint-hearted to pass respectably for a man, or even a boy. "You a man! You lack a man's heart," says Oliver to Rosalind. Within the world of *Marius & Delia*, such a rebuke would be out of place. A man's heart is not impressively brave or bold. Men only talk the talk. In chapter 2, Ferdinando Bye meets his death when the party of young men intent on joining the ill-fated Lammas Day uprising turn and flee as soon as they encounter an army patrol. Significantly, his fatal injury results from his lack of familiarity with the weapon he bears. He becomes trapped under his foundering horse when his "lended sword" gets in his way. The young men's martial venture, abandoned at the first threat of an armed skirmish, is merely the impulsive outcome of an evening of boastful guzzling and frat-house-style bravado. The text hints that it would require greater courage to refuse than to comply: "No gentleman of spirit and mettle could decline such a proposal; certainly none of the young sparks present dared to do so" (14). Another drunkenly boastful party of men surfaces in chapter 10. The dragoons quartered in the alehouse consider themselves "heroes and doers of great exploits," even though these exploits were limited to harassing "poor strollers and suspected Papists" (101). The tale of the maimed soldier denies the reality of glory and heroism. He gives "a soldier's account" of the battle of Steenkirk, "all smoke and confusion, a hellish noise of guns, shouting and cursing, and groans of dying men" (103). The troops were marched into an ill-planned attack by incompetent generals, their position so untenable that the retreat required more courage and produced more casualties than the battle itself. In expressing his contempt for cowards and shirkers, Major Boyle represents the worldview of the seasoned professional soldier. Nonetheless, he practices *sauve qui peut* when he fears the Jacobite plotters have been betrayed by Jack.

Given that the text offers such a skeptical take on masculine bravery, Jack does not "counterfeit to be a man" badly (to continue the comparison with Shakespeare's Rosalind). Oliver's criticism is made when Rosalind swoons at the sight of Orlando's blood. Fainting and weeping are marked as stereotypic behaviors that reveal the woman's heart. Jack trembles tearfully when s/he is roughed up and threatened by the rival gang of coiners. Far from suspecting a counterfeit manhood, the coiners express surprise at Jack's unexpected refusal to betray his fellows. When, a short while later, Jack discovers Gryce intends to murder him *pour encourage les autres,* he is "close to falling in a swoon" (145), but as a physical response to a seemingly inescapable threat this hardly registers as gender-specific.

In *Marius & Delia*, a man's heart is not so much courageous as argumentative. In that regard, Marius Bye is thoroughly masculine. Though he may lack a knack for bawdry, he showed early on "his genius for inventing taunts and jeers" (12). In his gout-ridden retirement, he prefers his guests to be quarrelsome men who "washed down their meat with a dispute" (67). By contrast, Delia in her petticoats is submissive and unquestioningly obedient, even when her father strikes and abuses her: "she had never disobeyed or disputed with him, and she did not now" (82). Out of petticoats and into breeches, s/he undergoes a corresponding, though gradual, change in behavior. Setting out from London through Southwark, Jack initiates a quarrel with the chapwoman over money, but is soon forced to relent and make peace. This, significantly, is cited as Delia's one failure to counterfeit a man. "Jack was not man enough" to insist upon fixing a monetary value on the chapwoman's services and instead submissively expresses gratitude. However effective the chapwoman's "fraudulent indignation" might be in out-disputing her companion, the narrator attributes Jack's capitulation to being still new to breeches: "Jack indeed was so newly out of his coats and into his breeches, still so much the dutiful and compliant child, that he could not endure arousing her displeasure" (92). The language here adds another dimension that further blurs the significance of gender. Children are also dressed in "coats" until the age when boys are put in breeches; submission and obedience are thereby positioned as social rather than gender roles, expected of women and children as well as servants, apprentices and other subordinates. It is only because he is newly breeched that Jack lacks a man's bold, quarrelsome heart—which he does later demonstrate. In chapter 13 Jack shows "an itch to object" when his belligerent new master demands an oath of loyalty, engaging him in a debate upon the ethics of coining. Jack acquiesces only after Gryce puts forward a pseudo-republican argument equating the royal monopoly over the coinage to an act of tyranny. The narrator draws the reader's attention to the exchange by remarking:

> I noted that the longer he was in breeches, the more he gained assurance and even displayed a certain quarrelsomeness, at least (like his father) in words. I wonder how such a transformation should come to pass: whether it might be due to the frictions of the garment upon the skin, which thicken, congeal, and coarsen the animal spirits, which then transmit their occult qualities to the brain; so that the meek, soft, and pliable person in coats, becomes a bold, forward, contentious being when breeched. I must note that this operation obtains also in reverse: for Delia is by no means shrewish or froward when she is in the habiliment belonging to her sex. (136)

Breeches command; petticoats submit. Breeches are bold and contentious, petticoats meek and eager to please. The text sets up a metonymy for gender identity which is subsequently interpreted literally. Gender is not merely signaled by dress, it *is* dress or is at least an accessory of dress. Although it is Jack's ignorance of same-sex attraction that leads him to wonder "if the priest knew the difference between male and female," that difference is only in those "privy parts" between the legs (121). There are no constraints to Jack's ability to pass as male as long as he can keep those breeches on—and keep prying hands out of them. Jack fears exposure on four occasions. The innocent caresses of Sally, the amorous maidservant, risk an accidental discovery. Yet more urgently Jack fends off the assault of the pederast priest. Later he is embarrassingly probed for sexual ripeness by the experienced hand of Mrs. Peatfoote, who is the female complement to Bevil Maynard, only subject to societal constraints regarding her freedom to choose (and dominate) a partner. The final threat is presented by the rival gang of coiners searching his pockets, who might make "a discovery that outslipt both the amorous Mrs. Peatfoote and the mass-priest" (143). The fear is not that a searcher would discover womanly breasts (we are reminded more than once that Delia is thin), but rather would identify Jack as a counterfeit by the absence of external male genitalia. The menservants of Sir John's house are not far off in mocking Jack as a neuter who keeps "his nutmegs in a box" (119).

However lean and lacking in salt she may be, every Jill has her Jack. Delia charms her misogynistic master by her androgynous traits—her masculine-styled calligraphy and vocabulary, her lack of coquetry and of the usual feminine attainments of singing and dancing. She is of course biologically female and she soon presents her husband with an heir. That heir is presumably a changeling, the child of his nephew and namesake. It's possible that Sir Maynard is in fact sterile, neutered by his severe case of syphilis. Contemporaries certainly believed the disease could result in male sterility. Gossip had attributed James II's difficulties in producing an heir to a "revenge pox" passed on to him by Robert Carnegie, Earl of Southesk, the resentful husband of one of his mistresses.

If a Jill may pass herself so easily as a Jack, then the sartorial social contract, as Terry Castle terms it, is vulnerable to deceit and double-dealing.[5] The text hints at the pervasiveness of cross-dressing. The old clothes dealer in Houndsditch claims that many gentlewomen come to him for breeches, "it being a more convenient attire" (89). The convenience is not elaborated upon and raises questions. Is it simply more convenient to be a man than a woman? Nan the chapwoman views breeches as standard travel apparel for young women.[6] "You would go better in breeches" (88), she tells Delia after she is again sexually harassed upon the road. On the run from Jacobite plotters and double-crossing coiners, Jack is compelled to hide himself inside female dress. He shifts clothes to become she once again in a dirty corner of Alsatia that is likened to the one where she was raped by her supposed husband—the parallel registering the gender switch as a descent into an exploited and abused class. Jack is once again Delia, "a Delia who dropped a few tears" (161). She is distressed at being cheated out of her keepsake scissors, but the tears are perhaps also shed over the loss of status and security consequent to being gendered female. The inconveniences of gown and petticoat quickly surface. Fearful to be abroad at night, she is put to the added expense of staying at an inn. There a sneering manservant initially refuses to provide her with pen and paper. Taking employment as a chambermaid in the Maynard household, she is subjected to inferior wages, to the misogyny of her master, and to continual sexual harassment inflicted by the nephew and the two footmen. The inconveniences of wearing a gown are so evident that the masculine-appearing housemaid in the Maynard household is remarked upon for the oddity of *not* choosing to cross-dress, "'twas a wonder she did not pass herself for a man to improve her wages" (164). This sturdy, hairy maid-of-all-work, who is never named, receives only two subsequent mentions, including one that asserts her between-the-legs womanhood in conjunction with the masculine strength of her arm. The other servants warn Delia to avoid the nephew who "would leave no woman alone ... he would even attempt the amazon, were he not afraid of her arm" (165). Delia initially "feared" she would have to share a bed with "the viraginian housemaid," which suggests she perceives her fellow servant as a sexual threat. The ambiguously sexed housemaid has so little relevance to the narrative that she seems to be introduced purely as a (partial) denial of instrumentalized biological difference, a questioning of narrow dichotomous gendering.[7] As a final instance of the convenience of breeches, the Roman Catholic priest in Sir John Herewige's household has left off wearing a cassock in order to avoid persecution, dressing in the style of an upper servant or poor relation.

The chief cross-dressing imposter within the text of *Marius & Delia* is of course the narrator, posing as a Tory/Jacobite male, a poor hack writer in a garret who expresses decidedly negative and dismissive views of both republicans and women. The narrator's cross-dressing is discursive and indirect, taking advantage of the reader's sex-typing assumptions. Beyond a passing reference in the mock dedication to a well-worn shirt (an article of clothing that was not strongly gendered), there is no overt claim to breeches. Rather, the narrator offers misogynistic generalizations and represents her/himself as moving about in society in a way that would be largely reserved for men. In the abortive first chapter or "Exordium Scandali," the narrator backs up claims to truth-telling by a first-hand report: "I myself have passed along that road, it is the North Road, and looked up to see the old man at his window." In chapter 15, Delia looks up to see her father at the window after she is chased from the door by her new stepmother, but the reader is presumably not expected to note the parallel. In the "Defensio Interjecta," the narrator is treated to a good dinner and a good deal of claret by a company of men "flattered to be thought judges of literature" (55). Nettled by a poor reception to the first five chapters, the narrator details various sources for the narrative, an account that includes a visit to various booksellers; an urgent stop at the public jakes; careful perusal of those pages of Marius Bye's work that escaped defilement; efforts to prompt the daughter's parrot-like memory for her father's sayings; and the provision of a treat in a Southwark tavern to an alcoholic ex-plotter and "Newgate pettifogger" who had preserved the narrator from a stint in debtor's prison. None of these activities would require a penis, but they do imply a freedom of movement that no woman, rich or poor, would be likely to enjoy. When Delia is in her maidservant dress, she is harassed by day and fearful of assault if she goes abroad at night. As a wealthy citizen's wife with a coach and servants, respectability limits her mobility: "I may not go anywhere without at least one footman" (183).

The stated motive for working "a deception" upon the reader is to gain trust and credibility. Even patched breeches have more authority than petticoats. So much may be granted; however, by dropping her assumed breeches to flash the reader in her final paragraphs, the narratorial maneuver self-destructs the text's credibility without attaining its stated (presumably disingenuous) purpose. The reader's impression of Marius Bye will not reverse itself. Moreover, the fact that it is so difficult, within the narrative, to distinguish republicans from Jacobites would itself undercut any non-ironic attempt to represent republican political thinking.

The epilogue thus presents the reader with an irresolvable paradox: this is a true history told by a liar. If one ventures to take the narrator at her (final) word, any attempt to reconcile the newly merged identities of narrator and protagonist takes one into the literal-minded, character-focused territory occupied by mediocre student essays. (I can readily imagine one of my students arguing that Lady Maynard slips back into her patched breeches—we never hear that she discarded them, after all—to tear around London upon cross-dressing adventures, such as visits to the Peatfoote tavern in Southwark.)

If the epilogue has a purpose beyond the surprise element, if it does not fracture the narrative into incoherence, that purpose is not to fool the reader into accepting republican ideas so much as to further undermine the possibility of perceiving gender and political identities, given the endless and multifarious deceits of speech and dress. By mimicking the opposing faction/gender successfully, s/he undermines the distinction. There is no essential difference to gender beyond the genitals; and there is no essential distinction between the political factions, since self-interest is the only abiding determinant. Just as the difference of male and female diminishes to nearly neuter, so the warring political factions prove difficult to distinguish, due to the presence of changelings. As noted, the too-aptly-named Ned Shift exemplifies the double-crossing deceits of party. But there is also Sir Maynard, a Jacobite by conviction who passes himself as a Williamite Whig for the sake of his business interests. The reader may legitimately interrogate the ending and raise issues concerning intentionality and the thematic unity of the narrative. Nonetheless, it does succeed in pushing the one-sex theory to its logical extreme (or well beyond it). It succeeds as well in representing a social order at continual risk of being destabilized by the deceptions of cross-dressing neuters and double-crossing changelings.

Notes

1 As any such tally is somewhat subjective, I will detail mine: 1) Delia is raped by Bevil Maynard in the street and then has sex with him in an alehouse; 2) Delia is beaten by the amorous rustic after she resists his sexual demands; 3) Delia is "grasped in a disgusting embrace" on the way to Houndsditch; 4) Jack is courted by Sally, the maidservant in Herewige's house; 5) Jack is assaulted by the priest, 6) Jack is groped by Mrs. Peatfoote; 7 & 8) the two footmen repeatedly grope, kiss or otherwise harass Delia; and 9) Delia is harassed by Bevil Maynard twice, and subsequently spends the night with him, having sex three times.

2 Although Laqueur's work has been criticized as overstating the dominance of the one-sex model, this model, as we shall see, shows a good fit with the presentation of sex difference in *Marius & Delia*: Thomas Laqueur, *Making Sex: Body and Gender from the Greeks to Freud* (Cambridge, MA: Harvard University Press, 1990).

3 On the literary tradition asserting a pen-as-penis or pen-requires-penis relationship, see Sandra M. Gilbert and Susan Gubar, *The Madwoman in the Attic* (New Haven, CT: Yale University Press, 1979, 1984), 3–16.

4 See, for example, Marjorie Garber, *Vested Interests: Cross-Dressing & Cultural Anxiety* (New York: Harper Perennial, 1992).

5 Terry Castle, *Masquerade and Civilization: The Carnivalesque in Eighteenth-Century English Culture and Fiction* (Stanford, CA: Stanford University Press, 1986), 56.

6 See Rudolf M. Dekker and Lotte C. van de Pol, *The Tradition of Female Transvestism in Early Modern Europe* (New York: Macmillan Press, 1989) for evidence suggesting cross-dressing was a common self-protective strategy for women traveling alone in this time period.

7 Wahrman has proposed that the late seventeenth century was open to more free play in the understanding of gender as a social construct, with "the willingness to accept the possible freedom of an occasional biological 'woman' or 'man' to sidestep the cultural expectations of 'femininity' and 'masculinity'." Dror Wahrman, *The Making of the Modern Self* (New Haven, CT: Yale University Press, 2004), 34.

Commodification of Self and Others in *Marius & Delia*

Gavin Mettrick

CHAPTER 14 of *Marius & Delia* opens with a trope depicting animated money, jingling in the purses of rural laborers, crying out to be spent at markets and fairs. A vision of harvest celebration, seemingly communal and egalitarian, is undercut by the "Spend! Spend!" clamor of pocketed wages. Only a few "grum misers" are able to resist the demands of money to circulate. Coins are thus attributed an agency that renders humans passive and powerless to resist their demands, thereby effecting a subject/object reversal. It is one of several junctures in the text which assert money's determinative influence upon behavior. Marius, upon taking his first pamphlet to the booksellers and discovering he has missed the market, refuses to write upon the suggested themes: "Marius (with money in his pocket) was no hireling" (17). The parenthetical qualifier serves to doubt his integrity—implying he would succumb to wage-labor in need. Yet the reader discovers, not many pages further, that he does not do so despite his descent into poverty during the plague year. Moreover, the implication contradicts the text's overriding portrayal of him as obsessively and quixotically fixed upon his brand of radical politics: "For the sole mistress of his heart, that he loved above all else, was the Good Old Cause" (32). With an interesting inconsistency, the not-entirely-trustworthy narrator suggests at one point that Marius' devotion to his cause might not have been all-consuming and unwavering, that he might have settled down to a comfortable life as a rentier landlord, given that "levelling notions suit poorly with full purses and fine expectations" (22), "had his kind father lived to guide him" (24), presumably by teaching him the fundamentals of estate management. There is, additionally, an undeveloped implication that his expectations *were* disappointed and his purse never full, providing a financial motive for his ongoing political discontent: "When Marius went to view the estate, he found it weakened and impaired from the depredations and exactions of the army, the Protectorate, and his brother Roger" (24). The impurity of his political motivations is implied as well in his lifelong resentment of goldsmith-bankers. Marius does have money in his pocket: yet it is never quite enough money, and he later engages in alchemical investigations that are inadequately explained by his daughter, "laboring to exonerate her father" (31), as motivated purely by empathy for the poor. The money-in-pocket questioning of Marius' sincerity makes a minor contribution to establishing the narratorial voice's pretense to a royalist-tinged cynicism. Its principal effect, however, is to draw the reader's attention to the potency of money, albeit with conspicuous redundancy.

The mock dedication which opens the text presents the author-image as a Grubstreet hack in a garret, making a memorandum of debts to be paid down with the earnings from his book—*his* being the default gender that readers are prompted to assign to this narratorial voice. His book, the product of "sweaty labor," is thus characterized from the outset as a commodity, to be furnished with a dedication as a ploy, a marketing gimmick, for "fooling the reader into a belief that the book and its author are something considerable and well worth his shilling" (2). The reader is thereby aligned with the rustics Hodge and Nell of chapter 14, while the author and his book perform the same mass-entertainment function as "the peddlers, mountebanks, sorcerers, jugglers, strolling players, pickpockets, and all-cause rogues of England" (147). At the precise juncture that the authorial presence boasts of producing something entirely new, never thought of before, the text undermines itself by an association with hucksterism, with conning people into its purchase by false pretenses. The text thus enacts Eagleton's observation that "it is just when the artist is becoming debased to a petty commodity producer that he or she will lay claim to transcendent genius."[1] A demystification of authorship as labor for hire is accompanied by a corresponding elevation of the potency of money. Money and its impact upon human relationships are core issues in this text, both acknowledged and unacknowledged. The animated coins jingling in the pockets of rural day laborers play upon a recurrent theme of reification and its consequences.

The shilling and the soldier

Midway through the text of *Marius & Delia*, an ordinary young man undergoes an extraordinary metamorphosis. Tricked into touching a coin, "the King's shilling," he is converted into a commodity via a mysterious mechanism which cannot be undone nor effectively resisted. He is warehoused with a stock of other unfree bipedal commodities ("friendless young men like myself") until they are brought before officer-purchasers "like cattle at market" (105–06). His "soldier's tale" emphasizes the buying and selling aspects of his ordeals, the dehumanizing loss of autonomy and freedom, rather than the physical suffering of illness and lasting injury. The Midas-fingered touch of the powerful commodifies the powerless—and yet the powerless also do it to themselves. As conscious commodities, he and his fellow soldiers contrive to resell themselves by deserting and reenlisting, thereby realizing money to buy supplemental food. His degradation is permanent: on his return to England, he is rejected by his family and social connections. He is given five pounds by his uncle with an understanding that he resume his wanderings and make no further claims upon his family or his parish. He next attempts to change his storyline from picaresque to pastoral by a retreat to a cottage in Romney Marsh, shared with a poor drover whom he met on the road: "I am sure I have listened to many a sermon praising humility and contented poverty; I thought that this was such a humble, contented man, and I might learn from him how to accept my unhappy lot" (107–08). The drover's contentment, however, is founded upon the poverty that barred him from heavy drinking, which he is now enabled to indulge with his half-share of the five pounds. A drunken fall causes him to break his leg, an injury that may well be permanently disabling. The reader knows only that he is halting upon a stick at the time the soldier leaves him. If so, then the soldier's misfortunes might indeed be "infectious," a notion he attributed to his uncle and friends in shunning him. The possibility of the drover suffering a permanent injury that terminates his employability parallels the soldier's own experience after handling the shilling held out to him. Money has a potency to diminish autonomy, to impair or destroy integrity (physical as well as moral), and to reduce individuals to market commodity.

Reification of relationship and the alchemy of the market

The soldier's tale centers upon an account of the battle of Steenkirk, or Steenkerque, in August of 1692, in which a botched assault by the Allies resulted in casualties of over fifty percent. In the opening of chapter 11, Jack offers a commentary: "However dreadful and deadly the battle had been, it was his account of how he had been waylaid and held prisoner, then sold to the best bidder, that was most shocking to me" (110). But s/he should talk. Not one of Delia/Jack's relationships escapes the domination of the market and its valuations.

Early in the course of their travels through Kent, Jack is irritated into starting a quarrel with Nan over the money she pocketed from the sale of Delia's clothes and hair. Nan instantly retorts with "all the fraudulent indignation of her kind," accusing her companion of ingratitude, whom she had rescued from two possible fates, either "perishing on the roadside, or becoming a hedge-trull that lifts her coats for bread" (92). Surrendering to her counterattack, Jack appeases her with apologies and expressions of gratitude—an acquiescence that the narrator attributes to Jack's inexperience in asserting himself as a socially dominant male:

> Jack was not man enough to answer, that the value of her services to him was not more than five or six shillings, say it were six; then the men's clothes, being coarse and shabby, and the coins delivered over to him amounted to about seven shilling sixpence; so that, setting the value of the hair at two pounds and the clothes at six shillings (though it was probably greater), there was a difference of one pound four shilling sixpence that was owed beyond any debt of gratitude or claim of fellowship. (92)

The narratorial stance taken here, proposing that women are naturally submissive, whereas men view relationships in economic terms, is a(nother) textual misdirection. Nan made a parallel set of calculations when the two travelers were approaching London. Taking Delia's bundle from her, "she began to rummage its contents, mumbling of shillings and pence, as she pulled out and examined each item" (88). Delia stifled her resentment at this proceeding because she herself was currently struggling to put a proper valuation on the chapwoman's services, believing she had been guided faithfully to Cambridge and would be expected to offer compensation, either in goods or coin. Taken into the second-hand clothing shops of Houndsditch, she is subsequently trapped into the sale of her hair as well as her clothes. Understanding that her companion had realized more money than she shared out, Delia/Jack determines that she must "cleave" to the chapwoman to have any hopes of recovering the money (90). Their "apparent friendship"—these are the last words of chapter 9—is thus contaminated from its outset by mutual rationalization and the ongoing calculation of shillings and pence. Each attempts to extract money from the other, or in exchange for the other. The chapwoman's superior skills in such transactions are shown in her success in selling Delia/Jack several times over: first piecemeal to the dealers of Houndsditch, then whole-person to Sir John Herewige. She also trades her supposed concern for her companion's fatigue for a reduced reckoning from the innkeeper who was reluctant host to the dragoons.

This is the pattern set by all relationships within the text. Delia/Jack views Tom Found as a friend—"his only friend" s/he calls him upon leaving the Dog and Bear Tavern—yet it is a friendship established and sustained by money, through giving Tom a share of the tips dispensed by the gentlemen in the upstairs rooms. In the end, of course, as a wealthy city-knight's wife, Delia commands Tom's loyalty by becoming his employer, providing him with wages and a livery. Delia has never known a relationship that is free from instrumentalization. Her father's attachment to her is based on utility: "She became a necessary furniture of her father's study: pen, ink, paper, Delia" (64). She later augments her usefulness by serving her father and his fellow conspirators at table. The villagers, in gossiping about Marius Bye as "a brain-sick, scribbling gentleman," sum up the relationship of father and daughter as purely exploitative: "He had a daughter that he used as a servant until she run away from him the year afore" (188). The final sentence of chapter 17 draws attention again to her subservient and instrumentalized status, asserting that Marius never mentions his daughter to Jane. Out of use, out of mind, in effect.

Jane happily retails gossip of her master to Tom Found in exchange for a shilling (the default price for every relationship, it seems), but lacks the curiosity to ask who is paying for the information. No doubt she too has forgotten Delia, who had been completely under her care and control as a small child, until her father began to take an interest in her. Jane "almost fancied herself the [girl's] mother" in terms exactly comparable to her father's instrumentalization of the relationship: "For certain, she had come to view the child as a miniken maid who would in due time perform the hard work of the house under her direction" (61). The relationship of Jane and

Delia is portrayed in some detail, with a surface inconsistency ("sometime kisses and sometime blows, and sometime one after the other" [61]) that may be read as reflecting Jane's shifting perception of the costs and benefits of providing "rough fostering" to the child. At first Delia is kept "half-famished on waterish pap" in order to skim money from the housekeeping budget while her father is too preoccupied in plotting to notice "the disarray of his house and child" (52–53). When, however, Jane finds it relatively easy to profit from Delia's dependency and trust, she shows her affection by only overcharging her for the pies from her cookshop:

> Delia paid whatever price she named for whatever dish she urged upon her. I shall say in Jane's defense, that though she could have imposed upon Delia with rusty or corrupted meat, she was sufficiently fond of the girl, only to overcharge her for food that was fresh and toothsome. (74)

In the transactional world of *Marius & Delia*, this is as good as a relationship gets.

Like the conscripted soldier, Delia is regularly bought and sold: a price is paid for her clothes, her hair and for the use (short or long term) of her genitals. In chapter 8 her rape is perceived, both by her attacker and the narrator, in terms of commerce. Her stunned confusion and passivity allow Bevil Maynard to repeat his assault in the more comfortable setting of a private chamber in a nearby alehouse. He subsequently redefines the assault as a commercial transaction by putting money in her hand, as he will do again after using her sexual services in his uncle's house. But the narrator had already characterized his exploitation of her as a market transaction in a repellent simile, which follows a surmise that Maynard had spent the night in the company of prostitutes: "His condition was that of the householder who goes to market, where he is persuaded into buying a piece of old mutton, for which he pays too much; only to come upon another stall where he might have had fresher meat for less, if he had only waited. Delia was somewhat too lean, and lacking in salt, to make a market, but she was unquestionably a fresh and wholesome morsel" (80). *To make a market*, according to the OED, is to trade or to bring off a deal, but also to have sexual intercourse; the double meaning of *salt* is familiar from Shakespeare. A gender-reversed version of the trope is deployed to describe Jane's sexual interest in the baker's young apprentice, whom she would squeeze and pinch affectionately "as if checking his fatness for the market," until she at last gave sufficient hints to provoke "an offer of marriage to a fresh, plump purse of good silver and a pursy, one-eyed woman of near forty years" (74).

Delia's marriage to Sir Bevil Maynard is not provided with a fig leaf of sentiment to disguise its character as an economic transaction. In the final chapter, offering "the conclusion of this history, with the fates of many persons in it" (179), she is put before the reader fingering the contents of "a fresh purse of guineas from her husband" (185). The mockery of reader expectations at the outset of chapter

12, when "the author reminds the reader that this is a true history, not a romance" (123), recurs in Delia's fortunate, but not especially joyous ending. She might have been at risk of becoming a hedge-trull—the insult thrown at her by Nan and by her stepmother. Instead, she is, as viewed through Tom Found's eyes, "young, well-favored, and richly dressed," riding in a splendid coach and six with footmen in attendance. Her own perspective in regard to her new status is obscured, though the reader can draw a surmise when she says, in regard to her father's republican manuscript, "I would not for a hundred pounds that Sir Maynard should find such papers in his house" (187). Delia, with bags of guineas at her disposal, has begun to gauge feelings by their cash equivalents. Until she joined the money-in-pocket elite, it would be an improbable figure of speech for her to use. The refusal to depict the married relations of the Maynards as more than rational self-interest—perhaps rising to the "sufficiently fond" of Jane's attachment to Delia—underlines the mutually exploitative nature of their union. "It needs no great ceremony or delicacy for a wealthy gentleman to propose marriage to his servant girl, nor was Delia foolishly coy in accepting" (175).

If she was not foolishly coy, neither was she Pamela-style rapturous. The couple begin married life with little change from business as usual. In fact, she waits upon him at table after the rattled servants are dismissed. Then the new husband goes to his study to write letters, presumably including one to his nephew, while his lady calls the servants together and wins them over to enabling her exposé of the nephew's character to his uncle. Despite the fine clothes and the coach, or perhaps because of them, Delia experiences the marriage as a bartered exchange of freedom for security. She gives no indication of regretting her bargain, except insofar as she expresses unexpected nostalgia for her past life as poor threadbare Jack in her farewell letter to her cross-dressed self: "a poor body in breeches may go about freely, without anyone taking notice of him, but the same is not true of a rich knight's lady" (183).

Her memory might be playing her false here, transforming her own history into a romance, given that for much of the cross-dressed portion of the narrative, she was either exhausted or fearful (though fully cognizant of the advantages of being kicked rather than raped—a contrast twice suggested [91, 127]). This is a possible reading but not incompatible with a second possibility, that her nostalgia is focused on the idyllic fortnight spent roaming the Weald with the chapwoman. The interval in the Weald constitutes the romance element that the narratorial voice has twice rejected (at the opening of chapter 12 and in the false start at the outset of the narrative). The romance/bourgeois-realism axis corresponds to the organic/reified axis, and it is only in this episode that the suppressed elements are allowed to surface, in a set-apart realm of poverty, subsistence agriculture and isolation: "It was a wild, meagre, little-habited country of small farmers, such as possess no more than a dozen hens, a brace of thin-bellied pigs, and an old despairing cow" (95).

The pastoral turn: borderlands of bartering

The pounds, shillings and pence calculations that underlie the relationship between Nan Trundle and Delia/Jack recede from view during this fortnight passed in the remoter portions of the Kentish Weald, in the interval between the two visits to the Jacobite smuggler. This is also the interval when their interactions are characterized as evincing "great good spirits and apparent friendship," emblematized by their singing together the chapwoman's old songs. The harmony of this time period arises, at least in part, from their escape from the oppressive power of the marketplace. The chapwoman had furnished their packs with outmoded, shopworn wares that were, in effect, past their sell date in the metropolis. At the end of their first full day of tramping, the chapwoman is able, with much bargaining, to exchange her second-quality finery for surplus food at a small farm. When they are within the Weald, wandering presumably in the region of Romney Marsh, these bartering exchanges become an everyday routine. The chapwoman's wares are now viewed as desirable, but the inhabitants of this sparsely populated region are without money and the exchange is "eggs, butter, and peas for ribbons, pins, and thread-lace" (95). Delia/Jack adopts an ambivalent response to these transactions. She assumes that carrying outmoded goods to buyers without ready access to markets is the chapwoman's chief trade, which prompts the question: "what the profit might be, of walking so far, only to eat well for a season" (95). Although puzzled by the chapwoman's failure to accumulate, Delia/Jack is simultaneously content to enter into a novel mode of existence not driven by desire for profit—or desire for anything beyond idling in pleasant pastoral settings: "he thought his present existence delightful, and gave no thought to past or future" (95). In attributing to Jack an unresolved split view of a barter-based mode of subsistence (querying the absence of profit while rejoicing at the gain in leisure), the text might be read as implying another breeches-versus-petticoats dichotomy; but the two conflicting views are not further elaborated and certainly not reconciled. The confliction and inconsistency that surface here in the views attributed to Delia/Jack remain unresolved and problematic for the text as a whole.

The sojourn in the Weald, bracketed by the two visits to the smuggler, is overtly positioned as a pastoral retreat, in which the urgencies of place, time and acquisition fade to insignificance. Each day the chapwoman barters her goods for food, supplemented by salads assembled from wayside herbs. The two companions have no destination or objective, sometimes idling at an inn or alongside a stream. The tensions in their relationship evanesce to the point that Nan volunteers an account of her life. Her mother was a ballad singer and an herbalist who had carefully saved her surplus earnings, burying hoards of coin in waste areas, with a view to acquiring wealth sufficient for a subsistence living on a small holding: "a cottage with a little land, upon which the two of them might shift to feed themselves, and sometimes carry a basket to the London market" (96). When it is time to act upon their plan, mother and daughter take separate ways to recover their coin caches, which are divided up among hidden pockets and pouches concealed in their clothes. But the mother never makes it to their rendezvous, murdered, apparently, by someone who knew or suspected what she concealed on her person. It will be her daughter's own fate, related in the penultimate chapter, after her fellow prisoners in Newgate see her pulling coins from her clothes. The parallel is striking and likely unintended, the incidental byproduct of the text's focus upon the unfreedom of commodification, of being transmuted, by self or others, into coin. It is an outcome which Delia, as the richly dressed Lady Maynard, who may go nowhere without at least one footman, will come to experience for herself.

The motivation for the chapwoman in providing an account of her early life and the death of her mother arose from a question about her improvisational style of singing, in which "the song was never twice the same." Nan explains her freely varied ballads as a feature of oral versus print culture: "it was the old way of singing, before books and paper made all the songs the same" (95–96). Her view of the stultifying effects of print culture may get a sympathetic nod from cultural theorists, but it does not hold up well for the Robin Hood ballad she sings. There are two versions of a Robin Hood and the Beggar ballad in the Child collection, numbered 133 and 134.[2] Child views the first, a broadside printed in the 1620s, with disdain. The second ballad is longer and far more developed but survives only in print versions of the late eighteenth century. Both belong to a late development in the Robin Hood legend, in which the hero becomes increasingly unheroic and is repeatedly bested by low-status figures such as a potter, a peddler, a shepherd or (the most despised of all marginalized persons) a sturdy beggar.

The Robin Hood and the Beggar ballad features a series of duplicitous and double-crossing maneuvers. Robin Hood, no believer in a fair fight, seeks revenge on the beggar for defeating him by sending three of his men in pursuit with orders to kill him. The captured beggar proposes to bribe Robin's men with a hundred pounds. The outlaws agree to the bribe while privately resolving to take both his money and his life. A deal having been falsely sworn on both sides, the beggar takes several bags out of his clothes. They contain meal, not money, which he scatters in their faces, momentarily blinding them and permitting his escape. The song thus harmonizes with the text's depiction of repeated acts of betrayal and deceit, the chapwoman presumably identifying with the beggar who purports to have a hundred pounds hidden in his clothes and who (unlike her mother) is able to outwit the killers and thieves who seize him. The ballad is thus no pastoral of the greenwood, no celebration of the freedom of living off the land, but rather a picaresque "cross-biting" tale of rogue versus rogue.

The chapwoman opposes the old way of singing to the leveling effect of the cosmopolitan print world, which homogenizes and commodifies the products of a disappearing oral culture. But the Robin Hood ballads generally, including her favorite, are themselves products of Grubstreet, passing in and out of the ballad-singing repertory, often fixed in print before they enter into oral circulation as an ersatz folk tradition.[3] The commodified knockoff is mistaken for—and thereby erases—the real thing, the genuine product of the itinerant singer. When Delia/Jack encounters her at Sturbridge Fair, the illiterate chapwoman, alienated from her labor, is selling a pack of printed ballads.

Hedges, whores and hirelings

As Braudel observed in his account of the origins of capitalism, "Above all, money everywhere contrives to insert itself into all economic and social relationships."[4] More recently Valenze has examined how the English of the long eighteenth century displayed a level of comfort with pricing human life that facilitated the enslavement of Africans and the brutal exploitation of native populations throughout the growing empire. "Most English people of the late seventeenth century would not have honored a sharp distinction that placed human beings, apart from things, in a separable and unique category," she asserts.[5] Within the text of *Marius & Delia*, everything and every person is, ultimately, for sale, or at least has monetary values appointed to them as markers of worth. As an apprentice Marius can match customers to the numbers in his master's ledger, which presumably constitute a measure of the deference to be shown them. When Delia denies wrongdoing after her voluntary sexual intercourse with Bevil Maynard, saying there was neither pleasure nor profit in the act, the small-change aspect of her wages of sin is prominent in her defense: "As for the ten shillings sixpence, truly, I would as soon turn dunghill-raker, or cry mackerel in the streets, as suffer the ropy kisses of that pimpled coxcomb" (167). On their first encounter Bevil transformed rape into a consensual act by putting money in her hand, in effect legitimizing a theft. The assumption that sex is a market commodity is not unique to the pimpled coxcomb. Delia's father reacts to her innocent account of her "marriage" with a blow and a barrage of invective, "vile trug, gaudy strumpet, flaunting trull, brazen-faced quean" (82), which—given his liberal views on matrimony—likely reflect his outrage at an illicit use of his property interest in her. Her new stepmother intensifies the abuse with "vile wretch" and "wicked hedge-trull" (162). *Hedge-trull* would seem to mark the lowest female social stratum. That was the probable fate, the sole alternative to perishing on the roadside, which the chapwoman scornfully assigned to Delia in her homelessness.

The OED records an extensive list of hedge- compounds in which *hedge* expresses contempt for the homeless, the outcast, the unsanctioned or illicit. There are hedge-lawyers, hedge-parsons, hedge-wenches, hedge-marriages, hedge-alehouses, hedge-wines, even hedge-presses and hedge-rhymes, the latter two presumably representing productions that are sub-Grubstreet in quality. The basic sense, at least when limited to persons, is: "born, brought up, habitually sleeping, sheltering, or plying their trade under hedges, or by the road-side (and hence used generally as an attribute expressing contempt)."[6] In his 1788 *Classical Dictionary of the Vulgar Tongue*, Francis Grose supplies a definition for "hedge whore" that weirdly juxtaposes entrepreneurship with destitution: "an itinerant harlot, who bilks the bagnios and bawdy houses, by disposing of her favours on the way side, under a hedge; a low beggarly prostitute."[7] The lexicographers are arguably fixed too literally upon *hedge* as a physical object, to the neglect of its cultural, economic and historical resonances.

A hedge is nature put to the service of capitalistic accumulation and social exclusion. Those of the English countryside were planted as a consequence of the enclosure of the commons and the engrossment of small holdings by the rentier class of gentry. The stereotyped Hodge and Nell of chapter 14 are classifiable as day-laborers, no longer able to obtain a living from the commons and accordingly dependent upon wage-labor for survival. As Raymond Williams demonstrated in his classic text, *The Country and the City,* it was the acquisitive innovations of seventeenth-century landowners that led to the formation of the capitalist state and a dependent class of propertyless laborers.[8] Over the course of two centuries, enclosure and engrossment combined to erase the self-sustaining independence of the husbandman, transforming him and his family into wage-laborers, if not homeless wanderers (i.e., hedge-dwellers) and forming the basis of the immiserated proletariat that would service the factories a hundred years later. In a sense, then, hedges truly did breed itinerant wanderers and outcasts.

Thus hedges marked, and greatly enlarged, the boundary between rich and poor, powerful and oppressed. Marius' alchemical ambitions were focused upon undermining just this aspect of the cultural formation: "For when every hedge-smith or strolling tinker can coin himself gold, where will the great men be?" (32). Grose's schizoid, possibly ironic gloss for "hedge whore" does however gesture toward an alternative view of hedge-dwellers as persons who have escaped the oppressive force of the power structure. It is implicit in Delia/Jack's idyllic delight in wandering aimlessly in the Weald:

> He scarce called to remembrance that, but a fortnight before, he had been only child and heir to a gentleman of respectable estate, and was now no more than

a hedge-bird, a runagate, a vagabond stroller. In truth, he thought his present existence delightful, and gave no thought to past or future." (95)

The text here draws upon a legendary tradition in which the lack of personal property, rootedness and community ties can be romanticized for its freedom. The concept is at the core of the Robin Hood legend but also transforms and romanticizes the representation of vagabonds, gypsies, pirates and highwaymen in ballads and chapbooks, as Christopher Hill has shown.[9] This sympathetic view of outsiders and outlaws is coupled, in the chapbook tradition, with a hatred for *hirelings*, for mercenary professionals who are viewed as upholding and enforcing the oppressive power of church and state. "Heed not the falsehoods of hireling priests!" are the words of the disruptive Quaker (10). Advocating for the elimination of compulsory tithes was a standard project of the radical sects in the commonwealth years, in particular Quakers and Fifth Monarchists. Marius Bye, however, ultimately takes little interest in sectarian reforms. Within the text of *Marius & Delia*, the hirelings are Grubstreet hacks, servile writers dependent upon wages and patrons, who occupy a literary position analogous to that of the suborned witnesses of the Popish Plot.

Base Grubstreet hirelings and the power of the marketplace

The text opens and closes by depicting the authorial image with pen in hand, writing the final portions of the manuscript and negotiating with the printer. In the epilogue the putative author dispatches the last words of the text and bundles it up for the printer. In the dedication, the fictive author is responding to the printer's subsequent demand for prefatory material that will promote it to potential buyers. Asked for a dedication that will serve to associate his work with a prestigious name, the putative author responds with a mock letter to a wealthy unknown Lord To-Be-Announced Your-Name-Here, a letter that relentlessly plays upon the themes of money, debt and borrowing. Dedications are relics of a precapitalist tradition of patronage and coterie writing, repurposed as disingenuous puffery. When the printer is not satisfied with the rejoinder that the book "is an entirely new thing never thought of before," the putative author resorts to a physical borrowing of language, cutting phrases out of other books in order to assemble a sufficiently "beggarly" dedication. That not only the implied author but the implied printer are given voices to dramatize the assemblage of the text emphatically establishes its materiality. The book is put before the reader as a work of manufacture, produced by sweaty labor, for sale at a stated price of one shilling, and thus equivalent in value to a shilling's worth of nails or buttons or second-hand clothes.

As a consequence, the putative author is unambiguously positioned as a Grubstreet hack, a class upon which the text comments critically as unprincipled opportunists, ready, like Ned Shift, to serve any party willing to pay. Marius Bye, though no hireling, does not escape the taint of Grubstreet when he permits Shaftesbury to control him: "He submitted to write under his guidance, almost, at times, upon his dictation" (43). Immediately following the text's depiction of Marius' uninspired writing upon assigned themes, a commentary is offered that divides the whig pamphleteers into two classes: "some few were men of learning and sincerity, whose works are yet read," whereas the rest were "base Grubstreet hirelings," by implication including Marius in the latter group, engaged, as he is, merely in "scribbling papers that were passed about for a week or two before ending in the bog-house" (43). *Hireling* is "a word always of evil signification," according to John Milton (the OED characterizes it more mildly as "usually opprobrious").[10] In the final chapter Delia thoughtfully attempts to alleviate the stigma by inventing a "Mr. Printer" who asks permission to republish one of her father's pamphlets, thereby elevating him to the higher class of authors whose works are yet read. However, the hedge-printer who is tasked with the actual printing does a Grubstreet job on it, thereby undermining the flattering pretense.

At this juncture, the narrator enters the narrative by offering to write a reply to Marius Bye's pamphlet; the reason given for the proposal is the reply's ephemeral character as "Grubstreet work, not fit for a lady's pen" (189). Grubstreet writes for guineas and for the moment, and thus cannot produce works of lasting worth or originality—although originality is exactly what the authorial image claimed for "his" work in the mock dedication. It is not many pages more, of course, before we are told that the text is in fact the product of a lady's pen. She impersonated "Jack Hack o' Grub Street" in order to gain credibility with the reader, who would sooner believe the words of "a pair of patched breeches inhabiting a garret, than of a silk mantua in an elegant closet" (191). The reader is thus prodded to fix upon the breeches-versus-mantua contrast, and to self-own as a misogynist. To do so, however, is to fall for yet another textual misdirection, and to ignore the text's expressed contempt for hackwork composition for the market. Here, alas, the ironies have spiraled out of control. The text cannot escape the marketplace in which it so insistently participates, and it thus fails to position itself outside the power-relations it has struggled to critique.

Notes

1 Terry Eagleton, *The Ideology of the Aesthetic* (Oxford, UK: Basil Blackwell, 1990), 64–65.

2 Francis James Child, ed., *The English and Scottish Popular Ballads* (Northfield, MN: Loomis House Press, 2nd ed., n. d.), 3:173–82.

3 In *Liberty Against the Law*, Christopher Hill characterizes the Robin Hood ballads as evoking "a lost world of apparent freedom" (London: Penguin Books, 1996), 56;

see also 71–90. However, the Robin Hood story was appropriated and commercialized multiple times, gentrified in the plays of Anthony Munday, and even adapted to royalist propaganda at the time of the Restoration. See Mary Ellen Brown, "Placed, Replaced, or Misplaced?: The Ballads' Progress," *The Eighteenth Century* 47, no. 2/3 (2006): 115–29; and Stephen Knight, "Robin Hood and the Royal Restoration," *Critical Survey* 5, no. 3 (1993): 298–312.

4 Fernand Braudel, *Structures of Everyday Life*, trans. Miriam Kochan and Siân Reynolds (New York: Harper & Row, 1981), 436.

5 Deborah Valenze, *The Social Life of Money in the English Past* (New York: Cambridge University Press, 2006), 224.

6 OED Online, https://www.oed.com/view/Entry/85371.

7 Francis Grose, *A Classical Dictionary of the Vulgar Tongue* (London, 1788).

8 Raymond Williams, *The Country and the City* (New York: Oxford University Press, 1973).

9 Hill's *Liberty Against the Law* (see note 3) explores not only the Robin Hood material but expressions of popular sympathy with other outcast groups seen as living communally outside the social order, as well as popular hatred for law and lawyers as instruments of oppression. "The first thing we do, let's kill all the lawyers" is a sentiment with a long history.

10 John Milton, *Complete Prose Works,* vol. 7, ed. Robert W. Ayers (New Haven, CT: Yale University Press, 1980), 279. OED Online, https://www.oed.com/view/Entry/87214.

Disabled and Undone: Suffering and Impairment in *Marius & Delia*

Brett S. Turley

THE MOCK opening of *Marius & Delia* attempts a lofty, idealizing tone, introducing Marius as a learned gentleman of distinguished birth, although we subsequently learn he lacks more than a rudimentary knowledge of Latin and is in fact the grandson of a yeoman and a city shopkeeper. The shift to a proto-realistic mode occurs abruptly in the third paragraph, as multiple topical allusions, delivered in slangy, colloquial diction, break in upon the narrative, thereby undermining its gesture at achieving a timeless, universalized relevance. Yet the idealizing tone of the opening was already undercut by the introduction of a secondary figure, a larcenous one-eyed maid who snores. It is highly suggestive that the maid Jane is introduced so early in the narrative—the second sentence—and in the same terms in which she will be portrayed with satiric realism in the narrative proper. She resists idealization, even for the momentary needs of the discarded opening. Marius Bye may be dressed up as a well-born scholar, but his physically impaired servant cannot undergo any such upward transformation into (for example) a faithful and devoted retainer with an unspecified number of eyes. Jane's visual impairment is coupled with her dishonesty, and it marks her in such a way that it cannot be disregarded, even momentarily.

Romance of course has its peasants and its villains, who are often marked, Cain-like, with deformity, so as to stand as unlovely contrasts to the handsome, high-born and virtuous heroes of the narrative. In this older tradition of prose fiction, Jane would be one-eyed *because* she is a thief: her appearance emblematizes her inner self. The repellent use of impairment or other non-normative traits as moral markers persists in the later novel, though often disingenuously disguised. Such a convention is presumably conditioning Jane's negative portrayal in *Marius & Delia.* Her thieving and spying are insistently recalled at virtually every point in which she receives more than passing mention.[1] The relationship between disfigurement and criminality in early modern culture is bidirectional. Mutilation was incorporated into the penal code, most commonly in the branding on the thumb (an *F* for felon) that accompanied a *successful* plea for benefit of clergy.[2] In a culture in which criminal actions are punished by the reality or threat of inflicted mutilation, any existing impairment or deformity marks a person *in advance* as criminal or morally suspect.

Latent, yet nonetheless traceable in the text, is an alternative reading of disability in which the relationship is reversed: Jane is a thief *because* she is one-eyed. Monocular vision fixes her in her place at the bottom of the domestic servant class as either a cook-maid or a drudging maid-of-all-work. Although she has acquired a repertory of culinary skills, "her appearance could not commend her to a squeamish mistress" (48). Her disablement is thus in the eye of the fastidious beholder, not in any functional limitations or loss of ability. Accordingly, she remains with her penurious master at an annual salary of twenty shillings, about one-sixth the usual London wages of a cook.[3] Jane supplements these wages by marking up the household accounts, a maneuver exactly paralleling that of the London broker employed to buy household furnishings, by whom Marius is "choused twice over," but whose form of cheating is legitimated, or at least tolerated, by society. The text remarks, moreover, on Marius' deliberate exploitation of the disabilities of his servants: "By reason of their extremes of age and their respective infirmities ... Marius paid them small wages." It is presented as a foolish rather than an immoral bargain since "the old witch and the young one" cost him money by "their thieving," i.e, by marking up the household accounts just as the broker did (25).

The narratorial voice focuses on externals but occasionally imparts inferences of psychological states, often with a rationalization appended. For example, a surmised account of Bevil Maynard's response to news of his uncle's wedding is supplemented with, "I do not know, of course, that Mr. Maynard reasoned thus to himself, for he was but slenderly supplied with brain; but he did have two days to consider it, and I believe he would indulge himself in the most easeful and soothing conclusion" (177). However slenderly endowed with brain he may be, as a privileged male member of the upper class, Maynard's interior state is at least assumed to be individual and unique. In contrast, Jane's unstated feelings and motivations are treated as transparent to view. Everything follows from her characterization as a one-eyed thieving servant. The narrator, without any hedge at a justification, confidently asserts knowledge of her emotions and intentions at multiple points in the text. She felt a spiteful joy when her fellow servants were dismissed without their wages. She intended to steal the valuables of her deceased mistress and sell them to peddlers on the road. "It was an agony" to watch when the broker returned to buy back these valuables. She planned to train Delia as an underservant or "miniken maid" to do the housework in her stead, but was thwarted when Marius manifested a dim paternal interest in his daughter. The critical gentlemen of the "Vindicatory Interlude" could have made a stronger case for questioning the narrative's veracity as history had they focused on Jane rather than Marius Bye. But of course the guiding intent of the narrative, despite the presence of unconscious dissonance, is that Jane should not be a focus of interest as an individual but function as a prop or prosthesis, in Mitchell and Snyder's terms, to support other narrative aims.[4]

The presentation of Jane is filled out in considerable detail over the course of the text. She is pursy, ill-tempered, acquisitive, libelous and lecherous, as well as an abusive or "rough" nurse to Delia. She is only once presented as manifesting socially positive behavior, grief for the death of her fellow servant, which (the irony is unintended in the text) only serves to heighten her perceived unattractiveness.

Viewed through the eyes of her new mistress she is cyclopic and grotesque: "a slatternly maid of hideous aspect, her one eye red and swollen from weeping her loss" (36–37). Although thieving and spying are insistently linked to Jane, they are hardly her exclusive domain. Ethically problematic methods for the accumulation of wealth are pursued by the unnamed agent who manages the Byes' purchases, Hull and his two sons, Nan Trundle, Wry-legged Bill, Gryce, Blank, Bushrod and Delia's own grandfather, in addition to one historical figure, the Earl of Shaftesbury, who "had always several projects in hand" (44). Spying or its corollary, betrayal for profit, is undertaken by various servants, Ned Shift, Bushrod, Wedge the joiner, the Irish witnesses and the infamous Titus Oates. Among this disreputable crew, Jane holds several distinctions: her antisocial behaviors of embezzling and spying are consistently presented unironically—called by their right name, in effect. She herself keeps "her right name of Jane" (8) when the others are furnished with protective aliases (or, in the case of Ned Shift, an alias upon an alias). Although Marius lives in fear of the King's Messengers and multiple characters are deserving of the noose, only Jane suffers punitive consequences for her actions. She is "the only person in this history who was detected in wrong-doing, punished for it, and subsequently underwent a reformation," although the narrator doubts whether she was in fact reformed or merely "properly terrified," the goal of punishment in Hobbesian terms (189). Thus she is marked down for punishment—her criminal acts catalogued by the narration and detected by the authorities—when her fellow rogues survive and prosper. Why does the text draw our attention to her lack of a concealing alias and to her subsequent brutal punishment—if not to mark her as a "predestinate" sacrifice to reader expectations (otherwise unfulfilled) that the fiction will conclude with a fair distribution of rewards and punishments? Her disfiguring (in a double sense) injury and her low origins in a family of poor cottagers designate her as unsympathetic and thereby disposable. It is her scapegoating punishment, related at some length in the concluding chapter, which keeps other necks safe from the pillory and the noose.

The narrator, impersonating the perspective of Marius Bye, reminds us that both Oates and Shaftesbury were physically stigmatized and caricatured in contemporary satire: "His [Marius'] queasiness must have been daily augmented by the sight of their two uncouth figures in conference: the one dwarfish, crooked, and diseased; the other framed like an ape, with a huge misshapen muns" (44).[5] The queasiness of Marius converges with the squeamishness of Jane's potential employers. Here it serves to imply that the two men's non-normative appearance confirmed his doubts regarding their integrity and their fidelity to the republican cause. He comes to detest Oates by some peculiar blend of authorial envy at his relative success and narcissistic dismay at being viewed as a "Junior Oates" by his faction and his patron, "yoked with Oates and compelled to draw the same load" (43). The metaphor prompts a visual image of Marius as a beast of burden paired with a figure "framed like an ape." There is a certain measure of self-loathing and fear of contagion implicit in his hatred, a fear that the mirror might reflect back the unsavory image of Oates. We will find this lurking fear of the non-normative body as a threat, as a potentially communicable disorder, surfacing elsewhere in the text.

The queasy Marius will go on to experience an impairment of his own and to be subjected to the narrator's mockery in turn. His first severe fit of gout occurs at the time of the Rye House Plot, when he is too ill or desponding, the narrator comments, to flee, though counseled to do so by a fellow conspirator. He is again ill at the time of the Monmouth Rebellion and the Bloody Assizes. The narrator, however, expresses doubt as to whether a simple diagnosis of gout is an adequate explanation for his prolonged and repeated attacks. Since "his symptoms observed a sympathy with the sufferings of his party," he might be suffering from "a new malady of politic gout"—a suggestion that plays upon the multiple senses of *politic* to suggest Marius is effectively hiding under the covers, paralyzed by the interplay of gout with "fear and conscious guilt" (59). The questioning of the diagnosis inserts an internal and incorporeal dimension to his suffering and subjects it to doubt. His symptoms continue almost unremittingly ("when he was not under present pain, he feared its return") for twelve years. When Hull (or his footman) delivers a hard knock to the door, leading Marius to fear the King's Messengers had come for him at last, he is unable to flee on "gouty stumps" (71). Shortly thereafter, in his fit of rage following Hull's departure, he paces up and down the room on "gouty pins" (73). Stumps and pins could both be used humorously for legs, but the first bears an association with prostheses and amputations that communicates his stationary freeze when he fears arrest. Gout is a wax-and-wane disorder, but not within the course of an hour. The psychic component of his disorder is not so much the "fear and conscious guilt" proposed by the narrator, adopting a conservative Tory tone, but his discouragement and melancholy. In chapter 17, after his daughter contrives a flattering letter from an interested publisher, followed by a flatteringly abusive rebuttal to his pamphlet, Marius attains a state close to cure. At the close of the narrative, he can move about without his crutch and take walks in his garden.

If Marius' disabling gout is given a strong psychic component, remarked upon in the text, the disability of Hull worsens inexplicably from his first appearance in the narrative, an aggravation which is possibly inadvertent but nonetheless serves as a token of the text's unconscious linkage of disability with (im)moral character. When Jane opens the door to him, "She knew him straightaway, despite a marvelous metamorphosis, from a crooked, lame, crump-shouldered, thin-gutted wretch, reeking of smoke—to a crooked, lame, crump-shouldered, richly dressed burgess, monstrously fat about the middle, smelling of musk and ambergris: Leviathan in person, he might have been" (71). Jane easily recognizes him but the attentive reader might not. In chapter 3 he was characterized as only "a trifle deformed" (29), a strangely vague statement, apparently employed (in conjunction with his humble birth) to position him as the less desirable option for husband and son-in-law in the Boult family. Nevertheless, the acquisition of wealth erases the stigma of deformity within this family. Once Hull has accumulated the resources to build a fine mansion-house in a prestigious neighborhood, "old Boult and his daughter might ever after bless the day that they turned Marius Bye without doors" (30). On his reappearance in chapter 7, Hull is both lame and redundantly crooked. The comparison to Leviathan encompasses corporeal and incorporeal features: Hull smells like a whale (scented with ambergris) and looks like a whale ([sea-]monstrously fat about the middle). Figuratively, in seventeenth-century usage, a leviathan is someone possessed of enormous wealth, not without a strong sulfurous savor of *the* Leviathan, the crooked serpent of Isaiah. The earlier characterization as "a trifle deformed" is put aside in the interests of heightening his disability as an index of greed and corruption. By the same logic, the description of Wry-legged Bill Grigg (grig was a cant word for money as well as a type of eel), the extortionate smuggler, bestows on him a comparable set of physical features, "squat, bow-legged, clump-gaited" (93). Corpulence, unsurprisingly, is the text's primary marker of greed. Jane (as seen by Tom Found) and the landlady who demands payment of the narrator are both "foggy." More significantly, characters become large-bodied as both a consequence and a sign of greed and moral corruption. Roger Bye, who survives as a card cheat and swindler, is greatly altered in appearance on his return home: "his form was corpulent, his behavior coarse and sowish" (17). Gryce, who applies his false coin primarily to dining well "grew monstrously fat"—the identical words applied to Hull.

Unhandsome does as unhandsome is, in effect—but the employment of physical difference to signify greed or corruption goes beyond narrative convention. There is also a fear of communicable corruption, which possibly arises from a guilty and subverted empathy. Marius' father, in dying, attributes his illness to "a taint" communicated to him by the touch of a madman. (The text begs the question of what would be irrational about an impoverished and desperate man attempting to steal a horse.) He is said to be crazed by sickness and hunger: perhaps more significantly he is "a *stark-naked* man" (22, emphasis added). There is a disgust of the body—even the normative body—latent in the text. The villains are loaded with deformity, but there is no countervailing emphasis on the desirable bodies of their (relatively) virtuous counterparts. Marius Bye and his offspring Delia/Jack are largely undescribed except for being several times depicted as thin or "lean-bodied." Their physically unattractive foils, Hull and Gryce, are identically labelled as *monstrously* fat. The slender, delicately built Delia/Jack is represented as handsome or well-favored, and thereby attracting amorous interest, only in the context of being *well-dressed*.[6] If normative bodies, undressed, can be a source of disgust and fear, then those who differ from them will be objects of abhorrence, suspicion and shunning.

Subliminally, though often very near the surface, the text aligns the metaphorical *disgust* or nausea that a "squeamish mistress" (or a queasy Marius) feels at the sight of deformity to the physical disgust and illness caused by corrupted food. Disability or difference sickens the normative-bodied beholder, with or without transmission through touch or prepared foods. This visceral disturbance, felt by the unimpaired in response to the impaired, gains a subliminal validation when wry-legged Bill and one-eyed Jane are both depicted as selling substandard or tainted food.

In an age when punishment of petty crime had largely moved indoors to the local bridewell, Jane's sentence for culinary fraud is crafted to satisfy traditional notions of justice as a ritual exaction of shame and pain—what Foucault termed "the gloomy festival of punishment" and "the penal ceremony." Her punishment is enacted in the public space of the market, the scene of her offense in vending substandard pies, on a market day when the optimal number of people may witness her ordeal. But the pillory was never merely a device for public shaming. The helplessly pinioned prisoner is at the mercy of a crowd that is rarely passive. A particularly notorious prisoner was at risk of being stoned or suffocated by filth or otherwise put to death, deliberately or accidentally.[7] The market crowd for Jane's shaming express their collective disapproval by a *lex talionis* reprisal, pelting her "with rotten vegetables, turds, bones, dead rats, and whatever else they judged fitting, as constituting a probable ingredient in her mixtures" (188). Her punishers are presumably aiming at her mouth so that she might be forced to swallow the same filth she is suspected of imposing on others. But this crowdsourced retribution comes dangerously close to becoming an eye for a pie, much in excess of her offense. Unelaborated in the text is the curious fact that her husband escapes, in dual senses. He takes advantage of his wife's helplessness to abscond with the child and the cashbox. In violation of the legal doctrine of coverture, by which husband and wife are one person, with the wife's actions viewed as her husband's responsibility, he apparently was either not charged or found innocent. Although the baker would surely know the contents of the pies he bakes, he had been positioned in village gossip as the passive conquest of "a pursy, one-eyed woman of near forty years," who "plucked him" before he was ripe (74). She is impaired, and she is the object of misogynistic and ageist censure for her role-reversed January-May marriage. The mob may take their intersectional pleasure in tormenting her.

"Rascal and rogue us not" say the carriers and porters Marius portrays in his pamphlet on the Great Fire, "for we would be pitiful fools, not to have learned from you, our betters, to withhold our wares from the market until we may command the best price" (29). Early modern writers were fitfully aware of the economic double standard by which various wealth-generating activities are criminalized in the poor but not in the privileged class. Jane's troubles originated in her dissatisfaction with the "modest income" available to her. She has raised herself from cook-maid to small-scale victualler. However skilled her hand in seasoning her pies, there is no further economic advance available to her by legally sanctioned means. Her betters had shown her the way. The Boult-Hull family begin their progress to great wealth by dishonest dealing in grain. (In his pamphlet on the fire, Marius, who would know, makes satiric allusion to the musty corn of a corn-chandler, distraught to find he would be unable to profit from the coming dearth.) War brings great profit to the next generation of the corn-chandler's family. Hull, on his visit to Marius, offers the chance to join a victualling syndicate (providing provisions to the navy, presumably) that will treble his money within three years' time—provided he has at least £4,000 to invest. The lack of accountability and excessive profit-taking of the Navy victuallers were notorious, as was the poor quality of the food.[8] The rich get richer by the same practices, on a grander scale, for which the poor are pilloried. But it is up to the reader to apply the metafictional insight of Marius' pamphlet upon profiteering during the Fire to Jane: she is given no voice to say that she learned her money-making tactics from her social superiors.

Marius made the abuses of wartime victualling one of his post-1688 pamphleteering themes, complaining of those "who starved the soldiers and poisoned the sailors with offal and offscourings" (70). The narrative introduces one such soldier in chapter 10, who gives his first-hand account of the dire conditions of the common soldier in Flanders: "There we got only enough coarse bread, hard cheese, and foisted beer to keep us on our feet" (101). While the dragoons are carousing, he "crept in from the rain" wearing a patched and tattered coat, as if "he were avoiding the host's eye"—presumably because his appearance is "beggarly," though in fact he does not beg (101). If Jack brings him food and drink "for pity," it is without being asked. His disabling war wound is concealed from view upon his entrance, and in the course of his narration, we learn that he has some money and is making at least a pittance as an agricultural laborer. Yet the text preemptively categorizes him as "a beggarly stranger" rather than a poor laborer, presumably because of his disabling, as yet concealed injury. In the typology of destitute wanderers, there were sturdy beggars, presumed to be lazy idlers at best, and maimed beggars (a subset of the deserving poor), who displayed their injuries or mutilations in an appeal for charity. In the course of his story, the soldier does indeed display his maimed hand, but not in order to beg alms. He raises his hand at the moment of describing the generosity of the Princess de Vaudemont, who not only took the wounded soldiers into her home, but tended them herself, "with her own white hands" (102). In this image of her white hands touching his maimed hand the Princess constitutes a vignette of the Renaissance ideal of true nobility, a survival from a pre-capitalist and pre-Reformation tradition, inserted into the narrative in explicit contrast to the Protestant officers "who enrich themselves and keep us half starved" (106). Returned to his home, the soldier discovers that his friends discredit his story and that he is presumed to be responsible for his misfortune and misery by some grounding moral failure: "They suspected instead that I fell into wicked ways while in London, so that I was obliged to enlist to save myself" (106). Despite reading his disability and poverty as consequences of unspecified ill-doing, his "pitiful" state also frightens them into shunning him: "They seemed to consider, that my disasters might be infectious" (107). The text does not contradict them, taking a similar stance of shunning and blaming. Jack's final response to his story, like that of his friends, is one of blame, remarking that his "bitter and unforgiving frame of mind" (110) is a disqualification for gaining the pity necessary to successful begging. This observation comes after the soldier concludes his story with a statement of his determined struggle against just such a subject position: "I am not yet reduced to begging, while I can get a little work in the fields" (108). All the same, the narrative insistently labels him a beggarly man rather than a poor one. His story occupies a substantial portion of chapter 10, yet he is one of the few figures in the narrative to make no reappearance, not even in the cursory summing up of the final chapter. Because he is maimed, because he bears the blameworthy insigne of impairment, his future is certain and needs no elaboration.

Notes

1 The editor kindly supplied a pre-publication PDF file of the text, which allowed me to word-search for mentions by name (86 in all), which I analyzed to draw up a rough contextual tally of negative characterizations, as follows: 25 Jane spies and lies; 10 Jane steals and cheats; 10 Jane is ill-tempered; and 6 Jane is hypocritical/deceitful.

2 J. M. Beattie, *Policing and Punishment in London 1660–1750* (New York: Oxford University Press, 2001, 2004), 305.

3 J. Jean Hecht, *The Domestic Servant Class in Eighteenth-Century England* (London: Routledge & Kegan Paul, 1956), 146. The "man-cook" in the household of Sir Maynard knows he can get a new place at any time (175).

4 David T. Mitchell and Sharon L. Snyder, *Narrative Prosthesis: Disability and the Dependencies of Discourse* (Ann Arbor: University of Michigan Press, 2000).

5 On Oates, see John Kenyon, *The Popish Plot* (London: Heinemann, 1972), 48, 50 ("grotesquely unprepossessing"). For Shaftesbury, see *Poems on Affairs of State*, vol. 3, ed. Howard H. Schless (New Haven, CT: Yale University Press, 1968), 57

("formidable cripple"), 407. We are also reminded in the text that Shaftesbury (aka Lord Tapski) was fitted with a drain to control an incurable abscess.

6 "Sally ... was besotted with love the moment she saw him in his livery" (119); "she looked handsome in her new clothes" (174); "young, well-favored, and richly dressed" (179).

7 J. M. Beattie, *Crime and the Courts in England, 1660–1800* (Princeton, NJ: Princeton University Press, 1986), 464–68.

8 Douglas W. Allen, "'The Lesser of Two Weevils': British Victualling Organization in the Long Eighteenth Century," *European Review of Economic History* 22, no. 2 (November 7, 2017): 233–59.

Gallows-worthy but Triumphant: Denial of Justice in *Marius & Delia*

Naomi Hoek

IN THE final chapter of *Marius & Delia*, the narrator sums up the subsequent careers of various characters that figured in the narrative. This forms an altogether conventional and unsurprising maneuver in prose fiction, as the virtuous and the vicious are sorted into their proper places upon the right and left hands of the narratorial presence. Yet the opening pages gave a preliminary hint that rewards and punishments would not be allotted according to conventional expectations. In the "false start" of the abortive opening, the reader is told that names will be changed to protect both the innocent and the guilty by a narrator who did not wish to betray the latter to the ultimate penalty, even though they are in fact "deserving of the gallows" (8), a phrasing that implies the text's unquestioning concurrence with the penal code. Thus, we are forewarned that an exemplary and morally satisfying ending will not be offered: those worthy of hanging will not in fact be hanged. In the "Defensio Interjecta," where the work is once again categorized as a history, not a romance, the narrator nonetheless asserts that the historical facts have been massaged to give importance to Marius Bye without endangering his neck. The narrator admits, however, to making his protagonist appear "somewhat of the fool," and persistently satirizes Marius' political views throughout the narrative (58). In the epilogue, the narrator unmasks to reveal a secret sympathy with Marius and republicanism. Thus the partial and misleading "informations" offered by the narratorial presence are ultimately revealed to be the half-truths of a double agent, yet another morally ambiguous inhabitant of the late seventeenth-century underworld of plotters and counterplotters, thieves and thief-takers.[1] Double-dealing, deception and betrayal loom over the narrative as normalized forms of social interaction and capitalist endeavor. As we shall see, the duplicity of the narrator casts a compromising shadow of moral ambiguity and complicity on the narrative and its incomplete resolution.

Denied the neat closure of a noose, the reader's desire to see justice done must be satisfied with learning that two of the principal "rope-ripe" malefactors, Gryce and Bushrod, do experience setbacks. Their separate attempts to earn bounty money or pardons by betraying their fellows seem to have backfired, and they are obliged to take flight to save themselves:

> Bushrod also informed upon the brothers Hull; for plainly 'twas he that betrayed Blank and Gryce to their rivals. Nonetheless, it was no idle boast of their father, that he had powerful friends: for not only did his sons come to no harm, but Bushrod was impelled to transport himself to the New World. Whereabout he settled I could not discover. He is such a nimble talker of religious cant that, whether he elected to be a Puritan of Boston or a Quaker

of Philadelphia, I make no question but he is prospering. Gryce also found the city grown too hot for him. He has taken a neat little box in Middlesex, where he busies himself in growing wall-fruit. (184–85)

We learn that Gryce is obliged to give up coining, only to relocate to what appears to be a charming rustic retreat, a neat little box. Why a box? The OED offers several glosses to apply to the word. It may mean: "a place of shelter for one or more men; as a sentry's, signalman's, or watchman's box; a sportsman's hiding-place while shooting." The night watchmen of London were provided with boxes, at least in the more affluent wards; these supplemented a network of more substantial shelters that included holding cells. If Bushrod is said to have transported himself, should we contextually decide that Gryce has imprisoned himself, put himself in his own protective custody? A further entry expands the meaning suggested by the sportman's stand: "a small country-house; a residence for temporary use while following a particular sport, as a hunting-box, shooting-box, fishing-box." The first citation the OED offers in support is from Thomas Ellwood's autobiography, where the rural retreat he found for John Milton and his family, fleeing London to escape the plague, is described as "a pretty Box." Here the word has become a modestly deprecatory term for a country residence (comparable to calling one's weekend house "just a shack"), without however shedding its history of use to describe a temporary shelter for evading danger or guarding against attack. We might take it that Gryce is merely laying low until his affairs cool down to a safer ambient temperature, if not for what immediately follows. He is cultivating his garden; more specifically, he is cultivating "wall-fruit," meaning apples, plums, quinces, or other orchard fruit, grown as espaliers, that is, trained upon a lattice or staked to a wall. The unnatural pattern of growth imposed on the trees, bound and straitened on a frame, lends an ironic contrast to his fortunate escape from deserved imprisonment. Only the plants suffer, and only that they may bear fruit more prolifically. He busies himself: it is one of two reflexive verbs in the passage cited—the reflexivity itself creating enclosure, fixing boundaries, boxing in. But the artifice of an enclosed garden also links him with literary traditions of pastoral and its edenic modes of fulfillment and contentment: "Fair Quiet, have I found thee here, / And Innocence, thy sister dear!" Well, perhaps not. But the text gestures ironically in that direction. Gryce has consistently shown a preference for safety, modest aspirations and self-imposed limitations. As a coiner, his ambitions were largely satisfied with being able to eat cheaply, getting "a shillingsworth of meat with a groatsworth of silver," and subsequently becoming "monstrously fat" (140). Blank describes him as a "dwarfish, big-bellied man with a thundering voice" (132) and his name, incidentally, can be etymologized as suckling pig. The reader may conclude he is comfortably snug, in swinely-ever-after fashion, within his well-provisioned box.

Gryce found the city grown too hot for him, and Bushrod was impelled to "transport himself." It's worth pausing to examine what the text omits here. Under the law, both men are "deserving of the gallows," although they have qualified for pardons in exchange for betraying their fellows. Given that the coiners claimed to be anti-government plotters, manipulating the coinage in order to undermine the Revolution state, they were potentially exposed to the counter-accusations of their intended victims. Thus, we don't know whether they take flight to evade the routine workings of formal justice or to escape a mafia-style retaliation by the Hull brothers. Or is it a distinction without a difference? The Hulls asserted a seemingly unconditional power to "rub 'em to the Whit" (144)—that is, to have the coiners sent to Newgate Prison. As J. M. Beattie lays out the parameters of the system of justice in 1690s London, corruption could be said to be baked in. Recommendations to the king's mercy were made to the Cabinet by the notoriously venal City recorder, Salathiel Lovell, who was widely thought to take bribes, and who regularly collaborated with thief-takers for mutual profit.[2] Both Defoe and Tom Brown attacked Lovell for venality and incompetence, and there is no reason why D. M. might not have aimed at him also with perfect consistency.[3] The text positions Bushrod as enacting the familiar plot pattern of the overreacher overreached, which would also have been within the compass of the fiction to elaborate. The narrative, having arrived at this minor crossroads, with one sign pointing to a timely segment of political satire and the other leading to a traditional wrap-up-the-plot maneuver, simply stops dead in the road. The chain of events leading to Bushrod's self-transportation to the New World are not specified. Nor can the reader be certain how to interpret "impelled to transport himself." Should it be read as a factual statement? Was he brought to trial, sentenced, then granted a pardon conditional upon transportation?

As an alternative to capital punishment, transportation had been fitfully applied since early in the century, with its most enthusiastic application coming in the first decade after the Restoration. It operated as a commercial venture: entrepreneurial ship captains and overseas traders would bargain for custody of conditionally pardoned felons, paying their fees plus shipping costs, in exchange for the right to sell them as indentured servants in the West Indies or the North American colonies. The duration of their bondage was stipulated in the pardon, usually as a period of six to ten years. By the 1670s, the limitations of the scheme were apparent. It was a buyer's market, and colonial planters were increasingly reluctant to purchase the labor services of felons, unless they were young, male, healthy and skilled. The colonies of Virginia and Maryland, which had been the chief North American markets for indentured felons, were transitioning to slave-based economies after 1675. Nonetheless, as the only sentencing option intermediate "between a whipping and a hanging," to borrow the chapwoman's phrase (112), transportation continued to be utilized, with the end result that Newgate and other prisons became dangerously overcrowded with unmarketable convicts: the old, the impaired and the female.[4] In a somewhat desperate maneuver to ease the pressure on the penal regime, the courts would enter into recognizances with prisoners sentenced to transportation, releasing them for self-deportation. It is thus entirely possible that Bushrod was brought to trial upon the evidence of informers and sentenced to self-transportation or banishment. There is, however, no suggestion of servitude. Bushrod will be a free agent, certain to prosper under the expansive opportunities of the New World.

The lack of elaboration here, despite the presumably tempting opportunity for satiric commentary on a well-known contemporary abuse, might result from simple authorial haste to conclude the final summing-up phase of the narrative. The heads-up hint that the guilty will be protected from exposure, positioned at the very outset, undermines such a conclusion. I would argue that the passage is better read as a deliberate refusal to offer the expected resolution of exposure and restorative justice, however limited or circumscribed. The reader is explicitly informed that the maid Jane was the only figure in the history to be caught and punished. Whatever *imp*els Bushrod's exile (*comp*els would carry a stronger implication of constraint or force), it is not positioned as justice exacted upon a malefactor. The emphasis is rather on Bushrod's anticipated triumph over a minor setback, his necessary self-transportation to a new base of operation.

The expectation is that he will settle in a town. But why should his options be confined to the either/or of the Quakers of Philadelphia versus the Puritans of Boston? Why not the Butterboxes and Patroons of New York? The Dutch colony of New Amsterdam came under English control in 1667, at the conclusion of the Second Anglo-Dutch war. Thirty years later, New York was the second largest town in the colonies, with a population of about 5,000, compared to 6,700 for Boston and 4,400 for Philadelphia. By way of explanation, the text references his facility as a nimble talker of religious cant, harkening back to a prior statement that he joined a gathered church in order to gain fluency in sanctified patois to support his projects. The desirability of religious cant for a con artist is not otherwise elaborated, but Bushrod fits the type denounced by Bunyan of the "carnal professor" who uses religion to improve his community standing and to gain the trust, and business, of his brethren.[5]

The word *cant* covered a remarkable range in seventeenth-century usage: referring to the whining, sing-song spiel of beggars, the argot of gypsies and thieves, the obfuscating jargon of the doctor or lawyer, and the phraseology of religious sects such as the Quakers. It could denote, on the one hand, a secret language (the "conspiratorial cant" Jack overhears at the Dog and Bear), and on the other, a meaningless or degenerate patter of clichés and set phrases. The common element would seem to be the abuse of language to deceive or obfuscate. At its core, cant is a specious medium of exchange, a coining of new words or significations not authorized in the King's English. The tailor wins over his prospective son-in-law by conversing in "an approved style of factious cant" (36): a usage that seems to draw upon multiple senses of the word. The bullies, adventurers and "false loons" who take advantage of Marius' hospitality need only to be able to speak "a plausible republican cant" or "the old levelling cant" to gain admission (65, 68). Although *cant* is used derogatorily throughout, the text nonetheless indulges in a slangy vocabulary that might have been lifted from such guides as Richard Head's *Canting Academy* and B. E.'s *New Dictionary of the Canting Crew*: blackguard, blow, cogger, coney, cross-biting, cuff, ferret-eyed, nab, peach, rub, scamper, sneak, snitch, squeak, tony, totty-head, Whit.[6] Gryce mingles (and mangles) sacred texts and doctrines with underworld cant, most notably in the conjuration he requires of Jack: "I swear upon the Holy Word of our Savior, by whose grace, and by whose grace only, I hope to be saved: that I will never blow, squeak or peach my fellow, or otherwise provide informations against any of our gang" (136). This merging of sectarian or "factious" discourse with thieves' cant is carried forward when the text limits Bushrod's possible destinations to Boston and Philadelphia. In the Puritan- and Quaker-dominated colonies, populated by a landowner and merchant class of rigid sectarians (escaping from persecution) who nonetheless preside despotically over an underclass of transported beggars and pardoned offenders (escaping from prosecution), the alignment rings true.

As a charlatan, nimble talking is Bushrod's stock-in-trade, and religious cant is only one of his lingos. His most profitable enterprise is undoubtedly dealing in counterfeit money but he is first and foremost a word-coiner, an utterer of deceptive or content-free language. He lards his talk with hard words that are "mere gabble coated in a Latin wash" (138). Although his cant-uttering talents will figure in his subsequent career, we are left to imagine how he will position himself in the New World. Deceptions that succeed in the world's largest city (London's population of a half-million eclipsed every other capital), or the greatest fair in England, might have a short half-life in a colonial town of four or five thousand. Nevertheless, his options were many: from their founding, the English colonies abounded in op- portunities to speculate, manipulate and exploit.

European settlement of the New World was achieved by a combination of germs, gunpowder and cant. By the late 1690s, many of the best opportunities had been seized; all the same, since Bushrod is prone to reviving tried-and-true scams such as scrying, he might well achieve prosperity by imitating the cant-speaking con men who had preceded him. There were, first of all, numerous opportunities for transatlantic quackery. The initial enthusiasm for sassafras as a cure for syphilis had faded, but it had sold for as much as twenty shillings a pound at one time. There were other native American remedies that might be touted as panaceas and marketed to "gouty, pursy, poxy persons" (138) on both sides of the Atlantic.[7] The best days of what Jennings called the "missionary racket" in Puritan Boston were over, but it might still be possible to convince an "infinitely gullible and easily jaded" public (147) to advance charitable donations for the conversion or education of the Indians.[8] The Puritan and Quaker merchants who were increasingly engaged in the slave trade would welcome a nimble speaker of religious cant among them to justify themselves.[9] Slavery came to the New World for the sake of expediency, to meet a severe labor shortage. The ideology of racism was yet in development. Ultimately, it would serve two vital aims by justifying the subjugation of dark-skinned people while mitigating the risk that dispossessed poor whites, native Americans and enslaved Africans would make common cause. If we look back at some puzzling junctures in the text, it can be shown Bushrod might well have useful aptitude for elaborating the ideology of linking darkness to supposed inferiority.

He had successfully imposed himself upon the coiners and subsequently gained a share of their business by advising them to expand, rather than curtail, their operation through the recruitment of the blackguard boys as workers. As homeless children, either orphaned or abandoned, these boys belong to the most vulnerable and oppressed underclass of the City. That is not, however, how they are presented in the text:

> They were the very refuse of mankind, being recruited from the ashes of the glass-houses, or found lying upon the filth under stalls and bulks. They might be supposed to have been generated or concocted from the combustive heat of their filthy beds, they could give so little account of themselves, beyond an uncertain recollection of some wretched doghole swarming with starveling brats. Those that outlived their brutal abandonment were not to be pitied, for they themselves were without pity or tenderness: knowing full well that they were despised, shunned, and destinate to the rope. Paid in coin of their own making, they applied themselves to every vice obtainable. Their youth might preserve them from the gallows for the moment, and they cared not a whit for tomorrow. They seemed to Jack the very confirmation of Gryce's dogmas, for it was scarce possible to imagine a crew more certainly reprobate and doomed to eternal torment. They seemed to think so themselves, without caring, considering the afterlife a jest. (138)

A few of these boys are referenced once or twice by a name, but the name in each case paradoxically reinforces their presentation as a threatening, undifferentiated horde: "They were all of them named John or Tom or Jack, with one or two being George or Bill; what other name they owned was only some byword with which they christened one aother" (138). To illustrate, we are provided with four such names: Jack Brawny, Jack Shuffle-Up, George Have-Face, Foul Tom. Otherwise, they are insistently lumped together and referred to only as blackguard boys. Why black and why guard? The word, so employed, appears to have been a very recent usage, substituting for older substantives that emphasized poverty, such as ragamuffin, tatterdemalion or beggar boy. In early use, black guard was often merely descriptive of servants dressed in dark clothing. Inevitably, the cultural aversion to blackness infused the word with feelings of disgust and contempt. In Elizabethan usage, the kitchen scullions in a noble household were known as the blackguards, the label here branding the lowest class of servants doing the dirtiest work, scouring soot and grease from cooking vessels. It could also refer to the menial kitchen servants of an army mess kitchen and more broadly to camp followers and hangers-on. Hence it was applied insultingly to characterize someone as menial and contemptible, the lowest of the low. The military association may have contributed to a subsequent shift towards describing persons or behaviors that were perceived as threatening, not merely contemptible. Or, as the word continued in use, its blackness grew, suffusing it with suggestions of evil and danger, with that sense of threat further intensified by the implications latent in *guard*. By the later seventeenth century the word blackguard was applied to criminals or vagrants as a class, according to the OED. The application to vagrant children (apparently restricted to boys) first surfaces as thieves' cant at the end of the century but thereafter came into general use. We find it cropping up again in Defoe. Speaking of blackguard children, Defoe sees their presence in London not as a failure of morality and charity but as an abuse to be put down: "above ten thousand wicked, idle, pilfering vagrants are permitted to patrol about our city and suburbs. These are called the black-guard."[10]

Following a parallel impulse to label and ostracize them as Other, nineteenth-century social commentators opted to call these children *city* or *street Arabs*. Once labeled with darkness and difference, the blackguard boys, as the text here asserts, are excluded from compassion or humane concern: "Those that outlived their brutal abandonment were not to be pitied, for they themselves were without pity or tenderness" (138). In other contexts, a stance of neither seeking nor offering pity would qualify as heroic, or at least martial, proper and becoming in a soldier. Major Boyle expresses just such an outlook: "If a man falls into a turbulent sea, he must swim or drown. I do not pity men that meanly despair, or struggle feebly till they sink beneath the waves" (113). Although Jack professes some shock at his stated readiness to murder a sleeping woman if ordered to do so, Boyle is viewed not with revulsion but with a curiosity that borders upon admiration. Delia/Jack will readily pity a poor tenant family or a maimed soldier, but such empathy is denied to the blackguards. Not only are they to be shunned and despised (destitute to the rope, predestinate to hellfire) but they are dehumanized as vermin. Their early abandonment to the streets, leaving them with little or no knowledge of their origins, occasions the suggestion that they might have been spontaneously generated from the heat of their "filthy beds," effectively equating them to maggots and worms—or, at best, to the snakes, rats, mice and crocodiles said to be formed from the mud of the Nile.

This is blaming the victim with a vengeance! Given that the passage appears to transmit Jack's own contempt for blackguards, held in common with Gryce and Bushrod, there is an almost comically karmic turn, unintended by the text, when Jack is himself blackguarded by Bushrod, his skin "embrowned" and his hair blackened in order to pass as "an exiled princeling of Arabia" (148). When he fails to enact his assigned part with sufficient polish, he is recast as "the visionary seventh son from a famous family of cunning-men in the Vale of Eden" (148). Does his dark skin now represent the deep suntan of a Cumbrian rustic? Or does it rather mark him as commodified Other, as chattel? The darkness of his skin seems more significant than any pedigree invented to explain it. It is significant as well that Jack does not think of running away until after Bushrod has given him a strong soap to restore his skin and hair to a European complexion.

Jack wishes to escape before he is again "dipped in atramentum," an odd pay-attention-to-me word, lifted directly from Latin. Latin tags and phrases are uncommon features of this insistently in-the-moment text, generally confined to the self-conscious maneuvers of the narrator in positioning the narrative (which are performed in a dog Latin not clearly differentiated from that linked to Bushrod's con games). *Atramentum* is the Latin word for ink or, more broadly, a black pigment. Jack's inky complexion gestures ironically to his past existence, in a state of relative innocence and comfort, as "an ink-spotted girl." He is not merely embarrassed to be more thoroughly dipped in ink in order to pass as an implausible hazel-eyed Egyptian, he is profoundly ashamed and feels both morally compromised and degraded. If he thinks the business "wickeder than coining" (149), there is lurking in this judgment his unexpressed horror of his own dark-stained skin. The clumsy rhetorical flourish that concludes the chapter inadvertently foregrounds the equation of blackness with criminality that had permeated the account of the homeless boys who are recruited into the coining ring: "Jack supposed he would again be dabbed with atramentum and put to telling fortunes; but in truth Bushrod intended to dip him in far blacker deeds" (157). The blacker deeds are of course the cascading series of betrayals which Jack puts into motion and then attempts, unsuccessfully, to reverse.

What, finally, should we make of the text's refusal to satisfy reader expectations for a fair distribution of rewards and punishments? Is it in fact a refusal, or is it a failure? One might cite the false start as demonstrating a firm and conscious intention: "I must falsify names and features and other such particulars. For many of the persons in her story are yet alive; and, though deserving of the gallows, I would not have their deaths upon my conscience" (8). But the opening is a false start in more ways than one. The narrator projects a stridently masculine and conservative persona from the outset. The civil wars are termed "the Great Rebellion," the phrase employed by the arch-conservative Edward Hyde, Earl of Clarendon, in his history. Women are belittled as ignorant and unintellectual: females "by their very natures, must be ignorant of political philosophy" (57). The ideas of the republicans are repeatedly mocked and derided; their supporters among the London citizenry are characterized as a rabble of fanatics. The reader is thus trepanned into accepting a woman-hating, royalist and patrician perspective, only to have it abruptly withdrawn in the final paragraphs. "But you have done more than pretend to wear a pair of patched breeches in a garret," the aggrieved reader might protest, "To sustain your alias and conceal your motives, the helpless have been betrayed to persecution and the guilty allowed to escape." By impersonating a Grubstreet hack upon the model of Ned Ward or Tom Brown, both misogynistic Tories, the narrator loses control of the narrative. The mask has stuck fast; sympathy resides with the winners, with the "moneyed men," "the masters of London, the lords and gentry of England" (11). Double-agents often end by not knowing which side they truly serve. At this juncture I am *im*pelled to cite a CIA source on the nature of double-agents: "Experience suggests that some people who take to the double agent role—perhaps a majority of willing ones, in fact—have a number of traits in common with the con-man."[11] From the opening pages on, D. M. was on Bushrod's side without knowing it.

Notes

1 On the activities of seventeenth-century double-agents, see Alan Marshall, *Intelligence and Espionage in the Reign of Charles II, 1660–1685* (Cambridge: Cambridge University Press, 1994, 2002), 200–43. The text itself, of course, has multiple paranoid reminders concerning the threat posed by "spies, trepanners, and informers" (19).

2 On Lovell and his role in mediating pardons, see J. M. Beattie, *Policing and Punishment in London, 1660–1750* (Oxford: Oxford University Press, 2001, 2004), 350–52.

3 Defoe's *Reformation of Manners, A Satyr* (1702) devotes thirty-four lines to him, beginning: "L—l, the Pandor of [the] Judgment-Seat, Has neither Manners, Honesty or Wit." Tom Brown, *Letters from the Dead to the Living* (1701), portrays the devil as complaining that Sir Senseless Lovel has not been sending him condemned souls in the usual numbers.

4 In practice, the sentencing alternatives were often between branding the thumb (for a clergyable offence) and execution by hanging, see Beattie, 304–05. Branding was considered a less severe penalty than whipping. For prison overcrowding resulting from untransported felons and the government's increasing willingness to release prisoners for self-transportation, see Beattie, 294–95.

5 Christopher Hill, *A Tinker and a Poor Man: John Bunyan and His Church* (New York: Alfred A. Knopf, 1989), 304–05.

6 B. E., *A new dictionary of the terms ancient and modern of the canting crew* (London, 1699), ESTC R171889. Richard Head, *The Canting Academy* (London, 1673), ESTC R9723.

7 Martha Robinson, "New Worlds, New Medicines: Indian Remedies and English Medicine in Early America," *Early American Studies* 1, no. 3 (2005): 94–110. Charles Manning and Merrill Moore, "Sassafras and Syphilis," *New England Quarterly* 9, no. 3 (1936): 473–75.

8 Francis Jennings, *The Invasion of America: Indians, Colonialism, and the Cant of Conquest* (New York: W. W. Norton, 1975), 53, 228–53.

9 Peter H. Wood, *Strange New Land: Africans in Colonial America* (New York: Oxford University Press, 1996). See p. 21 for Boston's involvement in the slave trade. The first shipload of 150 enslaved Africans arrived in Philadelphia in 1684. Joseph E. Illick, *Colonial Pennsylvania: A History* (New York: Charles Scribner's Sons, 1976), 63. Gary B. Nash, "Slaves and Slaveowners in Colonial Philadelphia," *William and Mary Quarterly* 30 (1973): 223–56. On the application of doctrine to the justification of slave-owning or trading in Boston and Philadelphia, see Betty Wood, *The Origins of American Slavery* (New York: Hill & Wang, 1997), 94–117.

10 Andrew Moreton [Daniel Defoe], *Every-body's business, is no-body's business: or, private abuses, publick grievances: exemplified in the pride, insolence, and exorbitant wages of our women-servants, footmen, &c. With a proposal for amendment of the same* (London, 1725), 24.

11 F. M. Begoum [John P. Dimmer, Jr.], "Observations on the Double Agent," *Studies in Intelligence* 6, no. 1 (1962): 58.

The Anxiety of Influence Revisited: Rereading the Post-Miltonic Novel

Kayla Norton

> *The fact is that every writer creates his own precursors. His work modifies our conception of the past, as it will modify the future. —Borges*

THE BRAND-NAME novelists of the eighteenth century, Fielding, Richardson, Defoe, attained their preeminence in the twentieth-century canon in consequence of the time-honored, time-beleaguered convention of awarding authorial merit badges for most original or first-on-scene. Yet, if one segment of the culture privileges priority over subsequency, while another, larger segment selects newness over oldness, can originality be anything other than novelty, the prime desideratum of consumerism? There is an inherent irrelevance to temporalities, to befores and afters, which reveal themselves as the product-positioning tropes of marketing campaigns. Evaluative criteria that valorize originality (however defined) have been subject to revision, indeed to outright scorn in recent decades. Nonetheless, these three novelists have retained their status as official founders of the Anglo-American tradition of the modern novel, despite having been dislodged from their hold on the college syllabus. It is a status derived from assertions of originality made within the texts. The implied author in *Tom Jones* plants a flag of conquest and possession on what is claimed to be a new, previously undiscovered genre: "For as I am, in reality, the Founder of a new Province of Writing, so I am at liberty to make what Laws I please therein" (77; Bk. II, ch. i).[1] Yet what if there was an indigenous occupier all along? If one inserts *Marius & Delia* as a foundational text of the late seventeenth century, a substantial shift occurs: the tradition gets rudely jostled by a fresh pair of sharp elbows. The purported originators of the new genre are now, in Bloomian terms, the epigones, strenuously attempting to suppress the evidence of their debt to their female progenitor. In post-Freudian theory she becomes the devouring mother who threatens to engulf her literary offspring, unless they suppress her power by attaching themselves to a quixotic paternal line, revising the family history to diminish or exclude her.

In what follows I am obliged to refer to authors and their works, applying humanistic labels of attribution to the texts under consideration; but I trust my reader will allow that I do not do so naively, from a failure to theorize the instability of texts and the vexed (ultimately irrelevant) issues concerning the conditions of their production. I, Kayla Norton, am an embodied consciousness situated exterior to the sequence of signs that I am now engaged in keyboarding (my diachronic persistence is a peripheral issue of identity we may set aside)—producing a text that extends the texts under discussion. However, Deborah Milton, Daniel Defoe (whose name is itself a fiction), Samuel Richardson and Henry Fielding need not be given real status as authors or determiners of texts. Rather, these proper names serve as categories of description, as pragmatic boundaries (or figural skins) separating one set of texts from another and, as applied here, usefully personifying intertextual dynamics.

In *Anxiety of Influence* Bloom applied a palette of Freudian, Nietzchean and mythological motifs to depict the psychic distress of post–[John]Miltonic poets in attempting to escape the withering shadow of their precursor.[2] In order to individuate himself creatively and to suppress a compulsion to repeat the parent poet, each new poet must make a perverse or reductive misprision of his precursor's poem—*himself* and *his* poem because Bloom conceives of the relationship in Oedipal terms. In *Madwoman in the Attic* Gilbert and Gubar retooled (or de-tooled) Bloom's fundamental insight in order to apply it to characterizing the anxiety of authorship experienced by women confronting an almost exclusively male tradition. Gilbert and Gubar's ahistorical and essentialist reading of the purported mental states of women authors subsequently came under attack; nevertheless, a psychoanalytic approach continues to have its uses when applied to demystifying relations between texts as well as with the culture that produced them. For their theory of influence, as for Bloom's, John Milton is the overbearing and demeaning parent who stifles the creativity and independence of his literary sons and daughters.

The eighteenth-century novelists had a very different relationship to their parental precursor, though no less problematic and psychologically fraught. The other Milton is *the* Other in Lacanian terms, the Mother not merely of a single influential text but of a new genre. In responding to *Marius & Delia,* Defoe, Richardson and Fielding had to confront not only their anxiety as authors but their anxiety as males, as the literary sons of a too-powerful mother who grounded the new genre as a vehicle for an irony-laden exposure of gender politics. To write, to gain success in the new mode, they had to devise strategies to *take back* the novel. They succeeded, perhaps beyond their expectations, to such an extent as to obscure their predecessor from the view of later generations. And yet, over the subsequent two centuries of male *and* female novel-writing, no perceptive reader can fail to detect the palimpsistic trace of a female presence in the very constituents of the genre, which is absent in male-devised forms such as epic and tragedy. Ian Watt, for one, intuited the origins of the novel even as he accepted Defoe, Richardson and Fielding as its progenitors. "The feminine sensibility," he wrote, "was in some ways better equipped to reveal the intricacies of personal relationships and was therefore at a real advantage in the realm of the novel."[3] More recently, Michael McKeon has remarked upon the gap, "the apparent discontinuity" in the development of prose fiction, the odd absence of significant texts between Deloney and Defoe, between the sixteenth- and the eighteenth-century developments in genre expansion.[4] The insertion of Deborah

Milton as a convention-shattering, subsequently marginalized and erased experimenter in prose fiction not only fills that gap but fully and satisfyingly accounts for it. In explaining some curious defensive maneuvers in the novels of Fielding & Company, the principle of parsimony requires that we posit a text with what Watt quaintly termed "the feminine sensibility" that arrived prior to the masculinist texts and their assertion of originality. As I hope to show, postulating the priority of Deborah Milton's novel as a hidden presence, a concealed intertext, has great explanatory power.

Among the belated novelists who succeed Deborah Milton, Defoe's relationship to his precursor is the least troubled. He perceived the commercial possibilities of the new genre without troubling himself overmuch with narrative mode or structure. His journalistic experience helped to ground and orient him, albeit at the cost of fomenting some confusion in his truth claims. He seems to have missed the irony of Milton's this-is-a-true-story frame, which he imitated enthusiastically and uncritically. In any case, the deceptive positioning of the narrator in *Marius & Delia* is a strategy that cannot be imitated or even repeated. We find therefore her earliest successors, Defoe and Richardson, choosing an irony-free first-person narrative. Or, to give Defoe more credit for understanding the genre's potential, the official response to "The Shortest Way with the Dissenters" may have led him to reject further experiments with irony. It cannot be pleasant to stand in the pillory, even if pelted with roses.

Defoe's initial response to his precursor came as a straightforward, reactionary swerve to the masculinist right. His first and most successful work of fiction excludes the female altogether. We learn every facet of Robinson Crusoe's inventive adaptations and his can-do self-talk techniques, which anticipate some twentieth-century psychiatric interventions. But for all that the speaking voice of the narrative tells us regarding his psychological state, what he does not acknowledge is most revealing. There is not one word of sexual longing. In his Adamic isolation, Crusoe desires many things (better cooking pots, a gross of tobacco-pipes, turnip seeds and so forth) but he does not desire an Eve. Moglen remarks that, "The realistic narrative of the possessive male individual, as Defoe constructs it, is a narrative that has no place for women."[5] But this exclusion is certainly a strange one: given a woman's utility as a domestic possession, she is at least as valuable as a cooking pot. The text denies, by its silence, a need that most men and women would find far more imperative than turnip seeds and tobacco. Defoe does not see how to reintroduce a topic that was given unacceptable inflections in the predecessor text. In *Marius & Delia* the patriarchal rationale for female chastity becomes hopelessly subverted when the unchaste heroine provides her husband with a legitimate heir (perhaps more than one, depending on the nature of the "little services" that Robin Cloudsley performs for his aunt). Defoe's defensive maneuver is to banish sex from Crusoe's island, inadvertently establishing the text as a perennial children's classic. In his later novels featuring female protagonists, Defoe lays it on with a trowel. Sexual intercourse itself is strongly gendered in these texts, positioned as a marketable commodity belonging to women. The texts are careful to ensure that the titular heroine of an anonymous first-person narration is not mistaken for an author. Neither Moll Flanders nor Roxanna is said to produce her own narrative, not without substantial editorial rewriting to correct deficiencies and indecencies. In a strikingly gendered contrast, the prefaces to *Robinson Crusoe* and *Colonel Jack* both imply the narratives have received little or no editorial retouching and assert their as-is literary and moral quality, even though the latter is fundamentally a reworking of *Moll Flanders* featuring a male protagonist.

In *Moll Flanders* and *Roxanna*, Defoe tries a have-one's-cake-and-repent-it-too maneuver. He presents readers with a heroine who violates social/sexual norms at the same time as he nests her adventures within a patriarchal value system. In *Moll Flanders*, the elder and younger brothers are an inverted substitution for the nephew and uncle of Milton's narrative. Defoe's two male figures preserve the sanctity of primogeniture, in that the elder is successful in his seduction and escapes without consequences; Moll's subsequent marriage to the younger brother, who is without an inheritance, does not benefit Defoe's impure heroine. *Roxanna* goes yet farther down the road of rejecting the political and moral values of *Marius & Delia*. In it greed and fiscal "prudence" are considered morally acceptable but sex outside wedlock is not. The book exemplifies Defoe's ambivalent and deeply conflicted attempt to have it both ways: to exploit the shock value of a transgressive heroine while still (stridently) justifying the ways of Providence to men. The abrupt ending communicates his dilemma and his failure. He cannot master the challenge of controlling his own and his reader's response to his heroine, wherein she must be both sympathetic and condemned.

Richardson could not (not even in his third and final attempt) escape the female embodiment of the novel genre. He, like Defoe before him, adapted by pretending to be the medium of transmission for a female author, to whom he stands merely as editor and publisher. He is quite consciously cross-dressing in his fiction, in weak imitation of the double transvestism of the protagonist and narrator of *Marius & Delia*. The structure of *Pamela*, the maidservant who becomes mistress, presents us with an author who is effectively cutting-and-pasting textual segments of his precursor. As Bloom writes, "Conceptually the central problem for the latecomer necessarily is *repetition*, for repetition dialectically raised to re-creation is the ephebe's road of excess, leading away from the horror of finding himself to be only a copy or a replica" (80). When Mr. B. repeatedly seizes Pamela's letters and diaries, we have Richardson's unconscious rendering (in effect, a confession) of his own theft and rape of Milton's writing. He cannot separate the act of literary creation from its female engendering. Thus, Pamela's concealed writings, stitched into her undercoat about her hips, become an unconscious simulation of pregnancy, merging authorship with motherhood. Even his epistolary write-to-the-moment technique fails to differentiate him from the precursor, since it had been introduced to good effect by Milton as the epilogue of *Marius & Delia*.

If Richardson could not stifle the female voice of the new genre, he could at least position a cryptic male protagonist who triumphs sexually over the female and thereby silences her. Pamela vows to give up her writing after her marriage and she meekly allows Mr. B. to lesson her on marital rules and regulations. It is as if Richardson needed to proclaim as a self-protective axiom that a woman who has been penetrated should not pick up a pen, not with any aim higher than quotidian business. Although the drugged and raped Clarissa has many letters to write before she dies, she can no longer wield her pen with confidence or coherency: "A distracted mind dictates to my trembling pen."[6] The myth of Philomela must be enforced if the genre is to escape its origins and become a vehicle for the moral values of a male-dominated society.

Richardson's purpose is to defend conventional morality, although he has trouble knowing what exactly it is, as if *Marius & Delia* unsettled his assumptions, or so outraged his masculine sensibilities that he could focus only on the physical. His muddled morality in evident in *Pamela*, where his heroine's motives are impure and unexamined, her behavior manipulative, but her hymen remains properly intact until marriage. Female chastity constitutes an obsessional theme of the mid-century novel, which cannot be ascribed simply to a me-too imitation of *Pamela* and *Clarissa*. It is hard to locate this theme either in contemporary culture or in precursor genres of fiction. It is present in romance but to a decidedly lesser degree. In the Hellenistic novel, the heroine certainly, and often the hero as well, must struggle to preserve chastity during their separation and wanderings, but fidelity that triumphs over various trials (not restricted to seduction or assault) constitutes the true measure of the heroic individual. Viewed as a reaction formation to *Marius & Delia*, however, this obsession can at last be understood. There is much in this foundational text on which the eighteenth-century novelists foundered in their attempts to evade or overcome their precursor. It seems to have provoked a reactionary fear of women in breeches wielding pens. As Watt observed, "the conception of sex we find in Richardson embodies a more complete and comprehensive separation between the male and female roles than had previously existed" (162).

Both Richardson and Defoe have received largely unmerited praise for psychological insight in their deep-dive explorations of character via first-person narration. I would argue instead that the moral obtuseness and materialistic hypocrisy of their protagonists are best understood as debased repetitions of the duplicity of the narratorial voice in *Marius & Delia*. Both writers perform what Bloom terms a *tessera*, a pretended completion of the truncated work of the precursor. Where *Marius & Delia* is tersely ironic, Richardson and Defoe spill ink over dozens of pages, as though a blanketing accumulation of language will in itself conceal and obscure their borrowings. It is a strategy of talking over, thereby covering up and undoing, the silences of the precursor, which commonly occur at disturbing junctures of the text. The descriptive excess of the later novelists is accompanied by abrupt reversals and oppositions: at every moral crossroad they set their protagonists on an opposing pathway. Whatever else they may be, however morally dubious or emotionally excessive their words and actions, Richardson's titular heroines must be distinguished absolutely from the predecessor's Delia. In her rape by a dissolute rake, to which she submits in a state of numbed surprise, Delia is the un-Clarissa. She expresses little perception that something psychologically shattering or even socially transforming has occurred to her, except, having confused rape with wedlock, she is sad to think she must leave her father, "even to live with a rich husband in the Town" (81). Her confusion regarding rape and wedlock results from her ironically portrayed misunderstanding of social norms; the confusion of wedlock and rape in Richardson's novels is a projection of the author's own guiltily ambivalent drives and motivation. When Delia's wealthy employer proposes marriage to her, she is the un-Pamela: we learn nothing at all of her emotions, only that she was not "foolishly coy in accepting" (175). In Richardson's revisionary rendering, the grateful Pamela casts herself down at Mr. B.'s feet so regularly that her clothes must have suffered for it.

Elaborating, concretizing and cataloging are the defensive maneuvers of both Defoe and Richardson in confronting their originator, maneuvers which are often pushed to a self-revealing excess. Richardson would not have compulsively listed the articles of clothing in Pamela's three bundles—an absurdity parodied by Fielding in *Shamela*—if the narrator of Milton's novel had not refused to provide just such a list of the clothing and accessories inherited by Delia. Here Bloom's theory of intertextuality and influence is again pertinent: "In the *tessera*, the later poet provides what his imagination tells him would complete the otherwise 'truncated' precursor poem and poet, a 'completion' that is as much misprision as a revisionary swerve is" (66).

Fielding had the crucial advantage, when he came to write in the new genre of prose fiction, of coming after Richardson. He could thereby pretend to mistake a fellow ephebe for the originator of the new form, countering him with a burlesque parody in *Shamela*. In *Joseph Andrews*, he continues his attack on Richardson while acknowledging a debt to Scarron's *Roman Comique*. However, there is nothing he derives from Scarron's example that he might not have encountered also in Milton. More significantly, Fielding attempts, as Defoe and Richardson did not, to deflect the gendering of the new genre as a gynocentric form.

The first-person narrations of Defoe and Richardson drew the texts into a sticky web of unironic double-voiced ambiguity. In contrast, Fielding, in his later novels, makes a defensive turn to a godlike narratorial presence that pronounces aphoristic platitudes and declares rules for the genre from a lofty prospect that combines features of Parnassus and Sinai. This voice of the purported author is suspiciously self-reflexive and metadiscursive, at the same time, and with an air of contradiction, as it claims to be purely mimetic, an imitation of capital *N* Nature. All texts are readings of other texts—but Fielding has hastily concealed a purloined text beneath mocking allusions to Richardson.

The preface of *Joseph Andrews* proposes to masculinize the new genre as "a Comic Epic-Poem in Prose." To elite readers schooled in the classics (the readers to whom Fielding addresses his narrative), such a hybrid label would be as ridiculous as the "tragical-comical-historical-pastoral" catchall of Polonius. Presumably Fielding would not have committed such a unforced solecism, if not for a psychically urgent require- ment that the new genre be repositioned in a male-dominated tradition. In *Joseph Andrews* Fielding displays a cock-a-doodle-doo confidence that he has outdone and outgone Richardson in his mastery of the new genre; his struggle to erase and undo Deborah Milton was far more fraught. In Bloom's system, Fielding is responding to Milton by a *kenosis*: he undoes the predecessor's pattern by a deliberate, willed loss in continuity.[7] Milton, matriarch of the genre, was his covering cherub, blocking Fielding from empathy with the women in his fictional world. In representing the female he becomes a failed Pygmalion, endowing his creations with virtue and beauty but denying them life.

Having put the chaste Joseph Andrew behind him, Fielding in his next two novels proves to be an obsessional advocate for, and rigorous enforcer of, the double standard in sexual behavior. This gendering of moral principle makes its first ap- pearance in the history of Mr. Wilson in Book III, chapter iii, of *Joseph Andrews*. In *Tom Jones* the eponymous representative of virtue, Allworthy, refers to the "Crime" committed by Jenny Jones as "the Violation of your Chastity" (51; Bk. I, ch. vii). If his phrase is intended only to stigmatize the surrender of female virginity outside of wedlock, it is a peculiarly old-fashioned usage, the implication of force being usually present. He tellingly compares the loss of a woman's virginity to leprosy, regardless, apparently, of whether the woman consented to intercourse or not. The comparison reveals an unconscious fear that female unchastity would be epidemic if not shamed and ostracized. Also shamed and blamed is any display of female intelligence, which, far from making the woman equal to a man, reduces her to the level of a beast. In a woman, says Allworthy, learning is "the Affectations of an Ape" (882; Bk. XVII, ch. iii)—an opinion shared by Dr. Harrison, his all-knowing counterpart in *Amelia*. (Can anyone wonder that Deborah Milton Clarke, in her old age, thought it prudent to pretend incomprehension when she recited Ovid and Euripides?) In the unlikely scenario that a woman may have a "superior understanding" to her husband, both novels suggest a remedy in her playing dumb and submitting to her less able spouse's authority (*Tom Jones* 595; Bk. XI, ch. vii; *Amelia* 408; Bk. X, ch. i).[8] The compulsion within Fielding's texts to revisit this topic, to force a context for it, is remarkable indeed.

In *Amelia*, compared to *Tom Jones*, there is an intensified effort to exclude women both as readers (by a heavier use of Greek and Latin quotation) and as active agents within the fiction. In *Amelia*, as in *Pamela* and *Clarissa*, the primary source of plot tension is female chastity (who's got it, who's lost it, whose is repeatedly threatened). In this last novel, Fielding's gender/genre anxieties are on full display. As the victim of her husband's serial selfishness, Amelia reprises the role of Patient Griselda, far exceeding Sophia and Pamela in submissiveness. She responds to crises with torrential crying fits (sometimes progressing to psychosomatic illness due to "her weak spirits") and submissive, self-effacing declaratory speeches. In case the reader fails to register her perfection, she is provided with two female foils, Miss Matthews (the bad girl) and Mrs. Atkinson (the smart girl), neither of whom is meek of spirit. The plot is provided with multiple Lovelaces, all of them in hot pursuit of Amelia, who evades Clarissa's fate only by virtue of the intervention of others. Reduced to utter passivity, she lacks even the one resource available to Richardson's heroines. She has no pen. In a howler of a parapraxis, one that was pilloried by Fielding's contemporaries, he even forgot to give his heroine a nose.[8] From here we arrive, by a natural progression, at that counter-sublime masterpiece of male anxiety, *Tristram Shandy*.

Marius & Delia constitutes the invisible black hole tugging at the narratives of the eighteenth-century novelists. Milton's male successors utilized the power of the patriarchy to erase their female progenitor, to push her into the literary unconscious, from which she would not emerge until our own times. Bloom writes, "Freud's vision of repression emphasizes that forgetting is anything but a liberating process. Every forgotten precursor becomes a giant of the imagination" (107). There was always at the core of the genre an inescapably strong bias to the female viewpoint, to female preoccupation with relationships, discourse and psychological insight. If not for the fortuitous recovery of *Marius & Delia*, the belated male novelists would have achieved what Bloom terms "the complex imposture of the positive apophrades," whereby the writer is able to reverse the relationship of indebtedness, reverse time itself, and carry off the illusion of "being *imitated by their ancestors*" (147, 141).

Finally, we may also trace a link, of perhaps unconscious inheritance, with Fanny Burney and Jane Austen. Their representations of the female begin where *Marius & Delia* concludes, fully adapted to a corseted and controlled life, where one is never a free agent, where even an arch or careless word may bring on socially destructive consequences. As George Eliot's Dorothea remarked, Deborah Milton was "a very naughty girl." Her female successors of the long eighteenth century purged themselves of naughtiness.

Notes

1 Henry Fielding, *The History of Tom Jones*, ed. Fredson Bowers ([Middleton, CT]: Wesleyan University Press, [1982]).

2 Harold Bloom, *The Anxiety of Influence: A Theory of Poetry* (New York: Oxford University Press, 1973).

3 Ian Watt, *The Rise of the Novel* (Berkley: University of California Press, 1974), 298.

4 "Literary scholars have long been troubled by the apparent discontinuity in prose fiction between Deloney and Greene and Defoe—or at least between the late-Elizabethans and mid-Restoration authors like Behn and Kirkman. If the English novel began to rise toward the end of the sixteenth century, why was this literary revolution abruptly curtailed after 1600 and postponed for the better part of a century?" (Michael McKeon, *The Origins of the English Novel, 1600–1740* [Baltimore, MD: Johns Hopkins University Press, 1987, 2002], 269.)

5 Helene Moglen, *The Trauma of Gender: A Feminist Theory of the English Novel* (Berkeley: University of California Press, 2001), 34–35.

6 Letter 295, dated Wednesday night, June 28. Samuel Richardson, *Clarissa* (London: The Folio Society, 1991), 2:974.

7 Bloom, 90: "in *kenosis*, ... he undoes the precursor's pattern by a deliberate, willed loss in continuity. His stance *appears* to be that of his precursor ... but the meaning of the stance is undone; the stance is *emptied* of its priority."

8 Henry Fielding, *Amelia,* ed. Martin Battestin (Middleton, CT: Wesleyan University Press, 1983).

9 We are told that "her lovely Nose was beat all to pieces" in an accident (66, Bk. II, ch. i). Fielding apparently intended to inform his readers that a skillful surgeon restored it to its former loveliness but neglected to do so.

Appendix 1 Notes on the Text

The copy-text for this edition was a legible photocopy of the transcription published by Angus Burdock (Leeds, UK: Scandalon Press, 1975), which had been kindly supplied to me by Angela Pruitt in the late 1980s. I initially attempted to obtain a physical copy of that edition but was unable to do so. Pruitt's copy had disappeared from view and no colleague I contacted possessed a text superior to my photocopy. Utilizing a proofread scan prepared by the publisher, I began work upon the text in March of 2017, based upon the publisher's assurance that a settlement to the legal challenge was pending (see Introduction, xxxiv–xxxvi).

Although my familiarity with the text goes back thirty years and uncounted re-readings (so many that, like Delia, I can repeat passages by heart), I was not fully cognizant of the issues presented by the problematic transmission of this text until I undertook my task. I became aware of numerous inconsistencies in accidentals, which were clearly the product of Burdock's hasty work in transcribing the original. In particular, spelling, punctuation and capitalization vacillated between seventeenth or eighteenth century and contemporary UK standards. Many of these inconsistencies were impossible to resolve without speculative emendation. However much I would have wished to present Deborah Milton's book as it came from her anonymous printer, it was not possible to do so.

Accordingly, I determined early on that I should prepare a text that has been silently modernized in capitalization and spelling. A modernized text has the merit of increased accessibility for both undergraduates and the literate public. But the primary rationale is that Burdock's hasty transcription displayed too many orthographical and typographical inconsistencies for an editor to feel confident in following it. I have largely retained the punctuation of the original, but this too has been modified or occasionally modernized where Burdock's transcription seemed doubtful. I have chosen not to introduce the use of quotation marks, since the author has set out direct speech with a fair degree of consistency according to the conventions of the times; thus there are few passages where the reader has more than momentary uncertainty as to speaker or voice. Where an apostrophe appears in past participles (e.g., walk'd for walked, to mark an -ed that was not pronounced), I have spelled out the word in accordance with current usage. I also elected, in the interest of clarity, to insert missing apostrophes to indicate possessives; the copy-text followed seventeenth-century usage in omitting the use of an apostrophe with the plural as well as following a sibilant, as in "Marius house." The occasional periphrastic, in the form "Marius his house," I have left unaltered.

Subsequent to the negotiated settlement of the legal challenge to publication in June of 2017, I was provided with the copy of the 1975 edition that had served as legal exhibit. This is, or was, a royal crown octavo, bound in red cloth, set in 11-point modern-face roman, comprising 240 pages: front matter of five unnumbered pages [half-title, blank verso, title, copyright; table of contents]; a foreword numbered vi–xxxii; and text pages numbered 1–202, each chapter opening on a recto, with three blank leaves following the text. The text block was identical to that of the photocopy in every regard. In accordance with the terms of the settlement agreement (see p. xlvi, note 103), both the photocopy and the original hardcover volume have since been destroyed.

Mr. Burdock's testimony under oath in his January 9, 2017, deposition was not supplied to me at that time, although it was clearly pertinent to the preparation of the new edition. It came to me five months later as an enclosure (possibly inadvertent) in a mailing from the offices of the publisher's attorney, the purpose of which was to present me with the document I was required to sign, acknowledging the negotiated redistribution of royalties by which Mr. Burdock would receive a half-share. I endorsed the revised agreement with a shaky signature that called to mind Deborah Milton's own, upon receiving her scanted share of her father's estate.

When I read the enclosed deposition (see Appendix 2), I had still greater cause for agitation. In it, Mr. Burdock's account of his transcription differed very substantially from that provided in his 1975 foreword, upon which I had based my editorial decisions. The latter had given a tediously self-involved account of the discovery of the text and of his diligence in performing his transcription. A fair bit of emphasis was put upon the haste and secrecy of his procedure, which took a childishly cloak-and-dagger tone. All the same, nothing in this preface implied that the transcription was *not* reasonably accurate and reliable as a first-pass effort, given that it was undertaken by a specialist in textual scholarship. Fifty years later, in his sworn testimony, intended to support his intellectual property claim, Burdock admitted to the most egregious sloppiness, asserting that the text was heavily contaminated throughout by untold numbers of errors.

I had devoted many hours, many years, in fact, to understanding—attempting to understand, across the centuries—Deborah Milton Clarke's mind, her thoughts and intentions in creating her fiction. It is hopeless even to guess the thoughts of the person seated across the table, but an editor must attempt such assessments in producing a text: every decision to add or delete a comma, or to correct even patent errors, must be founded upon the editor's imaginative identification with the author in producing and/or revising her text. Now I must also consider the intentions and the

mental state of her transcriber. Should I trust the 1975 foreword with its hyperbolic claims of concentrated effort—or the 2017 avowal of cringe-worthy incompetence? Was the latter to be understood as a late-life confession, or merely a desperate ploy to retain a financial stake in the text? I will not detail my considerations at length, given that Mr. Burdock is a person of litigious impulses.

I had considered my editorial work on the text to be largely complete. I had modernized the text according to my first intentions (which also suited the publisher's market-oriented preference). I had detected and emended a significant number of transcriptional errors of the *lectio difficilior* sort, mostly careless substitutions of a modern word for the historically appropriate one. These (roughly 250 in total) had been scrupulously logged with the intention of providing a textual apparatus once the text was in page proof. Now it was necessary to re-examine the whole for grossly corrupted readings that might span whole sentences. (Mr. Burdock, as the deposition shows, contends that the work is a "unique, inevitably faulty transcription" contaminated with "numerous errors"; when asked, twice, he did not deny the possibility that he might have deliberately introduced errors.)

I had noted words and phrasings that that seemed surprisingly archaic for the 1690s, in contrast to others for which there was no record in the OED of their use before, say, 1750. Of course, Deborah might naturally tend, at times, to echo the cadences of her father's old-fashioned, Latinate prose style, even as, at other points in the text, she faithfully reproduced elements of everyday speech not previously recorded in writing. But now I was obliged to re-interrogate every line of text: Has a word been omitted? Has a word been added? Have phrases been transposed or even substituted? These unresolvable questions occasioned many sleepless nights and distressful days of proposing, then deleting, revisionary readings.

I was aware that I must consider my obligations to the contributors, who had been provided with a PDF of what I had believed to be the all-but-final text. It was a considerable relief to find that they perceived no insuperable problem to publishing the text, and certainly no barrier to writing their planned contributions to the volume. Naomi Hoek helpfully let me know which passages she wished to be stetted, and I have done my best to oblige her, though some of her selected readings were marked by a melodramatic tone which I found to be suspiciously redolent of Burdock's foreword. Gavin Mettrick remarked upon the artificiality of set texts, in contrast to the indeterminacy of speech and of media such as Wikipedia, which oscillates, like a living organism, through different states over the course of a few days or even hours. Janet Spurway drew a comparison to the texts known synecdochically as "Shakespeare," which are accretions of borrowings from source materials, adaptations for specific performances, revisions by multiple hands, transcriber's and compositor's errors along with in-press corrections, and which likely bear only a generalized resemblance to the manuscripts produced by an individual named Shakespeare. Kayla Norton similarly expressed her view that all texts have multiple authorships, that an individual human hand might have formed the words in time, but originated nothing. Texts achieve their meanings in the minds of readers, for whom the identity and intentions of the author-function are irrelevant.

None of these views were entirely new to me, of course, but it was one problem out of the way to know that my colleagues were comfortable with their shares of the project. My own editorial dilemma persisted: I was unwilling to propagate a text laden with hidden Burdockisms. Certainly it ought to be possible to distinguish the words, the ideas, of a brilliant

seventeenth-century Englishwoman, exposed from childhood to the conversation of leading intellectuals, from those of an underachieving twentieth-century male with a slippery sense of ethics and a thoroughly undistinguished résumé.

I stared at my computer monitor so long and so fixedly that the words seemed to dance on the screen, like the electrons that they are in truth. Shadowing the words I saw on the screen were other words, absent, yet leaving a trace—the words that might have been, the rejected, the erased. They come to me from the limbo of lost intentions and unknowable minds. Which were Deborah's? Which were imposters? Which words did Deborah choose? Which would she choose if she could choose again? There is nothing from her hand, no spoken words recorded by reliable witnesses (see Introduction, ix–xxiii), to guide me. There is only her signature, reproduced below. I examine it again—or rather, I examine an enlarged (400%) PDF image of a facsimile (presumably lithographic) appearing in a scanned nineteenth-century text preserved online [archive.org/details/ramblingsinelucioosothrich], *Ramblings in the Elucidation of the Autograph of Milton,* by Samuel Leigh Sotheby.

The initial capitals are curious in that they descend below the imaginary baseline rather than above it. Neither is as tall as the ascenders of *b, h* and *k.* The *C* is shaped like a left parenthesis, inclosing *l-a-r*—perhaps enclosing the whole surname, circumscribing it as doubtful. Only now do I see that the malformed *k-e* of *Clarke* are in reality the *l-t* of *Milton.* The pen returns to print the angled strokes of the *k* and a terminal *e* on top of them, laying down a broad dark trace of ink without obliterating the ghostly presence of the Miltonic *l-t.* The *D* floats, defying the invisible rules that confine the lower-case letters to the x-height; it is ornamented with two loops, the only flourishes given to her workaday signature. She discovers, belatedly, that the pen provided to her is poorly cut; as she turns it to form the upstrokes of her Greek *e* and the *l,* a notched or uneven edge interrupts the flow of ink. It must have contributed to her aggravation and revelatory distraction.

There is a rich text to be read in these characters. The writer writes rapidly; she returns to revise; she must revise, always, from the pressure of her double self, the Miltonic one shrouded by *Clarke,* by her containment in a conventional, possibly stifling marriage. And the irony that her marriage should rechristen her a mere clerk, a scribe, an instrument of writing under the domination of another, first a father, then a husband, something she experiences, if only subliminally, at this moment, revealed in the signature shaped under duress.

The letters of the transmitted text of *Marius & Delia* are displayed on my monitor in Linux Libertine, lending a spurious crispness and clarity that is in fact a levelling and mechanized degradation of sense. Supposing it a faithful transcription, would she still recognize it as *her* text, so transmuted and dematerialized? Or would it seem to her, rather, a forgery or imposture, the uniform glyphs on the glowing screen being nothing like those that she shaped with her hand on the dingy, speckled paper available to her.

Still studying her signature, I attempt to extrapolate from eleven letter forms (*a, b, C, D, e* [medial and terminal], *h, k, l, o, r*), supplemented by a facsimile manuscript page of her father's *De Doctrina Christiana* (likewise reproduced in Sotheby's *Ramblings,* which resembles, to my untrained eye, her autograph), how her text appeared as she wrote it. I take up a ballpoint pen—then recall that I have a steel nib fountain pen, inauthentic, certainly, but one minute degree closer to the quill held in her hand. With that pen I attempt a hand resembling hers, improving with repetition. *Marius Bye is a man of vinegar wit and frustrate ambition: a Roundhead of our Latter Days, a belated but convinced Republican.*

And yet, even if I could impersonate her hand, correctly fabricating her *M,* her *B,* how she strokes the *f* that occurs three times—how can I know where the pen, held lightly, raced forward, where, hesitating, it left a thicker trace, where it returned and revised? Perhaps, intent upon the substantive sense, and of subsequent sentences pressing urgently in her thought, she wrote *was a man*—slipping unconsciously into the once-upon-a-time of the conventional storyteller—then returned, moments or days later, to write *is* above a now-crossed *was.* I cannot know. I could not know, even with the printed book, circa 1695, put before me. The procrustean rigor of the justified page crushes the unconforming phrase, erases the expressivity of the living hand.

Timorous printers, says the text (scrying its own fate), expunge passages, knavish printers rewrite them. Nor does any compositor set the text, letter by letter, from the author's fair copy (itself the dilute product of chilly second thoughts and late-come prudence) without a confounding haze of error and whim. The text of Deborah, the invention of her hand and mind, is betrayed and sullied at its first setting out in the world. That text is unrecoverable. If the text, as I must transmit it, cannot be truly hers, there is one thing in my power as editor to achieve. I can ensure that it is *not* the text of Angus Burdock. It is an undertaking that requires countless hours of focused, unremunerated effort. I regret being now unable to provide a list of textual emendations, as it would run to a prohibitively large number of pages, effectively requiring a second volume.

Appendix 2 Oral Deposition of Angus Burdock

IN THE UNITED STATES DISTRICT COURT FOR THE EASTERN DIVISION OF
PENNSYLVANIA, CIVIL TRIAL DIVISION

Angus Burdock, Ph.D.
Plaintiff
v.
Carol Hart, Editor & Publisher, SpringStreet Books
Margo Quigley, Ph.D.
Defendants

Monday, January 9, 2017
Oral deposition of ANGUS BURDOCK, taken pursuant to notice, was held at the law
offices of Chatterton & Rowley, 1799 Youngsford Road, Gladwyne, Pennsylvania,
commencing at 10:05 a.m., on the above date, before CHERIE SUPER, a Professional
Court Reporter and Notary Public in the Commonwealth of Pennsylvania.

APPEARANCES:

RICHARD CHAVEL, ESQUIRE
MACPHERSON & ASSOCIATES, P. C.
1322 Laurel Road
Suite 44C
Lindenwold, NJ 08021
Counsel for Plaintiff

WILLIAM CLACK, ESQUIRE
CHATTERTON & ROWLEY, L. L. P.
1799 Youngsford Road
Gladwyne, PA 19035
Counsel for Defendants

ALSO PRESENT:
Carol Hart

EXHIBITS:

EXHIBIT NO.	DESCRIPTION	PAGE FIRST REFERENCED
Burdock-1	*Marius and Delia*, 1975 edition	3 [279]
Burdock-2	*Marius and Delia*, print-on-demand edition	3 [280]
Burdock-3	Burdock résumé	7 [283]

PROCEEDINGS

(It is hereby stipulated and agreed by and between counsel for the respective parties that sealing, filing and certification are waived; and that all objections, except as to the form of questions, be reserved until the time of trial.)

ANGUS BURDOCK, after having been duly sworn, was examined by Counsel for the Defendants and testified as follows:

BY MR. CLACK:

Q. Mr. Burdock, we are here today to examine the facts regarding your claim to the ownership of intellectual property rights in the work of fiction entitled *Marius and Delia*. Under U.S. law, during a deposition, I am permitted to ask you any and all questions that I judge to be relevant to the case. Your counsel may object to a question on a variety of grounds. For example, he might want to state an objection because the question is vague or because it's really two questions in one. I might take the hint and decide to rephrase or withdraw the question, but if I don't, the question will still need to be answered by you. Is that clear thus far?

A. Yes.

Q. Because the deposition will be recorded and transcribed, we need to follow a few ground rules in order to have a clear record of your testimony. When you're asked a question, remember to respond in words, yes or no, or say I don't know if you don't know the answer. Also, even if you see where I'm heading with my question, wait until I'm finished speaking before you begin your answer. That way your counsel will have an opportunity to put his objection on record if he doesn't happen to like the question for some reason. Is all that clear to you?

A. Yes.

Q. Do you have any questions?

A. No, I don't.

Q. I should add that if at any time you need to take a break, you want to use the bathroom or you just need to relax a few minutes, just say so.

All right, so I have here a cloth-bound book bearing the title, *Marius and Delia*. On the title page this title is repeated with a subtitle added, *Or a Pleasant and Profitable History of the Times*. On a separate line there's a byline that reads "By D. M." Underneath that are the words, "The First English Novel, Attributed to Deborah Milton." Beneath that, there is a line that reads: "Edited by Angus Burdock."

Mr. Burdock, would you confirm for the record that your claim to a copyright violation regards the text of this novel?

A. Yes. If you'll turn the page, you'll see it was copyrighted in 1975 by me.

Q. Mr. Burdock, copyright pages can also be works of fiction. We are here to investigate the basis of that assertion.

MR. CHAVEL: Angus, you only have to say yes or no. Let him ask for details if he wants the details.

MR. CLACK: Your opportunity to instruct your client is over and done with. Don't you suppose I was about to turn the page and read that into the record too? Let's not waste the time Mr. Burdock just saved us.

I would like this book marked as an exhibit, make it Burdock Number 1.

(Whereupon Exhibit Burdock Number 1 was marked for identification.)

BY MR. CLACK:

Q. Mr. Burdock, you chose an obscure, little-known publisher for this book. Was there a reason for that?

A. Yes. I had difficulty interesting the major publishers in undertaking it. They mostly caviled over the attribution. If it wasn't mentioned in the standard literary histories, it wasn't real as far as they were concerned. My editor at Scandalon Press was able to appreciate the work for its literary merit.

Q. Did you receive royalties or an advance on royalties from the publisher?

A. No. I received a number of copies for my personal use but no advances or royalties. Scholars aren't always remunerated for their work. Sometimes they even have to contribute to the costs of publication.

Q. Did you do so in this instance?

A. Yes.

Q. How much? How much did you pay to cover the costs?

A. I don't recall.

Q. I have here another volume, a paperback with the same title, *Marius and Delia*, and with the title page and copyright page bearing the same information, including the same date, 1975, only the publisher named on the title page is called InRequest Press.

I'd like this book marked as an exhibit, Burdock Number 2.

(Whereupon Exhibit Burdock Number 2 was marked for identification.)

Q. Mr. Burdock, was this paperback edition authorized by you?

A. Yes.

Q. This publisher is a print-on-demand company, correct? You paid for the publication?

A. Yes.

Q. Why did you decide to put out another edition?

A. The 1975 edition had been long out of print, and I wished to make *Marius and Delia* available to readers again, that's all.

Q. When did this paperback edition come out?

A. I don't remember the precise date. About twelve years ago.

Q. 2005? 2004?

A. Something like that.

Q. And you do receive royalties on it, correct?

A. Yes.

Q. Has it proved profitable? Over and above your initial investment?

MR. CHAVEL: Objection.

BY MR. CLACK:

Q. You can answer.

THE WITNESS: I'm not an accountant. I don't keep a balance sheet. A deposit shows up on my bank statement from time to time. Modest sums overall.

BY MR. CLACK:

Q. What would be an average or typical amount for these royalty payments?

MR. CHAVEL: Objection.

BY MR. CLACK:

Q. You can answer.

A. I don't know. They vary a great deal.

Q. Mr. Burdock, is this paperback print-on-demand version a straightforward reprint of the 1975 edition? Without additions or deletions or other substantial changes?

A. I certainly hope so. I paid a fairly substantial sum to have it scanned and proofread.

Q. Then, for the purposes of this deposition, we will refer to the 1975 edition, with the understanding that there are no substantive differences, no additions or omissions in the print-on-demand version of the book.

The table of contents lists a foreword, running 27 pages, with roman numerals for the pagination, followed by the text of a novel called *Marius and Delia*, divided into seventeen chapters, totaling 202 pages. Now this foreword has your name printed at the end. So we may take it that the foreword is your original work, correct?

A. Yes.

Q. Was it written expressly as an introduction to the text of *Marius and Delia*, for the 1975 publication?

A. Yes.

Q. Now that we have established that you wrote the foreword, could you tell us who wrote the novel itself, pages 1 to 202 of this book?

A. It has been attributed to Deborah Milton.

Q. Now I am not an English scholar, but you mean the daughter of John Milton, the epic poet who lived in the seventeenth century—not some other Deborah Milton?

A. Yes.

Q. Could you tell us when Deborah Milton lived?

A. I don't remember the dates of birth and death. They could be readily ascertained.

Q. Could you give us approximate dates, for the purpose of the record?

MR. CHAVEL: Objection.

BY MR. CLACK:

Q. Roughly speaking, her lifetime fell between the middle of the seventeenth century and the first quarter of the eighteenth, is that approximately right?

A. Yes, give or take a few years.

Q. Do you consider this novel, pages 1 to 202 of the book to which you contributed a foreword, do you personally consider this novel to have been written by Deborah Milton?

A. I think the attribution is credible, on current evidence, on the face of it.

Q. Am I correct that the attribution originates with you?

A. Not entirely, no. I took the attribution from the original title page. The name Deborah Milton was handwritten on the page as a gloss on the author's initials, D. M.

Q. Do you have that title page?

A. No.

Q. Is there a copy of that title page available?

A. No.

Q. Was there a date on the title page?

A. No.

Q. Was there a publisher named on the title page?

A. No.

Q. I am not an English scholar, so could you tell me if those two omissions would be unusual in the time period we're talking about?

A. Unusual, yes, but not unheard of. If a book was potentially controversial or indecent in the judgment of the authorities, the printer might choose to publish without an imprint. The date of publication was often omitted.

Q. Would it be unusual for the author to be unidentified as well, or identified only by initials?

A. Not at all. Many works in this time period were published anonymously.

Q. When you say "in this time period," could you be more specific?

A. I am speaking generally of Restoration and eighteenth-century literature, or publishing in general during that period, from 1660 to 1800.

Q. I am going to read to you a passage from your foreword, and I would like you to follow along to check that I have read it correctly. It's on page xi. That's lower case roman numerals x-i. Have you located the page?

A. Yes.

Q. The passage is as follows:

"In the course of researching my doctoral thesis, I visited a Gothicised Georgian country house in southern Dorset which possessed a creditable collection of seventeenth- and eighteenth-century editions, although carelessly maintained and incompletely catalogued. As I was scanning the titles on an inexcusably dusty and disorganized shelf, I noticed a slender volume with a blank spine. I pulled it out to examine it. The title page at once arrested my attention. As I began reading the opening chapters, I realized that I had stumbled upon a major literary find. It was a work of prose fiction that fully met the criteria defining the novel as a genre, which had been composed some decades before the work of Richardson and Fielding— indeed, before the works of Daniel Defoe.

"My first impulse was to shout to the world about this extraordinary book—and I knew it was extraordinary within a very few pages. The only part of the world within earshot, however, was an elderly housekeeper, half-daft, half-shrewd, and one-hundred-percent paranoid. She had admitted me with obvious reluctance, warned me what not to touch and where not to go. She had followed me across the Ivanhoe-inspired hall and up the gimcrack Gothic staircase, equipped with a carpet sweeper and a tin of wood polish to expunge any trace of my passage. Her head would reappear at the library door at almost predictable intervals, like the mechanical cuckoo of a pendulum clock. My second, much wiser impulse, therefore, was to keep it to myself. After indulging myself by reading a few more pages, I began to transcribe, as rapidly as possible, for I had very few days allowed me in that library, and I still had to do my work on textual variants in the *Eikon Basilike*. I kept the latter volume open on a stand before me, so that I could quickly shuffle D. M.'s little book under my papers whenever the disapproving housekeeper slipped into the room, as she frequently did, to peer through her bifocals at my inexplicably slow progress. I worked frantically whenever I wasn't under the scrutiny of the bifocals. At the end of three days of sore eyes, writer's cramp, and intense, secret excitement, I had a full transcript of *Marius and Delia*. I had even finished my dry but necessary work on the library's unremarkable copy of the *Eikon Basilike*."

Do these two paragraphs represent an accurate account of the circumstances in which you discovered the novel and made your transcription of it?

A. It is perhaps a bit over-dramatized. I wasn't under oath, you know.

Q. You are under oath now. Are there significant details you would add, or any corrections that you would make now?

A. No.

Q. I will read another passage from your foreword, which comes after the two paragraphs we've already covered. Again, please follow along and check that I read it correctly. We're on page xiii now, that's small roman numeral x-i-i-i:

"Back at my university, after I had caught up on my sleep and managed to straighten my fingers out of a pen-clutching claw, I considered what to do. I wanted, of course, to contact the lady of the manor in order to tell her what she owned and to get her permission to bring out a proper edition, edited, of course, by its discoverer, Angus Burdock. Then reality reared its ugly hydra heads of yes-buts and what-ifs. She might say no. She might choose another editor, someone she happened to know or someone with more impressive credentials. I had merely exchanged a pair of formal letters with the lady: mine asking permission to visit the library and hers granting that permission. And I was only a graduate student. Reluctantly, I put Deborah Milton's *Marius and Delia* in the file cabinet and got on with the *Eikon Basilike* and its now terribly uninteresting textual variants."

Did I read that correctly?

A. Yes. Well, actually it's pronounced EYE-KON BA-SIL-I-KEY, but that hardly matters.

Q. And is this passage that I just read an accurate account of your considerations at the time, and of your initial disposition of your transcription?

A. Yes, with the proviso again that it's a trifle too literary-ish about the edges.

Q. Can you provide a date for this time period, when you made your transcription?

A. It was in the summer of 1969. August perhaps. Quite hot as I recall.

Q. I have here a copy of your résumé and I'd like it labeled Exhibit Burdock Number 3.

(Whereupon, Exhibit Burdock Number 3 was marked for identification.)

Your résumé states that you were awarded your Ph.D. in 1971. What month was that?

A. July.

Q. So you put your transcript of Deborah Milton's work aside for two years so that you could earn your Ph.D. degree?

A. Yes.

Q. In that time, did you show your transcript to anyone?

A. No.

Q. During that time, did you tell anyone about discovering a previously unknown early novel, presumed to be written by Deborah Milton?

A. No.

Q. Why not?

MR. CHAVEL: Objection.

BY MR. CLACK:

Q. It must have been difficult to keep a discovery so momentous to yourself for so long. Didn't you ever want to confide in someone, get a second opinion on its merits?

A. Colleagues are not always completely honorable when it comes to claim jumping. There really wasn't anyone qualified to form a judgment who I would trust that far.

Q. Once you had earned your Ph.D., was it your plan to move forward with Deborah Milton? Did you now contact the owner of the country house?

A. It was a trifle more complicated than that. I think this is all in my foreword.

Q. It is, but the relevant sections are too long to read into the record, so it would be better to have you retell it.

A. I didn't immediately take up the project again. I was preoccupied with getting a job, naturally. And I thought a good academic post would add to my standing and to making my case that I ought to be the editor of a scholarly edition of *Marius and Delia*. However, those sorts of jobs don't simply drop into one's lap. Especially since my doctoral supervisor, he wasn't fully behind me. I ended up taking a post as instructor in literature at a boarding school in Yorkshire. Quite a good school, but not what I had hoped for. That all took time and then there was getting settled into my job, before I felt ready to move forward, as you put it, with Deborah Milton.

Q. How much time are we talking about here? Dating from when you got your degree in July of 1971?

A. Two years, two and a half years really.

Q. So late in 1973, perhaps?

A. Yes. About that. I decided to see if I could get permission to go back to the library over Christmas break, say that I was preparing my thesis for publication and needed to check something. I could get another look at the book and perhaps with luck find the owner at home and introduce myself.

Q. And the owner was—

A. Well, the owner, as it turned out, was dead. I hadn't realized she was old. I had never met her, you know. She had died about a year back, and the estate had gone to a second cousin, or some such relation, and because of the death duties the second cousin had sold everything that could be picked up and carted off, including of course the library.

Q. Did you attempt to trace who had bought the collection?

A. Yes, yes, I did. It wasn't handled very intelligently. The library wasn't a collection in any real sense, just an accumulation over many generations, some of those generations more literate than others. Hardly a first edition in the lot and much of it valueless. It was partially catalogued but only partially, so it would have taken time and expertise to appraise it properly. That was never done, as I learned from a phone call to the new owner, who was then in London as best as I can recall.

I told him, honesty being the best policy, that I was very interested in a book that I had seen in the library and was it at all possible to trace it. Probably not, he told me, and was about to ring off, so I quickly said I should like to buy it, if it hadn't been sold already. That got his attention for just the tiniest minute. He gave me permission to look over what was left: he would call the caretaker and tell him to let me in. And he also gave me the name of the book dealer in Weymouth who had bought the lot.

I decided to start with the bookseller, who struck me as being an honest but not especially knowledgeable individual. He had put together a catalog of books for sale from the estate, which he was happy to show me. There was the copy of the *Eikon Basilike* I had examined, but no D. M., no *Marius and Delia*. It was a short list, just over six hundred titles. I asked the dealer about that, and he told me that the owner had set aside the books he wanted to keep and had required him, the book dealer, to clear the shelves of everything else. A van full of waste paper it was, he said.

Well, I feared the worst at that point, but there was still a chance that I would find *Marius and Delia* quietly gathering dust on its old shelf. I was disillusioned of that notion once the caretaker had admitted me to the library. The dim-witted philistine had simply held onto anything bound in morocco or calf—collections of sermons, second-rate histories, county annals, deluxe club editions, and so forth.

Q. So what did you conclude? What had happened to the original?

A. I suppose there's a chance it was salvaged. Most likely it went straight to the waste-paper mill to be pulped and turned into, oh, butcher paper, packing cartons, something like that.

Q. Now, you said that you considered the attribution to Deborah Milton, John Milton's daughter, to be credible. Is that correct?

A. Yes.

Q. Is it fair to say that if it were not by Deborah Milton, in your opinion it would have been written by a contemporary of hers, someone who lived in the late seventeenth century? Or early eighteenth century?

A. Judged by the style, yes.

Q. You presumably examined the physical copy from which you made your transcript. Did it appear to you to have been printed during that time period?

A. I am not a paleographer. I am not qualified to make such a determination.

Q. Could you define that term, for the record?

A. A paleographer is an expert in dating books and manuscripts and determining their provenance, based on the paper and the script if a manuscript, or the characteristics of the typeface if a printed book. I do not have that training, and in any case I would not have had the tools or the time to determine the provenance, other than the information on the title page.

Q. Your dissertation research involved examining original editions of a seventeenth-century work, correct?

A. Yes.

Q. As a result you must have been reasonably familiar with recognizing a seventeenth-century book, as opposed to, say, a book published in the twentieth century?

A. There are obvious differences, certainly. But I would not claim to be able to detect twentieth-century presswork that carefully imitated the paper and printing conditions of the seventeenth or eighteenth century. I don't know that there are such works. I am simply stating a hypothetical. Only a paleographer expert in the period could make a differentiation of that sort.

Q. I would like to call your attention to another statement in your 1975 foreword. It's on page xii, small roman numeral x-i-i, and it comes after the first passage I read, and it describes that now-missing title page. It reads:

"The initials D. M. had been annotated in a typical, if somewhat cramped and ill-formed seventeenth-century mixed italic hand."

Although you are not a trained paleographer, you felt confident enough to date the style of the handwriting, correct?

A. Again, I have, as you say, a familiarity from examining books and manuscripts from the period. But I would not be able to recognize a forgery. I do not have those skills.

Q. You have mentioned the possibility of forgery twice. Did you consider at the time that the book you found in this private library, which you then transcribed, did you consider the possibility that it might have been a forgery?

A. I cannot recall what I may have been thinking fifty years ago.

Q. Would you have taken the effort to transcribe, under difficult circumstances, this volume you discovered if you considered it likely to be a forgery, a modern forgery?

A. No.

Q. You were then fully convinced it was a genuine work of fiction from the late seventeenth or early eighteenth century?

A. Yes.

Q. At this time, do you remain convinced that the work you examined was genuine?

A. Well, I have not seen the original for close to fifty years, so I cannot reevaluate.

Q. In other words, you have no basis for revising your original assessment, based on your familiarity with the style of the period, that this was an original work of fiction dating from that time period. Correct?

A. Yes.

Q. And the transcription you published in 1975 in this book, with a foreword written by you—that transcription is an exact and faithful copy of the book you found in 1969, which you believe to have been written by Deborah Milton?

A. I did not say that. I never said that. I have never said it was an exact copy. I did the transcription under very difficult circumstances and inevitably there are errors. Perhaps you know what scholars always say when making their acknowledgments, my errors are my own. Well, that's true here. The text as printed is a unique, inevitably faulty transcription. Were another copy of Deborah Milton's novel to be discovered, as I'm sure we all hope, that text would be different from my text.

Q. What proportion or percentage of the text do you estimate to be faulty, half a percent, a tenth of a percent?

A. I have no way of knowing that.

Q. You must be able to make some sort of estimate. This is your edition and you're an expert. Is it fair to say that 99.5 percent of the text is the original, with only a few scattered typos of spelling or punctuation?

MR. CHAVEL: Objection. Asked and answered.

BY MR. CLACK:

Q. Is it fair to say, given your training, your occasional slips, your errors, would have been a word here or there, or at most an occasional short phrase?

A. Again, I have no way, now, of knowing that.

Q. It was your intention to make an accurate transcription, even under difficult circumstances, correct?

A. Yes.

Q. Did you at any time deliberately introduce errors into the text?

A. I certainly cannot recall what I may have done in transcribing, hastily, fifty, I suppose it was forty-eight years ago.

Q. Would you have had any motive for introducing deliberate errors into your transcription?

A. Again I cannot recall what I may have been thinking forty-eight years ago.

Q. Is it usual for literary scholars to deliberately introduce errors into their work?

A. Errors always occur.

Q. There are procedures or best practices to avoid errors, or to minimize errors in reproducing a work, correct? Proofreading techniques?

A. Yes, there are. However, that is precisely the issue. I did not have the opportunity to proofread. I made a transcription in haste and was not able to read it against the original. Properly, that should have been done multiple times, letter by letter, word by word, ideally backwards. Regrettably, I was not able to do that.

Q. Can you give me some examples? What errors are you aware of in your transcription?

A. If I knew what the errors are, I would have attempted to fix them in advance of publication.

Q. There are some critics of the novel who have questioned the attribution. They have identified what they consider to be anachronisms. Would these be examples of your errors, potential errors?

A. They might be. I may have, in haste, slipped and substituted a modern word or phrase. I worked very rapidly and was often exhausted.

Q. An authoritative edition of Deborah Milton's novel, prepared by a team of scholars who, like you, are familiar with the style of the period, might identify and eliminate such errors. Aren't there examples, precedents, of that sort of reconstructive scholarship? Some of Shakespeare's plays, for example. A suspect word or phrase is amended to something more plausible.

A. That sort of textual scholarship is done very conservatively, to replace sheer nonsense. An emendation that replaced a possible transcriptional error that was not nonsense would be no closer to the original. It would be necessary to cite the disputed phrase, and that phrase, if in fact an error, would be my original—my original if unintentional contribution to the text of the novel. Until and unless another original is found, the text inevitably includes my errors and those errors belong to me and may not be reproduced without my permission.

Q. Your Ph.D. thesis involved a kind of textual scholarship, correct? You read line by line, looking for small variants?

A. I was unable to employ the skills and techniques needed for my doctoral research on this very rapid transcription.

Q. All the same, professional techniques often become second nature. My wife, for example, sometimes accuses me of trying to cross-examine her. So don't you think that someone trained in textual scholarship would do a better job, produce a more accurate transcript, than someone—me, for example—who was completely without training and without a deep knowledge of the period?

A. I would not say that, not at all. Someone who knew the period and the style might make what we call predictive errors. Predictive errors occur when someone anticipates a word or phrase by recognizing a familiar context. Given the conditions, I may well have made many such errors. These could not be identified and emended by other scholars, however well trained and familiar with the period.

Q. Given your training and your field of research, isn't that exactly what you were trained to do, to avoid predictive errors while you were comparing different editions of the same work? Otherwise your Ph.D. research would have been valueless; every copy of the work would have seemed to be identical.

A. In fact, as it turned out, I discovered few significant textual differences in the editions I examined—none that were new and publishable, that is.

Q. Do you consider that this disappointing outcome was a result of poor skills or carelessness on your part? Or were there simply few differences to be discovered?

MR. CHAVEL: Objection.

BY MR. CLACK:

Q. I will rephrase: Did you consider at the time, or do you consider now, that you lacked the necessary skills to do your dissertation, an exercise in textual scholarship?

A. No. I passed my viva exam and my thesis was accepted with minor amendments.

Q. When you were preparing your 1975 edition, did you identify and correct any of these transcription errors?

A. I really can't recall.

Q. You were aware then of the possibility of transcriptional error?

A. Yes.

Q. You reviewed the text prior to publication?

A. That was forty-odd years ago. I don't recall the process of preparing the manuscript for publication.

Q. Your transcription was handwritten, correct?

A. Yes.

Q. Was it typed before sending it to the publisher?

A. Yes.

Q. Who typed it?

A. I did.

Q. So you necessarily reviewed the text word by word and letter by letter, didn't you?

A. Yes, although of course there is a renewed possibility of error, likewise with proofing the galleys.

Q. Do you have that typescript?

A. No. It remained with the publisher.

Q. Do you have your original transcription, either the original or a photocopy of your transcription?

A. No.

Q. Do you have notebooks or work journals from the time period in question, 1969 when you made the transcription, to 1975 when you published your edition?

A. No. When I retired, which was fourteen years ago, I pulped all my files, all my teaching and research files.

Q. You didn't consider that posterity might be interested in your transcript or your notes?

A. I am a tired old man. I didn't care to be encumbered with masses and masses of paper.

Q. Let me step back and summarize. You say you are certain that you made errors, inevitable errors, though you cannot identify any. Is that a fair summary?

A. Yes.

Q. Did you make any deliberate changes in the text, either in the course of transcription or in preparing for publication in 1975?

MR. CHAVEL: Objection. Asked and answered.

BY MR. CLACK:

Q. We were talking about errors before, not changes, but I'll rephrase. You have said that there would be no reason to deliberately introduce errors when transcribing. What about when you were preparing your transcription for publication?

A. I don't know what you mean. I may have corrected obvious errors, such as upside down letters or other obvious typographic errors.

Q. Did you make any attempts to improve the text? For example, rewrite a sentence to make it better or more literary?

A. I certainly do not recall doing so.

Q. So you made no attempt to improve or enhance the text. The changes that you may have made were all errors, all inadvertent. They would have been more or less random, wouldn't they? Such as a mistake in punctuation, or misreading a this for a that?

MR. CHAVEL: Objection.

BY MR. CLACK:

Q. You would agree with me that errors, by definition, are inadvertent and do not fall into any particular pattern or are predictable in any way?

A. No, I wouldn't agree. There are often patterns to transcriptional errors. A semi-colon can be mistaken for a comma and vice versa, homonyms can be confused, nonstandard spellings might be simplified, typographical oddities, the long s can be mistaken for an f so that, for instance, the word see is misread as fee. Those are all more likely than random.

Q. These errors, the errors that you feel certain you must have made, they wouldn't be thematic or substantive, you would agree with that?

A. I don't know what you mean by thematic. They might, just by chance, be substantive. A minor misreading might nonetheless change the meaning of a passage.

Q. I'll give an example. You have said that you would have had no motive to make a deliberate effort to transform or improve the text. So in making your errors, you wouldn't, say, have changed the word ugly to beautiful throughout, or changed the word yellow to the word red throughout? Or given the heroine a moustache and a funny little beard?

MR. CHAVEL: Objection.

THE WITNESS: I don't see how those particular errors could occur consistently, no. But there are undoubtedly errors, numerous errors.

Q. Surely you don't mean to claim that your edition is so riddled with errors, so degraded by faulty transcribing, as to no longer be the work of Deborah Milton?

MR. CHAVEL: Objection.

BY MR. CLACK:

Q. Wouldn't such a work would be fundamentally valueless; no better, in fact, than a modern forgery?

MR. CHAVEL: Objection. You aren't asking a question, you're making insinuations.

THE WITNESS: I would nonetheless like to respond to Mr. Clack's insinuation, if I may.

MR. CHAVEL: Go ahead if that's what you want to do. But there's no necessity of responding.

THE WITNESS: No one in possession of even a modest level of literary taste and training who would read *Marius and Delia* could doubt for a moment that it is a unique and a very great work of fiction. There is, however, an unknown level of error unavoidably introduced by the circumstances of making my transcription. Those errors might be trivial or substantive, brief or extensive. A poor thing but mine own, to paraphrase Touchstone. Those errors are my intellectual property.

MR. CHAVEL: I hope we can move on now.

MR. CLACK: Oh, absolutely. I have what I want. Thank you for clarifying, Mr. Burdock.

BY MR. CLACK:

Q. Now I would like to ask a few questions about the place where you made your remarkable find. You stated that it was a private library in a country house. Where was it located?

A. Southern Dorset.

Q. Where in southern Dorset?

A. In a thoroughly hideous Georgian manor that had been done up in Victorian Gothic. Battlements and turrets jumbled together with fan lights and sash windows. That sort of thing.

Q. I recall the description from your foreword, but it doesn't help us here with identifying the location of the library. What was the nearest town?

A. Well, it was in Purbeck, in the Purbeck district, that is, but quite isolated. There wasn't a town, not even a hamlet nearby. Very rural. At the time, that is. It's been built over a great deal since, I believe, but of course I've never been back. It's quite possible the building has been pulled down by now. It deserved to be.

Q. You were able to locate it. It must be on the map, near some road.

A. I took an express train, followed by a bus, and then had my legs to carry me for a good mile or so further. As I said, it was quite isolated.

Q. Houses like that have names, don't they? What was it called?

A. I believe it was more something.

Q. Try that again?

A. More something. Or something more. At this late date I can't remember whether it was M-O-R-E or M-O-O-R, but I'm fairly certain it had a "more" in it.

Q. Who did it belong to?

A. Well, extraordinarily enough, as I later learned, the owner turned out to be the housekeeper, or rather, the woman I mistook for a housekeeper was actually the owner. She never gave her name and just let me make a natural assumption. I suppose the expense of keeping up such a place reduced her to doing her own dusting and what-not.

Q. What was her name?

A. Lady Dee, as she was known to her friends and to the society pages—not of course that I was a friend, or for that matter a regular reader of society pages— Lady Dee had been married three times, as I believe I remember reading, and the title came with her first husband, a life peer—who died, conveniently enough, and left her the title but not much else. Now, the estate came with her second husband, and that marriage I believe ended in a divorce.

Q. Mr. Burdock—

A. But I suppose the ex- was happy enough to get rid of the unfashionable manor along with the wife, and—

Q. Mr. Burdock—

A. And then there was the third marriage, which I really know very little about. The titled husband was related to the—

Q. Mr. Burdock—

A. Anstruther-Gough-Calthorpes, but—

Q. Mr. Burdock, I do not want a marital history or a family tree. I am asking you for the first and last name of the lady who owned the manor.

A. But don't you see, that's just the point. She was married three times and divorced twice and changed her name as many times, and though she held onto the title, of course, she took the current husband's name, at least in certain social contexts, and so—

Q. Mr. Burdock, you wrote a letter to this woman. You must have been able to write her name on the envelope. What is or was her name?

A. I really cannot answer that, as I'm trying to explain. And of course I could have gotten the address right and made a little mistake or two with the name, and then that was, oh, forty-eight years ago, I suppose, so I really don't know how I might have addressed her.

Q. Do you really mean to suggest that you do not know her name? You had her permission to visit the library for your dissertation research. You corresponded with her. You were able to track down her obituary or otherwise learn of her death.

A. I cannot recall her precise name.

Q. Mr. Burdock, that is not even remotely credible. You are a scholar. You are trained to keep careful records of your sources. You did some of your dissertation work in her library. You discovered a rare, a unique literary work in her library. You must know her name. What is it?

MR. CHAVEL: He says he cannot remember. It was a long time ago. Is this really relevant? You've been going down this road for too long.

MR. CLACK: Of course it's relevant. These questions are entirely relevant to establishing what claims, if any, Mr. Burdock might have to any part of the text beyond the foreword. If your client continues to refuse or evade answering my question, we will file for sanctions under Rule 37.

THE WITNESS: May I speak to my solicitor?

MR. CLACK: Okay. We'll take a short break. But you understand that there is no attorney-client privilege to your discussion.

(Whereupon, a recess was taken at 11:44 a.m. and resumed at 12:03 p.m.)

BY MR. CLACK:

Q. Mr. Burdock, I will ask my question again. What was the name of the owner of the library where you discovered Deborah Milton's work?

A. I refuse to answer on the grounds that I would incriminate myself.

Q. You're taking the Fifth?

A. Yes.

Q. Mr. Burdock, we are speaking of events that took place forty-eight years ago. There are statutes of limitations on these things. You can't be charged with theft or misappropriation, or any other property crime. Unless you're going to tell me you murdered that old lady, you're home free. You can't be charged.

MR. CHAVEL: We don't think that's true. Not under English law, and that's what applies here, in terms of self-incrimination.

MR. CLACK: Are you telling me—they may call it something different—are you telling me there aren't time limitations for criminal and civil prosecution in English law?

MR. CHAVEL: There are, but they work a little differently. And, based on what Mr. Burdock just told me, which is frankly new to me, this is a case of deliberate concealment that has not been discovered—in fact, cannot be discovered until and unless Mr. Burdock incriminates himself. And in British law—it's Section 32 of the Limitation Act of 1980, I looked it up during the break—the six-year limitation period doesn't begin to run until then, until a fraud or deliberate concealment is discovered or could reasonably be discovered.

MR. CLACK: I have no idea what you're talking about and neither do you. You're wasting time and interfering with the deposition of this witness.

MR. CHAVEL: Angus, you'd better tell him what you just told me.

THE WITNESS: Yes, well. The account I gave in my foreword was not entirely accurate. I was compelled to work very hastily, as I said, in making my transcription. In fact, there was really no possibility of finishing the task during the three days I had permission to use the library. So I was compelled to sneak the book out of the library. I put it down my trousers, in fact.

BY MR. CLACK:

Q. I do not see how—

A. Let me finish, please. This is really very difficult for me. I have never told anyone about it until now. I took the book back to my room to transcribe, that was my intention. I sat up all night at it for two nights so that I could return the book on my final visit to the library. I never meant to keep it, you know. I was going to return it and then, at some future date, request formal permission to make a transcription—everything proper that way, you know. But after sitting up two nights I was exhausted and not thinking clearly, and in fact, I believe I left it on the train.

Q. On the train? You believe you left it on the train?

A. That must have been it. I fell asleep on the train, you see, and got up in a fluster when the stop was called, and it wasn't until I reached the library that I realized that I didn't have the book.

Q. Did you attempt to trace it? Did you contact the railroad?

A. Oh, yes. Oh, yes. It went missing somewhere between Waterloo and Hamworthy. I tried every station.

Q. Do you have any theory, any guess as to what happened to it?

A. Well, it was wrapped in brown paper and someone might have taken it hoping it was something smutty, and then left it somewhere when they were disappointed. Or tossed it in a rubbish bin.

Q. That is certainly very unfortunate, Mr. Burdock.

A. It has saddened every day of my life.

Q. However, it seems to me that you and Mr. Chavel have greatly exaggerated your risk of prosecution. You said that you intended to return it, and that you were only prevented from doing so by the accident of losing the book. So I think the most you could be charged with is misappropriation. And after forty-eight years, you cannot be charged at all, even with theft.

A. Ah, well, there's more to tell. When I realized I had lost the book, I funked it. I was afraid of getting caught, somehow, so I pulled the catalog card when the old lady wasn't looking.

Q. You did what to what card?

A. I took the library catalog card. It was filed under M, and it simply said M period comma D period comma *Marius and Delia* parens n dot d dot end-parens, meaning no date. And it gave the shelf location, which I do not remember.

Q. Do you have that card?

A. No. No. I wouldn't keep something like that, would I? No, it's gone. And Mr. Chavel tells me I was guilty of fraud and deliberate concealment by doing so. Because that was the only record of the book's existence in that library.

Q. You don't need to dot the i's and cross the t's for me, Mr. Burdock. I understand the position that you and Mr. Chavel are taking. And I also understand that it's based on fifteen minutes of research into English law. We have yet to find whether the trial judge will find it persuasive, or whether you will have to answer the question you have refused to answer today.

I have no further questions now.

(Whereupon, the witness was excused.)

(Whereupon, the deposition concluded at approximately 12:35 p.m.)

Appendix 3: Journal Prospectus

𝕯ᴇʙᴏʀᴀʜ 𝕸ɪʟᴛᴏɴ 𝕾ᴛᴜᴅɪᴇs will provide a forum for scholarship addressing the interpretive challenges presented by D. M.'s *Marius & Delia*. The journal seeks to provoke dialogue and debate concerning canonicity and intertextuality in early modern prose fiction. We do not limit contributions to any particular theoretical-methodological paradigm: new historicist, cultural materialist, feminist, psychoanalytic and Marxist readings are all welcomed—as are, of course, Bakhtinian, Baudrillardian, Deleuzian and Derridean approaches. We do not publish undertheorized readings, nor are we interested in belletristic expositions of meaning or authorial intention. The editors prize richly textured, theoretically sophisticated explorations of the text's unsettling discourses of gender, patriarchy and class. We invite contributions from both emerging and eminent scholars who perceive the path-breaking significance of this text for an intellectually fruitful reconceptualization of the origins of the English novel.

Prospectus: Deborah Milton Studies

Deborah Milton Studies is planned as an annual publication with an anticipated launch date of February 2022.

Contents in preparation:

Deborah Milton and the Recovery Project
 Margo Quigley

Crack-brained and Fit for Bedlam: Madness and Subjugation in *Marius & Delia*
 Terence Mackey

The Semiotics of Gout in *Marius & Delia*
 Claudia McCracken

Who did you say you were again? Diegetic Levels in *Marius & Delia*
 Aimee Sunderland

"The peculiar vessels required to serve it": The Social Life of Things in *Marius & Delia*
 Lynda Cardoso-Kenworthy

Debtors and Downright Thieves: Recontextualizing the Formation of the Novel
 Denice Baird

J. M./D. M.: Author[iz]ing Authorship
 C. A. Borengasser

Submissions and other correspondence may be addressed to: query@springstreetbooks.com. Please name the journal in the subject line.

www.ingramcontent.com/pod-product-compliance
Lightning Source LLC
Chambersburg PA
CBHW072318020726
47501CB00002B/553